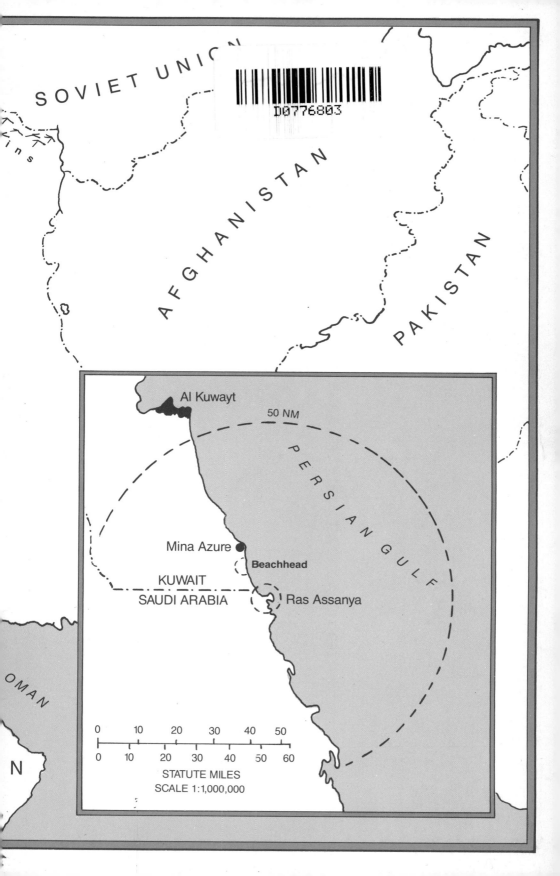

THE WARBIRDS

THE
WAR

BIRDS

A NOVEL BY
RICHARD HERMAN, JR.

DONALD I. FINE, INC.
New York

Library of Congress Cataloging-in-Publication Data
Herman, Richard.
   The warbirds.

   I. Title.
PS3558.E684W37   1988   813'.54   88-45380
ISBN 1-55611-097-9

Manufactured in the United States of America

10 9 8 7 6 5 4 3 2 1

I would like to extend my thanks and gratitude to George Wieser and Donald I. Fine
who saw something in a very rough manuscript and decided to take a chance; and
to George Coleman and Rick Horgan who taught me how to tell a better story.

For Sheila, who waited.

AUTHOR'S NOTE

This novel is a work of fiction and is based on my experiences and extensive research. My goal was to tell a story with realistic scenarios using facts available in the public sector. As an author, I did take the liberty of changing things around and putting them together in new combinations, creating fictitious places, organizations, weapons systems, etc. There is no RAF Stonewood, Ras Assanya, Watch Center, Outpost, RC-135, Stealth reconnaissance aircraft, etc. as described in this story. They are composites based on ideas and facts that I picked up while doing research and are a product of my imagination. If they seem realistic and add to the story, so much the better.

TECHNICAL TERMS

ACT: Air Combat Tactics; dogfighting.

ACTIVE, THE: Main runway in use.

AILERON ROLL: A rolling maneuver along the longitudinal axis of an aircraft induced by the aileron controls on the trailing edge of the wing.

AIM: The designation for a U.S. air-to-air missile, e.g., AIM-9.

AIRCRAFT COMMANDER: The pilot in command of an aircraft regardless of the rank of any other officer on board.

ALCE: Airlift Command Element. A small command post in MAC used for controlling the movement of cargo and aircraft.

ATC: Air Traffic Control or an air traffic control agency.

BACKSEATER: A Weapon Systems Officer.

BANDIT: A hostile aircraft.

BARREL, THE: Slang for alert duty, being on alert, or the alert facility.

BARRIER: Arrestment cables stretched across each end of a runway. The hook of a fighter aircraft can be lowered to catch the cable for an emergency stop, much like an aircraft carrier landing.

BDA: Bomb Damage Assessment: a post-attack evaluation of results.

BM-21: Soviet-built, truck rocket launcher. Carries forty 122-mm unguided rockets.

BOGIE: An unidentified aircraft.

BRICK: Nickname for a small hand-held radio; a walkie-talkie.

CAP: Combat Air Patrol. A protective umbrella of fighters.

CBU: Cluster Bomb Unit. An aircraft-delivered anti-personnel weapon that spews baseball-sized bomblets over a wide area.

COIC: Combined Operations Intelligence Center.

COMM OUT: Communications out. Operating without radio or telephone communications.

DEFCON: Defense Condition. A state of warning/alert. DEFCON ONE is highest.

DIA: Defense Intelligence Agency.

DM: Deputy for Maintenance.

DO: Deputy for Operations.

FEBA: Forward Edge of the Battle Area, i.e., the front, the battlefield.

FEET WET: Flying over water.

FIR: Flight Information Region.

FLOGGER: NATO code name for the Soviet-built Mikoyan MiG-23 fighter. Comes in different models, e.g. Flogger B, Flogger J, etc.

FOX ONE: Brevity code for a radar-guided air-to-air missile.

FOX TWO: Brevity code for an infrared-guided air-to-air missile.

FOX THREE: Brevity code for an aircraft's cannon.

FRAG ORDER: The operations order that sends aircraft into combat.

GCA: Ground Control Radar Approach. The GCA controller "talks" the aircraft down.

GCI: Ground Control Intercept.

HSI: Horizontal Situation Indicator: the main instrument the pilot uses for navigation. Incorporates a compass rose, bearing pointers, and range indicator.

IFF: Identification, Friend or Foe: a radar transponder used for aircraft identification by ground-based radars.

IG: Inspector General.

INSPECTOR GENERAL: A specific organization in an armed service that conducts inspections and investigates complaints.

IP: Initial Point: a small, easily identifiable, easily found point on the ground close to a target. It serves as the last checkpoint and points the way to the target.

JINK: Continuous random changes in altitude and heading to defeat tracking by an enemy.

JUDY: Brevity code for the aircrew taking over an air-to-air intercept from a GCI controller.

JUSMAG: Joint United States Military Advisory Group. They are in charge of U.S. military aide and advice in a foreign country.

LOX: Liquid oxygen.

MAC: Military Airlift Command. Formerly MATS.

MARK-82. Designator for five-hundred-pound bombs.

MAVERICK: An electro-optical guided anti-tank rocket.

MC: Mission Capable: an aircraft ready to fly its mission.

NOTAMS: Notice to Airmen. Published notices warning pilots of hazardous or unusual conditions.

NOSE GUNNER: Nickname for pilot in two-place fighter aircraft.

NRO: National Reconnaissance Office. Manages U.S. spy satellite program.

NSA: The National Security Agency. The largest and most secret Intelligence agency. It uses satellites, huge computers, and other sophisticated technological means of gathering intelligence. Also breaks codes.

OB: Order of Battle: listing of hostile armed forces by type, strength and location.

OER: Officer Effectiveness Report: the report card issued on an officer by his commander, critical to promotion and career advancement.

PITTER: Nickname for a Weapon Systems Officer.

PUZZLE PALACE: The Pentagon.

ORI: Operational Readiness Inspection: an inspection of a unit's ability to carry out its assigned wartime mission. Conducted by the IG.

PSI: Fictional. Abbreviation for People's Soldiers of Islam, the military arm of the Iranian Communist Tudeh Party.

RADAR CONTROL POST: a Ground Control Intercept (GCI) site that controls and reports on aircraft.

RAMP: The concrete or asphalt apron used for parking aircraft; the sloping entranceway for loading an aircraft.

RDF: Rapid Deployment Force: a highly mobile, quick-reaction, combined-unit combat force.

RECCY: Slang for *reconnaissance.*

RED FLAG: A recurring exercise at Nellis AFB, outside Las Vegas,

Nevada, that tries to create a battlefield environment, simulating combat. Used for training aircrews in the disorientation and sensory overload of combat.

RHAW: Radar Homing and Warning: Equipment that warns aircrews about radar threats.

RTB: Return to base.

SA: Designation for a Soviet-built surface-to-air missile, e.g., SA-3.

SAM: Any surface-to-air missile.

SNAKEYE: Five-hundred-pound high-explosive bomb that can be selected in flight for either "slick" or "retarded" (high-drag) delivery.

SPO: Special Project Office: A specific organization in the Air Force responsible for developing a specific weapon system, e.g. the F-15.

STINGER: U.S.-built, shoulder-held, surface-to-air missile. Extremely effective.

SUU-21: A dispenser hung on a wing pylon carrying six practice bomblets for use on a gunnery range.

TAC: Tactical Air Command.

TAC EVAL: A NATO Tactical Evaluation, similar to an ORI but much more focused on results.

TDY: Temporary Duty: assignment away from home station for short periods of time—supposedly.

TLP: Tactical Leadership Program, NATO's version of Red Flag.

TOT: Time over target.

TRASH HAULER: Slang for cargo aircraft or aircrews that fly them.

TRIPLE A: Anti-aircraft artillery.

TWEAK: Slang for tune-up, or to slightly improve.

UAC: Fictional. Abbreviation for United Arab Command, the military arm of a political alliance between Saudi Arabia, Iraq, and Kuwait.

VOQ: Visiting Officers' Quarters.

WEAPON(S) SYSTEMS OFFICER: Flies in backseat of fighter. Combination radar operator, bombardier, electronic countermeasures operator, radio operator, observer, and co-pilot. By nature a very trusting soul.

WEAPONS TIGHT: An air defense term ordering air defense weapons to only engage targets positively identified as hostile.

wizzo: Slang for WSO (Weapons Systems Officer).

zsu-23: Soviet-built 23-mm Triple A, an excellent air-defense weapon. ZSU-23-2 is two-barrel version. ZSU-23-4 is mobile, radar-laid, four-barrel version—to be avoided.

THE SETUP

Every man and woman was standing at attention well before the general entered the small briefing room next to his office in the Pentagon. The general's aide still called the assembled generals and colonels to attention as General Lawrence M. Cunningham, the Air Force's chief of staff, invaded the room and swept it with a hard gaze before sitting down. The colonel giving the briefing stood behind the narrow podium next to the screen, wishing he were anywhere else. Anxiety twisted the knot in his stomach tighter as Cunningham said, "Please be seated." The "please" was an order.

"Good morning, sir," the colonel began, amazed that his voice seemed under control. "I'm Colonel Fred Perkins, sir, and I'll be giving this week's Situation Report on the—"

"Perkins, I *know* who you are and that this is the SIT REP on the Middle East. We're not all retards here. Get to it."

The colonel pressed a button on the side of the podium three times, causing three introductory thirty-five-millimeter slides to flash in sequence on the screen in front of the general. He paused at the fourth slide. "The Grain King food relief flights in the southern Sahara are going smoothly. Our C-130s are moving in excess of one hundred fifty tons of foodstuffs daily into the drought-stricken region. Please note the exact tonnage delivered by type of food and date."

Cunningham had started the first Grain King flights three years before when he was commander of MAC, the Military Airlift Command.

Click. The colonel keyed up the next slide of Libya. "The Libyan situation remains unchanged. We have nothing new to report."

"Perkins, are you telling me that Libya's nut-case colonel isn't up to something? He's been chewing nails since our F-111s bombed him in April of '86. He needs to even the score."

Perkins could feel the sweat trickling down his back. "Sir, he apparently hasn't found an opportunity as yet. We believe he will move against us, but right now he is facing some stiff political opposition at home and is putting on a front to look like a rational leader. We are monitoring Libyan communications for any indication that something is about to go down. So far, though, the situation is normal."

"Who's doing the monitoring?"

"The 6096th Reconnaissance Squadron out of Bergstrom AFB has a RC-135 on station over the Mediterranean. Its crews are staging out of Athens, which allows a short turnaround time. They are backed up by Outpost, a surveillance site in Egypt. Their information is fed to the Watch Center here, where it is correlated with intelligence from the National Security Agency and the CIA. So far, the five-day rule seems to apply." Perkins regretted mentioning that last even as he said it.

"*What* is the goddamn five-day rule?"

Perkins slowly answered the general, fully expecting Cunningham to live up to his nickname, "Sundown," by relieving him of duty on the spot and ordering him to clear out of the Pentagon by sundown. "The Libyans must stay focused on a subject or idea for at least five days before we consider it a serious matter. Otherwise, we assume it is customary rhetoric. Words, not action—"

"You *believe* that, Perkins?" There was danger in the softly spoken words.

The colonel plunged on, feeling suicidal. "It seems to work, sir. We are dealing with Arabs. They prefer to make us act without taking action themselves . . ."

Cunningham reached into his shirt pocket and pulled out a cigar. He rolled it between his fingers before fitting it unlit into the left side of his mouth. "Perkins, kindly get out of here and be gone by sundown." Cunningham turned to the three-star general sitting behind him. "Beller, get someone up here to finish this brief. Make sure he doesn't make dumb-assed assumptions. Five minutes." He lit the cigar and settled back into the leather armchair. His aide handed him a folder containing proposed budget figures to study while he waited.

General Beller half-ran out of the briefing room, grabbed the nearest phone and called the Watch Center, telling them to get the top Middle East analyst on duty to the briefing room in three minutes. Four minutes later Captain Sara Marshall was standing behind the podium recently vacated by Colonel Perkins. Her face was flushed from the run to the briefing room. She glanced at the slide of Libya that was still on the screen and looked at the general. "Anymore questions on Libya, sir."

The general shrugged, a response that Sara took for "none," and she keyed up the next series of slides on Egypt, Israel and Lebanon. With each slide she quickly summarized the current situation. She continued until the briefing's last slide of Iran flashed onto the screen. "The Ayatollah's power base is being parceled out among the other Ayatollahs. This is due to his advanced age and failing health, long rumored and now true. While he still has tremendous influence and prestige as the Shiites' lawgiver, he is becoming increasingly a figurehead."

Cunningham took the cigar out of his mouth and stared at the screen. "If fighting should break out in the Gulf again and the president wants a force projected into the region, how soon can the Air Force react?" The question was not directed at the captain; however, no one else volunteered an answer. The memory of Perkins was too fresh.

Sara pushed the button on the side of the podium and brought up the first slide of the Situation Report, a map of the entire Middle East, and broke the heavy silence. "The Rapid Deployment Force can have three squadrons of F-15s from Langley AFB in place within seventy-two hours for an active role in the air defense of Saudi Arabia and

Kuwait. Two AWACS can be in place and operating out of Saudi Arabia within twenty-four hours."

Cunningham leaned forward in his chair, impressed with the captain. "And what if the president wants to drop iron bombs on the enemy? F-15s and the AWACS can't do that. Does the Navy get the honors—again?"

"Not this time, sir." She tapped the map at Alexandria, Egypt, with a pointer. "The 45th Tactical Fighter Wing is now operational at Alexandria South Air Base. They report that they are capable of deploying two of their three F-4E squadrons within twelve hours. They can one-hop it into the gulf without refueling." She paused and thought for a moment, "Approximately two hours and fifteen minutes flying time, sir."

"When did the 45th change their combat-status rating?"

"This morning, sir," Sara quickly replied, determined that she would answer the questions she could. "They are still reporting an overall 'two' because they are not current in air-to-air combat, only air-to-ground, and can only mobilize and deploy two of their three squadrons within twelve hours."

"When will they be a 'one' and fully mission ready?"

"Sorry, sir. I can't answer that. There will be an answer on your desk within the hour."

Satisfied, the general stood up abruptly, all five feet five of him, and barreled out of the room, tossing the budget folder at his aide. "The captain did good, Dick," he muttered.

13 July: 0610 hours, Greenwich Mean Time
0810 hours, Alexandria, Egypt

Locke's name was right there, correctly spelled and underlined in the Security Police report. The wing commander reread it slowly, savoring what was between the lines. He could just picture the tall, ruggedly handsome pilot sowing some wild oats. But he could also picture real trouble, and that was something he didn't need.

He read on. The girl's name hit him. Colonel John Shaw's face flushed with anger and he bolted in his chair, his square chin hardening as he reached for the hotline to Locke's squadron. Then he thought better of it. He needed time . . . time to sort out what had suddenly become a very real problem.

Air Force protocol dictated he should pass the incident on to his deputy for Operations (DO) since it involved a pilot in one of the three flying squadrons that made up the business end of his wing. But his deputy, Colonel Sam Hawkins, was taking a much-needed leave in Cairo. Shaw shook his head and wondered how much longer he could carry Hawkins. He liked the tall, cadaverous colonel and respected his ability as a fighter pilot, but the man let too many details slip through the cracks. And the last thing Shaw needed was to be left holding the bag.

Back to Locke. Shaw decided to handle this problem himself. He knew what had to be done. He hadn't become a colonel and earned the command of the Air Force's newest base at Alexandria, Egypt, by being slow or stupid.

Shaw understood the system well and knew that perhaps one out of every hundred colonels was qualified to command a combat-ready wing. But all were motivated by their inner fires to order and lead. It was for the generals to consult their crystal balls and decide who should be given the chance to command and prove his ability. However, the same generals kept a stable of colonels in reserve, ready to take over the reins from their fellow colonel who faltered or drew up lame.

And Shaw knew that the activities of Lieutenant Jackson D. Locke had the potential to get him relieved of duty.

He picked up the hotline to Locke's squadron, and made a mental note to count the rings before the duty officer answered. The phone had not even completed its first ring when it was picked up; all very satisfactory.

"Have Lieutenant Colonel Fairly report to my office ASAP," he ordered. "And have Lieutenant Locke in my outer office on the double."

Jack Locke buffed at his boots with unusual ferocity, bringing them to a high shine.

"I don't think that's going to save your butt this time," the duty officer, Captain James "Thunder" Bryant, observed.

Jack looked up at his friend and grunted before returning to his task.

"Have you told Colonel Fairly yet? The boss doesn't need any surprises this early in the morning."

"He isn't in yet. He flew late last night with Johnny Nelson. He should be here in five minutes or so." Locke's dark blond hair flew back and forth to the beat of the brush strokes. He tried very hard not to sweat, even though he had reason to . . . Thunder picked up the rhythm and beat a tattoo on the desk, adding to Jack's discomfort. "Knock it off," he said, throwing the brush into its box. "I think I've really stepped on it this time." He glanced out the window toward the empty spot reserved for the squadron commander's car, biting his lower lip.

A group of pilots and their backseaters straggled up to the duty officer's station, a chest-high counter in front of a scheduling board, garnering Thunder's attention. While Thunder gave the crews a last-minute update on the weather and field conditions, Jack focused his gaze on the concrete ramp in front of the building, studying an F-4 waiting on the expanse of concrete that reminded him of a beach without sand or water, with the hint of its purpose hidden over the near horizon and lost to his view. "God, I love that beast," he muttered. "How the hell did I ever let last night happen?"

Getting into the cockpit of a Phantom had been a long and tedious road for Locke. Now it was all in jeopardy. Jack's turn in Egypt had been less than a success. Within a month, he had been thrown out of the Officers' Club for practicing carrier landings on a beer-sloshed table; arrested for speeding on base in a dilapidated Ferrari he had recently brought from an Egyptian; and reprimanded for being too aggressive on the gunnery range while practicing dive bombing. He prayed everything would blow over in a few days. Other things in his life had . . . He had been washed out of the Air Force Academy because he flunked military science. He still couldn't take the subject seriously. But he had learned from it, and pushed himself even harder at Arizona State, where he enrolled to finish college. It had been a walk-through after the discipline of the Academy. The Air Force's ROTC program at Arizona had opened another path into pilot training. The advice of his ROTC instructor, an unrestrained fighter pilot, had proved good so far; "If you keep your boots shined and your hair cut short, you can screw off until you make captain. After that, you'll have to play the game."

Locke had thrown himself into pilot training and finished at the top of his class, but when the assignments came down, all the choice F-15 and F-16 slots went to Academy graduates. Locke went on a drunk, in the privacy of his apartment, but didn't give up.

Another instructor, a cynical, overweight lieutenant, kept him on track. "Bide your time and use the F-4 to your advantage. It's an old fighter but a good one. If those pricks that got the F-15s and 16s can't fly, being a Zoomy isn't going to help them. You can fly better than any student I've trained. Use the Phantom to prove how good you are and work into the F-16."

Upgrade training in the Phantom had come shortly after that, then an assignment to Alexandria South Air Base where he and Thunder, a big, affable black man, were teamed on the same crew. An immediate rapport sprang up between the two.

Jack complained to Thunder, whose attention was free since the last of the crews left the squadron to fly. "All I want to do is fly. Why do we get hammered for what we do on our own time?"

"There's more to the Air Force than just flying and chasing around, man. Hey—Fairly just drove up. Catch him quick."

Locke darted out. Lieutenant Colonel Mike Fairly, squadron commander of the 379th Tactical Flying Squadron, listened to Jack's story on the drive over and had also decided that was the reason behind the phone call, but it escaped him why the Old Man should be bent out of shape because some fighter jocks were whooping it up at a party. Everyone knew Shaw had raised hell in his time. But Fairly knew from personal experience what a discrete phone call from some general in a higher headquarters could do to a wing commander's disposition.

Fairly knocked on Shaw's door. Colonel Shaw waved Fairly to a chair and handed him the incident report with a curt, "Read that." Before the younger man had read half of the report, he could hardly control his grin. The Security Police had received a noise complaint from the BOQ (Bachelor Officers' Quarters) at 0207 hours that morning. A team consisting of Technical Sergeant Robert Kincaid and Sergeant Irene Bush (the last name being underlined) had responded to the call and upon entering the BOQ, heard loud music and the sounds of a party. They found the door to Lieutenant Locke's room fully opened (again, underlined) and the room occupied by approximately fifteen people. The people were shouting and clapping for a couple dancing on a table in the middle of the room. The woman was totally nude and the man was wearing a pair of shorts. The woman was taken into custody by Sergeant Irene Bush (again underlined).

The two individuals were subsequently identified as Lieutenant Jackson D. Locke and a civilian, Miss Abigail Pearson. Miss Pearson's father was called and picked up his daughter from the Law Enforcement Desk at 0513 hours. An initial investigation revealed that Miss Pearson had been attending a party given by Lieutenant Locke in honor of her eighteenth birthday.

The squadron commander gave an expressive shrug of his shoulders as if to say, "Fighter pilots will be fighter pilots," when he handed the report back to the colonel.

"Obviously, Colonel Fairly, you are more amused than worried about this incident. Perhaps you'll feel differently knowing a member of your squadron has been cavorting in the buff with the daughter of the U.S. ambassador to Egypt, the Honorable Frederick Pearson, and that the same Honorable Frederick Pearson was on my base this morning retrieving his daughter from our Security Police. A business that I knew nothing about. Still amused?"

"Colonel, if you want, I'll start checking on all the fornicators in my squadron and brief you every morning."

The color in Colonel Shaw's face started to rise. "Good God, no! With that bunch you sit on, it would take all morning, every morning. Besides, I lost my yen for pornography about fifteen years ago. But we are going to have to do something. Tell me about Locke."

"Pretty much your standard-issue fighter pilot," Fairly answered. Twenty-four years old, came into the service right out of college AFROTC. He's a bachelor and makes an impression with the ladies. Also with some of the young married lovelies, but he cools that. And, he's the best pilot in my squadron. All he needs is seasoning."

"Is he such a big skirt-chaser that it's going to influence his judgment?"

"He's OK, he only needs maturing. Like I said, he's had some pretty obvious propositions. He's always handled that well. My wife claims that I wouldn't be half as restrained." Fairly's answer satisfied the colonel. Too many of the fighter jocks in his wing were getting caught up in the fighter pilot image and losing their way, finding sex, alcohol and general hell-raising more to their liking than the daily business of responsible flying. Locke looked worth saving.

"OK, Mike, I'll buy what you say. But I'm going to have to take some action. We need to put some salt on his tail and slow him down a bit. We've got to get his attention. Got any ideas?"

"Well, sir, I'd recommend some strong words and putting him in the Barrel for a week. That would be the same as confining him to quarters and he'll have to hang around the squadron without a chance to fly. He'll get the message."

Shaw mulled over the suggestion for a few moments. His wing had a commitment to keep two aircrews on alert twenty-four hours a day. Two pilots and their wizzos, or more properly, Weapons Systems Officers (WSOs), had to be ready to man their aircraft within five minutes, ready to start engines. Because of the time requirement, the aircrews had to remain in the squadron or alert shack, and while there were eating and sleeping facilities available, it was very confining. Normally, two pilots and their backseaters would only stay on alert for twenty-four hours before someone else would replace them and go into the "Barrel." One of the three squadrons would "pull" alert for a week, then pass it on to the next squadron.

The crews had never been able to figure out exactly why the wing had an alert commitment. Since Maintenance only kept the twenty-millimeter cannon loaded and the aircraft were never launched, they did not see much sense to it all. There was one point of common agreement: they hated it.

The look on Shaw's face warned Fairly that the colonel wasn't convinced. "Sir, outside of flying, there is not a hell of a lot for my troops to do around here. Keeping them busy on the ground is a real headache. Take away the chance to fly, and you're really punishing them."

Fairly had touched on Shaw's biggest morale problem: how to keep his people occupied in their spare time. It distressed the wing commander that it was affecting his pilots and wizzos. "OK, that's what we'll do," he decided. "Bring him in."

Fairly checked the outer office and found the young lieutenant talking to the secretary. Typical, Fairly thought, he practices charming any available female. Jack Locke marched into the office and reported with a sharp salute. The wing commander kept him standing at attention for a full thirty seconds before returning his salute. Shaw sized Locke up, noticing his properly trimmed hair, brightly shined boots, and flight suit that was properly adjusted, probably within the last few minutes. He fits the image of a fighter pilot, Shaw decided: just under six feet tall, a trim and athletic build, clear blue eyes.

"Lieutenant Locke, your conduct last night was reported on the Security Police blotter. It goes without saying that such actions cannot be tolerated and are unbecoming to an officer. I will not have my officers dancing bare-assed with young ladies around the BOQ. *Especially* a young lady who happens to be the ambassador's daughter. Lewd conduct such as this is punishable by court-martial or nonjudicial punishment under Article Fifteen of the Uniform Code of Military Justice. Granted, there are mitigating circumstances in this case. Since this is the first time you have been in trouble, I have little desire to end any career you might find in the Air Force."

Shaw paused, partly for effect. "No doubt, you are aware that the presence of the U.S. Air Force in Egypt is new and we are having a difficult time convincing the Egyptians that we belong in the Middle East. We are here to help encourage the hotheads to leave their neighbors in peace. Any publicity resulting from such an escapade with the ambassador's daughter will not help our position with the Egyptians.

"Therefore, pending conversations with the ambassador, you are ordered to go low profile. It will depend on the ambassador's reaction as to the final action I will take. To ensure your low profile, and as your squadron assumes alert tomorrow, you will be in the Barrel for the next seven days. Any questions?"

Jack studied the colonel, knowing that any rebuttal would be wasted breath. Forget mentioning that it had been a private party and the cops should not have entered his rooms unannounced in the first place. "No, sir."

"One last thing, Lieutenant. If you ever again run around in public with your pecker hanging out, I'll hang you up by it. Dismissed." Fairly and Jack saluted the colonel and left the office.

Outside, Fairly said, "You were lucky this time, Jack. I don't think the ambassador is going to say a thing about it."

Jack glanced at his squadron commander. "Colonel Fairly, it was a private party. I don't know who opened that door last night. Probably the same clown who made the complaint. For *this* I don't get to fly for a week? A *week?*"

GRAIN KING

The changeover crew of the reconnaissance aircraft slowly gathered outside base operations in the soft, early-morning dark. Colonel Anthony J. Waters glanced out the window as he and the aircraft commander, Captain Kelly, went through the routine of debriefing the crew they were replacing, checking the weather, and filing a flight plan for the upcoming flight. "I haven't seen Cruzak yet," Waters said.

"No sweat, Colonel," the young captain beamed. "He won't be late for a flight again. He's already here doing loadmaster duties, helping the other crew clean the bird up before we take it. He's going to be the highest flying janitor in the Air Force until he cleans his act up."

Waters glanced at Captain Kelly with a look of resignation. The colonel liked the captain and he was a good pilot who could fly the RC-135 with a smooth and cool hand. But Sergeant Stan Cruzak was only the latest in a string of problems that plagued his crew, and Waters doubted that making the joker an acting loadmaster would help the situation.

Because of the highly sophisticated equipment in the rear of the aircraft, only personnel with a Top Secret Crypto clearance were allowed in the reconnaissance module aft of the flight deck. So when they were TDY (on Temporary Duty) away from their home base, only the crews that kept the aircraft constantly in the air had the necessary clearances to clean and service the cabin. The enlisted crew rotated the cleanup responsibilities, calling it "loadmaster duties," hating every minute of it.

Normally, pilots in charge of Air Force aircraft were the commanders of the crew regardless of rank, and the captain of this particular RC-135 insisted on maintaining every inch of his control over the radio specialists and translators that manned the module. But Waters was the module commander and in charge of their mission—intelligence gathering and monitoring communications. Supposedly, he didn't have to concern himself with the more mundane problems of flying the airplane and looking after the crew. That fell to the aircraft commander, who took his orders from the module commander. So Waters felt like a highly paid passenger, something he chalked up to the Air Force's having too many colonels and not enough jobs for them.

First Lieutenant William G. Carroll was waiting for them when they walked out of Ops and headed toward the heavily guarded plane. Waters liked the young intelligence officer, who was also the best translator on the crew. Carroll was dark complected, slender, of medium height, and had an easy manner that hid a high intellect. "Anything new for us to be worried about on this go-round?" the colonel asked.

"No, sir," Carroll said. "All the crazies are quiet and nothing has changed since the last time we flew. Should be a quiet twelve hours. I'll brief the flight crew after we take off."

The two security guards who would fly on this mission met the crew at the break in the rope that surrounded the RC-135. The Air Force had assigned a security team to maintain a constant guard on its latest and most valuable reconnaissance platform. The RC-135 never took off without two guards and a K-9 guard dog on board in case the aircraft had to divert into a civilian field for an emergency. Although the guards knew each of the crew, they carefully checked the restricted area badge of each person before allowing them past the barrier. Waters was the last through and paused, aware that once they launched, the guards would be restricted to the small compartment at the crew entrance door with the dog for the long flight. "Hell of a way to mess up your day," Waters said.

"No problem," one replied, "if Cruzak will stop bothering the dog."

A ground power unit was roaring nearby, supplying power to the aircraft, and Waters could barely hear the angry barking and howling of the well-trained K-9 coming from inside the aircraft. "What the—" Waters strode quickly up the steps leading to the crew entrance door. He had never heard the dog bark before.

He caught up with the pilot as they pushed through the knot of people standing and laughing in the entrance. Inside, Cruzak was crouched on the deck on all fours, barking furiously at the dog that was in its cage, ready for the flight. The dog responded in kind and the two were setting up a tremendous wail. Waters stifled a smile and brushed his dark, unruly hair back, shaking his head in amusement.

"Cruzak! What the hell are you doing?" Captain Kelly shouted, adding to the confusion.

The sergeant twisted his head and looked at the pilot. He did not move from in front of the cage. "Sir! I'm the loadmaster on this United States Air Force aircraft, right?"

The pilot nodded, dumbfounded.

"I checked the regulations, sir! As loadmaster I am required to brief all passengers who are not regularly assigned crew members on safety procedures." With that, he turned back to the dog and resumed his barking and growling.

The pilot stepped forward, reaching for the collar of the young sergeant. Waters grabbed the captain's shoulder and pulled him back before he touched Cruzak. "Get this beast into the air, Captain Kelly. I'll sort this one out." The young pilot looked at Waters, relieved that he had taken charge of the problem, and retreated into the cockpit. Waters motioned the rest of the crew into the module. "Hold on, Stan. We need to talk."

The dog quieted as the sergeant stood up. "What's going on, Stan? You can do better than this."

"Aah, Colonel," he shrugged, holding his head down in front of the tall colonel, "the captain just gets bent out of shape over the wrong things. If he were like you, there'd be no problem."

"Captain Kelly has to run the crew, you know that. You've got to help him or he can't do his job."

"That's the problem, Colonel. He won't *let* us help him. He doesn't tell us *when* to do our job, he tells us *how* to do it. And I know how to do my job better than anyone."

Cruzak was right. The problem was not the sergeant; it was Captain Kelly. "OK, cool it for now. We'll talk later."

"Thanks, Colonel. I'll do it right." Cruzak hurried to his position, ready to work.

Waters had known for a week that Kelly needed to be replaced, but he had hoped the captain would get the crew under control. He hated the thought of making a decision that would ruin Kelly's career. But he decided to do what was necessary after the mission was over. It's time to retire, he thought. You're going nowhere, in command of nothing, and hurting people you like.

16 July: 0515 hours, Greenwich Mean Time
0715 hours, Alexandria, Egypt

The alert shack was an afterthought tacked onto Alexandria South Air Base. When the Americans had finally wrangled the Egyptians into letting them occupy the base built by the Russians during the early 1960s, they had found the buildings poorly constructed and in need of massive repairs. It would have been cheaper to tear most of them down and start over. But the Egyptian government would not allow any new construction on the base and the Americans were forced into a major renovation project using Egyptian labor.

After the wing had picked up the commitment to keep two Phantoms on alert, two trailers had been towed to a spot near the flight line for the crews to stay in. For some reason, that satisfied the Egyptians. The four crew chiefs that launched the alert aircraft occupied one trailer, and the pilots and WSOs the other. The sergeants had scrounged around and turned their trailer into a plush lounge where the air conditioner always worked. The officers' trailer remained as it was delivered: barely livable. The two trailers' official title, "Quick Response Alert Facility," was quickly redubbed the "alert shack."

Thunder Bryant rapped on the door of the bedroom where Jack was sleeping. "Yo', Jack. Colonel Fairly has scheduled himself with Johnny Nelson in his backseat for the Barrel today. He'll be out here in about twenty minutes." That would get the pilot's attention and stir him into action.

A groan came from behind the bedroom door. "Can you meet me in the chiefs' trailer in a few minutes?"

A crew chief welcomed Thunder with a mug of fresh coffee before returning to the window overlooking the flight line. The captain joined him, waiting for Jack to come out from the officers' trailer. A dark frown drew his eyes into a squint when he saw a pretty young girl come out of the trailer first. "That boy is *thick*. Will he ever learn?"

"She was here two nights ago," the chief said to Thunder. "The ambassador's daughter? Where does he find 'em around this hole?"

Bryant shook his head. "Who knows? One day, that boy . . ." Thunder was aware that sooner or later he would have to stop running interference for his pilot. But protecting people and blocking for them was his nature. After all, he'd worked his way out of the ghetto in South Central Los Angeles by being the best guard in the history of L.A. high school football.

A scholarship to UCLA was a natural fringe benefit. There, he learned how much a guard could hurt someone when he didn't do his job. In his sophomore year, the team's phenomenal quarterback had become his best friend and during a hard-fought game, Thunder missed a block that let two opponents swarm over his teammate. The quarterback's wrist was broken in the pileup and never correctly healed, ending his career in football. And while no one blamed Thunder for the accident, he saddled himself with responsibility for it.

After that, the young black man lost his enthusiasm for football and turned to his studies. Eventually, he was cut from the team and lost his athletic scholarship. But the Air Force offered him another one in ROTC, and with student loans he was able to graduate. Once in the Air Force, less than perfect eyesight kept him out of pilot training and led him into navigator training. Thunder found flying and the Air Force deeply rewarding. He mounted a well-thought-out attack on navigator training and graduated at the top of his class, sweeping every honor the program had to offer. He was not surprised when he was assigned to F-4s, his first choice.

The young officer found a home in the fighter community and rapidly developed into the best WSO in his wing. When the Air Force asked for volunteers to open the base in Egypt, he jumped at the chance, instinctively aware of the opportunities that existed in a new unit. Three things happened to him at Alexandria South: he made captain, met Jack, and learned how to play. Out of desperation, Mike Fairly teamed Thunder with Jack, hoping the WSO could control the young lieutenant. It was a perfect match. Thunder was able to curb most of Jack's impulsive behavior and Jack taught Thunder how to relax and have some fun.

Jack kissed the girl good-bye near the alert area's parking lot and sprinted back to the chief's trailer, bursting through the door. "Coffee, amigo?" he asked the crew chief.

"Later," Thunder told him. "Maintenance is switching the alert birds. It's preflight time. Tail number is 512."

Jack faked a groan and headed out the door with the same enthusiasm as when he entered.

"Man, I'm teamed with a puppy," Thunder grinned, picking up his flight gear and following Jack out to the bunker, where the Phantom sat.

The crew chief trailed after Jack during the preflight, proud of the conditioning of his bird and ready to question the pilot if he found anything wrong. "Take good care of her this time," the sergeant told Jack. "OK? If you fly, don't bring her back broke like last time."

Jack nodded. 512 was the best-kept Phantom in the wing. It gleamed with the loving care the crew chief gave to an only child. Unfortunately, the chief's personal hygiene did not meet the same standards. His fatigues were filthy and he needed a shower and shave.

"Hey, Chief, you want to stand downwind a bit?" The sergeant ignored Jack.

"Why are you back on alert?" Jack asked Thunder as they walked back from the preflight. He felt bad about his backseater pulling a second alert shift with him.

"Would you believe I got lonely?" Thunder changed the subject, not wanting to embarrass his friend. "Besides, we can lift some weights, maybe run some laps around the flight line."

"What are you, a bloody drill sergeant?" Jack laughed.

16 July: 0930 hours, Greenwich Mean Time
0930 hours, a village in Niger, Africa

The navigator, Major David Belfort, was lying on the floor of the flight deck next to the copilot's seat, studying the heat-cracked landscape through the lower quarter window at the copilot's right foot. The desert village the C-130 Hercules was circling for the third time was eighteen hundred miles to the southwest of Alexandria, Egypt, and nestled against small hills that helped protect it from the fury of the Sahara's harsh climate. Belfort was wearing his headset to muffle the noise of the turboprop engines and didn't like hearing the pilot and copilot argue whether they should land.

"I think we ought to hotfoot it back to Kano before we have to divert into a field to the north," Toni D'Angelo argued.

"Relax, Toni," Sid Luna told her. "We've got plenty of time to land, offload the food and still make it back. Besides, these people are hungry. That's what Grain King is all about." The copilot did not reply, accepting the pilot's decision. She nudged Dave with her foot and gave him a thumbs-down gesture, indicating they were going to land.

Belfort's gut told him the copilot was right—they should heed the latest weather warning she'd received. An unexpectedly large sandstorm was descending on them. But he didn't say anything. After all, she could hold her own in any argument. She was also an excellent pilot, which surprised her macho skeptics.

The pilot turned onto final approach, calling for her to read the landing checklist. "Sid," Toni warned, "those people are crowding the right side of the runway. Shade it to the left."

"I've got 'em. No sweat," Luna replied. The pilots were not surprised to see the villagers crowding the narrow runway. They had seen it many times when they landed: starving, gaunt people, desperate for help.

Toni D'Angelo rechecked the landing gear and placed her left hand over Luna's right hand, which controlled the throttles. It was a backup technique they had developed to prevent the pilot's hand from bouncing off the throttle quadrant on a hard landing. Sid flew the big cargo plane onto the exact point he wanted on the approach end of the runway. He planted the C-130 hard in a controlled crash, letting the main landing gear absorb the shock before slamming the nose onto the narrow dirt runway. He jerked the throttles back, throwing the four propellers into reverse to help brake their landing rollout.

The Hercules abruptly jerked and skidded to the right, running off the packed dirt of the runway. Luna shouted over the interphone, "Differential thrust!" He fought for control of the Hercules as its props picked up dirt and gravel and threw it in front of them, seriously reducing his visibility.

One of the propellers on the left side had not gone into reverse, which let the props on the right create more drag, flinging them to the right. Both pilots' hands bounced off the throttles. Luna fumbled for the controls as he fought to keep the Hercules from skidding further to the right. Finally, he found the levers and instinctively threw number four prop on the right out of reverse. On a normal runway, he would have returned all four to idle, but he needed braking action if he was to stop the heavily loaded cargo plane in the little space that remained.

With a prop on each side giving him even braking, Luna regained control of the big cargo plane as it hurtled straight for the crowd of scattering villagers.

16 July: 1100 hours, Greenwich Mean Time
0700 hours, Washington, D.C.

Colonel Eugene S. Blevins stalked into the Watch Center in his normally dismal early morning mood. If anything, his natural state of depression was more intense, for he had convinced himself that his career was in jeopardy. The brigadier general selection board was to meet soon and nothing spectacular had happened to him. And unless his sponsor could do something for him, Belvins was going to be just another "nobody" name for the board to consider.

A scan of the big situation boards did nothing to improve his disposition.

The on-duty watch commander, Tom Gomez, was sitting in the battle cab, the glassed-in balcony that overlooked the entire operation, and had seen Blevins studying the boards. When he caught Blevins' eye, Gomez motioned him to come up the stairs for an update briefing and go through the motions of a change of command.

The Pentagon tried hard to promote the image of a formal, serious procedure, and Blevins believed that it should be one, given the responsibilities involved. But off-going Watch Commander Gomez was of an entirely different disposition and not concerned with formalities that he considered meaningless. His total disregard of established procedures infuriated Blevins, smacking as it did of unprofessionalism. But Gomez was a colonel and slightly senior to Blevins, so what could he do about it? Besides, the man was nothing but a broken-down fighter pilot on his last assignment before retirement. It irritated him that a pilot had been placed in such an important position only because he wore wings and had combat experience in Vietnam. Big deal. He, on the other hand, had done yeoman labor in Intelligence, working up through the field. He knew the subject inside and out; he was one of the people who knew how to make the system *work*. The other colonel was a Johnny-come-lately, and all because he wore wings on his chest.

The sergeant monitoring the entry control point into the battle cab had been watching Blevins since he stepped onto the main floor. Master Sergeant John Nesbit had worked many shifts with Blevins and knew what the colonel was thinking. He shuddered at the thought of spending a twelve-hour shift with a man full of self-pity.

Colonel Tom Gomez read the sergeant's mind. "Hey, Sarge, he won't hurt you. Might frighten the staff a bit if his coffee is cold, but he knows this business. He's not a twenty-watter, that's for damn sure."

Blevins arrived at the door, awaiting entry. Nesbit pushed a button, unlocking the door. The sergeant gave an audible sigh, looking at the two colonels. Blevins resembled a field grade officer, slightly over six feet tall, carefully styled dark hair, with an immaculately tailored uniform. Tom Gomez was two inches shorter, stocky, cut his graying hair in a brush cut, and shambled about unconcerned with his uniform.

The Watch Center in the Pentagon was a pivotal fusion point between Intelligence, Communications, and Command and Control. During a crisis involving the military, it was the primary intelligence center for the War Room. When a crisis started to form, the colonel on duty recalled the three Air Force generals that made up the Watch Center's battle staff. The generals gathered in the battle cab overlooking the main boards and decided what information should be up-channeled to the War Room. Their function was critical in preventing the higher echelons of command from being inundated with irrelevant information.

Also, the generals or the watch commander could initiate orders to certain Air Force operational units should a fast-breaking situation require an immediate response. Each colonel was aware of the visibility that went with the position; provided the right incident happened, a good performance could result in promotion. However, there was a risk. If the colonel produced an interpretation of events that ran counter to the preconceived notions of the generals on the battle staff, the watch commander was in for some rough handling.

Over the course of a year, Nesbit had seen both Blevins and Gomez in action during a number of crises, or "flaps." Blevins had proven himself to be very adept at avoiding any controversy or producing his own estimate for the generals to scrutinize or criticize. He always had an intelligence analyst from the main floor available to analyze the situation and take any heat from the generals. Gomez was totally different and the junior officers still talked about the way he had handled the latest in a long series of incidents in the Persian Gulf.

General Lawrence Cunningham, the Air Force chief of staff, had put in an unexpected appearance in the battle cab shortly after an unidentified fighter had bombed a Kuwaiti oil refinery. He had permanently relieved the on-duty watch commander before Gomez reported in for not giving him the answers he wanted. As soon as the colonel had cleared the door, Cunningham had hit him with a barrage of questions, a few well-chosen expletives, and a very pointed comment about Gomez's career expectations if some sense wasn't made out of the situation.

Gomez had only said, "Excuse me for a moment, sir. I have to get my ducks lined up." He had left the general to stew for three minutes while he reviewed the message traffic. After a brief scan of the situation boards, he was sure of the situation and had turned to Cunningham. "This was a hit-and-run raid by the Iranians. There won't be any follow-up. Right now the only fires being lit are here, not in the Gulf."

Cunningham's reaction amazed everyone in the cab, most of whom had just put Gomez down as a candidate for castration. He nodded in agreement and left the battle cab. The Watch Center reverted to its normal routine, monitoring the military disposition, Order of Battle (OB), of potential enemies. The analysts liked to think of their job as guarding against the "Pearl Harbor option."

Most information received by the Watch Center was already processed and evaluated. However, something happened to common sense when raw data moved through the system. Tom Gomez had learned a valuable lesson when one of the analysts correctly interpreted a series of events that had almost increased the nation's DEFCON status. A large portion of the Soviets' civil air fleet, Aeroflot, had been suddenly grounded after landing at the Red Army's collection bases for deployment. The analyst, a female captain, had called it correctly when she pointed out that the aircraft had gone into the bases to pick up the annual replacements for the Red Army in Eastern Europe. They had not launched because the weather at their drop-off points in East Germany was below landing minimums. Further, she observed that the number of aircraft grounded in Russia was the same as that used every year for the redeployment of troops to Eastern Europe.

Gomez learned something else from that incident. He had concentrated on the analyst's legs and not on what she was saying. He later realized that he had brought too many preconceived ideas about women over from his operational experiences in tactical fighter aircraft. It came as a shock to him that a woman could think and be pretty at the same time.

He never made that mistake again.

Master Sergeant Nesbit resigned himself to the next twelve hours as Blevins adjusted his controlled area badge, insuring its straight alignment. The sergeant groaned as Blevins marched up to Gomez who was sitting in the center captain's chair at the main console. Blevins snapped a smart salute and reported in. "Morning, Colonel Gomez. Colonel Blevins reporting for duty."

Nesbit groaned louder.

Tom Gomez waved a salute back to Blevins. "It's all yours, Gene." An intriguing thought tickled the back of Gomez's mind. With a little effort, he could arrange to have a series of perfectly valid, yet totally insignificant facts funneled to the pompous colonel. If he did it right, the man would screw himself into the floor before he decided what to do. There were plenty of willing conspirators down on the main floor.

Erasing the thought, Gomez gave Blevins a quick rundown of the current situation. "Europe's quiet. The Fourth Air Regiment in Romania has stopped its conversion to Flogger Gs. Not sure why yet. Captain Marshall thinks the aircraft are being diverted to Ashkhabad, near the Iranian border."

Gomez began to type a series of commands into the computer, calling up different display maps on the situation boards. He paused over North Africa. "The Grain King food and relief flights for the UN are still going full bore in the southern Sahara. The buildup at Kano in Nigeria as a central staging base is working well. There are six C-130s operational down there today. But Sara is worried. She believes the Libyans are starting to get antsy again.

"Well, she's wrong," Blevins said. "The Libyans have bought into the UN food relief missions as a way to create some good will. That should be perfectly *obvious* to everyone in the Watch Center. They've even given the UN permission to use their airfields and airspace."

What a shame, Gomez thought, that he doesn't have the courage to argue with the generals this way when he knows he's right. "Nothing has changed in the Mideast," Gomez continued. "Iran is its usual mess, quiet for the moment. Most of the analysts think the fighting will start up again. They don't have anything definite."

Blevins interrupted him, nodding in agreement. "Like I've said many times, the analysts don't have the big picture, but they are right this time. Iran and Iraq have worn themselves out but Iran is still spoiling for a fight."

Gomez continued, "The reports of an alliance between Iran and Afghanistan were only rumors. The Kurds are back at it, fighting both Iraq and Iran." He sped over the rest of the world, ending on the Soviet Bloc. He called up the Warsaw Pact's OB by type, strength, and location. "No major changes other than the normal seasonal ones. Just that glitch about the Fourth Regiment Floggers. Any questions?" Gomez asked.

"Thank you, Colonel Gomez, no questions," he replied, stiff as a board.

"See you next time around," Gomez said, rising from the captain's chair and disappearing down the stairs onto the main floor.

Blevins leaned over the main console, peering at the situation boards. He noticed that Gomez was still on the main floor talking to Captain Sara Marshall. They were engaged in an intense conversation and Blevins hoped that the colonel was reprimanding her for the length of her skirt, which was always shorter than the regulations allowed, revealing her shapely legs. Blevins wished he could make the junior officers see the relationship between meeting the Air Force's regulations on dress and appearance and doing the job right. Too often, he'd seen shoddy job performances and sloppy appearances go hand in hand. If her sudden laughter meant anything, Gomez was not talking hemlines.

Frustrated, he turned his attention to the boards and called up NATO's Order of Battle, placing it opposite the Warsaw Pact's. Nothing had changed since his last shift. Although the display was exactly as he expected, he still found it frightening. He doubted that any politician could survive an election if the American public could see and understand those numbers the way he did. Blevins was echoing an article of faith held by the generals on the Watch Center's battle staff.

The state of depression that had curdled the colonel's existence returned to dominate his thoughts.

Something *had* to happen if he was to shine.

He clicked over possible scenarios in his mind, and what he would do in each.

If something didn't happen soon, he would never make general.

16 July: 1200 hours, Greenwich Mean Time
1400 hours, Alexandria, Egypt

"What I need is a ghost writer for these damn things," Fairly muttered, disgusted with himself. Normally he would write an efficiency report in fifteen minutes. The squadron commander glared at the blank Officer Effectiveness Report (OER), AF Form 77, and willed the words to appear on the OER. Nothing happened. He carefully printed Jack's full name in the appropriate space in neat block letters. No other words came to him.

He tried to find the right phrases by staring at Jack, then Thunder. Both were slumped in the two most comfortable chairs in the alert shack. Jack was thumbing through an old Playboy magazine while Thunder was reading a book on the Civil War. Fairly threw down his pencil. "Jack, let's go into the kitchen. I need to talk to you."

Jack immediately followed the older man into the small kitchen, pausing to shoot a glance at Thunder, who arched one of his bushy eyebrows in reply.

"I guess this is why the boss pulled alert," Jack mumbled, calculating there was bad news waiting for him. He followed Fairly into the small kitchen and closed the door behind him.

"Sit down and relax, Jack. We need to talk about your career." Relief flowed over Jack; he had been certain that Ambassador Pearson had sent down the word to crush him. The lieutenant colonel was going through the motions of doing annual career counseling of junior officers as the regulations required. Fairly was doing "square filling," Jack decided.

"Jack, I'm worried about you. You're one of the best pilots in the wing. But you're all balls and no forehead once you crawl out of the cockpit. Get your act together. Try to remember that the Air Force wants you to act like a responsible officer on the ground. Because if you don't . . ."

"Excuse me, Colonel, with all due respect, isn't our job, like they say, to 'fly and fight' and not worry about playing Mickey Mouse games on the ground?"

"Listen, you and I both know there's no fighting in a peacetime Air Force. We're trainers. Training to fight. That's the glitch. You'll probably never see combat in your entire career. Or if you do, you'll be in a command position. You've got to learn to use good judgment and be responsible in *all* your actions. I've teamed you with the best WSO in the wing, maybe the Air Force. Thunder is going to make general because he is good, very good. And not because he is black. Right now he's serving time as a technician, just like you. As soon as I can, I'm going to move him up to headquarters where he can get more experience in making decisions and get out of the cockpit.

"If there's a war, he'll be ready. But for now I've entrusted him to you. For some strange reason he likes flying with you and wants to stay in your pit. Now it's your job to keep him alive and not drag him into trouble with you. That's what leadership for a lieutenant is all about. Think about what I've said and what you want to do in this Air Force."

Jack returned to the trailer's lounge, shaking his head. He flopped back into the chair next to Thunder. "Career counseling, no biggy," he muttered. Thunder visibly relaxed. Jack felt a rising itch of frustration as he recalled his commander's words. He didn't like the implications behind what Fairly had said. All he wanted to do was to fly fighters and avoid all the rest of the Mickey Mouse that Fairly was telling him was so important. To him, the Air Force started and ended in the cockpit, and he was not merely a "technician"; his job was what the Air Force was all about. And he didn't like the idea of losing Thunder as his backseater.

The reality of the Air Force was much different than he had imagined as a fourteen-year-old ninth grader in Phoenix, Arizona. He could always remember seeing jets from nearby Luke Air Force Base maneuver around the cloudless sky, catching his imagination and drawing him out of his everyday world. And then one day in the ninth grade he knew he was going to fly fighters. After that, everything he did had one purpose, to get an appointment to the Air Force Academy. He took all the science and math courses his high school had to offer and went out for sports every semester. An Air Force Academy liaison officer had told him making Eagle Scout would help him in the fiercely competitive selective process and he had dutifully worked on getting the required twenty-one merit badges. He suffered a slight distraction when he discovered girls and sex. Had he been less attractive, a girl might have persuaded him that marriage was preferable to the celibacy offered by the Academy. However, he soon discovered that lack of female companionship would never be a problem.

What bothered him now was that the service was asking more from him than being the best fighter jock that ever strapped on a Phantom.

16 July: 1230 hours, Greenwich Mean Time
1230 hours, over the Sahara

The flight deck of the C-130 Hercules was quiet. But with everything that had happened in the last three hours, Dave Belfort couldn't find the rest he needed. The navigator was sitting in the copilot's position jotting down notes in the small notebook he always carried in his navigator's bag. He glanced at Toni D'Angelo, who was sleeping. Belfort was relieved that the co-pilot had been able to catnap for a few minutes. He looked at the crew bunk at the rear of the flight deck to check on Sid Luna's condition. The loadmaster, Leonard McCray, was bent over the inert pilot, wearing his headset.

"How's Sid doing?" he asked the master sergeant over the interphone.

"The bleeding is just oozing. He's conscious," McCray answered. The slight improvement in the pilot's condition helped to buoy Belfort's sagging spirits.

The exchange on the intercom did not disturb the sleeping flight engineer Riley Henderson. The old sergeant had learned years before how to tune out unwanted noise, doze off in his seat, and be wide awake at the first hint of mechanical trouble on the Hercules.

Belfort decided to let him sleep.

Toni D'Angelo stirred in her seat, then snapped awake in a moment of panic when she realized she was in command of the C-130. "I slept too long," she said, putting her headset on.

"No problem," Belfort replied. "Sid's conscious and his bleeding's almost stopped."

"Dave, did I cause the accident because I wasn't strong enough to hold Sid's hand on the throttles?"

"I don't see how. It's a shitty technique anyway. Besides, the problem was differential thrust. I thought Sid did well to keep us from going all over the place."

"I never felt us hit the girl," Toni murmured.

"First time you've ever seen a mangled body? It's always tough. I've never seen anyone hit by a prop before. No wonder the villagers attacked Sid. Jeez. Thank God, McCray knew enough of the language to calm them down."

"This is the second time I've been on Grain King," McCray interjected, "and I had to manage the cargo sheds at Niamey for three months. It sort of rubbed off, you know, associating with the locals."

"I'm glad you know something about first aid too," Toni added.

"Hell," the loadmaster said, "with all that blood from the knife wound, I thought for sure he was dead. They thought he was dead, too. He's lucky he was kicked unconscious."

Both officers became silent, recalling how McCray had quieted the raging villagers by yelling in Berber, telling them the C-130 was carrying food for them. After that, it had been easy for McCray to get the injured pilot onto the flight deck and arrange for the cargo of rice and vegetables to be offloaded.

The high-frequency radio crackled into life. "Grain King Zero-Three, N'Djamena Center. How do you read?"

Belfort answered the call from the Air Traffic Control center, "Read you five-by, N'Djamena. Go ahead."

"Roger, Grain King," the heavy French accent replied. "You are cleared as requested. Tripoli Center has cleared you to enter their airspace. Report crossing the FIR. Contact Tripoli on upper high-frequency channels eight-niner six-niner or eight-eight six-two."

Dave keyed the mike again, "Grain King copies, N'Djamena. Please confirm that Tripoli knows we are a UN food relief flight and diverting to Alexandria South due to weather. Also that we have an injured crewman on board in need of medical attention and are requesting priority handling. Please recheck the weather for us."

"Stand by Grain King," N'Djamena answered. The flight deck was quiet while Belfort waited for the reply.

"Grain King, this is N'Djamena," the flight control center radioed. Tripoli acknowledges your status. Also be advised that all stations to the south and west are now down due to blowing sand and dust. Alexandria will remain clear for the next eight hours."

Dave thanked N'Djamena for their help and leaned back in the co-pilot's seat, still not able to rest. "Never hurts to double check," he said to no one in particular.

"It's OK to overfly Libya?" Toni said.

"They've given us a clearance," Dave answered. "We've got to go northeast because of this granddaddy of a sandstorm and we need a hospital for Sid. There's an American hospital at Alexandria South. The weather prophets blew this one big time." The weather warning they had received after launching from the village was far worse than the first. They had to divert.

"It'll be OK," Belfort said as the C-130 approached the extreme southwestern corner of Libya and he started to establish contact with Tripoli Center. I hope, he added to himself.

16 July: 1235 hours, Greenwich Mean Time
1235 hours, over the Mediterranean

The U.S. Air Force Reconnaissance RC-135 carved a lazy orbit over the Mediterranean while it monitored and recorded all the high-frequency radio transmissions made by the Grain King flight. As module commander in the rear of the big four-engine Boeing, Colonel Anthony Waters accordingly annotated his log while an old and familiar tingling signaled something was wrong. Experience had taught him not to ignore the warning. He rummaged around in his briefcase and pulled out a map of North Africa. He pressed the button keying his intercom. "Stan, can you play back the tape where Grain King gave N'Djamena Center its route to Alexandria South?"

The radio technician retrieved the transmission Waters wanted and played it back over the interphone.

The colonel frowned as he drew the C-130's route from Niger, through the southern part of Libya, and on into Egypt. The tingling grew stronger. Again keying his interphone, Waters called the flight deck and directed Captain Kelly to fly to an orbit south of the island of Malta, as close as they could get to Libya. He unstrapped from his seat and walked down the narrow passage to Bill Carroll's station, stretching and thinking at the same time. "Bill, what's the Mad Colonel been doing lately?" he said, spreading out his map on the lieutenant's desk and pointing to Libya.

"Been quiet ever since the F-111 raid on Tripoli in April '86. He's got lots of internal problems to keep him busy."

Waters mulled it over. "We've got a Grain King flight crossing the southern part of Libya. Here's their route. I don't like it. It doesn't feel right."

Carroll shrugged. "But Grain King is a UN operation that Libya is backing."

"I know," Waters replied, still not satisfied. Waters had not always been in the intelligence-gathering business and had only recently been made a module commander in RC-135s. When his last position had been phased out, colonel assignments at Headquarters Military Personnel had looked hard to find him a last assignment that matched his background before he retired. Unfortunately, there was nothing available and he was plugged into the only available slot.

Waters had accepted the assignment with resignation, unhappy at losing a job he enjoyed. His career had been like that since he returned from his second tour in Vietnam as a captain. His combat experience in F-4s had led him to the Air Force's Fighter Weapons School at Nellis AFB outside Las Vegas. Once there, he had worked his way up from an instructor to become Red Flag's key project officer—Red Flag was the Air Force's combat training program that tried to simulate an actual combat arena for its fighter pilots. Waters had become very adept at blending tactics and technology into believable wartime exercises.

Finally he had become too controversial a figure with his constant challenges of testing weapons systems and employment plans in the cold reality of combat scenarios and had infuriated the policy makers when he demonstrated the F-15 should be a two-place aircraft. The SPO (Special Projects Office) that drove the development of the F-15 had been dominated by old-line fighter pilots who believed fighter aircraft had one pilot and one engine. It had been a bitter compromise just to put two engines in the jet. When Waters proved repeatedly that a single pilot would be overwhelmed at low altitude in a high-threat environment, the SPO solved the problem by getting Waters reassigned.

After Nellis, he had been assigned to the fighter wing at Bitburg Air Base in Germany, and again had worked his way up, this time reaching squadron commander when he made lieutenant colonel. But that ended when Bitburg transitioned to F-15s and he had been reassigned stateside to Weapons Testing and Development at Eglin Air Force Base, Florida, which led into an assignment in Foreign Fighter Support at Kelly Air Force Base, Texas, where he had met and negotiated with many Arabs.

Through those contacts Waters had learned something of how the

Arab mind worked. Rather than move logically from one step to the next until a conclusion was reached, the Arab circled his objective, often going off on a wild tangent or goose chase but always returning to circle—so what was the Libyan leader's objective this time?

"Bill," Waters finally said, "I've moved our orbit closer to Tripoli. So far, we've only picked up routine messenger traffic, nothing to worry about. We may be spinning our wheels, but pay special attention to the Libyans for a while."

He waved for Stan Cruzak to join them. "Stan, as soon as we start picking up the Libyan's command net, see if you can crack into their frequency rotation."

One of the RC-135's most closely guarded secrets was its ability to break into the method of scrambling radio messages the Russians had provided the Libyans with. The Libyans could not handle encryption, and out of exasperation the Russians had sold them a scrambling system that rapidly rotated voice radio transmissions over many frequencies. The frequency shift was so rapid that the users did not even notice it. The idea was that an enemy could not follow the frequency changes. But a skilled radio operator on the RC-135 could slave the plane's computer to the monitoring sweeps and lock onto the frequency rotation. He also had to work with a translator to know if what he was receiving made sense and he wasn't missing frequency changes. Carroll and Cruzak were a well-rehearsed team.

"Tell me when you start to get something," Waters said. He left the two men and walked back to a sealed compartment in the rear of the module that held the aircraft's most classified equipment. The man that occupied the small space had jokingly painted the door green in homage to the movie *Behind the Green Door,* reminding the crew that what went on behind the door was none of their business. Only the operator and Waters knew what the equipment did and each held one half the code that activated the self-destruct mechanism that would destroy the sensitive equipment, which could, under the right conditions, pick up unshielded land-line telephone conversations from as far away as one hundred miles. Waters had the Libyans wired for sound. He explained what was happening to the operator and told him to buzz his position if he monitored anything significant.

At first Bill Carroll could not understand the flood of Arabic that started to crackle through his headset. But as the recon bird moved south, and as Stan refined the frequency shifts, the transmissions became stronger and clearer.

"Goddamn," Carroll said. "The Libyans are acting like they've got an intruder!" For five more minutes he monitored the transmission, wanting to be sure he understood exactly what he was hearing, then called Waters.

"Damn," Waters muttered. His internal warning sensations had turned into alarms. The action light from behind the green door flashed for his attention.

"Colonel . . ."

Waters cut him off and keyed the communication circuit for the green door. The operator's information was sketchy, "Sorry, Colonel. I can't break out what is being said, but the lines between the Soviet Embassy and Libyan Headquarters are hotter than hell."

The colonel broke the connection and patched his interphone into a conference line to talk to his translators and radio technicians. "Has anyone got unusual flight activity inside Libya or approaching their airspace?" The replies were negative. He punched up Carroll's circuit for a private conversation. "Bill, I think the Libyans are getting ready to scramble interceptors. I can only see one logical target—Grain King. You're an expert on these people, am I reading this wrong?"

"It's hard to tell, sir. They don't react like we do. It's a possibility . . ."

Which was enough for Waters to act on. He cut him off and called the flight deck. "Pilot, this is Waters. Go to Rose Orbit. Climb as high as possible. *Now.* Words why later." Everyone looked at one another, knowing that Rose Orbit was the optimum location for downlinking with Washington, D.C. RC-135s were required to maintain radio silence—their job was to monitor and gather information for analysis later on the ground, and not to talk to the world.

One of Waters' most important duties was to protect the capabilities of his reconnaissance platform from compromise, and if the Soviets monitored communications from the RC-135 that coincided with the actions of the Libyans, they would soon figure out what the bird could do. Waters knew a normal high-frequency radio transmission as well as an ultra-low-frequency message transmitted through the trailing wire antenna that stretched two miles behind the aircraft would be picked up immediately.

That only left an Apple Wave, which had never been used operationally.

The colonel rapidly drafted a message outlining the situation. He could anticipate some searching questions about breaking radio silence, probably be subject to an official enquiry, and worst of all, have to personally debrief Sundown Cunningham. Screw it, he thought, remembering when he had met the troublesome general at Red Flag. Maybe he could retire before that. Besides, he was willing to take the chance if other airmen were in danger and he could do something about it.

A computer technician fed the colonel's message into a computer bank. The computer encoded the message into a one-time use code, then split it into several parts. All of the parts would be transmitted simultaneously; however, the second part would start its transmission a fraction of a second after the first and on a slightly different part of the frequency wave and so on until all parts of the message were being transmitted at once. But before that happened, the computer would send a series of command signals to the aircraft's power sources and to the phased array antenna that punched the message into the atmosphere. Huge amounts of power were needed to overcome any jamming attempts by an enemy, to narrowly focus and to bend the beam over the horizon. Relays in junction boxes would open and close at the command of the computer, readying circuits that for a few seconds drew electrical power from other equipment on the aircraft.

Less than five seconds after the computer technician had finished typing the message into the computer, two ready lights flashed at the colonel's panel. Waters read the soft copy of his message spat out by the computer's printer. The computer had encoded, then decoded, the message before printing it out, accomplishing two things: first, the computer signaled that it had completed its self-tests, and second, it verified that it had properly encoded the message. It was up to Waters to check the most fallible element—human error in writing the message and inserting it into the computer.

There were no typographical errors, and as he had determined, it was not a bad message to end a career with. He pushed the TRANSMIT button. At least he had given the generals enough information to make a timely decision. He had done his part, he hoped the command network would do theirs.

Every light on the RC-135 dimmed or went out, the two radar sets automatically went to standby, drawing less power than a hundred-watt bulb, and the big computer went into a reduced operating mode, using only the power needed to control the transmission and keep its memory banks alive. Only the electronic counter-measures warning gear remained alive. A sharply focused burst of radio energy drilled the message over the horizon. The entire sequence took less than ten seconds before all systems on the aircraft reverted to normal.

If the Soviets monitored the Apple Wave, they would never decode the message, but they would soon make the connection between Grain King and what the RC-135 could do. Every module commander knew that possibility as well as General Cunningham.

Muddy Waters knew that he was in big trouble unless he was absolutely right.

16 July: 1327 hours, Greenwich Mean Time
0927 hours, Washington, D.C.

Master Sergeant John Nesbit jerked the message out of the high-speed printer. He had studied and been forced to learn the various types of messages, their format, sources and priority for handling. This was the first time he had seen an actual Apple Wave. The fact that it was being used indicated that the sender judged the message to be of critical importance.

Nesbit also knew better than to hesitate. He pushed the "Immediate Action" button for Colonel Blevins, wishing Colonel Gomez was on duty. This will certainly get Ramrod's attention . . .

Blevins was out of the cab and at the coffee bar when he saw the summoning lights come on. He sat his coffee cup down and waddled up the stairs to the cab.

Nesbit handed Blevins the message as soon as the puffing colonel cleared the door. Blevins scanned the message, then reread it slowly:

USAF C-130, CALL SIGN GRAIN KING ZERO THREE, TRAN-
SITING SOUTHERN LIBYAN AIRSPACE ON APPROVED
FLIGHT PLAN ENROUTE TO ALEXANDRIA SOUTH AIR BASE.
CURRENTLY MONITORING INCREASED COMMUNICATIONS
BETWEEN INTERCEPTOR FIGHTER UNITS AND HEAD-
QUARTERS TRIPOLI. ACTIVITY INDICATES PROBABLE LIB-
YAN INTERCEPTION OF GRAIN KING.

"What in *hell*, " Blevins exploded. "Some fool has used an Apple
Wave because the Libyans are talking to each other and have OK'd
a UN flight over their country?" He sat down and reread the message
for the third time, ready to ignore its significance and file a security
violation against the sender for a possible compromise.

Then he remembered Tom Gomez's changeover briefing. Glancing
at his watch, he picked up a phone and pressed the button for the
analysis section. "Send up Captains Marshall and Williamson *ASAP.* "
He had asked for the two best analysts on the shift, two officers that
Blevins disliked for their ability and did not trust because of their
informality.

The two captains ran up the stairs to the cab. The entire staff of the
Watch Center had seen the Immediate Action lights and the hurried
reaction of the analysts confirmed something was about to break. A
computer technician banged his head on a console, moaning, "Not on
a Friday."

Blevins handed the captains the message without a word. They
stood side by side reading it.

"I'll call up the boards, Don, if you'll search the status file. OK."
Don Williamson and Sara Marshall were a well-rehearsed team, each
intuitively understanding the other. Their casual approach to their
duties irritated Blevins, but he had to use them because he didn't stay
current with the masses of information they dealt with each day. The
colonel had discovered from past experiences that if he tried to inter-
fere with the way they did their job, the two officers would only do
exactly what he told them. And if he missed anything important, they
would never mention his oversight.

Blevins stopped Sara Marshall before she left. "I may have to notify
the battle staff. How soon before you can tie this into the big picture

with an assurance and coordinate with the Defense Intelligence Agency?"

The captain halted and turned to look at the portly colonel, "No idea, sir. No one's been working this. It may be hours before we get anything definite, and it takes days to coordinate with DIA."

Blevins turned to Williamson and asked for an assurance.

Williamson took off his glasses and rubbed the bridge of his nose. "This one is going to go down fast, Colonel. I doubt that we can work up an assurance before it happens."

"Before *what* happens, Captain?"

Sara looked at Don and raised an eyebrow.

With a shrug the junior male partner told him, "Like the Apple Wave says, the Libyans will intercept the Grain King. That in itself is not a hostile act, but knowing the Libyans, they'll most likely try to shoot it down. Other than that, they might force it to land at one of their bases and intern the crew."

"Bullshit. I don't believe that," Blevins snapped.

"It's not bullshit, Gene." Tom Gomez's voice cut through the air.

Blevins twisted to look at him, puzzled that he was still in the Center. Why hadn't he gone home after the shift changed? How had he entered the cab unobserved? How did he know what was going on? The too-innocent look on Nesbit's face told him the answer to his last two questions.

"If I were in your place I'd do two things," Gomez continued. "First, relay the situation to the base at Alexandria South and have them bring two fighters up to cockpit alert. Second, call the heavies now."

"But we need to coordinate this information first, I need an assurance, goddamnit."

"You don't have time for that," Gomez told him.

The decision had been made for him. Blevins hated Gomez for taking it from him and made a promise to himself to even the score.

As the on-duty Watch Center commander, Blevins had the authority to change the alert status of fighters at Alexandria South. He could even launch those fighters into a holding orbit. It was justifying his actions after the fact that frightened Blevins. Reluctantly, he turned to Nesbit. "Establish an open channel to Alexandria South. Have them bring two fighters to cockpit alert status immediately. Keep the channel open but do not, repeat, *do not* relay any other information to them at this time."

Blevins straightened his shoulders. He scanned the generals' meeting schedule to find out what was slated for the morning. What he saw was not reassuring: a meeting of the Contingency Budgeting Committee was in progress. He believed the generals would not like having that one interrupted.

Reluctantly, Blevins called the Emergency Actions Cell in the War Room. "This is the Watch Center commander. A situation is developing that requires the presence of the battle staff in the Watch Center. Notify the appropriate individuals this is a Priority Three. Standing by to authenticate." The Emergency Action Cell challenged Blevins with a two-letter code. The colonel studied the page with the authenticator table that Nesbit handed him and gave the proper two-letter response and hung up the phone. If he was lucky, only the generals assigned to the battle staff would respond and not the Air Force chief of staff, General "Get-the-Hell-out-of-Here-by-Sundown" Cunningham.

Gomez regarded Blevins. The colonel was having a hard time controlling the quiver in his voice. "Relax, Gene. This is not a Priority One. It's only a Three, a potential incident involving Air Force resources within six hours. You did it by the book." Gomez almost felt sorry for Blevins.

16 July: 1343 hours, Greenwich Mean Time
1543 hours, Alexandria, Egypt

The controller in the command post at Alexandria South Air Base saw the incoming light on the teletype bank flash. In quick succession the sergeant hit the wing commander's page button and unlocked the cover on the highly classified teletype. Colonel Shaw's voice came over the intra-base radio before the message started to print. "What's up, Barry?" he asked.

"Sir, I have a priority message coming in that requires your immediate attention."

"I'll be right there," the colonel answered.

The controller read the message as it started to scroll out of the printer and immediately hit the button sounding the scramble horn in the alert area and the squadrons.

Shaw came through the door of the command post, followed by two anxious deputies. Colonel Sam Hawkins, his DO, whose hawklike nose matched his personality, was right behind him. He was closely followed by a shorter, heavyset man, Colonel Clayton Leason, his deputy for Maintenance (DM). The wing commander read the short message and handed it to his deputies.

"Fun and games," Shaw said, "telling us to bring our crews up to cockpit alert doesn't tell us much. Any ideas?"

Sam Hawkins rubbed the back of his neck. "Beats me. Intel hasn't said anything is brewing. But that's not unusual, they never have a clue." He didn't think much of Intelligence.

"Barry"—Shaw turned to the NCO sitting at the main console— "patch the landline into the loudspeaker so we can talk to the crews when they get plugged into the drop cords." The colonel was referring to the long, extensionlike cords that hung from the ceiling of each bunker and connected their helmets to a secure telephone landline running to the command post. The crews could sit in the cockpit and talk directly to the controller without using their aircraft's radio. Without an engine start to run the F-4's cooling system, heat buildup limited ground use of their radios to ten minutes.

"Stinger One-One is up." Fairly's voice crackled over the loud-speaker.

"Stinger One-Two is up," Jack answered in quick succession.

Shaw picked up the controller's phone and keyed the transmit button. "Roger, Stinger flight. We received a flash message bringing you up to cockpit alert. Other than that, we don't know what's going down. This is *not* an exercise. You'll have to be pretty flexible on this one."

"If we could get some ordnance besides a gun on these birds," Fairly replied, "we might *be* more flexible."

Shaw wanted to give his crews more to fight with, but he had been denied permission by higher headquarters to upload the alert birds with the most effective air-to-air ordnance he had. Hell, he thought, this is what I get paid for. AIM-7 radar missiles could be uploaded, but that was a time-consuming process. If missile rails were already on the planes, AIM-9 Sidewinder missiles could be uploaded much quicker. "Do the birds have missile rails on them?" Shaw asked his deputy for Maintenance.

A sober look was on the DM's face. "We're not allowed to upload the alert birds."

"Do the alert birds have missile rails on them?" he repeated, anger in his voice.

"Yes, sir," the DM admitted, not happy with what was coming next.

Shaw made his decision. "OK, get the missiles on the way. Upload the AIM-9s first. Hurry."

"But we haven't practiced emergency missile loading," the DM protested. "It'll take about an hour to break the missiles out of the dump, form a convoy, and move them to the alert pad. Then it's another fifteen minutes to upload the AIM-9s."

"Then do it faster," Shaw warned, his anger rising. Christ, he had directed Maintenance to start training on emergency missile uploads months ago.

The wing commander mashed the transmit button on the telephone: "Stinger One-One and One-Two, AIM-9s are on the way, followed by AIM-7s. If you are scrambled before the missiles are loaded, go without them."

"Control, Stinger One-Two," Jack answered. "I've been running some numbers in my head. With two wing tanks, we've got about two hours and twenty minutes flying time to play with. That gives us a cruising radius of maybe six hundred nautical miles. A tanker for inflight refueling would be helpful if they send us out over the Mediterranean for escort."

His adrenaline was flowing. For the first time in months he felt that maybe all the trivia, paperwork and "square filling" they endured might be worth it. A slight smile creased the corners of his mouth as he thought about the party and "punishment" that had gotten him onto alert.

Shaw knew he should have thought of inflight refueling, but hadn't. He was impressed with Locke's quick thinking. He wondered if he could get the Strategic Air Command tanker unit on his base to respond quickly enough and get one of their two KC-135s airborne. They'd probably dig in their heels and claim they had no requirement to support the alert birds—that nothing was on the schedule. Still, he'd try. "I'll see if I can pry them loose," he told Jack. "You know how SAC is."

16 July: 1430 hours, Greenwich Mean Time
1430 hours, over the Sahara

"Grain King Zero-Three, Tripoli Center."

"Go ahead, Tripoli. This is Grain King," Toni answered, handling the radios on the C-130 while the navigator and loadmaster racked out. She had ordered them to get some rest; both were well into their twelfth hour of crew duty. The radio call woke Belfort from his troubled nap in the navigator's seat. Tripoli Center read out a new flight clearance for the C-130 while Toni and Dave copied it down.

"Copy all, Tripoli." Toni acknowledged the new clearance automatically. "Dave, what's that going to do to us?"

Belfort was bent over his work table, studying the chart and scratching new numbers into his log. "They've given us a new route with a dogleg going due north instead of letting us go direct to Alexandria South. That will take us right into northeastern Libya. Hold on a minute." The navigator worked quickly. "The dogleg will add almost thirteen minutes to our en route time and cut our fuel reserve to twenty-five minutes."

"Why would they do that?" she asked.

"Probably to get us on an established airway to enter Egyptian airspace. That's pretty routine. But I'd like to get Sid on the ground and into a hospital ASAP."

Toni looked worried. "McCray, how's Captain Luna doing?"

"No change," the loadmaster replied. "He's conscious, the bleeding has stopped. He seems OK."

She made her decision. "Thirteen more minutes shouldn't make too much difference. We'll go with the clearance. Couldn't get it changed to go direct anyway if they want us on an airway. Hell, we have to do a lot of things we don't want to do on these missions. Like airlifting food into every little village like the one where they clobbered Sid. They ought to be using trucks to deliver this stuff, like in Ethiopia, not C-130s."

"Lieutenant, there's no roads in the southern Sahara that can handle heavy trucks," McCray told her, "and by delivering the food we at least can keep it from getting stolen. Getting ripped off was our biggest problem in the cargo sheds at Niamey."

The mission they were on was part of Grain King III, the third year that the U.S. government had mounted the relief program bringing food to the starving inhabitants of the southern Sahara. Grain King I had not started as a pure airlift operation but had turned into one after its first faltering steps. It had started out as a massive but straightforward logistics problem. The Air Force brought food and relief supplies into central staging points and delivered them to the local authorities for distribution to outlying areas by trucks. Every pound of grain was duly accounted for and the data fed into the appropriate computer. Grain King I was judged to be a resounding success.

Nevertheless, some disturbing reports were still coming out of the area about widespread and growing starvation. A meeting of the UN General Assembly had resounded with bitter accusations from Third World ambassadors about the United States propaganda efforts being greater than its attempts at food relief. Economic imperialism and genocide had been openly mentioned. The U.S. ambassador had been forewarned and was prepared with a commanding battery of charts and statistics outlining the size of the food deliveries under Grain King I, comparing them to the size of the annual grain production in each of the stricken countries.

The figures were imposing and should have carried the day. But the ambassador from Mali had produced a series of photographs showing potbellied, starving children, mothers nursing emaciated babies, and gaunt, hollow-eyed old people with death as their companion. With each photo, the ambassador had stated the date and location where each had been taken. All were in the area of Grain King operations and less than two weeks old. "So much for Operation Grain King. My people continue to die."

The commander of MAC (Military Airlift Command) who had been responsible for the first Grain King, General Lawrence Cunningham, was rumored to have once kept a pet piranha until he discovered that it was too even tempered and not aggressive enough. So he ate the fish. Cunningham had never been content as the commander of MAC ("Trash hauling is not my bag") and his disposition hadn't improved after getting a call over the Pentagon's hot line. The subject had been Grain King and the UN. For once, Cunningham did the listening. His rage, not to mention vocabulary, after that phone call was well remembered at MAC. Four colonels had been relieved from duty and ordered to be off base by sundown because they had produced the same figures as shown at the UN. What had gone wrong?

The answer came from a young major running the Airlift Command Element at Ouagadougou, the capital of Upper Volta. Corruption had been responsible for diverting the food supplies into the hands of local merchants once the grain had been transloaded onto trucks for final delivery. The kickbacks had been enormous. Over eighty percent of the food had been shipped south into prosperous areas that could afford to buy it.

Cunningham was ordered to restart Grain King and he gave a decisive order: airlift it all down to the local level, to the people who were starving. That directive became the single-minded marching order for Grain King and had not changed after Cunningham left MAC for command of the Air Force. The basic tenant of Grain King had been established and chiseled in stone: airlift it and get it to the people. *All of it . . .*

Belfort broke the silence on the flight deck, "Time to dogleg north."

"Rog'," the copilot responded as she turned the C-130 onto a northerly heading—right into the heart of eastern Libya. She contacted Tripoli Center . . .

16 July: 1458 hours, Greenwich Mean Time
1058 hours, Washington, D.C.

Colonel Eugene Blevins' shirt was damp with sweat. General Cunningham had been sitting in the Watch Center's battle cab for over five minutes and hadn't said a word. He was staring directly at Blevins, rolling an unlit cigar in his mouth.

"Sir," Blevins said, "we have just received a second Apple Wave message. Grain King's route has been changed. It is flying north into Libyan GCI radar coverage and the Libyans have placed two fighters on runway alert." He handed the message to the Air Force's legendary gorilla.

Sundown Cunningham continued to stare at Blevins, not bothering to read the message. "Who the hell is sending these? Get me a *name.*" He dropped the Top Secret message to the floor.

Blevins hurried the short distance to the waiting Nesbit. "Get on the line to the reconnaissance unit that flies these missions. You heard what the general wants—*move.*"

"I haven't got a clue what unit that is, Colonel." The sergeant knew Cunningham was listening.

"Well, find *out,* Sergeant."

Suppressing his smile, Nesbit assumed a worried look and placed an unnecessary call. He knew what unit to contact and whom to talk to. He enjoyed the thought of what he was doing to Blevins by stalling.

Cunningham continued to wait, chewing on his cigar. After a long pause, he barked at Blevins, "What do you recommend that I do about this Apple Wave?" Cunningham believed the hardest thing for any man to learn was how to think under pressure. The general already knew what his decision was but wanted to gauge the mental agility of his Watch Center commander.

Blevins admitted to himself that he didn't know what to do, and worse, he didn't know how to escape the general's undivided scrutiny. The best he could do was stall for time. "I'm waiting for my analysts to correlate this information with an area situation report. I'm confident, sir, that they will give us a level of assurance on which to make the proper decision." The general continued to glare at Blevins, who turned to one of the repeater consoles in an attempt to appear busy while frantically devising a way to shift the general's attention away from himself.

Tom Gomez joined Blevins at the repeater console. "Jesus H. Christ," he said *sotto voce.* "Cunningham wants you to make a decision. You're in charge of the battle cab. Get some people in action before he rips us apart."

There was desperation in Blevins' voice. "My job is intelligence, damn it, not, not . . . "

In a low voice Gomez quickly outlined what Blevins should say. Blevins listened, then steeled himself for what he had to do.

He walked over to Cunningham and met the general's direct stare. He paused and looked at the four other generals and six colonels who had crowded into the battle cab. "General, I have placed two F-4E fighters on cockpit alert at Alexandria South Air Base. I recommend you scramble them into an orbit close as possible to the C-130. Keep them in friendly airspace. Sergeant Nesbit has the details worked out."

The cigar rolled in Cunningham's mouth for a moment. "Not bad, Blevins. *Do it.* Relay everything we've got to Outpost. And tell them to get Grain King the hell out of Libya." The general did not bother to tell the colonels what or where Outpost was; he simply expected them to get the message through and damn quick. Gomez and Nesbit knew that Outpost was an intelligence-gathering unit in northwestern Egypt near the Libyan border that operated under the guise of a radar ground control intercept site. Outpost would be able to find the C-130 on its radar and establish radio contact to relay Cunningham's order.

"Excuse me, General," Nesbit called from his console. "The module commander in the RC-135 sending the Apple Waves is Colonel Anthony J. Waters." The sergeant knew Blevins had wanted to give Cunningham the name and take credit for himself.

The general remembered the name. From the depths of his memory, everything became clear. *So, that's where you've been hiding. I wondered what had happened to you after that F-15 fiasco. I was sure the Air Force had lost one of its better tactics men.* Cunningham had participated in one of Waters' Red Flag exercises and had been trounced by the complex scenario Waters had thrown at him.

The general had thoroughly enjoyed it.

16 July: 1511 hours, Greenwich Mean Time
1711 hours, Alexandria, Egypt

"Stinger One-One, scramble. Stinger One-Two, scramble."

Lieutenant Colonel Mike Fairly and Lieutenant Jack Locke hit their start buttons simultaneously when they heard the first "scramble" from control.

Fairly acknowledged, "Roger, control. Scrambling now. Standing by for words."

Bryant's low voice came over the cockpit intercom. "The boss would rather die than sound bad on the radio."

"You've got to look good and sound good to be a squadron commander, me lad. I want to make them eat their hearts out at the bar tonight, so let's try to be as good," Locke said.

"Goddamn Air Farce!" Bryant exploded. "Here come the missile trailers now. Too damn late. We get to go to war with only a gun? Well now, look at that. There's a crew headed for one of the tankers. I didn't know them SAC fellows could run."

Control came over the radio. "Stinger One-One and One-Two, you are scrambled to Point Hotel. Contact Outpost on primary frequency two six-five point eight, backup frequency two eight-three point five."

And Fairly again answered the controller, "Roger, control. Copied all."

"Thunder, where in all the United Arab Republic *is* Point Hotel and *who* is Outpost?" Jack asked.

"I'll dig it out while the inertial nav system aligns," the WSO answered. Got to keep the boy cool, he thought.

"A wonderful thing, the inertial navigation system," Jack said. "All ready to go and here we sit while that damn little black box tries to make up its mind where it is."

"Patience, patience," Bryant urged, pulling his aircrew aid out of a pocket on the leg of his anti-G suit. He thumbed through the small book until he found what he wanted. "Point Hotel is over two hundred nautical miles to the west. Glad for that tanker. Outpost is a radar control post. OK, the inertial nav system is aligned. Cleared primary-sync."

At Thunder's words, Jack flipped his compass and nav systems to their primary mode of operation, slaving them to the gyros in the inertial navigation system. It was a long delay. Jack gave Fairly a thumbs up, signaling that he was at last ready to taxi. Lieutenant Johnny Nelson, Fairly's backseater, tapped his forehead. When he saw Bryant nod in acknowledgment, he simultaneously rocked his head forward and closed his rear canopy. Bryant keyed on Nelson's head nod and closed his canopy in unison with Nelson. Fairly repeated the procedure for Jack and their front canopies came down together. Only the four crew chiefs launching the aircraft saw the synchronized canopy routine that was the first step in the aircrews' coming together as a team.

Colonel Shaw and his lanky DO were sitting in the commander's pickup truck, monitoring the radio and watching the two fighters as they taxied out, lined up on the runway, and started their takeoff roll. Shaw watched, with a critical eye, the two F-4s as they made a precision formation takeoff while the sound of the SAC tanker's engines filled the truck. He was satisfied with the response of the SAC tanker unit. Maybe, he thought, SAC *does* understand what the Air Force is all about.

"Your boys look good," he said to Hawkins.

"Good enough," the DO said. He hoped.

16 July: 1523 hours, Greenwich Mean Time
1523 hours, over the Mediterranean

"Colonel!" Bill Carroll shouted over the interphone in the RC-135. "The Libyans scrambled the MiGs. They're going after the Grain King—"

Cruzak was continuing to refine the frequency pattern. The computer was almost locked onto the entire shift pattern the scrambler used. Cruzak calculated they would break the system wide open in another five minutes. It was a significant breakthrough.

Anthony Waters reacted calmly to this latest intelligence. "Downlink that to Washington." He was sure a battle was going to start in a few minutes and there was little else he could do. He also hadn't felt so alive in years.

The colonel unfolded from his seat and stretched his cramped legs. He could see the agitated lieutenant talking to Cruzak. Waters had been monitoring U.S. communications and walked down the narrow aisle, knowing the two needed reassurance. "Hey, you did good. Help is on the way from Alexandria South."

16 July: 1528 hours, Greenwich Mean Time
1728 hours, Western Egypt

Cunningham's order to establish contact with Grain King and order them out of Libyan airspace had been received over Outpost's command communications equipment. "Grain King, Grain King, this is

Outpost on Guard. Do you copy?" The transmission on Guard—the frequency reserved for emergencies—surprised the C-130 crew.

"Read you five-by, Outpost. Go ahead," Toni answered.

"Roger, Grain King. Turn right to a heading of zero-niner-zero degrees *now*. Leave Libyan airspace ASAP. Repeat, *leave Libyan airspace ASAP.*"

"Outpost," Toni replied, "we are under the control of Tripoli Center on an approved flight plan, on a weather divert into Alexandria South with an injured man on board."

"Grain King, Outpost. You are in danger of being intercepted by hostile aircraft. Do you copy all?"

"Copy all." Toni reached for the yoke, disengaged the autopilot, and spun the big cargo plane to an easterly heading. By pushing the throttles up and nosing the plane into a gentle descent, the airspeed increased to almost three hundred eighty knots. "How far to the border, Dave?"

"About a hundred miles, fifteen or sixteen minutes at this ground speed." He looked over the flight engineer's shoulder at the fuel gauges and rapidly calculated what the increased airspeed would do to their fuel. "You can keep this fuel flow up for about eighteen minutes." If we don't rip the wings off first, he thought. "Then you'll have to shut one engine down for long-range cruise. It's going to be tight."

16 July: 1531 hours, Greenwich Mean Time
1731 hours, Western Egypt

"Outpost, this is Stinger One-One with a flight of two. How read this frequency?" Fairly queried the radar control post.

"Read you five-by, Stinger," a female voice answered. "Situation is as follows. Grain King Zero-Three, U.S. C-130 cargo aircraft, is transiting Libyan airspace with approved flight plan. Two bandits reported scrambled to intercept Grain King. Intentions of bandits unknown, suspect hostile. I have contact with Grain King. On your nose bearing two-six-five degrees, one-niner-zero nautical miles from your position. Will have a tanker on station in fifteen minutes."

Fairly stepped on his rudder pedals, wagging the F-4's tail. Jack broke out of his loose formation and moved two thousand feet to

Fairly's right and five hundred feet above him. The fighters had moved into a tactical formation from which they could support each other in an engagement. Fairly calculated how he could set up an interception on the C-130 that could be switched into an engagement with the bandits should it be necessary. It all depended on how good Nelson was at running intercepts and if he could find the bandits on his scope. "How's the radar?"

"It's a good set," the young lieutenant replied. "All the test checks were OK. I've got it set up for air-to-air, fifty-mile range. It's not much good beyond that. Don't worry, I'll get the first radar contact on Grain King."

Fairly hoped it was not a false show of confidence. "Jack, listen up," Fairly said over the UHF radio. "If we have to rendezvous on Grain King, the first one with a radar contact will run a standard intercept to the stern of the C-130. If we have to engage the bandits, the first one with a radar contact or visual on the bandits is lead. Run a hot intercept head-on into the merge. Number two will fall in trail two miles. Lead will blow on through the bandits and reverse. We want them to turn and two will go for a sandwich. Don't let them get on Grain King. Support whoever's engaged."

"Roger," Jack answered his flight leader. "Thunder, trade your mother for the first contact on that magic box of yours," he told his backseater over the intercom.

"Stinger, Outpost. Say state." The radar post was asking for the fighters' armament, fuel and oxygen.

Fairly answered, "One-One and One-Two are guns only, fifteen minutes play time, lox sweet." The radar site understood he meant they had internal gatling guns, could stay in the area for fifteen minutes before fuel would force them to the tanker, and had plenty of liquid oxygen.

16 July: 1540 hours, Greenwich Mean Time
1740 hours, Western Egypt

"Stinger One-One, Outpost. Grain King is on your nose, five-five nautical miles from you. Altitude twenty-five thousand feet, heading zero-niner-zero degrees. The bandits are at your one-thirty position at five-five from you. They are intercepting Grain King. Do not intervene unless a hostile act is committed."

Thunder's voice came over the radio, deep and clear. "One-Two has a radar contact at twelve o'clock, five-four miles, level." He touched the radar's elevation wheel, raising the antenna's elevation a whisker. Slowly, he played the gain, breaking out the target.

"Roger, Stinger One-Two. That is Grain King," Outpost replied. "Rendezvous on Grain King. Fly heading two-six-five."

Outpost's orders were clear. The radar controller was still in control of the developing intercept. Fairly cursed his bad luck, radar set, and backseater.

"Jack, arm 'em up," Fairly ordered, directing the pilot to throw the sequence of switches that activated his gun and made it "hot" while he did the same. Jack's fingers moved over the switches, just as they had so many times on the gunnery range before he strafed the target panels. But this time he paused and went through the sequence again, making sure that all his switches were in the right position. No switch-ology errors, he thought as he lifted the switch guard and threw the final Master Arm toggle.

Jack glanced at the radar scope in front of him, satisfied to see the bright return of the C-130 sliding down the scope. He noticed that Thunder did not reduce the scope's range to fifty miles when Grain King moved inside forty-nine miles. Thunder was searching for the bandits, a much more difficult target to break out on the old radar set. Hell, the pilot thought, we need a pulse Doppler radar. But if anyone can make this set work, it's Thunder.

"Stinger, fly two-six-eight." Outpost ordered the two fighters to adjust their heading a few degrees. Thunder was working out the mental geometry of the intercept and still letting the controller direct them. He needed an accurate indication of how competent the un-known personality was at directing aircraft. After a short break the controller continued, "I'm bringing Grain King over to this fre-quency." Another slight pause was followed by, "Grain King, how read on this frequency?"

For the first time, the F-4 aircrews heard Toni D'Angelo. "Read you five-by, Outpost."

"Be damned," Jack spat over the intercom. "Two women!" Two women in the Air Force, caught up in combat. Not the role he had put them in.

Outpost calmly queried the C-130. "Do you have the bandits in sight? They are at your eight o'clock, ten miles."

"Negative," Toni groaned.

"Jack, punch off your tanks. Now," Fairly ordered his wingman. On the word "now," Jack pushed his jettison button, causing the two empty fuel tanks attached to the underside of his wings to separate in unison with Fairly's wing tanks. The two men were welded into a tight team. Both fighters had reduced the drag the tanks created and were fully configured for combat.

Toni called over the radio, "They shot a missile, repeat, they've fired. Missile went ballistic . . ." She turned and dove her plane as hard as she could without tearing the wings off, taking the big cargo plane into a sixty-degree dive. She flew for a small cloud deck lacing the sky eight thousand feet below her as the two MiGs repositioned for another attack.

"Stinger flight, you are cleared to engage. Repeat, *cleared to engage,*" Outpost told the Phantoms.

Now Thunder's voice came through. "One-Two has contact on bandits, Judy." With the code word "Judy," Bryant told the controller and the flight he was taking over the intercept. He would direct the two fighters into the engagement.

The controller acknowledged and fell silent, continuing to monitor the radar scope in case she could be of more assistance or had to disengage the F-4s if more bandits joined the flight.

Fairly buried his left foot in the rudder pedal and took spacing behind Jack, who was now flight lead, as he had briefed.

"Come right. Roll out." Thunder was directing Jack into a head-on radar intercept with the bandits.

"Tallyho," Jack yelled over the radio as he got a visual sighting on one of the bandits. "It's a Flogger." Jack had caught sight of the Soviet-built MiG-23 fighter, code-named "Flogger" by NATO. He had read the reports by U.S. pilots who had flown the swing-wing fighter in secret tests and had a healthy respect for its capabilities. If the single-engine fighter was carrying its normal armament, he could expect the MiGs to have two Apex and two Aphid air-to-air missiles along with a twin-barreled twenty-three-millimeter cannon.

"Where's the C-130?" he shouted at Thunder. The wizzo lifted his head out of the radar scope and twisted his large frame around in the cramped seat.

"Seven o'clock, six miles, twenty degrees low," he shouted back. Jack would not take his eyes off the MiG, not daring to lose sight of the slightly smaller aircraft. He was "padlocked" onto the MiG-23 Flogger. He jerked the Phantom to the right, dove and jerked back to the left, putting the MiG on a head-on collision course. He intended to shoot the other pilot in the face from a frontal cannon attack. As the Flogger surged into the target ring on the head-up display in front of him, Jack squeezed off a short burst of cannon fire. He had set the gatling gun on high rate of fire when he went through the arming routine. At six thousand rounds per minute, the six hundred forty rounds of twenty-millimeter shells in the ammunition drum would last less than seven seconds. The gun made a short burring sound as he expended one hundred eighty rounds, sending a near-solid stream of high-explosive ammunition toward the Flogger.

It was the first time the lieutenant had fired a shot in combat. He missed. He snap-rolled the fighter to the left, bringing the MiG aboard on his left, passing canopy-to-canopy with less than fifty-feet separation, his reflexes faster than the other pilot's. Instinctively, he pulled the F-4 up into the vertical, counterturning onto the escaping aircraft. Thunder's voice came over the radio, telling Jack and Fairly what the MiG was doing. "He's six o'clock, going away. Hey, they're both on Fairly—"

"Jack," Fairly blurted over the radio, "come back left, I'm engaged . . ." The command was for Jack to turn hard to his left, returning in the opposite direction of his original flight path.

Jack wrenched the big fighter through the pitch back he had started, pulling five G's as they came across the top, inverted. Both he and Thunder grunted, fighting the force of the G's created by the maneuver. Sweat was rolling off their faces. The fighter headed down, rapidly accelerating as they returned to the fight.

At the end of the arc, Jack saw Fairly about four miles in front and below him. The older man was jinking hard, attempting to shake the two Floggers and keep his tail turned away from the MiGs. One was less than three thousand feet behind Fairly and trying to get in a position behind the Phantom where the infrared guidance heads on his Aphid dogfight missiles could pick up the heat-signature of the F-4's jet exhaust. So far Fairly was denying the Flogger pilot a missile shot and keeping out of the effective range of the MiG's cannon.

The other bandit was doing a high yo-yo, a vertical roller-coaster maneuver, three miles behind Fairly, trying to kill his high overtake speed and fall in behind the first bandit by trading forward momentum for altitude. He would then pull his aircraft back down after his prey.

"You are dead meat," Jack swore at the tail-end MiG. "Boss, pitch back left, bandit coming into your twelve o'clock. I'll clear your six." And he headed for the MiG directly behind Fairly.

Fairly followed Jack's command, reefing his Phantom into a vertical turn to the left.

To Jack, it looked like Fairly was executing half a loop toward the Flogger doing the yo-yo. "Get him," the lieutenant shouted. But the nose of Fairly's F-4 only crossed the flight path of the Flogger for a fraction of a second, not enough time for a snap shot. The new Sidewinder missiles the wing had would have nailed the Libyan from any angle.

Jack slashed past the Flogger on Fairly's tail, managing to squeeze off a snap shot as the gatling gun gave off a short burring noise.

"Save it," Thunder commanded. The wizzo twisted in his seat, his eyes glued onto the Flogger. He quickly told Jack and Fairly what the MiG was doing . . . "Bandit is six o'clock, going away, disengaging. Going for the deck. Lost him." The Flogger had disappeared through a break in the clouds, running from the fight.

"Boss, what the hell are you doing?" Jack grunted over the intercom at Fairly, who was in a scissors maneuver with his Flogger, the two aircraft weaving back and forth across each other's flight path. Jack knew it was a good defensive maneuver, but that it was hard to go on the offensive from that position and harder yet to disengage. Jack was pleased, though, when he realized his own six o'clock was clear and maneuvered to fall in behind the Flogger, sandwiching him for a kill.

The Libyan pilot saw Jack at the same time and headed down, trying to disengage.

"They don't seem to want to hang around and fight," Jack said to Thunder.

"He'll outrun us," Thunder decided, trying to find the Hercules and the other MiG. But Jack wasn't ready to let the MiG escape. He turned hard, pushed his throttles into full afterburner, and shoved his nose toward the ground, chasing the Libyan. Again, Thunder buried his head in the radar scope, trying to lock-on the fleeing MiG. Jack was astounded as the gunsight's analogue bar clicked on, giving him the exact range to the MiG and telling him his backseater had managed to acquire the bandit on the radar scope in the midst of the fight.

"Shit hot," was all the pilot had time to say, signaling approval to his Weapons Systems Officer. Now the fight had descended to below five thousand feet and the F-4E was in the element it had been designed for. Jack's bird was turning like a witch and accelerating with the Flogger. He was still in a tail chase with the MiG. Fairly was following him. All three planes were in a steep dive, dangerously close to the ground as their altimeters unwound in a blur. Jack calculated how much lower he could go before pulling out. He was totally committed to chase the MiG into the ground.

Now the Libyan leveled out and jinked back and forth in short little left-and-right turns.

Thunder had turned around in his seat, still trying to find the other MiG. But all he could see was Fairly, less than four miles behind them. Knowing that the two F-4 pilots were fully occupied with the Flogger, he queried the C-130, "Grain King, say position."

Toni answered. "Circling at twenty-two thousand, hiding in this goddamn cloud deck."

Thunder scanned his RHAW (Radar Homing and Warning gear). "Good. Stay there." He twisted back and forth in his seat, still trying to find the first MiG, which would appear behind them at their six o'clock position—if it came back.

Jack was padlocked on to the MiG, slowly closing as the Flogger pilot tried to outmaneuver the bigger F-4 and started a left turn seventy-five feet above the ground. Jack also turned his bird hard to the left, getting the nose of his Phantom inside the MiG's arc. Slowly, the distance between the two closed as the F-4 turned inside the MiG, coming into gun range. Jack expected the Flogger pilot to roll out and accelerate away, but the Libyan, apparently confused, continued the turn, allowing the American to close on him.

Again, Jack had a MiG fill his lighted target ring and squeezed off a second shot. This time, determined not to miss, he tried to empty the remainder of his ammunition drum at the Flogger. The gun fired over three hundred rounds before it jammed. Four of the stream of bullets found the agile fighter, cutting into the right wing, tearing it off.

The MiG cartwheeled into the ground going over 600 miles per hour.

Jack let out a whoop. What had they always told him? A kill is a kill, there are only two kinds of airplanes—targets and fighters.

Jack pulled the throttles out of afterburner and started an easy spiraling climb above the wreckage of the MiG, which was sending a pillar of smoke into the sky, a dark beacon marking the funeral pyre.

Thunder's words broke the quiet of the aftermath as he called the radar post, "Outpost, Stinger One-Two. Any more trade?" Outpost immediately responded that there were no other bandits in the area.

Jack's backseater friend had not mentioned the downed MiG. Then he realized that Fairly had also been silent as he joined on the right. Jack keyed his radio. "Outpost, Stinger One-Two. Bandit splashed at this time." Both he and Thunder studied the wreckage in silence.

As they climbed above it, a peculiar sense of sadness came over Jack. He had just killed a man. His stomach tightened in a knot. His heart burned. He wasn't so sure it was something to be proud of . . . But he could have just as easily been the pilot in the burning wreckage. "Poor bastard," he said, mostly to himself.

Thunder lifted his visor and rubbed the sweat off his forehead and from around his eyes with the back of his glove. He was grateful for the subdued reaction of the pilot. Just maybe, he thought, the man might make it.

In the aftermath of the engagement, the burning wreckage fading behind them, Fairly took charge. The squadron commander understood what his wingman was going through. It was a feeling that he had experienced in Vietnam. Savor it now for what it is worth, he thought, because I'm going to chew the hell out of you later in the debriefing. "Well done, Jack." The lieutenant colonel patted his left leg, trying to vent the intense pressure generated by the fight. He smiled as an image came to him: the embarrassment Shaw was going to suffer, explaining why Jack had been on alert for a week. "Jack, fuel check." Fairly's own fuel was at a low level and he suspected that Jack's was even lower after the prolonged engagement.

"One-niner squared," Jack said, subdued. He had nineteen hundred pounds of fuel remaining, all in his internal fuselage tanks. He calculated how far his remaining fuel would take him. He sure as hell didn't relish the thought of meeting an accident board and having to explain to them how he had shot down a MiG, then run out of fuel on the way home. One Flogger exchanged for one F-4 because he had forgotten to check his fuel while engaged . . .

"Outpost, Stinger One-One. Request immediate rendezvous with the tanker. Request the tanker head our way. Now." Fairly had resumed lead of the flight.

The controller at Outpost came right back, still very much a part of Stinger flight. "Roger, Stinger. Fly heading of zero-seven-eight degrees. Climb to flight level two-four-oh. Tanker has already departed orbit and is moving your way." Twenty-four thousand feet, Jack thought. It was a long way to climb with the fuel he had, and he was thankful the controller had brought the tanker in for a rendezvous before they asked for it.

Toni's voice came over the radio. "Outpost, Grain King proceeding on course. Declaring minimum fuel at this time and request priority handling."

All four of the F-4 crewmembers noted how calm and controlled the C-130 driver had become. They also understood her fuel problems could only be solved by landing. At least the Phantoms could refuel in flight. Outpost cleared Grain King over to an air traffic control frequency. Before her flight engineer could switch the radio over, Toni stopped him and keyed her mike. She could see the two fighters climbing past on the left. "Stinger flight, Grain King."

"Go ahead Grain King," Fairly answered.

"Mucho thanks. I'm buying the bar tonight. Can you make it?"

"Wouldn't miss it, Grain King." There was no doubt in Fairly's mind that between the trash hauler's and Jack's generosity, the bar was going to be very wet.

16 July: 1635 hours, Greenwich Mean Time
1835 hours, Alexandria, Egypt

It was one of those magnificent desert sunsets that escaped description, frustrated artists, and defied the poets who knew how many similar sunsets had witnessed the conclusion of battles in this scarred portion of the world. Colonel Shaw and his bird of prey DO had seen many Egyptian sunsets and were immune to the spectacular sunset before their eyes. The men were caught up in another emotion; the intense feeling of a commander when his crews returned from combat. Both had fought in Vietnam, where they had waited with growing concern for their comrades to recover. Time had not diminished the intensity of that emotion. The experience of making decisions and assuming responsibility for others had sharpened the feelings of pride, accomplishment and relief that they felt.

They were not alone in their vigil. Word that one of the wing's fighters had downed a MiG had gone around the base. The report the radar post had called in was classified Secret, but it was a secret the close-knit community could not keep, at least not from themselves.

The base had first stirred when a buzz went around that two Phantoms had been brought up to cockpit alert. The buzz didn't die down and kept growing until the entire base knew something big was going down. As facts changed the buzz to confirmed truth, a change came over the men and women who made the system work. The incessant complaining and grumbling—an everyday part of duty in the Air Force—died away. There was no rush to end the duty day. Wives were wondering why their husbands had not come home, and bars at the various clubs on base were empty. Instead, there was a migration toward the flight line. After the two Phantoms had launched, the command post filled with all who could think of a reason for being there.

Then the words that gave meaning to the long months of work, training and frustration that marked their existence were being passed: "Our birds got a MiG . . ." It wasn't a squadron's, or the wing's, but *ours.*" The feeling was older than the Air Force and probably had its roots in the First World War when air combat was still in its infancy.

Not everyone reacted with jubilation. The four crew chiefs who were really the two birds' parents were waiting on the flight line for their charges to come home. No one intruded on their solitude. Each knew in his heart that it had been *his* bird that had downed the MiG, and each wanted his Phantom to be safe. Later on, after uncounted beers, the hard veneer of the professional crew chief would be back in place. He'd claim that the heavy-handed "assholes" that flew his air machine had abused it unnecessarily. They should be permanently grounded for being such "dumb shits," he'd say, and it was pure luck and the fine condition of his warbird that made the kill possible. But that would come later. For the moment, the crew chiefs were four very worried young men.

Shaw watched the two Phantoms touch down two thousand feet in trail and pop their drag chutes. "Nice recoveries," he said under his breath. "Thank God, Locke didn't do a victory roll." Turning to his deputy for Operations, he rubbed the sweat off his bald head and relaxed for the first time since responding to the call from the command post. "Your boys did good, Sam."

"Good enough," was the only answer Hawkins would allow.

16 July: 1700 hours, Greenwich Mean Time
1300 hours, Washington, D.C.

The atmosphere in the Pentagon's battle cab was blue with cigar haze. Colonel Blevins' face was flushed and his shirt was mottled with sweat. He knew his performance in front of General Cunningham didn't look good and he had to recover his standing. All messages were now coming in over the normal circuits and the RC-135 had been silent since its third transmission. Slowly, the situation reports were filtering in, giving a more detailed account of the engagement.

Cunningham was his usual brooding self, deep into what the incident had revealed. The general understood the way of combat and how Intelligence, Command and Control, and Operations had to work together for the effective management of violence. All three had been players in the Grain King incident and he wanted to use the experience to improve his Air Force, to get his people more ready to fight.

The general focused on the men who had made the decisions. He sized up Blevins: a standard bureaucratic approach to business. If nothing else, the Blevinses of the Air Force would never act in haste.

Still, he had placed the F-4s on cockpit alert and had recommended their scramble. Those were excellent, timely decisions, especially since Blevins was a ground-pounder. A three-star general on the battle staff, Hiram Stanglay, had also been impressed with Blevins' performance. Stanglay had been picked to serve on the promotion board that would soon be selecting new brigadier generals for the Air Force.

Cunningham's relentless mind continued, pressing for the truth . . . Had their actions been timely or were they only lucky? Should he rack Waters for breaking radio silence and possibly compromising the capabilities of the RC-135 or give him a medal for saving the C-130? Why had the F-4s launched without missiles? He made a mental promise to correct *that* particular problem. Someone had made a very bad decision. What was that damn C-130 doing in Libyan airspace in the first place? The general decided he wanted to see a detailed after-action report. He'd have to talk to Waters . . .

Every man and woman in the Watch Center knew the way the short, feisty general reacted, and not one was about to break into his brooding solitude. Blevins continued to search for a way to make himself look good. Relief washed over him and his sweating subsided when he saw the latest message traffic coming over the repeater on his console, and his confidence surged as he decided how to use the new information to his advantage.

"Excuse me, sir"—Blevins earned an admiring glance from General Stanglay for approaching Cunningham—"the C-130 landed safely at Alexandria South and ran out of fuel taxiing in. Also, we have received queries from the State Department and the National Security Council . . ." Blevins hesitated for effect, implying he fully understood the power the NSC wielded and the special relationship its chief had with the President. "They are requesting answers to what appears to be precipitate action on our part without advising them or the President." Blevins' self-assurance soared. He had an answer to each of those questions, by God, and he could make the Air Force look good in front of any group of policy makers.

"Tough," Cunningham spat, eyes sparkling at the challenge. "I've got questions, too. The most important is why in hell we only got *one* MiG." He stood, lit up a fresh cigar, and turned to Blevins. "Sort it all out, pronto. I want Waters here tomorrow and a briefing on this incident Sunday." Before leaving, he paused at Master Sergeant Nesbit's console. "Nesbit, you made your point." The sergeant wasn't sure if the general had given him a rare accolade or a reprimand.

Whatever, a collective sigh of relief went around the cab as the general left to prepare to fight another, even more difficult battle with the NSC.

16 July: 1845 hours, Greenwich Mean Time
2045 hours, Athens, Greece

The crew of the RC-135 was on the patio of the resort hotel in Glifada, a beach town near Athens the reccy crews had adopted while they were on TDY in Greece. The fatigue of the long mission was on each of their faces as they sat quietly drinking beer, waiting for Waters and Carroll to arrive from the post-mission debrief with Intelligence and the new crew that would soon launch the RC-135 on another mission.

Finally, the two officers walked in, equally tired.

Magically, a beer appeared in Waters' hand as he grinned at the waiting men. "You did good," he announced. "The C-130 made it." A ripple of applause and whistles spread around the patio. Because the details were highly classified, the crew would have to wait until they were back on the reccy bird to learn exactly how the cargo plane was saved. But for now, the knowledge that it had safely landed was enough.

Pride in what his crew had accomplished washed Waters' fatigue away. Hell, maybe it's too soon to retire, he thought.

The desk clerk came out of the hotel and stood at the gate leading to the patio. "Colonel Waters," he called, "there's an urgent message for you."

Then again, maybe not.

II

THE WING

After landing from their scramble, Jack and Thunder had gone through the mandatory debrief with Intelligence, expecting to spend hours with the Intel debriefer. Instead, the sergeant had produced a checklist and run through it, asking canned questions. They were through within twenty minutes and the initial report was sent out five minutes later, up-channeled to higher headquarters where it was eagerly awaited. Maintenance was next, where they quickly went over the condition of their bird. After that, Fairly had told them to report the next morning at 0800 hours for the flight debrief.

They had made a headlong rush for the officers' club, and Jack wore his hat into the bar—a signal that he was buying. But Toni D'Angelo and Dave Belfort had beat them there, also wearing their hats. Then the serious drinking began, celebrating Jack and Thunder's victory. Colonel Shaw told his security police to be "helpful" with the drunks, and they were put at a polite distance.

* * *

Breakfast had consisted of a beer and two cigarettes. Fortunately the crew chief who owned Locke's jet, tail number 512, had made it to work on time. Should have known the bastards would have a work-call after yesterday, the crew chief thought. At least the line chief had let him and his assistant off last night after a quick post-flight of the Phantom. By the time they had made it to the Service Club the place was jumping. Everyone was celebrating the wing's victory. The crew chief's hangover was monumental. Now if the chief would only leave him alone—and if his partner would drag his ass to work—six hours *might* do the trick.

The maintenance forms were lying in the gun bay, right where the crew chief expected them. He thumbed through the write-ups from yesterday's flight, deciding half the problems the pilot had written up couldn't be duplicated or fixed. Then he noticed two entries: "One star missing from left side of fuselage," signed off with the corrective action by corrosion control, "One star painted on left side of fuselage." Looking up, he could see the freshly painted light brown star on the variable ramp that led into the intake duct, signifying that his bird had shot down an enemy aircraft.

Suddenly everything felt better. He was so proud of his only child. Then he saw the second write-up: "Gun jammed on high rate of fire on third burst. Total rounds fired: 508. Altitude 185 feet, airspeed 620 knots at time of jam." The write-up was still open, meaning that he would have to get the gatling gun fixed this day.

He walked around his bird, a little more in awe of the machine than before yesterday's scramble. He doubted he would ever understand everything that his baby could do. But . . . something was wrong, he could feel it. He tried to clear the fog of his hangover . . . Finally his eyes found it . . . his bird had, in effect, tried to commit suicide. Rushing up to the nose, he gently stroked the gun port beneath the long radar cone. The opening was about four inches bigger than normal. He had never seen or heard of that before, yet instinct told him what had caused it. The gatling gun had malfunctioned. One of the six rapidly rotating barrels had fired prematurely before it was aligned with the gun port. 512 had blown away part of it's face. The crew chief's nausea swept back over him, only this time it was not caused by his hangover. He was sick near to death that his baby had so badly hurt itself.

Jack and Thunder arrived at the squadron as the crew chief reported for duty. Jack was in the same condition as the chief and doubted if he could afford to pay his bar bill from the night before, whatever it might be. He hated to admit it, but the trash hauler, Dave Belfort, had set a tough example to match.

"Thunder," he groaned, "who won last night?"

"Not you," his backseater said. Thunder had closed Jack's bar bill and carried the happily inebriated pilot back to the BOQ early in the morning.

The duty officer directed them now into the main briefing room.

Shaw and his deputy for Operations, Hawkins, were there along with the chief of Intelligence, the C-130 crew, and a female captain neither of them recognized. A sergeant was setting up a videotape recorder and camera.

"This is going to be a big deal," Jack said, under his breath, appraising the newcomer. She was a plain woman, very thin, and possessed the hardest blue eyes he had ever seen.

Colonel Shaw stood. "Okay, let's get this underway. The Pentagon wants the debrief on videotape. They've already received our initial reports and are more than passing interested in what went down yesterday—so interested that they've got a C-141 on the ramp to fly the tape to Washington as soon as you finish.

"Before we start the tape let me introduce Captain Mary Hauser. She is the controller from Outpost who worked you and will explain what her organization is all about. From now on everything you hear is classified top secret. It's all yours, Mary." The colonel sank into his chair. He had not slept the previous night and had been answering a series of messages and phone calls from headquarters since early morning.

The captain unfolded from her seat, astonishing Jack with her height. "Thank you, Colonel Shaw. Outpost is a covert surveillance site for monitoring the Libyans. Our parent organization is in Germany and we rotate every six weeks. Our cover is that we're a training detachment teaching the Egyptians ground control intercept procedures. The GCI cover has worked well and we'd like to keep it intact. I'm also a master controller and fully current, which adds authenticity to our story. The recordings of our radio transmissions and radar tapes are here for this debrief. I'll be taking them to D.C. with the tape of this debrief and your gun-camera film."

Jack had recognized her voice right away. She wasn't someone he wanted to mess with.

Because Fairly had been the flight lead for Stinger flight, he had the responsibility for conducting the debrief. He had been preparing for over an hour, and for the next hour he reconstructed the mission in chronological sequence, critiqued every action, sparing no one, including himself.

Mary Hauser brought up two new aspects of the mission. She asked if they had heard her warning call about approaching the border. All four said they did not. Careful reconstruction revealed the call came at the time they dropped off her radar scope, chasing the MiG. She then brought up the subject of the tanker. The SAC crew had kept pushing her to get as close to the engagement as possible, more than willing to jeopardize their bird to be in position to refuel the F-4s.

Hearing this, Jack decided he'd never criticize SAC again.

Fairly turned to Jack: "After downing the MiG, you were still flight-lead and should have immediately performed a fuel check, joined up the flight into a tactical formation and requested clearance to the tanker. Jack, you did not attend to business after the engagement. Further, you let your fuel state degenerate to a dangerously low level during the fight. The only thing that saved you from a flameout and fuel starvation was the tanker's early departure out of orbit toward us. That call by Captain Hauser saved you. You owe her. And that's all I have."

After the videotape was shut off, Shaw again stood. "I know having an audience for a debrief is highly unusual. But I felt it would be appropriate to have a live audience to serve as a constant reminder that a good many people are going to be seeing this tape. I think it's worked. Thank you and again, congratulations." The room was called to attention as the wing commander left.

Jack walked out of the room, steaming. "Fairly crucified us—and on tape." Nothing, it seemed to him, was ever good enough for the Air Force.

"We deserved what we got," Thunder told him. And we also got respect in there, Thunder decided, even if you didn't see it. That's all right. He'd mention it to Jack later. And also the fact that the squadron commander had seemed fairly proud of them.

17 July: 1315 hours, Greenwich Mean Time
0915 hours, Washington, D.C.

Sara Marshall stood beside Tom Gomez on the ramp at Andrews Air Force Base, waiting for the KC-135 to taxi in, drawing attention from others on the ramp, not that it was unexpected. Sara would draw attention wherever she went. He admired her cool composure and apparent disregard of the interest in her. Gomez was sure a lot of people only saw a pretty face framed by deep golden hair and highlighted by luminous brown eyes. He saw a lot more, but unfortunately —or fortunately—was a happily married man. The third person out of the KC-135 was a rangy colonel, over six feet tall. In spite of his fatigue he walked with the springy grace of an athlete. Halfway down the steps he shoved a battered flight cap over his dark hair, pushing it forward on his forehead and denting it in the back. Gomez liked him right away—he knew another fighter pilot when he saw one. His optimism did not fade when he could read the name tag over the colonel's right pocket: Anthony J. Waters.

Sara stepped forward, saluting the colonel. "Colonel Waters, welcome to Washington."

Waters returned her salute with an easy motion, pleased, and impressed, with the Pentagon's welcoming committee.

"May I introduce Colonel Gomez?" she said.

"Quit being so formal, Sara," Gomez said. "Welcome to the Puzzle Palace, Colonel. Name's Tom and I'll be your guide dog for the next few fun-filled days."

Water's handshake was firm. "Thanks, I go by Muddy, and I'm glad someone's in charge, because I haven't a clue about what's going on." They collected Waters' bag and walked to Gomez's car. Sara enjoyed the easy camaraderie that flowed between the two colonels and felt as though she was part of a real team.

In the privacy of Gomez's car Gomez turned to Waters. "There's bad news. Sundown wants a brief tomorrow on the Libyan incident. As usual, no one's really sure what he wants, but the spotlight is right on us."

Waters smiled slightly and shook his head. "Friday I was the honcho of an RC-135 over the Med. Hell, I was even minding my own business. Isn't Sunday a bit soon?"

Sara appreciated his easy acceptance of what they had to do and also noted he was not wearing a wedding ring.

"For Cunningham? He works seven days a week," Gomez said. "We're already at work on the briefing and need to finish it today. Hope you don't mind going right to it. Briefing Cunningham is always a problem."

Once they were at the Pentagon, they went to one of the back offices of the Watch Center and interrupted a heated discussion between Blevins and Williamson. Waters could feel the animosity between the colonel and young captain as Blevins outlined the briefing they were preparing and how he wanted it presented on thirty-five-millimeter slides for the general.

"Obviously," Blevins said pompously, "General Cunningham will only be interested in addressing the questions raised by the State Department and the National Security Council on this unfortunate incident."

The grim set of Williamson's mouth and his silence made clear he did not agree.

Waters found a chair and sat down, listening to Blevins and Tom Gomez discuss what to tell the general. He noticed that Sara and Williamson did not say a word. The two colonels could not agree and kept circling around the subject. Finally they both gave up and the whole room was silent. This is no way to get anything done, Waters thought; someone needs to take charge of this headless committee.

"What do you think, Captain Williamson?" Waters asked.

"What the captain thinks is irrelevant at this point," Blevins snapped.

Waters looked to the colonel, trying to fathom what was bothering the man.

Blevins turned away from his gaze and started to ruffle through a stack of notes. "We informed the War Room and they notified the White House. I called State's situation officer myself and he stated, 'Call us when someone gets shot down.' Those are the points we should be concerned with, hammer home."

"What do you think, Don?" Waters repeated.

Blevins shot Waters a look.

"I think General Cunningham wants to see the total incident, all the facts we can present and how they tie together," Williamson replied.

"I think you're both right," Waters said. "Let me kick it around a bit while you take a break."

Sara removed the jacket of her uniform while Williamson scampered out of the room ahead of Blevins and Gomez. She studied the new colonel who was doodling on a yellow legal pad. She liked the way he had taken charge without pushing.

Finally Waters wrote three words on the pad, threw down his pencil and leaned back in his chair. "Lousy way to ruin Saturday."

"We're used to it."

"Who was the on-duty watch commander during this flap?"

"Colonel Blevins," she said, wondering if she should confide in the colonel and tell him how Gomez had really made the critical decisions and forced Blevins into acting. While she wanted to trust this man, he was still of an unknown quantity and she had learned from experience how most colonels were only interested in advancing their own careers.

After the three men returned, Waters outlined his proposal. "Break the facts into three groups for the general: Intelligence, Command and Control, Operations. Do it in that order. Finish the brief on the points Colonel Blevins has made. Condense everything into less than fifteen minutes. Put all the information on slides. Cunningham can read faster than any of us can talk—"

"Colonel," Blevins broke in. "General Cunningham is a well-studied commodity at the Pentagon. I know what will work and, more importantly, what won't work when we brief him. I'm telling you, *my* approach will work."

"Does that mean you want to present the briefing?" Waters asked.

Sara noted a glint of amusement in his brown eyes. Waters had touched on the one point Blevins had wanted to avoid. The maulings that Cunningham handed out to briefers were well known, and Blevins didn't want to step into *that* line of fire. He stared at Waters.

Tom Gomez shrugged. "I can do it. But I'm not a golden orator. Sundown would have a field day on me."

"I'll do it," Waters told them.

Relief crept into the room as they settled down to work. Blevins relaxed, now that he was safe. "I think I've done all I can for you. Why don't I let you complete this and I'll be back tomorrow morning for the final run-through?"

"I thought we'd finish this today," Waters said.

"Brace yourself," Gomez told him. "You'll have to brief the chiefs of Operations and Intelligence before you brief the Big C. They always make changes. It's a real bucket of worms getting a brief put together."

Waters agreed with him, and an hour later the briefing was complete, to the surprise of the captains. Gomez congratulated Waters as they walked to his car. "It's a damned good brief . . . Muddy. You work well with Sara and Don. Why don't you stay at my place tonight? Beats the hell out of the Bolling VOQ."

"Thanks, I'd like that. They really are a matched pair of whiz kids, aren't they? I like them, but can't say the same about Eugene." He paused. "You know, I found Sara a little . . . distracting. It wasn't easy to keep my mind on business, and I'm an old bird of—forty-six."

"Yeah, I know," Gomez said. "You should see her in a pair of tight jeans. We're required to wear civvies when we work on weekends unless we have to wear a uniform for a meeting or something like picking you up at Andrews. Sara makes the most of it. I made the mistake when I first got here of looking at her and not listening to what she had to say. She's got plenty of smarts to go with the rest of her . . ."

Over a Saturday night pitcher of martinis at Gomez's home, Waters confessed that Sara and Don had put together a much better briefing than anything he could have created. "Why can't one of them brief the Old Man and get the credit for what they've done?"

"Sundown prefers colonels. He likes to eat them for breakfast."

They spent the rest of the evening swapping tall stories about war and peace and destroying martinis.

* * *

The next morning Gomez led Waters through the labyrinth of corridors to a small briefing room next to Cunningham's office, where Blevins was waiting. A few minutes later, two generals joined them. Waters walked to the podium at the front of the small room and nodded at the projectionist's booth to start the thirty-five-millimeter slides.

"Hit the advance button on the right side," the sergeant running the slide projector called, figuring the tall colonel was off to a very bad start if he didn't know that.

Waters found the button and noticed an engraved plaque on the podium that cautioned: "Never miss a golden opportunity to keep your mouth shut." Good advice, he thought, but a little too late for me.

Blevins sat quietly at the rear, content to see another officer being readied for the slaughter. But much faster than Gomez or Blevins expected, the generals accepted what they saw, only directing that one slide be changed to correct a misspelled word. The projectionist bolted from the booth before the generals could change their mind, amazed that only one slide had to be changed. Normally half the briefing slides were scrapped or modified.

Gomez admired Waters' cool but decided to give him some advice. "Don't let him rattle you. Don't start the briefing until he tells you. He likes to stare at briefers to intimidate them. God knows what else he'll pull. Sundown has a bag of tricks. Whenever we think we've seen them all, he comes up with a new one. But he won't use them on junior officers; he's partial to colonels. I've been in briefings where I have actually felt sorry for some bastard I can't stand. They tell a story here about the Russian pilot that defected with the Backfire bomber. He was the only man ever to stare the Big C down."

"Thanks, Tom. I've briefed him before," Waters said. "He was a colonel then and his wing was at Red Flag. I had run them through one hell of an exercise, the most demanding I could think of. His crews did okay, but you would have thought they had personally lost World War Three. This guy only settles for total victory. The out-brief was a major conflict in itself." After a pause he asked, "What does the bastard accomplish by it? Does he think fear is the spur? Well, hell, I guess this is part of what we get paid for."

A young colonel, Cunningham's aide, entered the room. "Gentlemen, the commander," and the room sprang to attention.

Cunningham walked quickly in, carrying a thin report. His eyes swept the room, pausing on Waters. He sat down in the center chair and started to read the report, ignoring the five waiting men. Waters returned to the podium and waited. Although he had met Cunningham before, he had forgotten how short the man was, a fact accentuated by the large overstuffed chair he sat in. His hair was almost totally white, with a few dark strands. The color of his hair blended with his pale complexion. The man is sick or needs some exercise and sun, Waters decided.

The general raised his eyes from the report and appraised Waters, who returned the general's stare, wondering how long this would go on and what purpose it served. All the stories he had heard about Sundown's habits replayed through his mind and he caught himself half-smiling at his own predicament.

"What's so funny, Colonel?"

"An irrelevant thought, sir."

"If you're going to give a briefing I suggest you be very relevant," Cunningham said, breaking eye contact and looking around the room.

Gomez gave Waters a look of congratulations at the results of round one.

Waters keyed the forward button as the lights dimmed. "Stifle it, Waters," the general snapped. "I'll run the slides." He hit a button on the arm of his chair.

Cunningham scanned one slide after another in silence. Waters had heard the general could read at a high rate of speed, but he wondered how much the man could understand at the rate he was running through the slides. Abruptly the screen was blank, a condition reflected in Gomez's face. Every man in the room knew that the briefing was far from over. The traditional words of British sea captains on Men-of-War about to receive a broadside flitted unbidden to Waters and another smile started to form.

Again Cunningham caught it. "Another irrelevant thought, Colonel?"

Waters caught himself, decided to play it straight. "I was thinking of an old prayer, General. 'For what we are about to receive, may the Lord make us truly thankful.' "

For a moment the general said nothing. Then: "Colonel, you probably managed to compromise the monitoring capabilities of my most sophisticated reconnaissance platform by downlinking. And now you make jokes. You've got thirty seconds to justify that compromise."

Waters leaned over the podium, knuckles turning white as he clenched the edges. His voice, however, was calm and his face did not betray the emotion he felt. "Sir, the decision was right because of the results. Five crewmen and one C-130 recovered, one Flogger splashed, and it was the first time an Air Force pilot has made a kill since Vietnam."

Cunningham liked the way the colonel thought. "And is that important, Waters?" He deliberately filled his voice with danger, testing, and also liking the way the colonel was standing up to him.

"Yes, sir. Very important. At least you know your Air Force can still fight."

"I thought our job was to fly and fight."

"There were many people who never fly that were part of that engagement," Waters replied.

"Such as?"

"The crew chiefs, the launch controller, the GCI controller—"

"You say it was important even if the Egyptians are protesting to Allah, the State Department and God knows who else, not to mention thinking about boating us out of Egypt. Do you also presume to play at geopolitics? You, a *colonel?* Northern Africa was stabilizing for the first time in years. Egypt and Libya were showing signs of getting along, which is a good thing considering they're neighbors. The U.S. needs a broader sphere of stability in the eastern Med and this incident has set that development back." Cunningham paused, waiting to hear the colonel's response.

"General, if the situation was developing along those lines, why were those MiGs up there in the first place?"

"To embarrass the U.S.'s presence in Egypt, Colonel, nothing more, nothing less. Besides, I could have taken the loss of a C-130 easier than the compromise of what your RC-135 can do."

Push a little harder, Waters thought, but not to the point of insubordination. "We watch Soviet activity very closely to see if they've got a clue about what we can do. So far, we've no indication that any compromise has taken place. Also, sir, an Apple Wave is a focused transmission wave, much like a laser. When I downlinked, we bashed the message the long way around, away from Soviet monitoring activity." Waters kept his gaze on the general, still wanting to appear respectful and not betray what he felt.

The general rolled an unlit cigar in his mouth. "You bashed the message the 'long way 'round'? Right over the entire Middle East and China. And you don't think a compromise took place?"

"General, I focused the transmission over the South Pole, downlinking through Hawaii, not east or west."

Cunningham almost smiled. So, you like to win, he thought, and don't mind setting me up to make your point about no compromise taking place. Well done, Waters. And where the hell have you been hiding? I need people like you.

Waters gauged Cunningham to be even more a cold-blooded bastard than he'd suspected, too willing to sacrifice a C-130 against using the capabilities of his reconnaissance platform. No question, he had done the right thing by downlinking.

Cunningham stood now and headed toward the door. As he went through the opening he turned and looked at Waters standing at the podium. "You, Gomez and Blevins. My office."

The three colonels instantly followed Cunningham into his office and stood at attention, while he settled behind his large oak desk, lit his cigar and waved the men to seats.

"Waters," he began, "downlinking was the correct thing to do. But I wanted to know if it was merely dumb luck or a deliberate, calculated risk on your part. I like the way you analyzed the situation. We're going to get heavily involved in that part of the world and there are some definite lessons to be learned from what happened. I want you"—Cunningham nodded at Waters—"to work up a detailed afteraction report. I want it circulated through Command and Control, Operations and Intelligence."

Cunningham folded his hands together and leaned forward over his desk, an unfamiliar look on his face, concern in his voice. "We've got to have our act together, but I'm worried. To give you an example, the Phantoms launched without missiles. We made a major commitment when those birds were retrofitted to handle the AIM-9L, the best Sidewinder in our inventory. I want to know what happened. Start your report by taking a look at the 45th. Also, I want you to have the 45th develop a plan for deployment into the Persian Gulf. I'll send more down in a memo outlining what I want before you leave tomorrow. Blevins, you go with Waters. Take along one of those whiz kids who works in the Watch Center. Good experience for him. Gomez, you stay here and find out how quickly the Priority Three warning was handled when it was sent out. I want that in the after-action report. That's all for now, gentlemen."

The three colonels left the room in a state of shock.

"I'll be damned," Tom said as they walked back to the Watch Center, "I didn't expect anything like that, I was sure we'd get the get-the-hell-out-of-here-by-sundown routine. I always thought he was in the tertiary stage of syphilis, and here he goes acting like a human being." Waters shook his head and smiled.

Blevins walked with the two men in silence, an inner anger boiling . . . I should have given that briefing; I know more about what went on than anyone and I made the critical decisions. If anything had gone wrong, Sundown would have crucified me, not him. And now this jet-jockey gets all the attention . . .

Actually Cunningham had given Blevins high marks for what he saw in the battle cab of the Watch Center. To the general's way of thinking, making decisions was what colonels were hired to do, and Blevins had done better under pressure than many other colonels he had seen. He had missed Tom Gomez's prodding Blevins into action. After the three had left his office, Cunningham hit a button on the intercom, summoning his aide. The colonel who had escorted Cunningham into the briefing room immediately appeared. "Dick," the general began, "have you gotten any feedback from State about what's got the Egyptians upset over the Grain King affair?"

"My contacts over at Foggy Bottom are working under the assumption that the Egyptians think we set up the Libyans with the C-130 and forced an engagement. So far our ambassador hasn't been able to convince them otherwise."

"What do you think?" the general asked.

Dick Stevens shook his head. "Sorry, General, I can't offer any better explanation right now. But I'll keep working it."

Cunningham grunted, accepting his aide's answer.

The relationship between the two would have left most of the Air Force staff in the Pentagon dumbfounded, for Stevens knew Cunningham as a thoughtful, even *polite,* commander. As a young up-and-coming officer, Cunningham had developed a philosophy of leadership he had practiced and refined as he moved through the ranks of command. He believed most officers in the Air Force possessed the necessary intelligence to do the job but were uneducated. To him, the majority of officers hadn't been taught to think under pressure or respond to rapidly changing circumstances. The men he valued had neither of these faults, and Dick Stevens was one of them. Once a promising candidate passed through the crucible of Cunningham's scrutiny, he was admitted into the general's inner circle, promoted *and* respected.

Stevens had been a junior major when he came to Cunningham's attention, the commander of an airlift command element in Africa during the first Grain King relief operation. The corruption he had witnessed in the distribution of food supplies had deeply angered him, and his rage had built when his reports describing the situation were ignored. During the final days of the operation he received a belated message from Headquarters Military Airlift Command requesting information on any problems he had encountered in the distribution of relief supplies. In six short paragraphs he summarized the situation and fired off his reply.

Which hit the bull's-eye. Two days later he was briefing Sundown Cunningham. During that briefing a colonel criticized the junior major for not telling higher headquarters sooner. A mistake. In answer Stevens read one of his earlier messages detailing the corruption he had witnessed, a message that had been sent to the colonel's office. The colonel, understanding it was over for him, stood and excused himself, to start packing. Shortly thereafter, Stevens was assigned to the general's staff, where he had been ever since.

Whenever Cunningham detected an "uneducated officer," he personally completed the man's schooling, and being an egoist he believed he could do it with the force of his personality and well-tested bag of tricks. Valuing efficiency, he always did it quickly. For those who got the message, no harm was done to their career. For the slow learners, civilian life was the only refuge. The back of Lawrence Cunningham's mind was not a pretty place, but it was an extremely efficient locale, and filled with a blood lust toward the enemy that he fought to control.

The general drew on his cigar, wishing the flight surgeon would let him smoke more of them, and considered the two problems before him: why were the Egyptians so upset, and was the 45th ready for a combat role in the Middle East? Normally he could have found an answer to the second problem by sending in an Inspector General team to conduct an Operational Readiness Inspection. But the cantankerous Egyptians would not give an IG team diplomatic permission to enter their country. He hoped Waters, the latest candidate for his inner circle, would find some answers to both questions.

"Dick, I'm sending a team to Alexandria South to write an after-action report. Am I getting too involved with the nuts and bolts of the Air Force again?" Cunningham was aware of his difficulty in controlling his urge to tinker with small details and relied on his aide to keep him on track, dealing with policy.

"Don't think so, sir. An after-action report should furnish some answers."

"I'm taking a good look at Waters. Make sure word gets out that I'm doing detailed after-action reports now. Should liven up a few dead asses . . . How long has Shaw been at Alexandria South?"

"Fifteen months, sir."

"That's about the average tour of duty for a wing commander. Maybe a new wing commander would be a bone to the Egyptians. Let's be ready to try that. Tell General Percival at Third Air Force to start looking for a replacement for Shaw. Get a list of possibilities from him."

The 45th fell under the operational command of Third Air Force, headquartered at RAF Mildenhall in England. Cunningham wanted to keep the 45th in the Middle East as a counterforce to the increasing destabilization he saw developing in that area, especially in the Persian Gulf. Too many hotheads were trying to increase their power base at the expense of their neighbors and by controlling the flow of oil out of the Gulf. Experience had made clear that any disruption in that flow was a threat to the U.S. and its NATO allies.

"I need a memo for Waters to take to the 45th. I want Shaw's wing to put together a plan for sending one, two or all three of his squadrons into the Persian Gulf area on twelve-hour notice. I don't want the usual deployment plan where they take everything they own. I need something that will get a small force package into the area. They've got to go in lean and mean, ready to fight and get out quick. We can't do that with the Rapid Deployment Force. It takes too much support to defend that large a force. Figure one week autonomous operations before resupply. Fuel, munitions and billeting already in place."

Cunningham stopped for a moment. He was deeply frustrated by his planners, who seemed incapable of thinking of force packages less than a full-scale commitment of the RDF. Common sense told him the Air Force had to offer the President a smaller-force option for operations in that troubled part of the world. It was a much different matter to commit a squadron or wing of aging F-4s, and much easier to withdraw them than a prestigious commitment of F-15s or F-16s.

Cunningham leaned back in his armchair, his stout body sinking into the soft leather, a signal to Stevens that he was dismissed to go forward and execute the general's orders.

The two captains had been waiting for the colonels to return from the briefing with Cunningham. Relief and confusion spread across their faces when they saw the three men walk in. Waters and Gomez were obviously in a good mood, Blevins in a sour funk. "I thought Colonel Waters was giving the briefing, not Blevins," Williamson said. "It looks like the horse's ass was nailed to the floor."

"I don't think they would change briefers this late," Sara said. "I bet it went well and Blevins is feeling left out."

Gomez motioned for the two analysts to join them in the battle cab. Blevins, however, stalked off to his office at the back of the main floor. Sara and Don hurried up the stairs after Waters and Gomez, ignoring the petulant colonel.

Gomez quickly related what happened, telling them how Waters had to take Blevins along with him to Egypt. "He's such an—"

"Asshole," the two captains chorused.

Gomez should have reprimanded them for their disrespect but found it impossible to censure them for saying exactly what he had been thinking. "One more thing. Another officer is to go on the team. Which one of you wants it?"

Sara Marshall looked to her junior partner, Don Williamson. Their working relationship was a finely balanced blend of intellect and personality and she did not want to upset it. While she badly wanted to go, she was reluctant to preempt the offer.

Williamson rocked back in his chair, arms and legs flopping down like a rag doll. "Sara, why don't you go? I've got a heavy date this Saturday, and if I miss it, she'll start without me." The lie was easy for Williamson, who loved Sara with every hungry bone in his body.

20 July: 1505 hours, Greenwich Mean Time
1705 hours, Alexandria, Egypt

The walk across the ramp had caused all the passengers deplaning at Alexandria South to break out in perspiration. Colonel Shaw recognized Muddy Waters long before they entered the air-conditioned small passenger lounge. Time had been kind to Waters, and although they were the same age, he looked fifteen years younger than the heavy-set wing commander.

"Welcome to Alex South, Muddy. It's been a long time."

Waters introduced Blevins and Sara. Blevins shook Shaw's hand and nodded, saying nothing.

The wing commander was perplexed by Blevins' withdrawn, cautious response. "The Puzzle Palace sent word you were coming but we expected you sooner," Shaw said, trying to break through the colonel's reserve.

"We broke down in Spain and had a twelve-hour layover," Waters said, annoyed by Blevins' behavior. "Actually I needed the chance to sack out. Never could sleep on an airplane, especially when someone else is driving."

Shaw nodded. "We can check you into your quarters and go right to work if you want."

"Thanks, John," Waters said, but I'd rather get a good meal and night's rest. We can start to work in the morning when we're all fresh. Okay with you, Gene? Sara?"

Sara was grateful. Blevins went along. The heat had made him especially irritable, but he was dreading the coming week in any case. Never mind Shaw's welcome, he still felt excluded, which he blamed on his being non-rated, a ground-pounder.

As they settled into the air-conditioned car the driver had left running to keep cool, Shaw leaned back over the front seat. "I know you don't want to get involved tonight, but the message didn't say why you were coming here. Can you give me a clue?"

"We're tasked with writing up an after-action report on Grain King, John," Waters told him. "Sundown wants it circulated through Intel, Command and Control, and Ops—"

"Colonel Shaw," Blevins broke in, "I would prefer discussing this in the privacy of your office tomorrow. *Not* here." Blevins punctuated his statement with a curt nod in the driver's direction.

Shaw smiled to himself, deposited the group in their respective VIP suites and invited them to join him and his wife Beth for dinner.

As he did, a rush of emotions went through Waters, remembering well Shaw's attractive wife. Long dormant memories had surfaced in bits and pieces during the flight from the States, and now they had all coalesced and focused. The acute pain of his loss had died away long ago for Waters, but the recollection carried a life of its own. "I'd like that, John. How about you, Gene? Sara?"

Blevins declined, wanting to maintain a personal distance from Shaw. Sara readily accepted, glad to escape the irritating colonel.

The reason behind the arrival of the three officers had not bothered Shaw nearly as much as the attitude of Eugene S. Blevins, and after dropping them off at the VOQ he pulled his first sergeant aside. "Mort, spend some of your Green Stamps and find out about Colonel Eugene Blevins ASAP. I don't need to be blind-sided."

Back in his office, the first sergeant checked the Air Force register, digging out details on Blevins and duly noting the colonel's current assignment to the Pentagon's Watch Center. Although his marching orders had only covered Blevins, the NCO also checked on Waters and Marshall. Chief Master Sergeant Mortimer M. Pullman, loyal to the colonel, wasn't about to let his wing commander be gunned down from any quarter.

Now he went into the command post, collared one of the sergeants on duty and explained what he wanted, collecting a long-overdue marker. While the younger NCO had never been stationed at the Watch Center, he had a friend who was.

Forty minutes later the chief paged Shaw, who was on his way to the Officers Club.

As Waters changed for dinner, images of the long-ago pain came surging back with renewed intensity. He and Shaw had been lieutenants learning to fly the new F-4 at Luke Air Force Base in Arizona. It was Shaw's wife Beth who had driven Waters to the hospital, where his wife and infant daughter had been taken after a serious car accident. Beth had stayed there helping Waters endure the ordeal of waiting. And when a young doctor told Waters that his daughter, Jennifer, had died, Beth had joined in his grief. Four hours later she again shared his despair when the same doctor, too old for his age, told them that his wife had died without regaining consciousness. It was Beth who had brought the young pilot back to some form of sanity and after that neither was ever quite the same.

The Shaws and Waters had parted when Waters was assigned to a different wing in Florida, but they had run into each other from time to time and had never lost contact. Still, it had been over six years since he had last seen Beth . . .

An hour later Waters and Sara walked into the officers club bar. A group of young officers and their wives standing at the bar quieted when the newcomers entered. Waters was learning what it meant to be seen with Sara. The attention she drew hardly bothered him, and he liked being with her. Why not? She was young, bright, witty and a looker.

Now a long-remembered voice took Waters' attention away from Sara. "You haven't changed a bit, Muddy."

Turning, Waters saw a plump, matronly woman smiling at him. Her short black hair was streaked with gray, although the large dark eyes and wide, full mouth were exactly as he remembered them. He quickly collected Beth Shaw into his arms. "Beth, it's good to see you—"

"Easy, Muddy," she said, not breaking the embrace, then drew back and studied his face. "It's not fair."

"What's not?"

"Men get better looking; women get fatter with double chins."

The two stood back, still holding onto each other. Memories of when they were all newly married came flooding back . . . images of floating down the Salt River on inner-tubes dragging six-packs of beer behind them, of sitting around the officers club drinking beer and singing lewd, crude drinking songs, of learning with John to fly the F-4 . . .

Beth Shaw knew all about memories and was more of a realist than Waters in putting them into perspective. She knew what time did to memories, how it could turn them into the unexpected. She knew they had all changed, and with a sure instinct she sensed that Muddy Waters' visit to Alexandria South could mean trouble for her husband, for his career, which had also become hers . . . "Muddy, I'm afraid at least one of us is getting old, like the F-4 . . . Well, who else do we have here?"

Waters introduced her to Captain Sara Marshall. Beth had not really noticed Sara until now. She saw the absence of an engagement or wedding ring and felt her age even more. She had seen too many middle-aged colonels change their wives for a younger model and did not exactly look forward to any temptations coming her husband's way. Still, she continued to play the perfect hostess as they sat down and ordered drinks. "Himself will be along in a few minutes. That damn telephone just won't leave him alone. He was paged on the way over."

The telephone page for Shaw was from Chief Mort Pullman. "Sir, we've got a real winner on our hands. According to some people who work for him, Blevins is a scumbag. Smart, but when it comes to common sense, he hasn't the brains God gave a fence post. The word is he'd sell his daughter into white slavery to make general, and not a single NCO in the Watch Center would follow him to the latrine. He never makes a decision and always passes the buck. There is some good news, though. Captain Sara Marshall gets a grade-A endorsement from the NCO. Apparently she can't stand Blevins but keeps quiet about it. Rumor at the Big P has it that Waters had a bad briefing with Sundown, stood up to him and walked out alive. Something else you ought to know—Waters was the guy who started the ball rolling on protecting Grain King."

Shaw understood that the sergeant could not say any more over the phone, but it was enough. It never ceased to amaze him, the inside knowledge NCOs had about what went on in the Pentagon, even right into Sundown's office. The chief had confirmed Shaw's impression of Blevins. The guy could be dangerous . . . At least Waters still had his head screwed on straight, and Sara Marshall wasn't a problem. You won some, you lost some . . .

He joined the three in the bar, offered his apologies and led them in to dinner, during which Beth's early worries about Sara faded some when she observed an attraction between the young woman and Waters. Good . . . about time Muddy found someone to share his life with again. Good for all concerned . . .

The next morning the two colonels made the short walk to wing headquarters. Sara would join them an hour later; the captain understood the unspoken protocol dictating that the first and last meeting between a wing commander and a team should be private.

Blevins immediately criticized Waters for having dinner with the Shaws, implying it compromised the objectivity of their report.

"We're here to write an after-action report, not ax anyone," Waters told him, trying to keep the irritation he felt out of his voice. "John and I go back a long way; you want me to ignore him?"

Blevins shrugged, said nothing. Besides, the damn heat had given him an underarm rash. He'd better see a medic.

Shaw met them as they walked into his office, offering coffee.

Waters was ready to get down to work. "John, Sundown sent us here to take an in-depth look at the Grain King incident. He's interested in everything that happened and sees it as a chance for us to learn some lessons about operating in this part of the world. He also wants to know why the alert birds were scrambled without missiles . . ."

Shaw allowed a grin. "I've got a classified file an inch thick on that. You should see some of the messages we've gotten back from headquarters in reply to our requests for permission to upload missiles on the alert birds. I think you should read the file. The general is going to get his eyes watered."

"Colonel Shaw," Blevins said, "are you saying higher headquarters specifically ordered you not to upload missiles for the scramble on Grain King?"

"No, it doesn't work that way. We—"

"Did you specifically request to upload missiles when you were placed on cockpit alert?"

"No, I don't think it would have done any good——"

"But you didn't even try to use your command net to get permission. Is that correct?"

Shaw nodded.

Blevins was on a roll now. While still a captain he had chosen the Pentagon's bureaucracy as the path to promotion, seeing the nice, orderly flow of information, orders, supplies and personnel as the real strength of the Air Force. To his way of thinking, jet jockies were just freewheeling incompetents who disrupted the proper way of doing business. In a way he felt it was his job to protect the Air Force from people like Waters and Shaw.

"Colonel Shaw, I'd like to have the complete file immediately."

Shaw stared at Blevins. Waters didn't try to suppress his shock. The wing commander's eyes narrowed as he dissected the man, grudgingly conceding that for all his flabbiness and rigid attitude he did at least present a neat and professional appearance: firm jaw, slightly gray hair, chiseled mouth—all fitted the image of the very model of a modern Air Force officer. The image earned the promotions, Shaw decided. He clamped a control on his anger at Blevins' insinuation that the file might be purged before he saw it, casually picked up a phone and called his first sergeant.

"Mort, bring in every scrap of paper, message, memo for the record, notes, anything and everything we've got on arming the alert birds to my office. Sign them all over to Colonel Blevins."

Sitting the phone down he continued to stare at the colonel, appreciating just how accurate Mort Pullman's report on Blevins had been. "I think you'll have everything you want in a few moments. Satisfactory?"

A sharp knock at the door announced Chief Pullman, who quickly entered and handed over a thick folder to Blevins. "Please sign here, sir," he said.

Blevins scribbled his name on the sign-out record, not recognizing the chief as the driver from the night before.

Shaw wondered why Cunningham had teamed Blevins with his friend Waters. Well, he never could understand Sundown's logic. Who the hell could? . . . He turned to Waters, "Any other reason Sundown sent you here?"

Waters set the coffee cup down and opened his briefcase, trying to hide the disgust he felt at Blevins' demand for immediate control of the file. An IG team would have done that. "I think this'll help. Here's the memo Dick Stevens gave me."

Blevins instantly felt threatened as Waters handed Shaw the memo drafted by Cunningham's aide. Any indication of such close cooperation made him uneasy.

Shaw read the memo and Waters felt better as he watched the colonel's face, knowing what was in the memo. After reading it a second time, Shaw's adrenaline was pumping. "Lord, Muddy, this is what we're all about." His excitement filled the room, crowding the problem of the missiles and Grain King into a corner, and with it Eugene Blevins. "Let me get my people working on it." Without waiting for an acknowledgment from Waters, Shaw was on the telephone, ordering up a staff meeting in thirty minutes.

Chief Pullman found two offices for Waters and Blevins in wing headquarters to work out of and a smaller office in the command post for Sara. Waters decided to send Sara over to the squadron to meet the aircrews that flew in the engagement and get a copy of the video-cassette tape of the mission debrief. He knew the F-4 jocks would try to do a snow job on her. Not realizing they were dealing with a first-class mind as well as body, they would likely reveal more than they should to impress her.

After Sara left for the squadron Waters closed the door for a private chat with Blevins. "Gene, have you ever been assigned to a fighter wing?"

Blevins shook his head. "I've been at headquarters at SAC, DIA and now the Pentagon. *That's* where the action is."

"Operational wings are the cutting edge of the Air Force, Gene. Shaw is responsible for about forty-five hundred personnel and their dependents, seventy-two aircraft, a munitions dump that can destroy cities and God knows what else. It's an awesome responsibility few men have to live with. Please remember that when you're dealing with him." Waters knew he would never convince Blevins but at least he figured to slow him down. "Most of the generals we work for have been wing commanders. They tend to support wing commanders when there's a pissing contest with staff officers like you and me. Remember, the commander of Third Air Force handpicked Shaw . . ."

Blevins well understood power struggles, and the commander of Third was a three-star general who might serve on the brigadier general promotion board. Waters had gotten his attention.

Sara waited in the 379th to meet Lieutenant Colonel Fairly. She had not been lonely, for Thunder and Nelson had exercised proprietary rights until Fairly returned from a flight.

Like most men who first met her, Johnny Nelson wanted to make a good impression, even hoped he had an inside track. "What the weapons systems officer is all about is this . . . They call us the GIB, for guy in back, or the pitter, because we fly in the pit or back-seat, or wizzo, which is short for Weapons Systems Officer, also known as WSO. Those are polite names they call us."

Thunder broke in then, steering the conversation. "We're sort of a combination bombardier, co-pilot, navigator and radar operator. We also operate the radio and the RHAW gear, that's our Radar Homing and Warning system. It can get pretty busy back there."

"You mean you can fly the plane like a pilot?" she asked.

"Sure." Thunder grinned. "Jack, my nose gunner, lets me fly it all the time, and sometimes land it. But the heavies would have fits if they found out."

Sara could sense she had been brought into their inner circle when Thunder trusted her with the information about his landing the Phantom. Bryant had deliberately mentioned it, testing her reaction and trying to develop an ally in the game of choosing sides that constantly went on in the Air Force.

"You call Lieutenant Locke your nose gunner when you mean pilot, and everyone seems to have a nickname. How do you keep things straight?"

"We do it to simplify things," Thunder said. "Our procedures tend to get complicated and it helps to balance out the formality the Air Force wants. You listen to the tapes of when we tangled with the

MiGs, you'll hear the boss call 'Jack' over the radio and not use our call sign, Stinger One-Two. We're assigned a different call sign every time we fly, which causes confusion when the heat's on. It's much easier to remember your wingman's nickname, his tactical call sign, when you're mixing it up in a fight."

"What does the Air Force want?" she asked.

"Official policy is that we'll use rotating call signs and not tac call signs. When the brass at headquarters hear the tapes they'll be all over us again to stop using tac call signs. They do get pretty bent out of shape over it."

"You don't seem too worried about it."

Another voice broke into the conversation: "There's not much anyone can do about it unless they want to fly themselves, and staff officers don't like taking risks."

Sara turned, suspecting that he had been standing behind her for a few minutes. She did not like being watched, even when she was aware of it. The name tag on his flight suit belonged to "Lieutenant Jack Locke—Fighter Pilot." She took him in: just under six feet, athletic and conditioned, an interesting face topped by darkish blond hair. She was glad he didn't have a moustache like his backseater. Scars over his right eye and along his left jawline marred the symmetry of his features—but his dark blue eyes reached out to her, and like many beautiful women, Sara knew when to bring up her guard.

"Well, Thunder, introduce me to your latest guest," Jack said.

Waters' talk about wing commanders moved Blevins to action. He'd show what a good staff officer could do. He carefully read the file Shaw had given him but didn't have the technical know-how to follow the arguments that went on between the wing and higher headquarters about missile loading and the tactical advantage missiles gave the Phantom. Now he handed the file over to Sara to keep in her office and turned his attention to wing Intelligence, reviewing Intel's part in the Grain King incident. His years as a photo interpreter for SAC had given him expertise in photometrics and he poured over the reconnaissance photos of the MiG's crash site. From the first he sensed that something was wrong. He stared hard—then it snapped into place . . . the crash site was in *Libya.*

He overlapped the photos and measured from known reference points, established the border on the photos in relation to the crash site. No question . . . the MiG had been shot down in Libya, but the actual border markers on the ground placed the crash site well inside Egypt. Again his photo-interpretation experience helped him. He needed a geodetic survey of the area, found what he was looking for in the back files of Civil Engineering. The answer was right there: a huge magnetic anomaly in the area had thrown off the original boundary survey. When Eugene Blevins attended to what he knew instead of what he pretended to know, he was very good.

Sara had read the thick file on the wing's request to upload missiles, then turned it and the tapes the squadron had given her over to Waters. The colonel listened as she relayed what the aircrews had said. His hunch about them opening up to her had proved correct: they had given her not only a copy of the tape of the debrief but their gun-camera film, which was really a video tape, and a cassette tape recording that Thunder had made of everything said in his Phantom during the flight.

"Sara, did they talk about missiles?" Waters asked.

"Thunder, he's Jack's pitter," she told him, "said the missile trailers arrived just as they were scrambled."

Waters grinned at her ready use of fighter lingo. "Okay, find out everything you can about the missiles. Read this file, if you haven't already. Talk to Munitions and Shaw. Try to get a handle on what happened . . ."

At ten she left. Waters spent the next two hours listening to and replaying Thunder's tape. He called Chief Pullman, who delivered a TV set and VCR. "Chief," Waters asked, "can you get me a copy of the radar tapes from Outpost?"

The first sergeant hesitated. All intelligence-gathering units carefully guarded and controlled their information. Outpost used a small room in the 45th's large walk-in Intelligence vault to store and process its material. Not only was the vault more secure than the radar site, it removed intelligence activity from Outpost and helped maintain its cover as a lonely GCI radar-control post. Well, Pullman knew how to back-door a copy out of the vault from a sergeant who owed him a favor. "How fast you need it, Colonel? I can have you one in twenty minutes, long as you forget where you got it. Otherwise I can get you one through official channels in about four days."

"Appreciate it, Chief," Waters said, understanding the sergeant now held his marker. More important, the sergeant was trusting him.

It turned into a long evening with the tapes. At two A.M. Waters knocked off.

The next morning Waters walked into the 379th, asking to talk to Fairly and the other men on the scramble. They found an empty briefing room and for the next three hours went through an entirely different debrief with Waters.

After he left, Jack shook his head. "Where did *he* come from?"

"Calm down," Thunder told him. "What did you learn?"

"That we flew a shit hot mission, fucked up by the numbers, could have gotten two MiGs without half the hassle if we had done it another way, the Libyans are flying better, and we should be congratulated to hell and back again, big joke."

"Was he right?" Thunder asked.

Before Jack could answer, Fairly broke in. "He's right. We've been a flying club around here."

"He didn't say that—"

"No, *I* did. But that was his message." I think it's time we started to get our act together.

Waters gathered his team together in Sara's small office and began by asking Sara what had happened with the missiles.

"Up front," she said, "it looks like the Pentagon simply denied the wing permission to upload missiles because the issue is very sensitive with the Egyptians. But it's not all the Pentagon's fault. The wing could have done more. They never practiced rapid upload of missiles even though Shaw had told them to start doing it. They could have built a missile-holding area right next to the alert birds. The Russians built weapons bunkers into every revetment. Modifying them would have been simple and cheap. And Colonel Blevins was right; they could have requested permission to upload once they were placed on alert."

Waters nodded. "And you, Gene?"

Blevins fought to mask the triumph he felt as he told about his discovery of the true location of the crash site. Waters said he had suspected the fight had strayed into Libyan airspace when he reviewed the mission-debrief tape.

"Colonel Waters," Blevins persisted, "I know they were in hot pursuit, but they were lost and should not have penetrated the Libyan border without permission. They didn't take the time to evaluate the situation. It's a good thing they weren't armed with missiles, that would have made it even more of a hostile act. This should be the major thrust of our report—"

"Gene, it's a minor point. How much more hostile could Lieutenant Locke have acted?"

Blevins picked up his papers and left the office, angry at Waters' refusal to focus the after-action report on the crash site. It seemed he was losing his chance to impress the generals on the brigadier general selection board.

"Gene," Waters' quiet voice stopped the colonel, "this needs to be up-channeled right away. Can you get a message on the wires? And tell Shaw, he needs to know."

Blevins nodded, feeling somewhat better as he left.

"What do you think he's going to do?" Waters asked Sara.

"He won't co-sign the report, but he won't dissent either. He'll look for a loophole and pass it along to one of his buddies in the right office. Not to you. No matter what happens, he's off the hook. His buddies have ammunition to fight the report, and you're left holding the bag when the report looks bad." Blevins was too much of a company man. She'd seen him burn his way through the Pentagon and land on his feet every time. She worried about Waters, wondered if he was a match for Blevins in the staff warfare that went on in a headquarters.

"What kind of loopholes you think he'll look for?"

"I'm not sure. He did mention the aircrews not properly evaluating the situation."

"In a way he's right . . . Well, I think we can start writing part of the report."

"I've been invited to go into Alexandria to see the marketplace this afternoon. Okay by you we start after that?"

"Go ahead. I've got an idea for our other intrepid investigator. I think Colonel Blevins needs to go for a ride in an F-4 tomorrow to see how much time you get to 'evaluate the situation.' "

Jack could see Sara waiting behind the glass doors of the VOQ when he drove up in Thunder's car. He watched her run down the steps, blond hair catching the sun. He was glad Thunder had lent him his bigger, air-conditioned car. As usual his Dino Ferrari was broken and he couldn't find the parts he needed. Besides, the Dino would have overheated in downtown traffic.

"I'm glad you could make it," he said as she slid in beside him. "I was afraid the report would get in the way."

"I appreciate the offer. You sure it's not too much trouble?"

"Hardly. By the way, what do your bosses think of you spending time with one of the subjects of the report?"

"They don't know."

He liked that, made him feel like a co-conspirator. Close to her, which, of course, was the idea. At least in his head.

The marketplace was just reopening after the heat of the day, full of the sounds and smells that had captivated Sara from the first. They wandered from quarter to quarter in the huge labyrinth, stopping to look at goldsmiths and copper merchants. Sara's bargaining impressed Jack, who liked the merchants, especially the ones in the antique quarter. "My mother is an antique freak," he told Sara.

After the sun had set and the day's heat broken, the market took on a quieter, softer hue as the stalls started to close and the crowds thinned. Jack had been concentrating on Sara, trying to figure the best approach after being turned aside more than once during the afternoon. Clearly she was onto his game.

Down a side alley they came to a lighted circle under a street lamp where a one-legged beggar boy was dancing to the music of a flutelike instrument and a small drum. The music rose and fell as the boy twirled and dipped, smiling, occasionally chanting in time to the drum and throwing his head back and stretching out his arms. When the dance ended, his curly black hair glistened in the light. Jack reached into his pocket and handed the boy some pound notes, not bothering to count them.

Sara broke the silence as they walked back to the car. "You really like the Egyptians, don't you?" For the first time she was less sure about this man at her side.

"Some of them. For me that kid is Egypt, crippled but full of life . . . Can I interest you in some dinner? We can go to the club or a fairly decent restaurant—"

"I'd like something quiet if you don't mind."

"Well, there's omelets or spaghetti at my place."

"The omelet sounds find."

"Good. My spaghetti is lousy."

She sat back on the couch in Jack's apartment in the BOQ. The spicy omelets and wine had hit the spot, and to her relief, Jack had given up the game. She stretched and relaxed as he came out of the small kitchen after clearing up.

"I've got a fresh pot of coffee brewed," he said.

She smiled, shook her head and raised her empty wine glass.

He returned carrying the half-empty wine bottle and a mug of coffee for himself. "Hope you don't mind my drinking coffee, I've got a flight to the range tomorrow." He sat down beside her.

"Sure. I'm just enjoying the peace and quiet." The time with Jack had emphasized a loneliness that normally didn't bother her. Probably it was because the afternoon had been so relaxing once he had given up trying to seduce her. Seduce . . . she liked the old-fashioned word. It had been months since she'd shared the company of a man who wasn't just trying to get her into the sack. She studied his profile, remembering he was four years younger than she was, then tapped the cocktail table in front of them with her toe. "Is this the table of ambassador's daughter fame?"

"You've read the report. I wish you hadn't seen that. I can do dumb things . . ."

"Join the club . . ."

Encouraged, he began to move closer, reached out to her . . .

She gave a low laugh, realizing the game was on again. "Jack, I like you, but it's late and I've really got to go."

She left his BOQ, wondering how much longer she'd be able to resist. She was, damn it, good at her job, proud of being accepted as a team member. But she was also a woman . . .

Blevins listened to Lieutenant Jack Locke explain how the Martin-Baker Mark II ejection seat worked, annoyed that he'd been convinced by Waters to take this flight with Jack instead of writing his part of the report. At least Jack wasn't using a lot of fighter pilot jargon, but he was upset to hear from the pilot that the Martin-Baker was made by an English company. "What's a limey ejection seat doing in an American fighter?"

Jack explained that the Martin-Baker was the best seat available when the F-4 came on line and still compared favorably with more modern seats like the ACE's II in the F-15. Blevins was skeptical but said no more as Jack fitted him with a helmet, G-suit and parachute harness, then took him out to a nearby F-4 and went through the strapping-in routine. Before buckling the lap-and-shoulder harness he showed the colonel how to attach the eleven other buckles and plugs that fastened him into the seat and to the airplane, finally showing how to lower and raise the canopy.

Instantly, a strong feeling of claustrophobia came over Blevins as the canopy descended into place. Only the lieutenant's continued instructions over the intercom helped control his panic. "Colonel, we need to practice an emergency ground egress. We'll simulate we've run off the runway and are on fire. When I say, 'Egress over the right wing,' you go through the actual routine of unstrapping and go out the correct side. Remember you're sitting on an ejection seat. I've got it safety-pinned, but Murphy is still alive and well."

"Is this necessary, Lieutenant?" Blevins rasped through his oxygen mask, irritation growing as the sweat poured off his body.

"Yes, sir, it is if you want to go for a ride in Big Ugly." And, he added silently, if you can get your fat ass and belly over the canopy rails.

Blevins dug at the itching under the parachute harness.

"Ok, you ready?" Without waiting for a reply, Jack shouted in a rapid staccato over the intercom: "This pig is on fire, egress over the right side." The colonel started the ground-egress routine. Opening the canopy, he tried to stand up, only to be jerked back into the seat. Then he remembered to release his parachute riser-straps on his harness. Quickly he punched the clips on each shoulder and climbed out the left side. Locke yelled, "Your *other* right, Colonel." But Blevins continued out over the left wing.

"So how was that, Lieutenant?"

"If this had been the real thing you would have burned to death. You went out the left."

Blevins had never before been criticized by a junior officer. "And how in the hell are you going to know the fire's on the left and not the right, Lieutenant?"

"By the fire lights, sir. There's one for each engine. I'll check them before we go out."

"Rat shit. How often does this happen anyway?"

"It happened to me. You took over a minute. Too slow."

"How fast can you do it?"

"My best time is eleven seconds," he said as he turned and walked back into the squadron without waiting for the colonel.

Once in the squadron Blevins endured the detailed mission prebrief. Every aspect of the coming flight was covered. He and Locke were to be Mike Fairly's wingman in a formation takeoff followed by a tactical split at two hundred feet. They would then fly a low-level route to the initial point (the IP) onto the gunnery range, where they would do another split for the run-in. At two miles from the target they were to do a pop maneuver and drop a practice bomb. After that he would enter the pattern, drop five more bombs and return to base.

In the air-conditioned comfort of the briefing room it didn't sound that complicated, and while Blevins didn't like the idea of flying with this lieutenant, he decided the experience probably would reinforce the point he wanted to make in the report.

Twenty minutes later they were taxiing out to the runway. "What happened to the air conditioning?" Blevins growled, drenched in sweat. Jack explained that on the ground, the bleed air used for air conditioning was mostly directed to *equipment* that needed cooling. Human comfort was secondary.

As they continued to taxi out, Jack said, "Remember, your mike is always hot. If I'm transmitting on the radio, anything you say will go out."

Fairly now called the tower for his takeoff clearance.

"Roger, Poppa Two-One," the tower responded. "Taxi into position and hold."

The two fighters moved onto the runway and lined up, their wing tips about fifteen feet apart.

"Poppa Two-One, cleared for takeoff," came over the radio.

Fairly made a circular motion with his left forefinger, the sign for Jack to run up the engines. The noise was deafening as the big J-79 engines wound up, screaming their power. The lead snapped his head back against the headrest of his seat, then with an exaggerated forward nod, signaled Jack to release their brakes in unison. The planes started to roll when the pilots lit the afterburners. The sudden acceleration kicked Blevins back into his seat as the planes thundered down the runway. The angle of the F-4s rose as the nose gear came unglued from the ground at 140 knots. The colonel was breathing hard and his eyes were fixed on the lead aircraft. They seemed much too close. He was sure they were going to collide. But at 175 knots both aircraft lifted off together.

No sooner had the gear retracted than Jack jerked the Phantom into a hard, four-G turn to the left, and a jolt of fear hit the colonel as the ground filled the left side of the canopy. Just as abruptly Jack wrenched the F-4 to the right, and back on course.

"What was that?" Blevins gasped.

"A tactical split. We do it to take spacing. We're now about two thousand feet apart."

Blevins could barely read the big letters *AX* on the tail of the lead aircraft on their right. The two aircraft had leveled off at five hundred feet above the ground, and the airspeed indicator was locked on 480 knots as they sped toward the range.

"We're flying this one high; it's not as rough up here," Jack said.

Blevins wondered how low "down there" would be but decided not to ask. They might show him.

"Coming up on the first turn point," Jack intoned. "We'll be doing communications-out turns. By the way, first time we've ever done them. Colonel Waters showed us how."

Just what he didn't need to hear, Blevins thought.

The lead Phantom turned hard left into them while Jack only turned sixty degrees to the left. For a split second Blevins was absolutely sure they were going to collide, until the lead aircraft slid behind them. Jack then wrenched his bird further to the left, completing the turn and banging Blevins' head against the canopy. They were straight and level again, going in another direction, still two thousand feet apart.

"Goddamn," Blevins muttered, forgetting that his intercom was hot.

"You okay?" Jack asked, wondering if the colonel would survive the flight if a few four-G maneuvers were going to upset him.

"Yeah, no problem."

After three more short legs, each ending in a hard turn, Fairly made their first radio transmission since takeoff. "Mirow Range, Poppa Two-One, flight of two, five minutes out."

"Roger, Poppa Two-One, you are cleared onto the range, first attack hot. Altimeter setting, two-niner-niner-eight. Report IP."

"Roger, Mirow, two-niner-niner-eight," Lead repeated the altimeter setting, and both pilots dialed the number into the Kollsman window of their altimeters.

"Poppa Two-Two, arm 'em up."

With the last command from his lead, Jack set the series of switches that would allow him to pickle off practice bombs. He continued his commentary for Blevins. "This is the first time we've flown a low-level to the range and then dropped a bomb on the first pass out of a pop maneuver. We've done low levels and pops before, but like I said, Colonel Waters showed us how to put them all together. I can't believe how simple comm-out turns are. It's a great mission profile."

Blevins gritted his teeth.

At the initial point onto the range Fairly keyed his radio again. "Poppa Flight, IP now."

Again the planes jerked onto a new heading, but now Jack descended to one hundred feet, the ground rush starting, the noise scary.

"You're cleared in hot," the range controller acknowledged, barely audible over the noise.

At their altitude Blevins could not see the range, but he did notice the two F-4s were moving further apart, both on different headings. Then the nose of Fairly's plane came up as he pulled into a sharp climb.

Fifteen seconds later Jack pulled his Phantom up and at sixteen hundred feet rolled the F-4 onto its back and pulled the nose toward the ground. The range filled the forward windscreen, and the noise increased with their airspeed climb to 450 knots as they rolled out and dove toward the range. Blevins could see the wisps of marking smoke blowing away from where lead's small bomb had impacted. Then they were off, pulling four Gs as they pointed skyward. Again Jack rolled the F-4 and pulled toward the ground, then rolled out and leveled off at one hundred feet, following Poppa Two-One in a racecourse pattern around the range.

Now the range controller called out the scores for their first bombs. "Two-One, eighty feet at seven o'clock. Two-Two, bull."

Five more times they repeated the maneuver, pulling up, rolling and diving toward the ground. Their escape maneuver was the same, and not once did their airspeed drop below 420 knots. Jack's scores for the first two bombs were better than Fairly's.

"Did you copy the scores down?" Jack asked after their last pass.

"Didn't have time," Blevins said.

Right, Jack thought. You get the message.

They came off the range, climbing lazily to twelve thousand feet, and headed for the base. Blevins was drenched with sweat in spite of the cool blast of air. Unexpectedly he felt nauseous and began gagging.

"You okay?" The pilot's query was greeted by retching sounds and heavy breathing. Jack keyed his radio transmit button, sending the sounds on the intercom out to the world.

Fifty-five minutes after takeoff the two F-4s made a near-perfect formation landing, with one sick colonel in the pit of number two still trying with diminishing success to keep his cookies down.

Sara had gone with Waters and Mort Pullman to the hangar where the crash-recovery team had collected and spread out the parts of the Flogger retrieved from the crash site. After poking through the wreckage and taking a few pictures for the report, Waters said, "Sara, you don't have to do this. We're going to the morgue and talk to the

Mortuary Affairs Officer. The Egyptians are picking up the remains of the Libyan pilot today. The Libyans are asking that the body and its personal effects be returned immediately, and the Egyptians are going along with their request."

"I'd like to stick with you," Sara said. What else could she say?

The base veterinarian, who doubled as the Mortuary Affairs Officer, met them at the door to the small building behind the hospital. "You're just in time," he told them. "An Egyptian army officer arrived to pick up the body about five minutes ago." The vet introduced them to Captain Khalid Shakir, who was poking through a cardboard box holding the pilot's personal effects. Most of the items were fragmented and charred beyond recognition. Shakir held up a large piece of a uniform and pointed out the Libyan insignia on the shoulder. He shrugged and held up part of a helmet, then threw all the pieces back into the box and closed it. "May I see the body? This business is sickening." He spoke with an English accent.

The vet pulled open a small door in the refrigerated cabinet that could hold six bodies and rolled out the long drawer. Sara gasped when she saw the three-foot lump in the middle of the green rubber body-bag.

"Yes, I did not expect much," Shakir said. "I understand I must sign some paperwork."

The vet introduced a thin stack of papers and handed them over to Shakir. The captain dashed his signature across the top sheet and ripped it off, handing it to the vet, snapped his fingers and two sergeants collected the box and body-bag and they all left.

Sara picked up a copy of the crash report and thumbed through it, hesitating when she reached the death certificate. "Cause of death: blunt massive trauma followed by immediate dismemberment and incineration." She paused. "Does that mean he was still alive when . . ."

Waters shrugged, not telling her the pilot was probably still conscious when his aircraft hit the ground.

Waters was beginning to accept that Blevins was at least an excellent staff officer. His analysis of the crash site was right on. He had torn apart the Command Post's response to the scramble on Grain

King, finding nothing wrong and praising them in some specifics. And he admitted things happened very fast during a flight. That, Waters thought, was a good sign. They could maybe forget about a critique that said aircrews weren't "evaluating the situation."

As Blevins gathered up his papers to return to his own office, Waters asked if he'd seen Sara that morning.

Blevins fairly licked his chops. "I haven't seen her, but you might check with Lieutenant Locke." Actually Blevins had only seen Sara with Locke when they returned from the marketplace and knew she had gone back to her own room in the VOQ early in the evening. Well, the price of playing poker with Eugene Blevins had gone up. He tried not to smile as he walked out of Waters' office.

Taking the bait, Waters stood there, feeling hurt and angry and foolish. He'd been a presumptuous middle-aged jerk. He didn't have any claim on Sara. Hell, he thought, one look at those two together . . . what did he expect . . . ? He jammed a new tape into the small cassette recorder he always carried, hoping the Prelude from Verdi's *La Traviata* would help. It didn't.

Chief Pullman had seen Blevins leave Waters' office with a shit-eating grin and didn't like it. Pullman had heard about the colonel's flight at the NCO Club, even heard the control tower recording of the colonel being sick. Now why would a humiliated man be smiling? Time to put out some feelers.

He spent the rest of the day contacting senior NCOs throughout the wing, being selective about whom he approached, aware of the favors he would owe if he found something useful. Twice he checked on the clerk who was typing the report for Blevins and collected a back-door copy of what had been completed. He didn't much like what he read but conceded the report was accurate and even fair. Colonel Waters was a hard man, and it was the loyal sergeant's wing he was talking about. Pullman filed the pages away in his secret Pearl Harbor file. By late afternoon, the chief had found much more than expected. He sat in his office trying to decide on what to do next. He could suppress the information but doubted if that was smart. He glanced into Shaw's outer office and saw his door was open, reluctantly walked into the commander's office.

Shaw looked up as he did so. "Mort. Sit down. Something bothering you?"

"The report Colonel Waters is writing lays it all out—"

"Is it accurate? I can live with the truth."

"It tells what you know. We should have gotten missiles on the birds, the aircrews could have been trained better and the command post did great. We do get high marks for what we've done in activating the base."

"What about the crash site?"

"We were in hot pursuit. The Libyans still think the crash site is in Egypt. We're the only ones who know where the real border is."

"Anything else?"

Pullman stood and threw a small blackened metal object on the wing commander's desk. "This was found in the MiG wreckage. It's a Russian dog tag."

26 July: 0810 hours, Greenwich Mean Time
0410 hours, Washington, D.C.

Anticipation hung in the room like a thick, heavy fog. Each man had a copy of the message from Alexandria South, and each understood why he was in an emergency conference at four in the morning. The six generals and four colonels from Intelligence were organizing their defenses. Cunningham quietly entered the room as the ten men and stenographer stood to attention.

"Please be seated," he began. "Linda Jean, I want to apologize for your being called in so early. We won't be needing your magic fingers this morning." The stenographer reluctantly stood and left the room. This was going to be a bloodletting, she decided, and quietly closed the door.

"All *right,* you pig-fuckers. I do *not* like surprises. You know that. Now, clear your shit-for-brains heads and tell me why I'm learning about the crash site and that Russians are flying for the Libyans from a wing in Egypt with presumably minimal intelligence capabilities? I thought it was your job to find out such things and tell the wing, not the other way 'round." The general poked a finger at the three-star general sitting closest to him. "Beller, I believe you're chief of Intelligence, how did the 45th find out it was a Russian pilot?"

"Sir, I called the wing on the secure channel in the Watch—"

"Beller, I don't give a rat's ass how you did it. Tell me how *they* did it."

"One of the sergeants at the crash site was poking through the wreckage and found the dog tag. He didn't know what it was and kept it as a souvenir. The wing's first sergeant, a Mortimer Pullman, saw the dog tag and recognized it."

"So by dumb luck we find out the Russians are flying for the Libyans after the Libyans get the body back. Did any of you dickheads think of sending the wing support, like a pathologist? He might have discovered it. And why was a photo-interpreter in a wing Intelligence unit the first to discover the MiG crashed in Libya? All those high-priced reccy-tech surveillance and geodetic systems I bought for you should have discovered that."

"Sir, it was Colonel Blevins who discovered the exact location of the crash site." Lieutenant General Beller had been in Intelligence for over fourteen years. He was a professional. He knew his answer wouldn't appease Cunningham. Okay, his sophisticated reconnaissance systems hadn't lived up to their billing. What it needed was a chance to demonstrate that the systems were worth every cent the Air Force had spent on them. He had to produce *results*. He also wanted a fourth star. "General, I don't yet know what went wrong, but I will within hours. We've taken enough pictures of the crash site from all types of platforms. I'll rip apart Intel to be sure we're supporting the units in the field. If necessary I'll have every one of my officers back in operational units to relearn what the Air Force is about."

Cunningham looked at him, letting the place resonate with silence, then said, "Pass along this information about the Russian pilot to the Secretary of Defense and the Joint Chiefs. Recommend telling the President. Coordinate with NSA to confirm the crash site. I want to see Waters and Blevins when they get back. Understand?"

The room emptied rapidly. On the way out Beller told his aide, "Send a message to Alexandria South. Get Waters and Blevins back here."

*　*　*

The driver of the Air Force staff car halted automatically for the guards at the east gate of the White House. Cunningham endured the routine security check as the driver eased the car over the detection and scanner plates recessed in the driveway. The summons from the Oval Office had come as soon as the President had been told about the Russian pilot.

A young Air Force lieutenant colonel assigned as a White House aide escorted him to the Situation Room in the basement. Michael Cagliari, the President's National Security Adviser, was sitting at the conference table in the middle of the fifteen-by-twenty-foot room, studying a wall map of North Africa. "The President and his aides will be here in a few minutes," he said. "We're waiting for Cy to arrive." Cyrus J. Piccard was the courtly Secretary of State whose statesman-like image provided the perfect cover for his rapacious nature.

Twelve minutes later an aide held the door open for the President, who entered briskly and sat down. "General, thanks for coming over so quickly, although I can't say I'm especially happy to see you. Your news about the Russians flying missions for the Libyans caught too many of us by surprise." The President glanced at the director of the CIA, the last of the six men following him to enter the room, then settled into his chair. "To be perfectly frank, general, a few of my advisers are questioning the validity of your evidence—the dog tag."

"It's valid," Cunningham said. "It will be confirmed once the spooks . . . Intelligence . . . start looking in the right direction."

The director of the CIA tried not to show his irritation. "General, we realize that if the Russians have a significant military presence in Libya the whole balance of power in North Africa changes. Which can mean trouble for Egypt, Tunisia and Algeria. It also represents a potential threat on the flank of the oil-shipping lanes to Europe. I'd say, however, that that's making some pretty big jumps based on a little square piece of metal."

"But we can't ignore it," the National Security Adviser cut in. It was a rehash of the argument that had started in the Oval Office. "Give the crazy-like-a-fox Libyan the capability to make trouble and who knows or can predict what his intentions will be—"

The President held up his hand. "How do you interpret the evidence, General?"

Cunningham knew it would come back to him. "Well, Mr. President, the Soviets are doing more than just advising the Libyans. They have enough people there so that a combat-ready pilot was available to sit alert or man a MiG on short notice. You don't do that with a few 'advisers.' "

"Except, why would the Russians do that now?" the Secretary of State asked. "They're sure acting friendly and seem interested in good relations—at least for the present . . ."

Cunningham wanted to chew on a cigar but couldn't. Not here. "I'd guess it's a case of one hand not knowing what the other's doing. It's been known to happen even here . . ." He couldn't resist the dig, then hurried on. "Maybe the General Secretary is still not in full control of the Politburo. They've invested in a large military establishment, and obviously someone wants to use it."

"Well, they're not going to use it in North Africa," the President said. He reached into his coat and pulled out a cigar; he smoked when he was angry. "We've worked hard and sacrificed too much creating a favorable balance of power in the Mediterranean. The Med is in our sphere of influence and I plan to keep it that way. I'm not about to let the Libyans screw it up." He waved his cigar at the map. "If I have to, I'll take them off the damn map. I'd prefer to lever the Russians out of Libya without a hassle, but I want them *out*. Any suggestions?"

Secretary of State Piccard leaned back in his chair. "Mr. President, I'm a believer in rolling shit downhill, if you'll pardon the expression, and I think I know how we can start some rolling in the Libyans' direction. May I suggest we discuss Soviet involvement in Libya with the Russian ambassador? In the same conversation we can surface some problems we're having with their inspectors who are here monitoring the INF treaty."

The President nodded, getting the point Piccard was making. He suspected that the Soviets might be engaged in a test of wills to feel out his new administration. Psychological gamesmanship. Well, he was an old player in that game. "And what are the inspectors up to these days?"

"You might say they've found it very hard to adjust to the benefits democracy has to offer in their off-duty time," Piccard said. "The chief inspector, it seems, has a mistress, a Mrs. Frances Crawley, and five of the team members are assembling one of the largest videotape pornography collections in the great state of Utah."

"And how reliable is this information?"

"Mrs. Crawley works for us," Cagliari said, deadpan.

The President tapped the ashes of his cigar into an ash tray. He was not happy with the situation or the performance of his staff. He did not like being in a reactive position. So, it was his move . . . "Very well, let's send a few signals to our Soviet friends. Cy, call in the Soviet ambassador, today, to discuss the conduct of the inspectors. He'll know from the short notice that we're serious. Make it a friendly meeting, though—concerned administrators—that sort of approach. At the end of the meeting give him the dog tag. Ask him to be so kind as to return it to the proper individuals. I want them to get the message that we'll link the continued observance of the INF treaty to their conduct in the Med.

"Second"—he jabbed his cigar at the Director of the CIA—"get your people looking for *hard* confirmation of the advisers. I want it to be obvious. I hope that won't be too tasking for your people."

The President turned to Cagliari and Piccard. "You two gents were supposed to watch for this sort of development. I don't like surprises. *Any* surprises. And Lawrence," looking directly at Cunningham, "your C-130 should not have been in Libyan airspace in the first place. Keep your people out of trouble, or I'll just have to get someone who can. Gentlemen . . ." the President stubbed out his cigar and left the room, trailed by his chief of staff.

27 July: 0220 hours, Greenwich Mean Time
0520 hours, Moscow, USSR

The General Secretary made the short walk from his office in the Kremlin to the lavishly appointed room where the Politburo held its meetings. In spite of the early hour the army guard at the door was fully alert and clicked together the heels of his polished boots as the General Secretary approached.

There was nothing in this room the General Secretary entered that spoke of a spartan communist ethic. Indeed, a czar would have felt comfortable surrounded by the priceless paintings and furniture of Imperial Russia. Contrary to popular myth, the room was not lit by only the green-shaded desk lamps on the table in front of each Politburo member. When turned on, soft, comforting indirect lighting filled the room with warmth.

Four of the twelve chairs surrounding the table were vacant.

No doubt the Defense Council is trying to firm up its position, the General Secretary thought. Give them all the time they need. At this point it will only work to my advantage. He sat down and reread the ambassador's message from Washington. The General Secretary had known from the first what the Defense Council was doing but had pretended ignorance or indifference . . . let them guess. If the gambit in Libya started to pay off, he would support the four men and direct appropriate praise toward them, implying, of course, that he had been giving his consent by silence. Then they would owe him. On the other hand, if it backfired, as it appeared to have done, then he could remove one or maybe all of them from the Politburo and replace them with his supporters. Either way, he would benefit. At the same time, the maneuvering on the shores of North Africa kept the United States and Western Europe from looking at his two most important objectives. How near-sighted they are, he thought. Our foreign-policy goals have always been the same: break up NATO and expand into the Persian Gulf. NATO and oil were the keys to Europe. We'll keep them looking at Libya while the situation in the Gulf develops. The plan was so wonderfully simple—always an asset.

The door swung open now, and the four missing Politburo members walked in, only nodding at the General Secretary as they sat down. It was going to be a stormy meeting, he realized.

"Comrades," the General Secretary began, "it seems your adventure in Libya has gone a bit sour. It would have been better if we had all known the full extent of our involvement before something like this happened . . ."

Rafik Ulyanoff, the chairman of the Defense Council, spoke for the group. "Comrade General Secretary, there is nothing gone sour here. We were only executing our agreed-on plan. Perhaps you recall—"

"Was stupidity our agreed-on plan? We *agreed* to sell the Libyans the necessary equipment to build a defense force and to train them in its use. The *goal* was to encourage the *Libyans* to use it, create an unstable situation for the United States and Europe to contend with, for the Soviet Union *not* to be directly involved. Is your memory becoming a problem?"

"A matter of interpretation," Ulyanoff said quietly. "Surely the Defense Council has that prerogative—"

"Is it a matter of interpretation that our pilots fly with their identification plates?"

The other members of the Politburo kept silent, in the best tradition of skilled bureaucrats waiting and watching to see which way the wind blew. Now the General Secretary had to find out if they supported him. "And how do we recover from this situation? The United States is linking our presence in Libya to the INF treaty, and the conduct of our inspectors has been called into question."

Fydor Kalin-Tegov, the party's theoretician, the keeper of the true faith, spoke up. "It is sometimes necessary, sir, to take three steps forward and two steps back. Now is—"

"Why should we retreat at this point?" Defense Council Chairman Ulyanoff broke in.

"Because we can always return to Libya at a more opportune time. Be patient," Kalin-Tegov told him. "You have laid the ground work for us, for the future. But now, we should withdraw most of our military advisers while expanding the staff of our embassy in Tripoli. Be proud of what you have accomplished."

A murmur of agreement went around the table.

The General Secretary knew he had won, temporarily, but that Kalin-Tegov was still supporting Ulyanoff. "We will direct our ambassador to advise the Libyan government that we shall withdraw our advisers beginning in sixty days. If the Libyans object, we'll tell them that we have no intention of cutting off the flow of new equipment and spare parts. They will understand. Sixty days gives them time to reestablish their position with their neighbors, and they will do it if they are as smart as I think they are, regardless of the posturing of their leader."

The General Secretary stood and nodded his head at the group. The meeting was over. Rafik Ulyanoff had survived another round, he thought. Which was more than the commander of the inspection team in the U.S. would enjoy. After all, somebody's head had to roll.

27 July: 1003 hours, Greenwich Mean Time
1203 hours, Tripoli, Libya

The Soviet ambassador to Libya, *al-Jamahiriyah al-Arabiya al-Libya al-Shabiya al-Ishtirakiya,* to use his proper name, waited patiently in the reception room of the huge tent. He could hear the ritual chant of the *Shahada* coming through the canvas walls.

"Allah-u Akbar, Allah-u Akbar. La illah illa Allah . . ."

The Libyan leader would soon be finished with the third prayer of the day. Thankfully, prayers did not take long. The veil that served as a door was pulled aside by an unseen hand and the Libyan colonel entered the room. His hands were clasped together as he gave the customary greetings the occasion required. With a sweeping gesture he then motioned outside and the ambassador followed him onto the ramp of the airbase, where the tent was pitched. The heat was building. Twelve new MiG-23 Floggers were lined up, a guard of honor. "Your government has been most generous. For this we pledge our friendship."

The translator relayed the words in Russian, a formality, since the ambassador spoke Arabic.

"Always in the past our visits have been the touchstone of my day," the ambassador said in Arabic, the signal for the translator to disappear. "Today this is not a pleasant occasion for me." He waited for the Libyan's reaction. The man could switch from reasoned calm to apparent irrationality in seconds.

"There are many problems we can solve together," the colonel said.

"The problem is Comrade Vitali Morgun"—both men knew Morgun was the pilot Jack Locke had shot down. "The Americans know . . ."

"But we have the body."

The ambassador shook his head. "They know and are pressuring my government. It is a delicate situation for us—"

"How delicate?" An undercurrent of anger caught at the Libyan's words. "He was flying at *your* insistence."

The ambassador wanted to avoid that subject. He had, indeed, been directed to "persuade" the Libyans to accept a Russian pilot on every flight, the theory being that the Libyan pilots would thereby improve their shoddy flying skills. "We need to send the Americans a signal that our advisers have completed their work here. Of course . . . whatever we do will only be temporary."

"I understand Russian 'temporary,' " the colonel said.

"I assure your excellency that everything else will be the same as before between us. But for now we must start to remove our advisers in sixty days."

The colonel said nothing for a few minutes—silence was a sign, the ambassador knew, that the colonel's temper was building.

"Go," he finally said. "And take your advisers with you."

As the ambassador's limousine drove off, the colonel waved his hand at it, as if ridding himself of one more infidel who one day, along with the U.S., would be very sorry. For the moment he might be delayed in mounting his vengeance against the Americans for bombing his country, but he would still retaliate if they should send F-111s against him. He would use the ordnance the Russians had given him . . . and his own people would just have to do without the Russian "adviser" pilots. No question, time was running out for both of them. Meanwhile, he would use them in every way he could, especially the Russians, who were so anxious to control his country. He would play one giant against the other, just as he had already done, and watch them move to their well-deserved destruction. And he would wave their bloody flag to win sympathy with the Egyptians and the Arab nations.

27 July: 1425 hours, Greenwich Mean Time
1025 hours, Washington, D.C.

Thirty-two hours after the Pentagon had received the message telling of the Russian pilot, Waters and Blevins were in Cunningham's office. The general glanced at the two colonels. Waters, he noted, seemed relaxed.

"I need your help," Cunningham began. "I'm getting signals that the political situation in North Africa is heating up thanks to Grain King and that Russian pilot. I need to reassure the Egyptians that the 45th is there for *their* benefit and do all possible to calm the situation. You were there. Ideas?"

Blevins ran through his mental organization chart of the Pentagon to locate the office that should come up with an answer for the general. He himself damn well was not going to touch the thing.

"General Cunningham," Waters said, "I dealt with the Egyptians when we transferred the 31st's F-4s to them in 1980. Pride is a very big thing with them. They probably believe *they* should have flown the scramble, not us. I suggest you have our air attaché approach his counterpart in Egypt with apologies and try to work out a way to integrate our alert birds into their air defense system for the western half of Egypt."

"You're suggesting we put our birds under the operational control of a foreign command?"

"We do it for NATO now, sir. We'll be facing the Libyans, not the Israelis. And . . . if the Egyptians have found out about the Russian pilot, they'll read a Soviet presence as a Libyan reaction to our base in Alexandria South, which it probably is."

Cunningham was impressed with Waters' thinking. Okay, Muddy Waters, he decided, you're on the team . . . "When will you be finished with the report?"

"I'll have the RC-135 section done in three days," Waters told him. "I need to talk to the lieutenant that did the translating and is a Middle East expert to fill in some blanks."

The general nodded and looked to Blevins, who was seething. It was going to take him two weeks to write the part on the Watch Center and coordinate it through the staff. He didn't like Waters' driving his schedule. He remembered General Beller's words: "Keep Cunningham off Intel's back on this one . . ."

"Sir," Blevins hedged, "it'll take me longer than that. The situation in the Watch Center was more complicated than at the 45th or in the RC-135." Cunningham was drumming on the desk with one finger. "By the end of the week, no later . . ."

Cunningham stopped drumming. "Just get the report to me," he said, dismissing the colonels.

After they had gone he sat behind his desk brooding over another problem that was troubling him—shoving the Egyptians and the 45th onto a back burner for the moment. He buzzed for his aide. "Dick, I was looking at the Combat Status Reports last night. I think some of our wing commanders are inflating their combat capability. Have the Inspector General start looking for that. The first one that gets caught rating his wing a one when they're not gets the can. All right, Dick, get it into the mill." And he told himself, I've got to know the real combat capability of my wings. Goddamn, a one tells me you can go to war and take on the enemy—if you can't do that, tell me so I can fix it.

Sara handed a copy of the finished report to Lieutenant Bill Carroll. "I think you'll like what it says about your translating the Libyan's communications. I didn't know the Air Force had officers who spoke Arabic that well."

"He speaks Farsi like a native Iranian," Waters put in. "Also some Berber, and who knows what the hell else."

Sara smiled at Waters. She liked working for him. Be honest, she told herself, you like him. Very much. For one thing, he doesn't have an ego that always needs massaging. He's confident about himself and willing to accept me as I am, not on some limited basis that makes him feel safe. He's a man, a good man . . . and like they say, a good man is hard to find. She had first seen him at Andrews, walking off the RC-135, tired and in need of sleep. Even then there had been something in him she found appealing. Vulnerability? Come on, Sara, you're acting like a damn schoolgirl. Well, maybe so, but what she felt was more than girlish. Maybe some of the magic of that evening with the Shaws would come back . . . if necessary, she'd help it along . . . maybe if he didn't ask her out, she'd just have to ask him. Jack was an attractive flyboy. Muddy Waters was a man who stirred deeper emotions . . .

She forced herself back to the report and the Watch Center. Bill Carroll had arrived two days earlier and had almost wagged his tail at seeing Waters. At first she had chalked up Carroll's reaction as being that of a young toady, but soon learned that the lieutenant was nobody's bootlicker. He also had a first-class analytical mind.

Blevins entered the office then. "General Cunningham has reviewed the report and wants to see us immediately." The colonel seemed pleased to be the bearer of this important message.

Waters pushed away from the table. "The moment of truth."

Outside Cunningham's office General Beller and General Sims from Operations were waiting. Beller was not thrilled to see Sara, a junior officer, but gave in when Waters said that Captain Marshall had written part of the report and might be needed to answer Cunningham's questions about it. Carroll was dismissed.

They found Cunningham reading the report when they were ushered in. He laid it down and motioned them to seats. "Good report, get it distributed to the field."

Blevins couldn't contain a wide smile, which Cunningham ignored and got to the point. "The President has been told about the Russian pilot. The CIA has confirmed a much larger Soviet presence in Libya than suspected. The spooks claim the Egyptians know about the Russians and are doing a lot of wheeling and dealing with the Libyans right now. The State Department sees the two of them working out a *quid pro quo*. That's bullshit for cutting a deal . . . the Libyans get rid of the Russians, the Egyptians kick us out . . . Of course the idiots don't realize the place is about to come apart. The President has already decided that if the Egyptians do shoot our base down we'll withdraw nice as you please. We've got to stay friends while they kick us out of Arabland so we can return to defend them when they get their ass in a crack. Fucking camel jockeys. Anyway, the President has authorized us to start looking for another base for the 45th when and if we are kicked out. He wants to keep the wing in the area. We've got a number of emergency wartime bases we've been maintaining in NATO for years. Maybe we can use one of them. That's where you come in, Waters. I'm assigning you to the Operational Plans Division under General Sims to find a base where we can bed down the 45th in a hurry. I'll open the subject with our NATO allies. You find a base.

"Also, this report tells me the 45th is not ready to play an active combat role in the Middle East should the President decide to use them. But that's why they're there. So, what's wrong with them?"

"Sir"—Blevins fairly leaped at the opportunity to impress Cunningham, and intended to do it at Shaw's expense—"I believe the problem is lack of leadership in the 45th. You can read it between the lines of the report—"

"I think it's more complicated than that," Waters said quickly. "The wing is brand new and has a lot of problems to solve all at once. Right now they're a hit-and-miss proposition. Their command post and Intelligence sections are very good, but their Maintenance couldn't get missiles on the birds. The pilots are good, although they did do some dumb things—"

"For example?"

"They'd never heard of Outpost. They briefed for the engagement enroute, after takeoff, and were switching lead back and forth depending on who had a radar contact. Lieutenant Locke opened up with a head-on cannon attack. That's gutsy but dangerous. Mostly what he accomplished was to let his wingman be jumped by both Floggers. Then he forgot to monitor his fuel, came close to flaming out."

"What *did* they do right?" Blevins shot at Waters.

"Locke got a MiG," Waters said. *"That* counts. I think the wing's making progress and should be okay in a couple of months. Maintenance hasn't gotten enough planes ready to fly to meet the daily training schedule but Shaw has that almost licked. They've come a very long way, considering the condition of the base they inherited. Bottom line so far, eighteen months ago the 45th only existed on paper. Now, it is a wing for real. *That's* an accomplishment."

Cunningham shrugged. "Okay, okay, let's go to it. Find a place to put the 45th's seventy-two F-4s. I'll try to convince the NATO members that having those F-4s in their countries helps them. After all, any commitment we make to shore up stability in the Middle East, especially the Gulf, helps keep the oil flowing their way. You can never predict the exact time or place for the next explosion in the Middle East, but it's on our heads to be ready when it comes."

"General, we're seeing some indications that things are sort of quieting down in the Eastern Med," General Beller said carefully. "Our allies are seeing the same thing. They might not buy your argument . . ."

Sims shook his head. "Doesn't apply to the Gulf. Too many factions to stay quiet for very long . . . Iran and Iraq, Sunni and Shiite, it's a real shatter zone. Like the general says, it may be quiet there today, but next week?"

"General Sims," Waters said, "I've got a Middle East expert who has a worked-out scenario. He's waiting outside."

"He's got five minutes," Cunningham said.

Waters went to the door and motioned to Carroll to come in, told the lieutenant *sotto voce* that he was to brief Cunningham.

Carroll felt his stomach hit the floor, he'd heard about the way Cunningham devoured briefers . . . He noticed a bank of maps rolled up on the wall opposite the general, pulled down the one labeled "Mid East" and was relieved to see it was the standard briefing map he had used before. "The scenario, sir, is based on two assumptions. First: the Iranians will not quickly be able to solve the problem of political succession when the Ayatollah dies or falls from power. Second: the Soviet Union will continue to support the Tudeh, the Iranian communist party . . ."

"We know who the Tudeh are," Cunningham broke in.

"Yes, sir, sorry . . . The Tudeh will make a power play for control. They'll ask their Islamic brothers in communism from the Soviet Union and Afghanistan for help. Well-organized and well-equipped so-called volunteers will stream into Iran in support of the Tudeh. It will be a two-pronged thrust"—Carroll was pointing at the map—"toward the head of the Persian Gulf, right at Kuwait and toward the strait of Hormuz. That will give the communists the strategic locations necessary to control the Gulf."

"And how do we forestall that, Carroll?"

"I suggest that our best alternative is to give military support to Saudi Arabia, Kuwait and Iraq. They must hold a line roughly along the Shatt-al-Arab at the head of the Gulf where the Iran–Iraq war stalemated. Also, we need a creditable military presence in Muscat and Oman, at the strait. If the communists have the strength, they'll simultaneously press at both points, exploiting their advantage. There will be fighting. We can't afford to let them succeed."

Cunningham squinted at the lieutenant. "What else can we do, Carroll?" Cunningham knew his questions were unfair, demanding too much of the young man.

"There are things we can do, but I doubt we can stop it from happening. We can encourage Saudi Arabia and Iraq to form a stronger alliance. We can encourage some European countries to actively support such an alliance; it's to their advantage—"

"And which of our dedicated allies would be most likely to do that?" The general was leaning forward over his desk.

"Only Britain, sir. They've probably already worked out a scenario like this one."

"Lieutenant," Beller said. "your scenario strikes me as simplistic, leaves out too many factors. You overlooked, for example, the Soviet Union's concern with increasing its ties with the West. If they supported the Tudeh like you said, it would ruin that and close a lot of doors to them for years. It's called linkage—"

"Not if the Soviets do it right, sir," Carroll said. "They'll be the friendliest you've ever seen them. *Glasnost* will be alive and well. They'll take the pressure off everywhere else and might even disown Castro for a while. All the time they'll maintain that it's a regional matter and they are not more directly involved than the United States. They will do everything possible to avoid linkage."

Waters picked pretty damn good subordinates, Cunningham thought, and knew how to use them . . . "Thank you, Lieutenant Carroll. You've made your point. That's it for now," he said, dismissing them.

The office started to empty when Cunningham called his aide back. Stevens automatically shut the door and returned to stand in front of the general. "Dick, the situation in Egypt is much more fragile than I let on. It can go either way right now. Too bad, but I'm going to have to use Shaw, even make him into a fall guy. He's due for reassignment anyway. Have the colonel in charge of assignments find him a better job, one that can help get him promoted, while I make unpleasant noises about him to the Egyptian air attaché."

After listening to Waters and Blevins argue about the 45th, Cunningham had decided Shaw had done a creditable job as wing commander and certainly did not want to block his path to promotion when he played political games.

"Has Third Air Force come up with names for a new commander?" Stevens nodded. "Who's at the top of the list?"

"J. Stanley Morris," Stevens told him.

"What do you know about him?"

"Well, sir, the men don't much love him, but he did some very good work activating the cruise-missile weapons storage-sites in England and Belgium, dealt with some pretty touchy political and public relations issues."

"Sounds okay . . . what does *J* stand for?"

"It's only the letter, no name. I believe he had it legally changed from Jesus before he entered the Air Force Academy."

"What some parents do to their kids," Cunningham muttered.

* * *

"Bill, you did a fine job with the general," Waters said as he retreated down the long halls of the Pentagon with Bill Carroll and Sara. "How would you two like to work for me for a while? Finding a new home for the 45th."

Both officers quickly accepted, one for professional reasons only, one for personal and professional.

6 August: 0640 hours, Greenwich Mean Time
0840 hours, Alexandria, Egypt

Chief Pullman stood beside his colonel at parade rest, holding the wing's fanion as the C-141 carrying the new wing commander taxied in. The chief held the staff of the small pendant carrying the wing's number and logo with pride. His stomach hurt like hell . . . medicine couldn't help . . . but he wouldn't give in to it as he kept his face as motionless as the fanion. The pain had started as his sources filled in the details on J. Stanley Morris, better known as "Mad Stanley."

He had passed on his information to every chief master sergeant on base, preparing them for the new commander. Everything he had learned spelled trouble. He watched Colonel Shaw greet the new commander. Morris was rugged, trim and athletic looking. There was no gray in his dark hair but the lines around his eyes and mouth spoke tension, worry and pressure. The colonel's voice, however, was calm, tightly controlled.

After a few minutes Shaw told Pullman to have a staff car brought around and the chief volunteered to drive them. Colonel Morris, it seemed, was not much interested in the flight line, maintenance or the general security of the wing. Instead he ordered Pullman to drive around the base while he made comments into a small cassette recorder on cleanup and beautification. Twice he had Pullman stop the car and get the name and the unit of an airman whose appearance he judged below military standards. The last stop was on the ramp in front of base Ops, where the change-of-command ceremony would be held the next morning.

"Chief, this is not acceptable. I want the time changed to fifteen hundred hours and I want a pass-in-review. It will be my first chance to meet the wing."

"Stanley," Shaw said, "we planned this for the morning, before the heat of the day. It will be a hundred and twenty degrees on the ramp at three o'clock—"

"I said fifteen hundred hours, and by the way, three P.M. is civilian talk, Colonel. That's what's wrong with this place . . ." He returned to the car, cutting off any response.

Jesus, thought Chief Pullman, the man's a regular Captain Queeg.

The next morning he called the hospital and spoke to Colonel Douglas Goldman, the hospital commander, telling him what Morris had done.

Goldman, a veteran of Alexandria South, knew how dangerous the heat could be. "I've already heard," he said. "We'll have ambulances and medics out there. We'll pass out water and salt tablets as they form up. The salt tablets don't really do much good, but the troops think they do. Have your NCOs watch their people. Carry anyone looking flushed and not sweating to one of the aid stations set up by the ambulances. I've got a new doctor who will organize the show on the ramp—Lieutenant Colonel Landis."

At 2:30 Goldman walked around the ramp with Landis and was impressed with the way Landis had organized the aid stations. He also enjoyed the man's dry sense of humor. Both men were drenched with sweat by 2:40 when the squadrons formed up.

Landis fumbled with the switch on the small radio he was carrying, "Check out the groups nearest you," he told his medics. "Pass the word to bend their knees and wiggle their toes. Watch for signs of vertigo. Sweating is okay but get anyone to an aid station if they look dry and flushed; that's heat stroke." He walked around the block of men and women nearest him, chanting, "Bend them knees, wiggle them toes."

When the order was given for the wing to pass in review, Landis keyed his radio, "We should be okay when they start moving."

One by one the squadrons marched out in order, struggling through the first three turns. By the time they passed the reviewing stand most had managed to align their ranks, but it was still a pathetic demonstration. Morris' temper built. After the last squadron had marched by, the new commander turned to the officers on the reviewing stand and ordered them to report to the O' Club at 1800 hours.

Doc Landis keyed his radio, telling Goldman the parade was over. "Our troops did good. Only six casualties and not one case of heat stroke. Keep the faith; Colonel Shaw may be in luck. He won't have to put up with Morris."

Later that day slightly more than four hundred officers crowded into the Officers' Club, answering the summons of their new commander. Doc Landis found a seat at the front of the room next to Mike Fairly and Jack Locke and introduced himself.

"Arrived two days ago," Landis said. I think I'm the flight surgeon for the 379th. Isn't that your squadron?" Fairly nodded. "I'm looking forward to flying with you. I've never flown in a fighter before."

Jack studied the flight surgeon, noting his new uniform and rank. An odd-looking duck, he thought. The doctor's body was almost pear-shaped. His soft face, large brown eyes and gently curling brown hair made him look like a misshapen doll. The lieutenant doubted Landis would fly much beyond the minimum flight surgeons were required to fly.

"Seats, please, ladies and gentlemen," Colonel Morris commanded as he entered and mounted the stage. "I've called you together so there will be no misunderstandings about my policies. As your new commander I'm going to require that each of you lives up to the standards of professionalism the Air Force expects of its officers. What I saw yesterday and today does not impress me. We've got a long way to go. The 45th Tactical Fighter Wing may be basically sound, but it is unpolished. We are going to change that, starting now. For example, the standards of military dress and bearing on this base are the pits. You've all read Air Force Manual 35-10 on dress and appearance. Make your troops conform. I know tomorrow is Sunday, but I want this base to shine when we come to work on Monday. This base will be a home we can be proud of. The march-by this afternoon was the sloppiest I've ever seen. We are going to practice marching. Every Friday evening we'll have a retreat ceremony in front of wing headquarters. The hospital tells me six airmen passed out on the ramp during the parade. That was due to poor physical conditioning. Get your people in shape. Questions?"

Landis looked around, decided to speak up. "Excuse me, sir, I'm Doc Landis, one of your flight surgeons. The reason those six airmen passed out on the ramp was heat prostration, not poor physical conditioning. Five them are new to the base and not used to the heat, the other one has high blood pressure."

Morris looked at the doctor, voice tight. "First, you are Lieutenant Colonel Landis, not 'Doc.' You are not in a MASH outfit. Let's cut the bullshit camaraderie. Second, I don't argue with my officers."

Landis kept his voice under control. "Sir, the sun and heat would argue with you," and sat down. Jack decided that he'd misjudged the new doctor.

"Doctor," Morris said, "I admire your concern for the men and women of this base. I share that concern. I also have a long memory." He signaled his protocol officer to call the room to attention as he exited.

Fairly held out his hand to Landis. "Welcome to Alex South, *Doc.* I hope we can get a chance to see you around the squadron and get you hooked up on some flights." They shook hands. "What do you think of our new commander?"

"Mike," the doctor said, "if I were a shrink I'd say he is scary, egotistical and ambitious. To use military jargon, I think you'd call him a 'they.' First one I've met . . ."

The next day Fairly and Locke were ordered to report to the wing commander's office at 1400 hours. When they arrived they found a line waiting to see Morris, including Colonel Hawkins, the deputy for Operations and their immediate superior, who joined them as they entered Morris's office.

"Let's make this quick," Morris said. "I've read the after-action report on the Grain King incident. It is not my intention to discuss the wisdom of engaging the MiGs. Too late for that. But one thing stands out. Stinger flight penetrated the Libyan border, which means one thing: you were lost. That is unacceptable and we are going to take corrective action. Lieutenant Locke, you were flight lead at the time of the penetration, so the responsibility falls on you and your

WSO. Colonel Hawkins, what is the current flying status of Lieutenant Locke and Captain Bryant?" Spoken as if Jack wasn't in the room.

"Locke has been checked out as a flight lead, and Bryant is an instructor WSO and the chief of the life-support section," the DO answered, his lined and weathered face not revealing his inner rage at what Morris was doing.

"I see. For corrective action Lieutenant Locke is reduced to wingman status and is not a flight lead. He will reenter the checkout program to be upgraded to lead status," Morris said, still ignoring Jack's presence in the room. "Remove Bryant from instructor status and as chief of life support. Replace him with an officer capable of being both a WSO and in charge of a section."

"Excuse me, sir," Jack said. "Thunder . . . Captain Bryant . . . is an outstanding wizzo. The best I've ever flown with. He doesn't deserve that. He was doing other things besides navigating during the engagement with the MiG—"

"Lieutenant Locke, I'll excuse your lack of courtesy because of your rank. I will not excuse Captain Bryant's poor airmanship. He was lost. I want pros on my team."

"Sir, where I came from a pro is a whore."

Morris looked directly at Jack, then dismissed him. After Jack had gone, Morris leaned back in his chair and stared at the two standing men. "I would suggest you instill more respect in your men. You get my meaning."

Fairly said, "Sir, may I ask you to reconsider your corrective actions?"

"Why?"

"Because it sends the message to every pilot and wizzo in the wing that the fight is not the most important thing, even after they've been cleared to engage. Sir, they've got to want to tangle, to meet the threat head-on. True, they've got to worry about fuel, navigation and survival. But most important, they've got to want to blow the other guy away. Otherwise they're not fighter pilots—"

"Colonel Fairly, what you do not understand is that an aircrew is responsible for *all* its actions. Everything they do must be deliberate and considered. My decision stands."

* * *

Hawkins stopped Fairly in the hall just outside his own offices. "Tell your troops to go low profile. I'll run cover as much as I can but I can't do a damn thing for them if they're setting off fireworks. I'll tell the other two squadrons."

"I guess I didn't handle that very well," Fairly said. "I feel like I let Jack and Thunder down. My job is training my pilots and wizzos to be tigers, willing to take on all comers. Now I've got to teach them to turn it off."

"You've got that right," Hawkins said. "You've also got to teach them one more thing: survival." He turned and entered his office.

Lieutenant Colonel Fairly walked back to his squadron, trying to decide what to say to Jack and Thunder. He hoped the two would understand his position, *their* position, and go low profile the way Hawkins had advised. He decided to speak to them together and be as open and honest as he could. At least Thunder would understand, he thought, as he entered the squadron, glad to escape the heat after the long walk. The duty officer handed him a note, asking him to call Chief Pullman ASAP. What now? The chief answered on the first ring.

"Brace yourself, Colonel," Pullman said. "Colonel Morris has just finished talking to the Judge Advocate. He wants to court-martial Lieutenant Locke for insubordination and disrespect toward a superior officer. At least the lawyers want to look into it before they commit. But that still means an Article Thirty-two pre-trial investigation. My best guess is they'd rather represent Locke. But they can do just so much . . ."

"Chief, I appreciate the call. I owe you." Fairly paused before committing himself. Goddamn, it was time to choose up sides. "It seems it's going to be us against him. Thanks again, Chief."

20 August: 1800 hours, Greenwich Mean Time
1400 hours, Washington, D.C.

Stacks of computer printouts and reports were arranged in Waters' office against the walls. But the two maps that Bill and Sara had tacked up were the most important documents in the office. Bill had created his scenario on a map of the Persian Gulf, sketching in the order of battle of force threatening Kuwait and Saudi Arabia.

Sara had tried to re-create the geography of Bill's scenario on her map of Europe. "We substitute the North Sea for the Persian Gulf, East Anglia in England for Kuwait and Saudi Arabia, and the continent for Iran. The distances are almost identical and both have over-water approaches."

"The weather's different," Bill said. "The Gulf has almost unlimited ceilings and good visibility. The flying weather in Europe is cruddy. The continent has less than fifteen-hundred-foot ceilings and five-mile forward visiblity about thirty percent of the time."

"True," Waters said, "but if a fighter puke can't handle the weather he's not going to do well when surface-to-air missiles and anti-aircraft artillery are hosing him down. The distances are much more critical. With a base in East Anglia we can run raids against NATO's Tactical Leadership Program at Jever Air Base in Germany and they can retaliate against us. The Luftwaffe should love it—World War Two all over again."

Waters stretched out in a dilapidated overstuffed chair he had rescued from a back room and plotted how he would use the Tactical Leadership Program, the TLP, in a training program. The possibilities excited him as he developed one training scenario after another. TLP was NATO's counterpart to the United States Red Flag and strongly supported by the German Luftwaffe and the RAF. U.S. pilots who had been through both programs gave TLP a slight edge over Red Flag . . . Waters broke off his brainstorming and returned to the immediate reality of finding a new home for the 45th.

"The computer boffins," he said, affecting his best, or worst, British accent, "assure me these stacks of printouts contain data on every base available to us in NATO. Supposedly everything is in here, including which toilets leak and the age of the grass. Let's find the base we want."

Six hours later Carroll drew a heavy red circle on the map around a base seventy miles northeast of London in East Anglia—RAF Stonewood. "That's it," he announced. "I don't think we'll find anything better."

Sara stood up in the middle of the clutter littering the floor and announced she was hungry. "It's eight o'clock on a Friday night. If either of you are interested, it's spaghetti at my place." Waters and Carroll looked at each other, tore the maps down from the wall, locked them and the other classified documents in a safe and were right out the door after her.

Waters had asked Sara to a Van Cliburn concert over dinner when a lull drew their attention to Sara's background music—a classical piano piece.

"I'm just a farm boy from a place near Lyndon, Kansas," he had said, "but I'm a music nut—especially classical. Go figure it, but there it is."

A man of parts, no question, Sara had thought. A complex man she wanted to know more about. Much, much more. From that day at Alexandria South when he had asked her what Blevins would do, the growing attraction she felt for this older man had tugged at her. And now she sensed the attraction was mutual . . .

She carefully dressed for the evening, choosing a sleeveless black dress her mother had made for her. By most standards it would be considered modest, even simple, with a modest neckline that formed a vee in the back just low enough to suggest she was not wearing a bra. A woven belt of the same material snared her small waist, and the full skirt ended below her knees. The dress was discreetly but emphatically sexy. Her hair was pulled back into a tight bun and her jewelry was small gold earrings and a matching necklace.

She answered the knock at the door.

"Well, what do I call you? Colonel Waters seems a bit formal."

My God, he thought, he barely recognized her. In mufti she was all woman . . . "Muddy, I guess, like everyone else. I've been cursed with that name for so long that it seems natural now. Hell of a thing to call a grown man. I can't even remember when I picked the name up, sort of goes with Waters, I guess."

"Okay, then, how about Anthony?"

"Whatever you say," he said, and meant it.

Sara loved the concert. Cliburn's virtuosity created its own magic with the audience and flowed over her. Afterward she suggested, brazenly, she supposed, but to hell with it, that they go back to her apartment for coffee.

While she made coffee Waters rummaged through her tape collection, selecting an artist he had never heard of. "Who's Liona Boyd?"

"A classical guitarist. Put it on, I think you'll like her," Sara said, bringing the coffee. She looked around the room . . . the lights were not too dim or distractingly bright. The neighbors were quiet and they did have the right music. She settled onto the couch, close but not touching him, and curled her legs up under her full skirt. "What happened to the Shaws after they left Alexandria South?" she asked, rather abruptly steering the conversation in the way she wanted, into his past.

"What? Oh . . . he's assigned to Headquarters TAC at Langley in charge of Operational Requirements. Beth likes Norfolk and the Virginia countryside. They may retire there."

"Really? I was born and raised in Virginia," she said, stirring her coffee, "near Fredericksburg. I enjoyed that evening with the Shaw's. She's so vivacious. I take it you've known them a long time . . ."

Waters felt himself unwinding, wanting even to confide in her, and told her how they had met in 1963 at pilot training at Williams Air Force Base outside of Phoenix. They were both married and had lived in the same apartment complex. He told her how poor second lieutenants were. "Base pay was two hundred and twenty-two dollars a month. Payday was a very big deal."

Sara sensed something was bothering him. "I never realized you were married . . . You and the Shaws never mentioned it."

Waters looked slightly pained and she instantly regretted bringing it up.

"I'm sorry," she said, "I didn't mean to pry." She leaned forward to pour more coffee, brushing his arm.

"You're not prying," he said. "It happened a long time ago . . . Life was much simpler, I'd known Sarah since I was a kid. Small farm towns are like that."

Sara, startled by the name, was staring at him.

He knew exactly what she was thinking . . . wanted to make her understand that he had never looked for a replacement for his first wife. "We were a couple in our senior year in high school and it seemed so natural, friends in common and a shared and surprising interest in music. We both went on to the University of Kansas. Along with baseball and playing in the orchestra, my life was complete with Sarah. Or so I felt. We were married in our senior year. I started out majoring in math but ended up in aeronautical engineering, which was why I joined the Air Force, to be around airplanes. I wanted to be a test pilot then. Sarah accepted it and we decided to start a family . . ."

Waters was staring into his coffee cup. Slowly he recounted the hours in the hospital. "That was the hardest time of my life. I couldn't have made it alone. Beth made it a lot easier. Something like that leaves a scar, I guess. Anyway, it was years before I could have what they call a close relationship with another woman. And by then I guess I'd turned into a crusty bachelor, too set in my ways and caught up by the Air Force."

Listening to him, Sara felt at once moved and excited. Tears actually started to form. Was this careful discriminating Sara? Falling in love with the man beside her that she had spent only a few hours alone with. It seemed so . . . Impulsively she put a hand to his cheek. "Please, I need to look at you when I say this." She turned his face to her. "I want you to stay with me."

"Why? Pity?" He turned away from her and she could feel the barriers of memories start to build again.

"How about need, feeling . . . maybe even love?" Her hand was still touching his cheek. "Anthony J. Waters, ever since you walked off that airplane at Andrews shoving your cruddy flight cap over your thick skull I felt something about you. *For* you. Don't make this crazy lady explain. I'm saying and doing things I've never done before—"

"And Jack?"

"I don't understand what he has . . . Oh, yes, well . . ." She searched for the right words, knowing how critical they were. "Please try to understand what I'm saying. Jack . . . I think I saw a young, a very young you in him. But I don't want you that way, I want *you* the way you are now."

Waters was staring straight ahead, not looking at her, not daring to.

She tried one last time to break through his reserve. "Jack only invited me to the marketplace in Alexandria. We had dinner. Period."

"Blevins," he muttered. "I should have known. That lying sack of—" But her lips on his cut him off, and he was grateful to find her pulling him close, and down, obliterating all thoughts except of his delight in this lovely woman actually seeming to want an old party named Muddy Waters.

Morning. Still in bed, Sara was saying how much she loved the concert, especially the final encore. "I know they planned it, but when that little old lady walked down to the stage and he bent over the edge while she whispered to him . . . well, I could have cried when he played the *Polonaise*."

"Show biz. Sentimental but it worked. Besides, it was only one of his *Polonaises*, number six in A-flat. Cliburn really did it the way I bet Chopin meant for it to be played."

"Well, aren't you the big-deal expert . . . Okay, go ahead, pontificate. What did he do so special?" she asked, nuzzling his chest.

Waters had to force himself not to be hopelessly diverted. "It's the four-note bit in the middle. Sort of heroic, and I think that's what Chopin had in mind—ouch, damn it. Don't bite . . ." he gasped as her head worked lower.

"I'll bite when you sound like the back of a record jacket," she whispered. "Now, stop twitching, you're as bad as that old man who sat next to me."

"That old man was Senator Leeds."

Sara raised her head and wiggled back up his body. "Him? A senator? He's a dirty old man."

"Right. So watch out for him. He has a reputation for twitching."

"How do you know?"

"Never mind . . . any man would want you. Especially the way you looked last night."

"How about this man? What about now?"

She cradled back into his arms. "Do you know how worried I was that I might have lost you tonight? I wanted you so bad I couldn't wait. Shameless, right?"

"You bet," he said. Now, please shut up and let's get serious."

* * *

The yellow slip of paper telling Waters to call Cunningham's aide was on his desk when he arrived at his office at 5:30 in the morning. The colonel was not surprised when Stevens answered on the first ring; the general had a reputation for coming to work at ungodly hours. Stevens was very polite, asking Waters to "drop by" Cunningham's office at his convenience for a word with the general.

Six minutes later Waters was standing at attention in Sundown's office. Cunningham leaned over his desk. "Sit down, Waters. It makes me nervous to look up to someone tall as you." He puffed on his cigar, sending a thick smoke screen into the room. The cigar was the key to Cunningham's mood. When he rolled it about in his mouth unlit he was worrying and chasing a problem to a solution. If he lit the cigar and puffed lazily away and savored the aroma he was, for him, relaxed. Waters had never seen him puff so hard and braced himself for an outburst of the famous Cunningham temper.

"The Egyptians kicked the 45th out of Alexandria South yesterday." Cunningham bit off each word as Waters settled into a chair. "Like we suspected, the Libyans made a deal with the Egyptians. They kicked out their Russians, Egypt gives it to us. The Egyptian ambassador told State late yesterday that his government had no choice but to close Alexandria South because of the political situation. All operational flying has been stopped and I've got a wing tossed into the wilderness." A fog of smoke swirled around the general's head. He was, Water suspected, blaming himself for losing control of the situation, for not being able to handle the Egyptians, even when he all but appeased the bastards. "I hope you've found a base for the wing in Britain because none of our other so-called friends over there are interested."

"Yes, sir. RAF Stonewood in East Anglia."

"Good. I'll talk to our air attaché in London and have the British send a negotiator to work out arrangements for a base activation. Have one of your people show him around and work out a technical agreement.

"There's something else"—he laid the cigar in an ashtray and leaned across his desk, clasping his hands—"the brigadier general's list will be released in the next few weeks and I wanted to tell you why you aren't on it."

The news did not surprise Waters. Still, he appreciated Cunningham telling him to his face.

"Muddy, this is crazy, but you're a bachelor and no single man makes general or command of a wing. I think the Secretary's wife made the policy. Find yourself an Air Force wife and you'll get promoted. It sucks, but that's the way it is."

Muddy Waters ambled back to his own office, distracted and intrigued, and less upset than the general could have imagined or understood.

Protocol had briefed Carroll on the proper care and handling of the British officer, Group Captain Sir David Childs. He first met Sir David on Monday afternoon when he arrived at Dulles and escorted him to one of the VIP suites at Bolling Air Force Base on the edge of Washington.

Sir David was average looking, and at first his funny high-pitched voice struck Carroll as ridiculous. However, the lieutenant soon learned there was nothing peculiar or amusing about what he said. The group captain displayed a first-rate intellect. Carroll had met Royal Air Force officers while serving as an intelligence officer, but this one was different. During the next week Carroll became Childs' shadow. He noticed that the vice air marshal in charge of the Permanent British Liaison Office located in the Pentagon deferred to Sir David's abbreviated suggestions about the base activation.

Finally Carroll was able to tell him that a meeting with General Cunningham was set for three o'clock on a Wednesday, right after the How-Goes-It briefing on Stonewood's activation to initial the technical agreement.

"Ah, yes. I see." It was the longest conversation that Carroll had had with Childs.

Cunningham twirled a pen, thinking about the document in front of him that created a new base. Once signed by the U.S. ambassador to England and the British Minister of Defense, RAF Stonewood would become a formal reality. In name it would remain an RAF base complete with a British base commander. But inside the main gate it would mostly be an American base.

"Waters, this is good," Cunningham said, tapping the Technical Agreement for the Operational Use of RAF Stonewood with his pen. "How did you negotiate it so quickly?"

"It was easy with Group Captain Childs here. We built on the other agreements worked out for Bentwaters, Lakenheath and Upper Hey-ford. Sir David made it clear that Stonewood can never be anything but an intermediate base for a forward deployment into the Middle East. That simplified things." Waters realized he was getting to feel at ease with the general as he got the hang of how the general worked.

"Tell me about Childs."

"Don't let his squeaky voice mislead you, sir. He's competent as hell. Oh, I'd like his escort officer, Lieutenant Carroll, to come along. He's been involved in this from the get-go. He's my expert. He also keeps his mouth shut and can think."

The general nodded. Waters' style of leadership, he realized, was different than his, but the results were in front of him—a well-executed Technical Agreement.

Group Captain Childs' entrance into Cunningham's office combined convention and showmanship. He had deliberately selected an old but well-tailored uniform that he wore with dignity and authority. It represented the traditions and lineage of the Royal Air Force. His hat was tucked under his left elbow as he walked quickly up to Cunningham's desk and snapped a British palm-forward, open-handed salute.

The general was not fooled. He knew what Sir David was up to, had half been expecting it. He returned the salute, stood up and shook hands with Childs. Cunningham knew the force disposition of the RAF to the last man. He also appreciated how the tightly knit organization could fight and how little short of decimation could take an RAF squadron out of action. Training, tight organization and a tradition of professionalism did much to offset its small size. Childs had managed to remind the general of all that by simply wearing the right uniform, and wearing it the right way.

Both men played their roles, understanding that they were committing their governments to a mutual endeavor that could take them both into war in the Middle East. Childs had a sense of history that few U.S. officers or politicians could equal or appreciate. The lessons of two world wars were not lost on him, and he had negotiated his government into a position based entirely on implied agreements. Her Majesty's government was under no obligation other than allowing the Americans the use of Stonewood. The British still had the flexibility to apply pressure on the Americans, increase their own involvement or withdraw.

During the casual conversations and low-keyed meetings Childs had in the Ministry of Defense before coming to Washington he had been shown a scenario remarkably similar to Carroll's. The British politicians appreciated the financial and political implications of that scenario and were aligning their slender resources to maintain a semblance of stability in the Persian Gulf. But they needed help from the United States. They also had no illusions about the U.S. developing a decisive foreign policy for that part of the world that would be certain to last through successive political administrations. Among other things, they understood the trade-offs each U.S. President had to make between Israel and Saudi Arabia.

Cunningham was aware of the same problem and wished the U.S. would develop a consistent course of action in the Middle East. But experience had taught him that hope for a coherent strategy was a pipe dream. His solution in the face of that reality was to create a wide range of military options for the President and have them available if the need arose to use them. *He* saw the 45th as a small, quick-reaction force for rapid insertion into the Persian Gulf.

As for the British, they were more than willing to bring the Americans into an active and decisive role in the Middle East, and David Childs knew he had an ally in Lawrence Cunningham.

After the formalities of initialing the agreement were over, the two agreed that the public announcement should be made at the earliest possible moment. Childs quietly mentioned that he would be the RAF base commander. Cunningham responded by naming a colonel from Third Air Force to be the interim wing commander until Morris could get in place. "He'll be responsible for implementing our side of the agreement and can negotiate any problems through your team. I'll send an advance party to back up our man. I assume your team will be in place when they arrive?"

"I'll be at Stonewood within a week, sir."

* * *

Sara had been at the Watch Center less than a week when she called Bill Carroll to ask if he had news of the brigadier general's list, which had been released that morning. She could hear the anger in Bill's voice when he said he would be right over with a bootlegged copy of the list. Muddy had already told Sara he wasn't on the list, but the analysts were curious about who had been promoted. Expectations were running high for Tom Gomez. Don Williamson looked at her expectantly when she hung up and told him Bill Carroll was bringing over the list.

Carroll stormed into the Watch Center. "Let's go into your office."

"Bill, I know Anthony wasn't going to be promoted; he told me last night. Sundown told him several weeks ago."

He threw the list on a desk. "Look at what those shitheads did."

Williamson sat down on the floor when he saw the underlined name and Sara looked into a corner . . . Eugene S. Blevins had made his first star. Tom Gomez didn't make it either.

"What's surprising?" Sara said. "I've seen the Air Force promote men like Blevins before. He *looks* like a general and goes by the book, never makes waves, gets along by going along. Plays it safe, lets other people take the heat."

A loud cheer from the main floor. Sergeant Nesbit stuck his head in the door. "Blevins got his star but there are no jobs open at the Pentagon that require a BG. He's been reassigned to a general's slot at Third Air Force in England, heading up Plans and Intelligence. By God, that's an intelligent plan if ever I heard one. Is the U.K. far enough away? Hell, be thankful for small favors."

Much lower on the list was a name they had missed—John Shaw.

27 September: 0935 hours, Greenwich Mean Time
1035 hours, The English Countryside

On a map the distance from the ferry at Felixstowe to RAF Stonewood appeared to be about seventy miles, not so far, Jack thought. It also looked simple enough to find—go through Ipswich and Norwich, head west toward East Durham, then turn north. The base was located at the village of Stonewood just outside the larger town of Fakenham.

At the first traffic circle Jack took the wrong exit and headed toward London. After getting traffic circles and driving on the left sorted out, he finally found Fakenham. When he asked for directions he discovered he was not the first Yank that had been through the town looking for Stonewood. He was also at the wrong Fakenham and wanted the other one, forty miles to the south. He turned his old Dino Ferrari around and headed deeper into the East Anglia countryside.

After driving some thirty minutes along the narrow twisty roads, he was, he realized, hopelessly lost, which didn't surprise him. His escape from Egypt had been nothing but trouble—two flat tires, a loose muffler and then a sheared gear in his Ferrari's transaxle. Why should this be any different? After waiting twenty-four hours at Zeebrugge for a ferry to cross the channel, he decided his luck had to change. And after he got used to driving on the left he found his little car was perfect for the narrow, twisting lanes of East Anglia . . . He was lost, but didn't care. The lush green of the countryside was a welcome change from the dryness of Egypt, not to mention the other problems he'd left behind.

His last weeks at Alexandria South had turned into hell as he waited for the court-martial that Morris had promised him. The lawyer the Air Force provided to defend him kept making reassuring noises that all charges would shortly be dropped. The cherubic-faced lawyer had beamed when he said the most Morris could hit Jack with was a letter of reprimand, nothing else, and that the wing commander was drawing out the pre-trial investigation just to punish Jack. After being grounded Jack had served as the squadron's permanent duty officer and watched as Morris drove the wing's flying program into a repetitious and dull pattern that stressed flying safety. He could only watch as the pilots and wizzos became like robots going through the motions of flying, not able to keep their fighting skills honed to anything like a combat-ready edge. He had left Egypt in a state of limbo, sweating out the looming possibility of a court-martial.

He floored the accelerator now, venting his anger at the Air Force. Now, on account of the delays on the trip, he had to worry about reporting in late. He probably should have telephoned but he didn't have a clue about how to place a long-distance call around here. He also hadn't had a haircut in three weeks. Fairly had briefed the squadron before leaving Egypt that they had better show up at least looking like officers. "I'll have anyone's ass that checks in looking like a Cro-Magnon. You may not be sanitary but you'll look military, make a good first impression."

Everyone understood that he was relaying Colonel Mad Stanley Morris' words.

Jack arrived now at a small village and drove through, not seeing anything that looked like a barber shop. On the far side of the village, at a traffic circle, he spotted a young woman washing the window of a small shop. A sign said: "The Hair Fair." Was his lousy luck changing? He pulled up in front, rolled his window down. "Excuse me, miss, can you tell me where RAF Stonewood is, and where I might find a barber shop?"

The woman studied Jack and his bright yellow car. "Take the second left"—she pointed to a road on the opposite side of the circle—"and carry on down the road a half mile. Can't miss it. We don't have a barber here, but I do cut hair, except we're closed on Mondays." She added, "You can get one tomorrow at the base. Their barber shop should be open then."

"That'll be about twenty-four hours too late. You know how the military is."

"No, I really don't, I'm afraid."

"Any chance of your shop doing some unscheduled business?" He got out of his car. "I'm in a jam. I'm new here and if I show up at the base with long hair my commander will probably shave my head and then slit my throat."

"Pity." She actually smiled then. "Well, come along, we can't have a bald corpse." She led Jack into the shop and sat him in a chair. She quickly combed his hair. "I would rather wash your hair first. It is a bit gritty."

"Well, I've been on the road for ten days. Go ahead, have at it." She took off her smock, revealing a pleasantly full figure, nice breasts, small waist and big hips. Her tight jeans accentuated her rear. A regular earth mother, Jack thought, built for comfort.

While she washed his hair he learned that her name was Gillian and she owned the shop. When she had finished trimming his hair she stood behind him, surveying her handiwork in the mirror in front of Jack. "That's great." And it was.

"Right. That will be three pounds-fifty."

He stood up and checked his wallet, and groaned, "I think I spent most of my English money filling up with gas at Felixstowe. Wait a minute." He rifled his pockets, counting what he had left.

Gillian stood back, irritated and amused.

"I've got one pound-ten. Can you take a traveler's check?"

"Not to worry. Pay me the next time you're through. I don't have my cash box here anyway."

"Thanks, I really appreciate it . . ."

Gillian watched him drive away, attracted to this Yank in spite of herself. "Wherever do they find them?" And then reminded herself of the old War War Two saying she'd heard from her father about the American GIs: "They're overpaid, oversexed and over here."

At RAF Stonewood four men were landscaping around a newly erected sign:

RAF STONEWOOD
HOME OF THE 45TH TACTICAL FIGHTER WING
U.S. COMMANDER—COL J. STANLEY MORRIS
RAF COMMANDER—GRP CMDR D. CHILDS

Two civilians were putting the finishing touches on a new guard shack, and Jack noticed that the big water tower to the immediate left had received a fresh coat of paint in the standard orange-and-white checkerboard pattern. A gate guard checked his orders and identification, then with a sharp salute stepped back and said, "Welcome to RAF Stonewood, Lieutenant Locke. Please obey the twenty-mile-an-hour speed limit."

An uneasy feeling came over him as he entered the base . . . he could see Morris' influence everywhere; the base sparkled with new paint and was squeaky clean. A sullen young airman cleaning up in front of wing headquarters gave him directions to his squadron. Driving slowly through the base he had to be impressed by the level of activity.

New construction was going on everywhere. From the number of men at work he guessed that a full-scale Prime Beef construction team was on-base. Near the Base Exchange a flash of familiar auburn hair caught his attention, and a second look confirmed that it was Connie Fairly, his squadron commander's wife. "Hey, lady," he called, "where's the action?"

"If you mean the 379th, carry on down the road, love, turn left and follow the crowds." Her attempt at a limey accent broke down in a laugh that had lost none of its charm.

Jack found the squadron near the flight line. Parked in the open were six F-4Es with the freshly painted letters "SW" on their tails. Inside the squadron everyone was busy with construction or painting. A burly dark-haired major Jack had never met ambled over, extending a huge hand. "I'm Bull Morgan. Glad to meet you."

Jack nodded. Morgan was a legend, infamous for his flying, drinking, womanizing and total disdain for constituted authority. They said that when threatened with a court-martial in Vietnam he had told a colonel to "fuck off. The keys are in the bird if you want to fly it." Morgan would never be promoted again, but Jack doubted if he cared. Never mind legend, though, Jack decided. He'd play it straight for now. He was in enough trouble. "Good afternoon, sir, Lieutenant Locke. I'm just off the ferry and need to sign in."

"Good"—the amiable giant grinned—"the admin office is upstairs. They'll take care of you. Check into the BOQ, get changed and get your buns back here. We've got a lot of poundin' and paintin' to do before Mad Stanley will let us start to fly."

Upstairs an efficient sergeant, newly arrived from the States, started the paperwork that would make Jack a part of Stonewood. Pounding on a typewriter, he kept up a constant stream of chatter. Within minutes Jack learned the black sergeant's name was Macon Jefferson, from Cleveland, and that Mike Fairly was still the squadron commander, the 378th had a new commander—Lieutenant Colonel Charles Jenkins—because Morris had fired the old one, the new squadron Operations officer for the 379th was Bull Morgan, and Mad Stanley Morris was indeed mad.

"This place," the sergeant told Jack, "is about to become Disneyland East. Worse, English beer is piss. *And* without my talents this squadron's gonna be swamped by chickenshit paperwork." He handed

Jack a ration card, an in-processing checklist, an appointment with the wing commander and some final advice on Colonel Morris.

"Mad Stanley wants to make general so bad he can taste it at both ends," Jefferson warned. "And he's going to use this wing to do it. He's trying to be a carbon copy of Sundown Cunningham, even rolls an unlit cigar around in his mouth. He's made early promotion on every rank since captain. He's a fast burner, uses people for fuel. Good luck on your interview with him tomorrow."

Jack only smiled, not telling the sergeant he knew all about Morris. At least the man was consistent. Morris had been on-base less than a week.

Within an hour Jack was back in the squadron, where Morgan put him to work with a paintbrush. When Jack asked Morgan why he'd been assigned to Stonewood, the major said an old friend, Muddy Waters, told him there might be some action in the 45th that he'd like.

Morgan reminded Jack of an aging heavyweight prizefighter, past his prime but still obviously in good condition as he shambled about the squadron, now and then shadow boxing.

Morgan suffered from a split reputation. As a young fighter pilot, only his ability as a pilot and his combat record kept him from being kicked out of the service. Later on he had been assigned as an instructor at the Fighter Weapons School at Nellis and became one of Waters' protégés, following him to Bitburg, Germany. Under Waters, Morgan had settled down some and become one of the Air Force's best weapons-and-tactics officers. He was an expert at "mud moving," getting fighter aircraft through hostile defenses and over a target, accurately dropping bombs and then safely escaping to RTB, or return to base.

Late that afternoon, having checked in from leave in the States, Thunder came down from the admin office with the same handful of in-processing paperwork Jack had. "Looks like we're seeing Mad Stanley together," Thunder told him. "Should be interesting." Jack was glad to see his backseater. He figured he'd need him on this flight.

Jack and Thunder presented themselves at Colonel Morris's office on the dot for their scheduled interview. Their class A uniforms and shoes were immaculate, and Thunder had carefully trimmed his moustache back so as to be well within standards. After a few minutes wait Morris' executive officer briefed them to report in a military manner and remain standing during the interview.

"Sounds like an inquisition," Jack said. Thunder shrugged in resignation.

The exec rapped sharply on the colonel's door, paused for a moment, then escorted them in.

Morris returned their salute and rocked back in his chair, rolling a pen between the fingers of both hands. He mentally dismissed Thunder with a passing glance and fixed on Jack. "Lieutenant Locke, your irresponsible flying got my wing kicked out of Egypt. I do not like that. They tell me you're a good pilot. I doubt it, because you're certainly not a good officer. However, I believe you deserve another chance and I am dropping charges and court-martial proceedings against you and returning you to flying status." It was no act of generosity. The Judge Advocate had convinced Morris that Jack would be acquitted in any court-martial and the charges should be dropped.

Relief washed over Jack.

"I want you to understand one thing and understand it well," Morris went on. "You have no second chances here. One slip and I'll break you. Follow? Do you understand everything I've said?

"And while I am giving you another chance, Lieutenant Locke, I am holding both of you responsible for what I consider irresponsible flying at Alexandria South, which will be noted on your next effectiveness reports. I'm a generous fellow, so I'm giving you an opportunity to demonstrate how well you've gotten my message. To build good will and interaction with the community, I am creating my Friday afternoon public tours. You two will be in charge of the presentation on Operations. That's all. Dismissed."

The two officers saluted and left.

Thunder spoke up first. "Come on, we're going to see Fairly. I'm no genius, but I know a nut case when he drives over me."

Doc Landis was in Fairly's office when they stomped up the stairs and Fairly motioned them to come in and find some seats.

"The Doc is here lining up flights in Big Ugly. Kind of unusual," Fairly said, trying to lighten the somber mood of the two men, "he wants to meet all his flying requirements." Air Force regulations required flight surgeons to "fly frequently and periodically" in their wing's aircraft. As a flight surgeon assigned to a squadron, Landis had to know at first hand the environment and stresses his patients were experiencing. Not only was he to treat their physical ailments, but he was responsible for evaluating their mental well-being. After all, in a war he had to watch for combat fatigue, a sure killer in high-performance fighters.

"How did the interview go?" Fairly finally asked.

"That man's asshole is synced to his brain with a direct force-feed mechanism—"

Fairly interrupted. "Jack, we've got a guest." The squadron commander did not want his officer to get in the habit of criticizing senior officers in front of others, even a medic.

"It's okay," Landis said. "Let him get it out."

The break was enough for Jack to regain control as he told them what had happened with Morris. Fairly sighed. Morris' decision to downgrade their OERs would make future promotion for the two very tough.

"Jack," Doc said, "it's anybody's guess what's going on in Colonel Morris's head, but I'd guess he's trying to establish his control over the wing and his ego is getting involved. There's some kind of feedback . . . the more control, the better his precious ego feels. He might well see you as a threat to his control."

"Why me?"

Thunder picked it up. "Once you're in Big Ugly and the gear is in the well, he doesn't have any real control over you. He's got to trust you up there and that's one thing he's afraid to do."

"We're talking about how ego and leadership get all mixed up. T. E. Lawrence wrote all about it," Landis said.

"Who?"

"Lawrence of Arabia. He ought to be required reading for every officer."

"All this bullshit about egos and your pal Lawrence is great, but what do me and Thunder do right now?"

"Well, for one thing, don't squawk identification," Doc said. He was alluding to the IFF (Identification, Friend or Foe) radar transponder beacon that sent out a signal for ground-based radars to identify an aircraft.

"Where did *you* learn about the IFF?"

"I'm a student of the F-4," Landis said. "I figured I'd better be if I was going to be any good at saving your ass, and mine."

18 October: 0200 hours, Greenwich Mean Time
17 October: 2200 hours, Washington, D.C.

Sara decided she was going to have to push Anthony "Muddy" Waters off dead-center. She went into the bedroom, selected an old-fashioned nightgown with a high neckline and long sleeves and got ready for bed. After brushing out her hair she walked into the living room, leaving the bedroom light on, hoping it would silhouette her figure through the nightgown. Waters, watching her, stretched out his arm.

Sara sat down close and nestled against his shoulder. "Anthony, I'm an old-fashioned modern girl . . ." She waited, hoping he understood.

He did. "Sara . . . there's a hell of an age difference between us. Do you think—?"

"I *think* if I'm going to have an Anthony Jr. or an Antonia, I'd like to be halfway respectable about it." She waited.

"Are you . . . ?"

"No, but I want to get on with it."

"What would you do if I said no?"

"Not be so respectable, I guess." She was forcing herself to sound light but was close to tears.

He wasn't about to protest too much. "Then like you say, let's get on with it . . ."

18 October: 0730 hours, Greenwich Mean Time
0730 hours, Stonewood, England

Anticipating the inevitable noise complaints, Colonel Morris mounted a public-relations campaign in the local community. The 45th had flown P-51 Mustangs out of England in World War II, and Morris built on that, claiming a long-standing tradition of service in the U.K.

"Jet Noise—The Sound of Freedom" was printed on thousands of bumper stickers. The colonel invited newspaper and TV reporters to tour the base and made the Officers' Club available to the "Friends of the Eighth" for their next banquet. The public tours on Friday afternoons were a hit and well attended. It was time to get to the real work . . .

At 7:30 A.M. on a Monday morning the quiet was ripped apart as the wing started its training schedule. Four Phantoms cranked their engines in unison, the first go of the day. Within two hours the 45th would launch sixteen aircraft; then a period of relative quiet would descend over the base until the early afternoon when another sixteen would be launched.

The action started the previous evening as Maintenance confirmed which aircraft would be launched. The section chief on the flight line had his people check each bird, insuring each one was fully mission capable and serviced. Two of the birds had maintenance problems: one had a slow fuel leak from a wing fuel-cell; another's LOX bottle was found to be at its lower limits. The chief had the LOX bottle replaced with a fully charged bottle and called for a fuels specialist to fix the leak. It would be an all-night repair job.

By 4:00 A.M. the first four Phantoms stood ready when the crew chiefs, the pilot who would be the flight lead on the mission and the squadron duty officer reported in. The two crew chiefs on each Phantom pulled a detailed pre-flight inspection, ending the pre-flight by removing most of the safety pins, down locks on the main gear and intake covers from the engines. Two crew chiefs sacked out in a van near their bird, five had time to get breakfast and one cleaned the canopies of his bird and made a note in the maintenance forms to have the light brown star under the left front canopy repainted.

While the crew chiefs were preparing their birds the flight-lead planned his mission. At 5:30 A.M. the other seven members of his flight reported for the briefing. For the next hour the flight lead went over every aspect of the coming mission, covering exactly what he wanted from each pilot and wizzo. At 6:30 he concluded his briefing and his flight hurried into the Life Support section to put on their equipment and make a last pit stop. They gathered around the front counter where the duty officer gave them a last-minute briefing on field conditions, the active runway and any special notices. At 7:00 the crews stepped to their fighters, where they would meet the crew chiefs, make their own inspection of the birds, strap in, start engines and taxi to make an 8:00 A.M. takeoff.

On that first morning of flying, the wing was composed of 4156 active duty personnel, of which 2237 were assigned to maintenance; seventy-two F-4E aircraft divided between the three squadrons, of which thirty-four were fully mission capable; three flying squadrons of thirty-eight pilots and thirty-six wizzos each; various support units comprising the remainder of the wing—and J. Stanley Morris, who walked into the command post and told the controller on duty to change the wing's rating on the Combat Status Report to a one.

Doc Landis would try to break away from his office for a few hours every day and meet Thunder for some impromptu training on the care and feeding of the F-4. The schedulers got to know the Doc as he tried to cadge as many rides as possible, and Thunder soon learned that the funny-looking, pear-shaped man had a quick intellect, an excellent memory, superb eye-hand coordination and a high tolerance to Gs. He also never complained and made quick progress in using the radar.

In many ways Doc Landis' progress toward becoming a WSO paralleled the wing's training program. He started out by becoming familiar with the local training area: learning how to find the base, what areas to avoid, and how Eastern Radar, the local air traffic control, managed the airspace. From there he progressed to the gunnery ranges. He loved it. He even enjoyed riding Big Ugly down the chute at 450 knots as the altimeter rapidly unwound. He could put his faith in the ability of the pilot in the front seat. He told his wife, "I know that I can keep us out of trouble on the range. Besides, it satisfies my basic kamikaze instincts."

Radar bomb deliveries were a delight for the doctor. The sweat would pour off him as he worked the radar, acquiring the target. Once he had the target broken out on the scope he would drive the radar cursors over it and activate the system. After a few fumbling attempts and one extremely long bomb—the British range controller told him that he was supposed to bomb the island and not France, even though he thought it was a fine gesture—Doc turned into a right-on bombardier who won as many bets as he lost.

But it was when he experienced dogfighting for the first time that Doc Landis came to know what fighters were all about. He needed every bit of his intellect and experience to follow the three-dimensional form of combat. His keen eyesight often got the first visual sighting, the tallyho, in the first critical opening of the most engagements, and pilots liked having him in their pit.

On his third air-to-air ride he was paired with Mike Fairly and the squadron commander explained that it was never called dogfighting, it was air-to-air or air-combat tactics, ACT. They were still climbing out when their opponent, another F-4 from the 379th, developed a minor electrical problem and returned to base. Rather than recover with the disabled F-4 Fairly took his bird out over the North Sea to give Doc a flying lesson and burn off gas. They had just cleared the coast when two RAF Tornados from the nearby Honington base jumped them and the fight was on. It should have been an easy thing for the swing-wing Tornados, but Fairly took the fight into the vertical and played the sun to his advantage. He refused to disengage and dragged the fight lower and lower toward the sea so that never once did the Tornados bring their sights to bear on the F-4. Finally the Tornado leader rocked his wings and flew straight and level. Fairly joined up on the two RAF fighters and the lead gave him a thumbs-up sign. The three flew a tight formation back to the coast.

Fairly told Doc Landis that what they had been doing was illegal as hell and Morris would have their asses if he found out they were rat-racing with the Blokes. Doc didn't care. That night, he went home and pulled Mrs. Landis into bed for an all-nighter. "The movie director Sam Peckinpah was right," he told her. "Fighting and fucking is what it's all about. Everything else is a surrogate."

"My hero," she said. "Now cut the crap, Doctor, and stop acting like an overaged teenager." She deadpanned when she said it, but there was nothing dead about what they did together that night.

Afterward she wondered if he and Sam might not have been right. Keep flying, darling . . .

That Saturday night the Fairlys and Landises had dinner at the Tudenham Mill near Mildenhall. Over coffee in the lounge Fairly quizzed the doctor about leaving his successful practice in the States to join the Air Force and losing his mind over the F-4. "I don't really know why I did it," the doctor said. "Maybe I simply got bored with my patients. I can't tell you why I like flying Big Ugly so much. Maybe the challenge. In medicine a challenge means the patient's life is on the line. In flying, it's your own life you're betting."

"He's a teenager that grew old, never up," his wife announced.

The major in charge of the command post, Vernon Yaru-Lau, hated going to Morris' daily stand-up briefing. Every morning the commander of each unit on the base had to keep standing while a series of slides summarizing the previous day's activity, the planned schedule for the day and the current status of critical resources on the base was flashed on the screen. Every wing in the Air Force had a similar meeting each morning.

When Yaru-Lau had tried to explain that the slide summarizing the wing's combat status was wrong Morris had silenced him with "I know the combat status of my wing; you don't."

"Royally pissed," to quote his sergeant, the major called the Inspector General's office at Third Air Force and filed an anonymous complaint—the wing's Combat Status Report was highly inflated.

The next day two lieutenant colonels from the IG appeared in Morris' office to tell him they were conducting a no-notice inspection of the command post. Morris' secretary told them that Morris and the wing's vice-commander were at a conference in Germany and wouldn't be back until the next day. The two IG officers shrugged and went to the command post, where Yaru-Lau laid out the problem for them. "Colonel Morris has directed that I report our combat status as a one. But we're only flying enough tactical training sorties to rate a five, maybe a four. Also, Maintenance is only keeping enough aircraft fixed and flying to rate a three."

The two lieutenant colonels reviewed the sortie and maintenance rates, drafted a one-page report and forwarded it to the Pentagon and Third Air Force. No one told Morris when he returned that two officers from the IG had spent an hour in his command post while he was away. What he didn't know could hurt him . . . they hoped.

> *2 November: 1945 hours, Greenwich Mean Time*
> *1445 hours, Washington, D.C.*

Cunningham had read the one-page report and set it aside, letting his anger cool down before he decided what to do. The report had been on his desk over a day when his private telephone rang.

"Lawrence"—Ruth Cunningham's voice sparkled—"we've been invited to a wedding this Saturday for two of your officers, a Colonel Waters and a Captain Marshall. I believe I've already met the bride at a reception. It'll be at the Marshall's home and I'd like to attend."

Cunningham grunted a yes and then buzzed his aide, telling him when he wanted Morris relieved and who was to replace him.

The two women hovered behind Sara adjusting the old Spanish mantilla over her hair. The white lace shawl had been in the Marshall family for over a hundred years and had been worn as a bridal veil by four generations of Marshall brides, ever since a young John Marshall brought it home for his bride after making his first voyage as a third mate on a clipper ship. Sara's mother, Martha Marshall, had selected a subtle off-white material for the wedding dress that blended perfectly with the mantilla, creating the soft effect she wanted. Sara stood up, letting her mother appraise the elegently simple knee-length dress for the last time. "It's perfect, Mother," was all she could say, seeing tears form in her mother's eyes.

"I was just thinking about our names," Ruth Cunningham said, changing the subject. "Martha, Sara, and Ruth. You'd think we were a bunch of minister's wives. Should we be stern and sour?" Her gambit didn't work. Martha began to cry, no longer able to hold back.

"I'm sorry," she said, "I'm happy for Sara, but Louis is upset because of their age difference."

Ruth brightened. "I wouldn't worry too much about that. Just *look* at Muddy. He's younger looking than most thirty-five-year-olds, and certainly in better condition. Your daughter is not marrying the most eligible bachelor in this town, only the most desirable."

Sara put her arms around her mother. "You're going to have some beautiful grandchildren."

The French windows had been thrown open, letting the unusually warm fall day spill into the room. The Air Force chaplain marrying them stood with his back to the French windows while the guests arranged themselves in a semicircle in front of him. Sara's father escorted his daughter to the chaplain and gave her hand to Waters.

And so they became Colonel and Mrs. Anthony Waters. After the couple had been congratulated by the guests and Sara thoroughly kissed by Cunningham, the general took the couple aside. "I've got a honeymoon present for you. I want you to go through the commander's refresher course for flying F-4s at Luke. Your class starts a week from Monday. It's important that you make this class, Muddy."

Waters' muscles tensed. "Thank you, sir. We'll make it." He silently was furious, suspecting that the general knew about his wife and daughter's deaths at Luke the first time he had been stationed there.

Sara read his thoughts. "There's no way he could have known about your first marriage and what happened at Luke," she said, after the general had walked off. "We'll do this one together, but I wonder why the rush?"

"I don't know, but it looks like we are going to an F-4 unit. And damn soon. Not much time, so let's make the most of it . . ."

15 November: 2035 hours, Greenwich Mean Time
2035 hours, Stonewood, England

The communications technician ripped the message off the telecommunications bank at Stonewood, annoyed at the garbled text. She was going to request a retransmission when she noticed the message was directed to the attention of the Communications Squadron commander for decoding. She called for her first sergeant, who took the message and told her never to mention that it had been received or she had seen it. The NCO sealed the message in an envelope and called the lieutenant colonel in charge of the squadron, who rushed over to the communications center.

Seeing that the first two lines were decode instructions, the lieutenant colonel dismissed the NCO and called the wing's vice-commander and judge advocate as witnesses before proceeding any further. The two men looked over his shoulder as he finished decoding the message:

EFFECTIVE IMMEDIATELY COL J. STANLEY MORRIS IS RE-
LIEVED OF COMMAND OF 45TH TACTICAL FIGHTER WING.
COL WILLIAM L. BRADLEY WILL ASSUME COMMAND
PENDING ARRIVAL OF NEW COMMANDER. COMMANDER
THIRD AIR FORCE IS ACTION AUTHORITY. ACTION AU-
THORITY WILL NOTIFY AND RELIEVE COL MORRIS NLT
2200z.

"Well, I'll be damned," the Judge Advocate said.

Colonel Bradley felt his stomach turn sour. "I'll contact General Percival for instructions. He has to act by ten tonight. Until he tells Morris, we do nothing. I'll be in the command post. Needless to say, don't tell anyone." The vice commander's call to Third Air Force was too late. Percival had received another message and was enroute to Stonewood.

James Percival, the commander of Third Air Force, entered the command post at 9:45 and directed the controller to get Colonel Morris to the wing commander's office immediately. "Bill, I am sorry this had to happen, but you'll have to be on hand when I tell Morris," the general said.

"General, just what the hell is going down?" Bradley asked as they made the short walk to wing headquarters.

"I got a message from Cunningham. It seems Morris lied on his Combat Status Report and rated the wing a one. You know a one means the wing is fully combat ready, ready to go to war. Cunningham treats the Com Stat like being pregnant, either you are or you're not. Morris getting fired shows how important the Com Stat is to the general. I'd say there are at least seven wings in the Air Force right now that are rated a two or three. Cunningham needs to know so he can supply whatever it takes to make a wing a one. Morris must have thought downgrading his wing from a one would make him look bad, like he's not using what he's got.

"I'm worried, Bill; I've done this chore before and I've seen what it does to a man's ego. It is hard to tell how Morris will react, but watch him like a hawk until we can get him transferred out tomorrow."

The door to Morris' office was open and he was sitting behind his desk when Percival and Bradley arrived. He stood and saluted the general, puzzled by Bradley's presence.

The general returned the salute and handed Morris the decoded message. "Colonel Morris, I'm acting as directed by this message. Colonel Bradley is now in command of the 45th."

"I see the message was decoded. An obvious mistake," Morris said, a tight slight smile spreading across his lips.

"There's no mistake. I have a separate, confirming message," Percival told him.

Morris wadded the message in his fist. "Bill, you've wanted command of my wing and now you've got it. Well, do you mind if I clear out my desk?" He sat down and wrenched a drawer open, staring at its contents.

Percival nodded at Bradley and the two left the office, closing the door behind them.

"It could have been worse. Much worse," Percival said. "I'm relieved."

The wing learned of the change of command the next morning at Stand-Up and for the first time felt some relief. After the morning's Stand-Up briefing in the conference room the commander's civilian secretary ran up to Chief Pullman, her eyes full of worry. "Chief, Colonel Morris is in his office and he's acting . . . funny. I've never seen him like this before. He told me to place a call to General Cunningham. When I couldn't get through—it's only two-thirty in the morning there—he called me terrible names, then pulled out a gun . . ."

"Go on down to the conference room and tell Colonel Bradley; I'll handle it here," Pullman directed. And while the secretary hurried down the hall the Chief called the hospital, asking for Colonel Goldman, saying that he had an emergency on his hands. Doc Landis cut onto the line and asked what he could do to help, that Goldman was in the OR. The chief quickly explained the situation. Landis told him he would be right over and tried to remember what he had learned about handling so-called nervous breakdowns in authoritarian personalities while he was at Brooks AFB training to be a flight surgeon.

When he arrived Landis snapped a sharp salute. "Lieutenant Colonel Landis reporting as requested, sir."

Morris was sitting in a swivel chair behind his oak desk, hands folded childlike in his lap. Mementos were neatly arranged on the desk as in the past. He returned an awkward salute. "I didn't ask to see you," he said in a low, husky voice.

"Sorry, sir, it must have been a mistake. I was told you weren't feeling too well. Might have use of a sawbones—"

"You're one of them." Morris' voice was abruptly calm, too calm. He raised his right hand, and aimed a .38 service revolver at the doctor. "This is a mutiny. No one is going to take my command from me." The muzzle of the gun was pointed directly at Landis' forehead.

Landis froze. The colonel's forefinger seemed to twitch on the trigger.

"Colonel, I'm not a professional military man. I have nothing to gain from any of this. In two years I'll be back in private practice. Until then, my only job is to support you, be a member of *your* team. So, please, tell me what you'd like me to do." Slowly, Morris laid the pistol back down in his lap, and as he did Landis' heart slowed its frantic beat, though he fought not to show his relief.

"Convince them what they're doing is illegal," Morris said, voice flat, and toneless.

"If what they are doing is illegal," Landis said easily, "then the proper authorities will end it. But, sir, don't you think we should give them time to come to their senses and not do anything illegal ourselves in the meantime? You mustn't weaken our position, and your own conduct must be above reproach at all times."

"Yes, of course, but I must . . . must be protected until then . . ."

"Sir, perhaps we could schedule you for a physical, at the hospital? I guarantee I can protect you there . . ."

"Yes, yes . . . good. That will work. Good . . ." Morris handed over the pistol. "You might need this, Doctor. I'll report for a physical examination in twenty minutes. Be careful."

Landis accepted the pistol, which felt like a hot rivet, and joined the waiting men in the outer office, where he quickly gave the pistol to Chief Pullman.

"What the hell happened in there?" Bradley demanded.

Landis shook his head, "Sorry, Colonel. Can't violate the doctor–

patient relationship. I can tell you that Colonel Morris is probably suffering from nervous and physical exhaustion. Let it go at that."

1 December: 2340 hours, Greenwich Mean Time
1540 hours, Luke Air Force Base, Arizona

The crew chief marshaling the F-4 into its parking spot on the ramp at Luke AFB crossed his wrists above his head, signaling for Waters to stop, then made a slashing motion across his throat, the sign to cut engines.

Waters' hands went over the switches, shutting the big fighter down. He unstrapped and threw his helmet and then the small canvas bag carrying his flight publications to the crew chief, who motioned toward the edge of the ramp, pointing out the waiting staff car. Waters scrambled down the boarding ladder and quickly walked around the Phantom during a post-flight inspection, before heading for the car. The wing commander, Boots McClure, crawled out from behind the wheel and stood by the car, a slight smile on his face.

"Congratulations, Muddy. You've got yourself a wing—the 45th at Stonewood. The word came down about thirty minutes ago." McClure grabbed Waters' right hand and pumped it.

Waters just stood there, unable to speak.

A command . . .

A wing . . .

The fulfillment of his dream. The years of hard work, loneliness and frustration suddenly evaporated . . . A wide smile came across his face. A warmth that he had only experienced at the birth of his daughter captured him. It was a high few men ever realized.

"It's going to be different from anything you imagined," McClure said softly, doubting that Waters could catch his meaning. "Why don't you tell your bride and get her away from the O' Club pool." McClure laughed and pushed Waters towards the car. "She's driving some of my young jocks bonkers . . ."

Later, Anthony was ragging Sara a bit about Boots McClure's randy comments, and acting—well, partially acting—a little teed-off.

She picked it up fast, and fed him a few more anxiety moments before playing it straight.

"I met Mrs. McClure the other day at a luncheon and liked her," she said. "She doesn't wear her husband's rank like some of the other wives do. God, what a sad crowd they can be. You'd think in this day and age they'd get out and do *something* besides eat lunch and sit around the pool and gossip, gossip, gossip. For some reason I think the lieutenant colonels' wives are the worst—do you suppose it's because they're bucking with their spouses for the big eagle and letting off *his* frustrations? Oh, never mind—now what about the big news? Where are we off to in the wild blue yonder and so forth?"

"No way, lady. You got to pay for your intelligence. Ante up . . ."

And she did, and afterward, his head against her bare breasts, as she checked carefully for more signs of gray—"I love a mature man, stop worrying"—he told her it was England, and she told him that that was too easy, that she had paid too much for such available info.

"You've just begun," he said, and proceeded to make love in a way he never thought he could again, the inhibitions from the tragedy of the past finally giving up the ghost.

5 December: 1805 hours, Greenwich Mean Time
1305 hours, Washington, D.C.

On Sunday the Gomezes met them at the airport. While waiting for their luggage, Tim Gomez told Waters that his interview with Cunningham was set for Monday morning, a VIP flight was leaving Andrews AFB for Mildenhall late Monday afternoon and they had seats on it, and that his DO, Sam Hawkins, had submitted his retirement papers.

Waters studied his friend for a moment. "Tom, would you take the job?"

"In a minute . . ."

That night Gomez told his wife about Waters' offer.

"It won't much help your career at this point," she said.

"Well, I don't think I'm going anywhere beyond colonel. Might as well do something I want and work for someone I like and respect. Would it bother you moving to England?"

"Honey, you know I'm just a camp follower at heart. So let's do it. Besides, Sara's going to need a friend over there, and I'll bet you two rolls in the hay she's pregnant or damn soon will be."

"You mean you get off the hook two times if you're right?"

"No, fool. The other way 'round."

Colonel Stevens met Waters as he entered Cunningham's offices on Monday morning. "Congratulations on your command," the young colonel said. "We need to talk a bit before you go inside." Stevens handed Waters the IG's one-page special report on the combat status of the 45th. "The general fired Morris for one reason—he rated his wing a one on the Combat Status Report and an inspection team rated the wing's readiness as a five. Moral: don't fudge about your combat capability."

"The report only says the 45th should be rated a five because of deficiences in flying training and maintenance," Waters observed. "Some details might have helped."

"Well, your job as wing commander is to fill in the details and fix whatever's wrong. Remember, the general trusts and relies on the IG system . . . If you're ready I'll take you in now."

Cunningham, as usual, was direct and to the point. "Waters, I hope your honeymoon is over because the 45th is not combat ready and I may need them in the Persian Gulf before too long, especially if your lieutenant was right about his scenario. Six months at the most. Do what you have to, but get them ready. Your deputy for Operations, Sam Hawkins, is retiring. Who do you want to replace him?"

"Tom Gomez, sir. And I want Lieutenant Bill Carroll to be my Intelligence chief."

"That's a major's position; you want to put a lieutenant in it?"

"I'll take any major that speaks Arabic and Farsi and thinks as well as he does," Waters answered quickly.

"You've got them both. Anyone else?"

"Major Charles Justin Conlan." Waters waited, studying the general's face for clues.

"If you want that skinny, bald-headed S.O.B. you've got him too." The general smiled and leaned back in his chair. "Conlan is the best air-defense suppression man in the business. Now you'll want some

Wild Weasels. I'll see what I can do. You'll need them if you get involved in the Gulf." Cunningham was pleased with the man standing in front of him.

Vietnam and the 1973 Yom Kippur war between the Israelis and Arabs had driven home two hard points: Soviet-built Triple A, anti-aircraft artillery, and SAMs, surface-to-air missiles, were very effective at blowing fighters out of the sky, and the Soviets had produced large numbers of these air-defense weapons to ring every target for protection against air attack.

Yes, Waters would need Wild Weasels, the F-4G Phantoms were modified to go in and hit the SAMs and Triple A where they lived so an attacking force could get through. Air-defense suppression was military jargon for all that. The United States had built only 116 Wild Weasels, and every fighter wing that got involved in air-to-ground dropping bombs wanted as many Wild Weasels as possible to escort its aircraft onto a target. *Who* got the Weasels was always a big flap.

The general's gaze was direct, serious. "You're the first new wing commander I've met that's been concerned with tactics. I understand Bull Morgan is already assigned to the 45th. Looks like you're collecting quite a crew. Anyone else?"

Waters shook his head.

"Good luck, then, Muddy," the general said, sticking his hand out, and trying to keep any evidence of concern out of his hazel eyes.

8 December: 0800 hours, Greenwich Mean Time
0800 hours, Stonewood, England

Waters entered his new office and told the chief, "Let's do it."

While the officers stood at attention, Pullman read the formal orders relieving Bradley as temporary commander and designating Waters as the new commander of the 45th Tactical Fighter Wing. After Bradley passed the wing's fanion to him, Waters placed the small pendant in its stand behind his desk, shook hands with the small group. "Please call Sir David and set up a courtesy call. I'd like to visit him at his convenience. Also, I'll be looking around the base today with Colonel Bradley and Chief Pullman. Nothing special, just to meet your people. See you at Stand-Up tomorrow morning."

* * *

After the next morning's brief Stand-Up, Waters headed for the command post, where he flopped into a chair next to Vern Yaru-Lau, the major in charge of the command center, and asked, "Major, what is our true combat status rating?"

Waters' tone said not to hedge his answer. "We're a five, maybe a four. Maintenance can't keep enough of our aircraft fixed and MC . . . mission capable. These are old birds, sir. Also, we're not meeting all our flying training requirements."

"I know what MC means, Major . . . All right, report what's driving our rating down in the remarks section of the next message and tell me how many planes have to be MC and what our shortfalls in training sorties are so we can get a one rating."

After leaving the command post Waters dropped by the small building that served as the RAF base commander's headquarters. Sir David Childs was waiting and ushered him into his office. "Colonel Waters, good to see you."

"Thanks for seeing me so soon, Sir David. I don't want to bother you but I was wondering if I might change the sign at the entrance to the base?" Childs gave Waters a look and waited, suspecting that this one was just like Morris. "I'd like to drop my name and add the motto of the 45th, 'Return with Honor.' "

"*Lovely* idea," Sir David said quickly. "And please remove my name from the sign as well."

"And are there any immediate problems I need to know about?"

"Ah . . . I think you will discover that your predecessor did not stress tactical flying. Which did tend to make my position less difficult, inasmuch as it reduced noise complaints." Child spelled out how every RAF base had the same problems and that local citizens were always complaining. "This island is too densely populated, of course, and so no matter where you fly someone will be disturbed. But on the other hand I do believe tactical flying is the reason your wing is here . . ."

"Would you be willing to be the point of contact for noise complaints?" Waters asked.

Child smiled, nodded; the American colonel got the point.

"How else can we help you?" Waters asked.

"Well, I'd say don't fly below a thousand feet unless you're on a low-level route, and please avoid the mink and stud farms, especially during the mating season. Try not to make any unscheduled landings in the countryside. Disturbs the copulatory patterns of too many species." The two men laughed, saluted and Waters left.

Twenty minutes later Waters entered the 377th Tactical Fighter Squadron, where the short stay he had planned turned into a three-hour ordeal. His mouth was set in a grim line when he left, and it was the same when Colonel Sam Hawkins saw Waters enter his office . . . he had been warned about the results of the wing commander's visit to the 377th.

"Why, Sam?" Waters asked, closing the door behind him. They both knew what he meant.

"Colonel Waters," Hawkins said, "our flying program is exactly what Morris made it. He was more worried about losing aircraft than the crews maintaining flying proficiency—"

"Just what in the hell is a tactical fighter wing all about? Last time I checked it's to train like you plan to fight. Your crews haven't been doing that. You must have gotten the word that the 45th is earmarked for possible operations in the gulf. Has wing Intel been monitoring the situation there? Have your weapons and tactics pukes been working on ways to counter the SAM and Triple A threats down there? Have you run any true low-level flights onto similar targets? Sam, you're an old pro, you've been around the damn flagpole as much as I have. You know how to use training sorties to get your crews ready to fight. Better to lose one or two birds in training than lose a wing in combat . . ."

"I couldn't convince Morris of anything," Hawkins said.

"Maybe you didn't try hard enough," Waters said, stood up and left.

Back in his office, Waters shut the door and slumped into his chair. Things clearly were worse than when the wing was in Egypt. Shaw had problems like lousy base housing and schools. Mine are worse, the wing has forgotten how to fight, Waters realized. Courtesy of Mad Stanley. Commanding a wing was something he'd wanted since his first combat tour in southeast Asia with the 8th Tac Wing. Taking men into combat *and* bringing them home was the ultimate challenge. Well, he had his chance to do that. But first he had to teach them how to fight without killing any of them. But if necessary—he cut off the unwelcome thought.

The Phantom rolled in on the gunnery range at twenty-two hundred feet and nosed over into a twelve-degree dive. The sight picture was perfect as the pilot, called Sooner, acquired the strafe panel in the lighted target-ring of his heads-up display. Gently he squeezed and released the trigger for a short burst of cannon fire as he passed through three hundred feet, then instinctively pulled the nose up and fire-walled the throttles. But the burring noise of the M61 gatling gun did not stop, warning him the gun had jammed on full-fire. Sooner jerked the nose to the right, pointing the gun out to sea, only to spot a small fishing boat in the range's restricted zone. Automatically he pushed the nose over to direct the stream of bullets toward the water. By the time he had reacted the gun was empty and he was dangerously close to the water in a dive angle that was much too steep. For a split second Sooner thought he had bought it. Then, however, his quick reactions got the nose up and the Phantom bounced off the water, ripping off the wing-tanks but still flying.

The two men in the fishing boat were nearly mesmerized by the sight of the F-4 barely touching the water. They could hardly be aware of the tremendous forces at play when a sixteen-ton aircraft loaded with four tons of fuel ricocheted off water . . . accelerometers in both cockpits pegged at over ten Gs, not able to measure the full impact of the Gs breaking the plane apart, four engine-mounts on the right engine and two on the left snapping under the load, wing spars cracking. Like hitting concrete . . .

"Mike," the pilot yelled at his wizzo, "you still with me?"

"Yeah, no place to go. We okay?"

"Beats the hell out of me," Sooner told him. For a few moments the two men just breathed deeply, trying to steady nerves as Sooner climbed to a safer altitude over the Wash. The English range controller kept requesting them to check in. Sooner answered him with a call declaring an emergency. And now Sooner's wingman joined up on his left and checked him over while he ran his emergency checklist.

"You're in one piece," his wingman radioed. "It looks like the

SUU-21 is hanging by its trailing lug and will probably fall off. Why don't you jettison it before we coast in?" Sooner selected the right inboard station where the practice bomb dispenser was hung, had his wingman check if the ocean's surface was clear, and hit the jettison button. But the bomb dispenser did not separate from the pylon. Sooner's panic was building. Rather than try anything else he called for a straight-in approach to runway 09, landing to the east. He would have to stay airborne seven minutes longer to get to that side of the base but at least he would avoid the village and other built-up areas. He hoped they had the seven minutes.

Two minutes later the Phantom started to fall apart as they crossed the coast. The F-4, an honest airplane, didn't do things without giving its crew warning, sending signals to both cockpits. First the pilot's warning lights flashed on and then off, then he got a momentary fire light on the right engine. "I've got smoke and fumes back here," his wizzo announced.

"Hang in, I'm pulling the emergency vent knob—Jesus, both generators fell off the line."

By recycling the generators he managed to bring the left generator back on-line, but smoke kept filling the cockpit.

"Jettison your canopy," Sooner ordered.

The wizzo pulled the emergency jettison handle and the rear canopy separated cleanly from the aircraft, venting the cockpit but increasing the noise level, making it difficult to hear. Sooner realized he had to get his bird on the ground or start thinking about ejecting. His wizzo was thinking the same thing as he told him that a straight-in approach to runway 27, the west runway, was the quickest way to get on the ground, much faster than returning to the North Sea for an ejection. Sooner called the tower, told them he had to land immediately or eject. The tower had already been notified by ATC he had a serious emergency and had scrambled the crash trucks.

Sooner brought the Phantom down final, electing to take the approach-end barrier, he lowered the hook to snag the cable that was stretched across the end of the runway. When the hook came down the SUU-21 separated from the underside of the right wing. The wingman was flying a loose formation as Sooner brought the disabled plane in and noted the location where the bomb-dispenser came off. Smoke started to trail from the right side of the bird as they crossed the approach lights and then engulfed the Phantom as the cable snatched the big fighter to a halt. The crash crews were still moving toward the plane when they saw two figures emerge from the smoke on the left side of the aircraft.

Anthony Waters looked at the map that pinpointed the locations where the canopy and SUU-21 had been found. Slowly he shuffled the map with photos of the burned-out hulk of the Phantom that had been given to the accident board investigating the crash. He flipped to the inspection record of the Phantom before turning to the men in front of him. "Sam, Sooner and Mike did well and I want to commend them for the way they recovered the bird." The DO stared impassively at his commander. "Please tell your crews to think about what happened and tell them I've got lots of Phantoms but only one of them. There are times when an ejection is the preferred approach and landing. I can't make that decision for them, but I'll back them up when they get their bodies in a jam like this one."

The anger he felt was not in his voice as he turned to his deputy for Maintenance. "Colonel Leason, the gun on that bird hadn't been inspected since the wing arrived from Egypt. The accident board will probably find that to be a contributing if not primary cause of this accident. Just what the hell is going on?"

"Colonel Morris, sir, waived that inspection since he would not allow the crews to practice strafing . . ."

"Well, I *do* allow strafing. In fact I require it. Never mind Morris. Didn't it ever occur to you to have the guns inspected after Ops asked for loads of TP ammo? TP does stand for 'target piercing'; what do you think it's used for?" No answer. "Get your inspections caught up, even if it means you have to work weekends and take birds off the flying schedule."

The maintenance officer understood the long holiday they had been enjoying under Morris was over.

Another thought occurred to Waters. "Do you have a bird that's totally current on all inspections?"

"Only 512," the DM told him. "The crew chief punched out a gun-plumber for not inspecting the cannon. We gave the chief an Article Fifteen for fighting and took a stripe."

"Okay, at least we've got one warbird on this air patch. Give the chief back his stripe and assign a pilot and wizzo to 512. Make it Locke and Bryant since they got a MiG with it. Paint their names under the canopies. That's their bird from now on."

"Colonel," the DM protested, "that's against regulations—"

"I'm waiving that reg, Colonel. Second, paint my name on a hangar queen, the worst bird you've got. Tell the crew chief that I'm flying it tomorrow and that it had better be on the schedule. I'll be out to check on my bird soonest. Sam," he allowed a grin at his DO—"team me with the worst wizzo in the wing. Put his name on the bird with mine and get him on the flying schedule with me tomorrow."

"Just how bad of a basketcase do you want?" Hawkins said happily, thinking that he was retiring too early. "I've got a few."

"The absolute pits of pitters, the guy who has trouble even recognizing an F-4." Waters looked at the group. "Also, I understand we haven't found all the practice bombs that fell out of the SUU-21. Get some volunteers to start searching for those puppies tomorrow."

The young crew chief was poring over the maintenance forms with Waters, trying to explain why his plane was the wing's hangar queen. Nothing Maintenance did seemed to cure the Phantom's ills, and aircraft number 744 spent more time grounded and in the hangar than on the flight line. A roly-poly first lieutenant scurried up to them, out of breath. "S-s-sir," he stammered. "Lieutenant Ambler Furry reporting as ordered." He made an awkward salute.

Waters took a deep breath; Lieutenant Furry looked like a walking disaster area—unkempt, out of shape, in need of fixing—like 744. "You don't need to salute in a work area," Waters told him. "It's considered inefficient."

"S-s-sorry, sir. No one ever told me that before," Furry said, following Waters and the crew chief as they walked around the plane.

The lieutenant's slight stammer and fumbling gestures tugged at Water's memory . . . My God, he thought, it's an overweight version of C. J. Conlan when he was young. Conlan was the air-defense suppression expert he had asked Cunningham for. Waters took a few steps away from the Phantom and pointed at the black letters and numbers painted on the tail. What's the *SW* stand for?"

"Stonewood, sir," Furry answered, his stammer disappearing now that he was involved in prosaics.

"And the number 80-744?"

"It's the aircraft's serial number," the crew chief said.

"And the eighty stands for the year it was built," Waters said. "This is the last Phantom built by McDonnell Douglas. Five thousand F-4s and we've got the tail end. Well, we're going to fly this baby tomorrow. You two get it ready."

"But, sir, what if it's not fixed—?"

"Then Ambler had better be damn good pulling the ejection handle," Waters said, and walked out of the hangar.

The birdwatcher leveled his long telephone lens on the tripod and sighted it down the runway. By zooming in on the Phantom he planned on taking a series of shots as the plane made its takeoff roll directly toward him. Then as the F-4 lifted off he would switch to the camera slung around his neck. He watched as the warbird hunkered down on its nose, caging the thrust of its engines as the pilot ran them up. Now the plane started to move and he could hear the crack of the afterburners kicking in. He shot three pictures before the big bird lifted off. He was pleased as the nose came steeply up, giving him a good shot of the underside of the craft. But something was wrong, the pilot ruddered the F-4 to the left, which brought the nose down and put the plane into a hard left turn, its wings perpendicular to the ground.

The plane was turning away from him when he saw the canopies fly off and the backseater eject parallel to the ground. Then the front-seater came out, but his vector was pointed slightly down and the birdwatcher was sure that he would hit the ground before his chute had time to open. Once the crew had separated from the Phantom, the warbird pitched back up and danced on its tail before flopping onto its back and crashing into the woods less than a thousand feet from the end of the runway. He watched the first parachute deploy and swing once before the strong east wind blew it back onto the runway. The second chute snapped open as the man hit the ground. The birdwatcher did not know if it had opened in time. The seat bounced less than twenty yards away from the pilot.

The birdwatcher had managed to capture the entire sequence on film. Should be worth a fair price to the media, he thought . . .

The controller in the tower reached for the crash phone the instant he saw the Phantom pitch up. He had seen films of F-100s doing their "Sabre Dance" from over-rotating on takeoff and prayed the Martin-Baker ejection seat was good enough to get the crew out. Instead of keying the crash net he kept shouting, "Left, left, goddamn it . . ." To the right of the runway he could see the village where his family lived. When he saw the F-4's nose come down and the canopies fly off he gave the warning, "Attention on the net, attention on the net. *Crash Alert, Crash Alert!* F-4 crash off departure end of runway zero-nine. Repeat, F-4 crash off departure end of runway zero-nine. This is not a drill. All units standby for coordinates. Two parachutes sighted. Parachutes at departure end of runway zero-nine. Crash at Juliet-Ten. Repeat. Juliet-Ten."

He could hear the sirens start to wail, and glanced at the flying schedule, checking the name of the pilot that had directed his disabled jet away from the village. "I owe you big time, Bull Morgan."

Normal activity on the base suddenly halted as the wing reacted to the crash alert. The emergency actions controller in the command post notified Colonels Bradley and Hawkins, then started an accountability check of all the wing's aircraft that were airborne. By the time Bradley entered the command post the controller had identified the aircraft, pilot, and weapons systems officer. "It wasn't Waters. He's dumping fuel and will land in about fifteen minutes," he told the colonel, then sent out a flash message to the three levels of higher headquarters above the wing. Now they had to wait.

"Ambler, now's when we've got to be cool," Waters told his backseater after the command post had called him for an account-ability check and given him an RTB, return to base. "We've lost an-other bird and my ass is in a crack. But we are going to recover by the numbers. What's the first thing I've got to do to get our baby on the ground?"

"Dump fuel to get our landing weight down," the wizzo said quickly.

"Rog, dumping fuel now." Waters' hand poised over the fuel-dump switch and waited.

"Not over land," Ambler shouted, "over water."

"Right. Now you're doing your job. You know how, so do it."

The ejection out of the F-4 provided Doc Landis with the wildest ride he'd ever experienced. When Bull had shouted, "Eject, eject," he had reached for the ejection handle between his legs, only to find it blocked by the stick that was full-back against the seat and the handle. He had reached above his head and pulled on the face-curtain handles, which also started the ejection sequence for both men. The ejection gun fired, propelling the seat up the guide rails, igniting the rocket pack under the seat and sending Landis out of the airplane with a twelve-G kick. In quick sequence he felt a series of jerks as first the controller drogue chute, then the stabilizer drogue chute and the main parachute deployed. In less than three-and-a-half seconds after he pulled the handle, Landis had separated from the seat, taken one swing in his parachute and landed on the runway. As he did, everything that Thunder had taught him came back in a rush. He hit the quick release clips on his chest, releasing the big chute before it could drag him over the ground, then ran toward the other parachute that was still inflated and dragging Bull through the grass. He jumped into the canopy's fabric, grabbing and pulling until the chute collapsed, quickly rolled the big pilot over, releasing the parachute risers from his harness should the parachute canopy reinflate in the wind. "Hell of a day, Doc," Bull Morgan said, looking up at Landis. "You wouldn't happen to have a beer on you?"

"Lay down," Landis ordered. "You may be hurt, are likely in a state of shock." But when he quickly examined the man he found him only bruised, scratched and filthy from being dragged through the grass.

Bull shook his head. "Doc, you went out too. Why don't you join me and we'll swap lies till the crash trucks get here."

The first crash truck on the scene found them lying in the short grass on their back, side by side, laughing like loons.

* * *

At the hospital they were just coming out of the lab where a technician had taken the obligatory blood samples for drugs or alcohol when Waters found them.

"What happened?"

Bull stood in the corridor, hands on hips and leaning forward into the colonel. "Maintenance again, Colonel. I'm going to nail their asses—"

"Bull, take it easy," Waters said. "You've been through ejections before. Save what you've got for the accident board." That's all we need, Waters thought, *two* accident boards on-base at the same time.

"What do we do now?" Landis said.

"The flying safety officer is around here someplace and will want to talk to us," Bull told him. "But right now I'm going over to Maintenance and find the flight-controls specialist that worked on the bird last."

"What the hell happened?" Landis pressed.

"The goddamn stick programmed full-aft when we lifted off; the bird was trying to do a loop. We didn't have the airspeed or the altitude for that. I used the rudder to roll us into a ninety-degree bank to the left, which put us into a tight left turn away from the village. Except our lift vector was perpendicular to good old gravity and we didn't have a hell of a lot of airspeed to help us out. That's when I told you to eject us. And *that's* what goddamn happened."

"But why are you going to Maintenance?"

"The bird was trying to do the same thing yesterday but I broke the stick free. I wrote it up in the maintenance forms and even told them it was a problem with a leaking actuator valve. Airman Siebold didn't do his job right when he signed it off and I'm just going to explain a few things to him . . ."

The doctor trailed after the Bull, trying to talk him out of going to Maintenance. But he went directly to the flight control shop and found the young airman who had repaired the Phantom. To Doc's surprise, though, Morgan sat the young man down and talked quietly with him, gesturing with his hands and, as he said he would, explaining what had happened. Then he took the nineteen-year-old to a work bench and disassembled an actuator valve like the one that had failed and caused the accident, showing what went wrong. Before he left he gave the airman's rear a swat and told him to take it easy.

"That's the way Colonel Waters handled things at Nellis and Bitburg," Bull said. "Works good with young troops. The kid will feel like a shithead for a few days, but he'll learn. He better. I stop being Mr. Nice Guy the second time around."

Waters thumbed through the pages of the London newspaper, ignoring the topless pinup on page three. He was concentrating on the birdwatcher's photographs that had made the first and second page of the national newspaper under the headline: "Death Crash of Fighter—Farmers Live in Fear." He threw the paper down. "No one was *killed,*" he snapped at the paper, then picked up the phone and called Childs.

The English group captain listened to Waters and agreed that the birdwatcher would probably be delighted to meet the crew he had photographed ejecting, hung up and called the president of the Suffolk Birdwatchers Club. He placed a second call to Anglia TV.

Later that afternoon he ushered Brian Philips into Waters' office. Philips was a tall and gangly man who kept bobbing his head when he talked, reminding Waters of a stooped whooping crane with two cameras hung around its neck. The three men then drove out to the hangar where the pieces of the wreckage were being collected and examined. Bull Morgan and Doc Landis were already waiting for them, and Philips was delighted as he shot roll after roll of film. When Philips seemed satisfied with the pictures he had taken, Waters rummaged through the wreckage until he found the actuator valve he was looking for. He and Philips then squatted on the floor while the wing commander explained how the valve had malfunctioned and how Bull Morgan had used the Phantom's rudder to guide the dying aircraft to the left away from the village.

After the pictures and a television interview with the birdwatcher, public opinion swung in favor of the wing. A few of the older citizens even went on record that they were glad to have neighbors like the 45th, men who would stay with an aircraft to guide it away from their village. Sir David Childs was a bloody genius. But the next time . . .

* * *

The Maintenance problem lent itself to no PR deal. After investigations were completed, slipshod maintenance was found the primary cause in both crashes. When Waters asked Colonel Leason to come into his office the DM had no illusions why he was there and fully expected Waters to fire him on the spot. He had seen other DMs replaced for much less.

"Tell me," Waters said, "why Maintenance can't hack it."

"Colonel Waters," Leason began, "I've been playing a survival game. Took the easy way out . . . I mean, Colonel Morris was only interested in flying the exact number of hours headquarters allocated to us each calendar quarter. As long as we kept on schedule and maintained the time line he stayed off our backs. Since he cut back on the number of demanding missions the crews were flying, we got out of the habit of keeping the birds fully tweaked—"

"History, Leason. I asked why Maintenance can't hack it *now*. All you've done is told me why you were screwing off under Morris."

"Given a chance, sir, we can do our job."

Given incentive was more like it, Waters thought. "How long will it take you to get the birds back in shape?"

"If we have to fly the time line and the required amount of night sorties, at least six months—"

"I'm thinking six weeks."

"Impossible—"

"Too bad. There's a brace of lieutenant colonels in your organization who are about to get a chance to prove you wrong. Am I clear?"

"Are you giving me a second chance?"

"Depends. I don't give a damn about flying out the hours headquarters has given us. I want productive training sorties for my crews so they have a chance to practice tactics and learn something. They can't do that with sick birds. Also, they won't get productive sorties by sky-hooking at night. All the ranges close at dark and there's not much else they can do at night, so starting tomorrow we're going on a flying schedule in the day and a fix-'em schedule at night. There will be no flying on weekends for the next month. You'll have all the birds to work on for twelve hours a day and over the weekends. You've got six weeks to have the fleet in top-notch condition or . . . let's just say you'll freeze your ass, or boil it, where you'll be going for your last tour in this Air Force."

"Colonel Waters, I don't know if you're giving me enough time but I guarantee to kick some ass—"

"Never mind the talk, just do it," Waters said, and dismissed him. Sundown, Waters thought. I'm turning into a Sundown Cunningham. Well, so be it. When you haven't got time, fear can work its wonders. He glanced at his watch. He was going to Mildenhall to meet Tom Gomez, his new deputy for Operations.

An hour later Waters, Sara and Chief Pullman met the Gomezes as they came into the terminal with their two teenage daughters and Bill Carroll in tow. On the way to Stonewood Waters summarized the status of the wing.

Tom stared at the passing countryside, then said, "Seems we're in big trouble, Muddy. I've had the analysts in the Watch Center looking at the situation in the Gulf since I last talked to you . . . Bill, this is really your area. You want to tell Muddy the bad news?"

Lieutenant Carroll nodded. "It's a mess, for sure, sir. Let me find out what information wing Intel has and I'll get back to you. I can tell you now, though, we're going to have to do something about the crazies down there. It's getting real bad."

4 January: 1325 hours, Greenwich Mean Time
1625 hours, Moscow, USSR

The mist escaping from the steam rooms rose above the icy-cold waters of the pool and drifted up past the horseshoe-shaped balcony to break against the hard cold of the bathhouse's skylight. During the summer the chains that worked the elaborate bronze fittings of the glass panes in the skylight would be pulled and swing open. But the Moscow winter had frozen them shut. The General Secretary swung his legs off the massage table in one of the large curtained alcoves that lined the balcony and tugged a soft white turkish bathrobe across his broad shoulders. He stared down at his body and decided that his belly would soon match his shoulders. Too bad, he thought. Once his body had narrowed to a slim waist and taut stomach. The poundings of a masseur could only delay the inevitable.

Although he was one of the three most powerful men on earth, the General Secretary liked to use the Royal Banya, a carefully preserved leftover from the days of the czar. The stern economies of Lenin, the purges and disruption of the Stalin years and the excesses of the Brezhnev regime had not reached the bathhouse, which still reflected the glory days of its origin more than one hundred years ago. And the news that the General Secretary preferred a public bath had been carefully leaked, adding to his considerable popularity, even though the Royal Banya was not a place that the average Russian male would be allowed to use even if he could find it.

The walking tree stump of a man who served as the General Secretary's personal servant, bodyguard and court jester stuck his head through the heavy curtains. "Comrade Rafik Ulyanoff wants to see you. Claims that he has pressing business. Politburo business no doubt."

"I suppose this is necessary," the General Secretary grumbled.

"I'll give him a quick drowning lesson if you wish to be left alone. Even the head of the Defense Council should try the pool waters from time to time." It was the Tartar's idea of a joke, but a smile never crossed his Mongolian features.

Rafik Ulyanoff was the third most powerful man in the Soviet Union and as head of the Politburo's Defense Council could demand access to the General Secretary at almost any time. But even he did not wish to antagonize the dwarf-like Tartar who guarded the Communist Party chief. It was rumored that the Tartar had killed numerous men and women with his bare hands, usually breaking their necks with ease, when serving the General Secretary in his rise through the KGB. Ulyanoff waited impatiently until the curtain was held aside for him to enter. Years before, Ulyanoff had made a promise to himself that the Tartar would experience a lingering, most unpleasant old age once the General Secretary was deposed . . . retired.

"We must talk about Ashkhabad," Ulyanoff said at once.

The General Secretary looked through him. "And I thought we were going to discuss something urgent. Perhaps a place with more privacy?" He heaved his body off the massage table and slipped his feet into freshly washed slippers.

The Tartar led the two men around the balcony to where it ended at a paneled wall. When he pressed a concealed button the panel swung open into a large room, almost fifty feet to a side. The red damask walls, Persian rugs, inlaid tiles in the floor and heavy furniture reminded the General Secretary of a harem. He did not like or approve of the room, but it was the most secure place for a private conversation in the bathhouse.

A girl rose from one of the chaise longues and walked toward them. On the streets of Moscow, bundled up against the cold, she would have passed unnoticed. But walking across the rugs, blonde hair swaying against her shoulders and hips moving rhythmically to some inner song, the naked girl was indeed breathtaking.

The General Secretary preferred the banya to remain an all-male institution and looked inquiringly at his bodyguard.

"Part of Comrade Rokossovsky's traveling furniture," the Tartar said, motioning the girl to leave. Rokossovsky was the youngest voting member of the Politburo and one of the four members of the Defense Council, well inside Ulyanoff's pocket.

The General Secretary found a wing chair near the fireplace and sat down. "Please be comfortable," he told the older man. "Enjoy the fire."

Ulyanoff did not take the invitation but paced the floor. "Why are you directing a buildup of forces in Turkmen around Ashkhabad? I've also learned that the arms shipments to Iraq are being redirected there. All this, sir, is not part of our policy." Ashkhabad was at the head of a mountain pass that led through the Kopet mountains into northern Iran. The border was less than twenty miles away. A buildup there, Ulyanoff reasoned, could only mean . . .

"A minor adjustment of our forces. Nothing more. This could have waited for our next meeting."

"To sustain such a buildup on the southern edge of the Tsentralnyye Desert is foolish. A waste of resources."

The General Secretary was silent for a moment. "You don't think Comrade Kalin-Tegov would approve?"

The mention of the Communist Party's theoretician and Ulyanoff's most powerful supporter on the Politburo didn't faze Ulyanoff. "You know Kalin-Tegov," Ulyanoff said, "three steps forward, two steps backward." He was clearly upset.

"Perhaps this time we'll take only one step back."

"The alignment of our defenses falls to the Defense Council." Ulyanoff had to restrain himself not to shout.

"The Iraqis are proving to be poor allies," the General Secretary said. "They don't continue to press for victory against the Iranians."

Ulyanoff was near-speechless. At last he saw a complete pattern before him. "You can't desert the Iraqis now. Let them carry out our goals in the Persian Gulf. An invasion of Iran out of Ashkhabad would be suicidal. The Americans would intervene. It would lead to World War Three . . . That's it, isn't it? Kalin-Tegov approves of this adventurism." Ulyanoff saw a pit before him. Kalin-Tegov had always favored a more aggressive policy in the Persian Gulf and now had thrown in with the General Secretary. Which to Ulyanoff meant his own position on the Politburo was crumbling. He left the room without another word, needing privacy to calculate how best to shore up his defenses . . .

The Tartar drew a cup of hot water from a samovar, dropped in a bag of Earl Grey tea, which the General Secretary preferred, and carried the steeping tea to him.

The General Secretary accepted the cup and settled into thought. "Did Ulyanoff know the girl was here?" he asked the Tartar.

"No. The look on his face gave him away. Ulyanoff agrees with you about banyas. It's the *only* point where he agrees with you. He didn't even know who she belonged to."

"That was a mistake."

"Rokossovsky is making many mistakes over her."

"Then Comrade Rokossovsky is fond of the blonde nymph?"

"I would say he dotes on her."

The General Secretary smiled. "Send her to a place where she can be of better use to our people."

"Abyy on the Yana River would be suitable."

"Not bad," the General Secretary said, amused. The small village of Abyy was isolated in a remote river valley of the Khrebet mountain ranges of northeastern Siberia, well above the Arctic Circle. "As soon as she is established, issue her a temporary visa to return to Leningrad. Contingent on her good behavior, of course. Let us find out if Comrade Rokossovsky's duties require his presence in places other than Moscow." The General Secretary smiled. Ulyanoff was about to lose another of his supporters on the Politburo, thanks to Comrade Rokos-sovsky's hard-on.

"Why did Ulyanoff choose this place to confront you with his discoveries?"

"If we met privately in the Kremlin everyone would know immediately. Ulyanoff wanted news of this conversation delayed as long as possible. You know how difficult it is to keep anything secret from the Politburo. He wants time to maneuver."

"Has Kalin-Tagov switched his support to you?"

The General Secretary smiled and shook his head. "Not yet."

"Ulyanoff is right about one thing," the Tartar said, an astute observer as well as a bodyguard, and secure in his position with the General Secretary. "An invasion of Iran would certainly risk a major war."

"And *I* am not going to be the one to start it. We can achieve what we want, piece by piece, and using our surrogates wherever and however possible . . ."

13 January: 1333 hours, Greenwich Mean Time
0833 hours, Washington, D.C.

"Director, Mr. Cagliari is on line one." Like everyone in the CIA, the secretary used the title that the Director of the CIA preferred. There was also a joke circulating through the Agency about how he had originally insisted on being called M but the British Secret Intelligence Service had filed a copyright infringement against him.

The Director picked up the line. To hear himself addressed as "Freddy" by the National Security Adviser. It was a name he hated. "Freddy," Cagliari was saying, "the Chief wants an update on the Gulf and the Gulf area. Situation Room, two o'clock this afternoon. You're the star attraction." Cagliari didn't have to tell the Director he was in trouble. The grapevine had already forwarded that message to him.

At 1:55 P.M. the Director walked into the Situation Room followed by a team of six specialists. Cagliari was waiting for him. "Sorry, Freddy. Just you."

The Director did not like his team being dismissed, but was not about to show it. He told his people to lay out the photos and documents they were toting and leave. A stack of photos was placed in front of each position around the table. Each photo was stamped TOP SECRET RUFF, the code name indicating they were obtained by a satellite system—in this case the CIA's latest Keyhole-12 multi-mode reconnaissance satellite. The team was exiting the room as the President entered, sat down and lit a cigar, ignoring the photos.

"Well, Freddy, talk to me."

"Mr. President, the situation in the Gulf is unchanged. Each pair of photos here shows a major military storage or marshaling area in Iran and Iraq. The first photo was taken four weeks ago; the second is less than thirty-six hours old. You will notice there has been little change over the past month in each area. Much of the same equipment is still in place. We have only monitored some movement out of the areas and none in. This seemed rather too good to be true, so we have been looking for other storage areas. So far we haven't found a thing. My analysts are of the opinion that the Russians have curtailed their support of Iraq and that the Iranians are more concerned with internal economic problems."

The President tapped a cigar ash into an ashtray his ten-year-old daughter had made for him and that he kept in the Situation Room. "You say you haven't found other storage areas. What about Ashkhabad, Freddy?"

The Director frowned, both at the repeated use of the name he hated and at his realization that his staff had scarcely mentioned that city in the Soviet Socialist Republic of Turkmen when they prepared the briefing for the President. Thank God he had a good memory. "Mr. President, we *have* monitored some unusual activity on the outskirts of Ashkhabad. If you will look at the last photo . . ."

"I've already seen it, Freddy."

The Director could hear the tone in the President's voice. Clearly some son of a bitch had been back-dooring information to the President. The Keyhole-12 belonged to the CIA, but the National Reconnaissance Office managed the satellite. Could that bastard who ran the NRO be out to get him? Or had the Defense Intelligence Agency been siphoning off Keyhole-12 imagery as it was downlinked through the Defense Special Missile and Astronautics Center at Fort Meade? Well, two could play this game.

"The information we have is fragmentary at this point, Mr. President. What we are seeing is a temporary storage area the Soviets are using as they withdraw from Afghanistan. At this juncture, nothing more. Our analysis will be confirmed when the buildup we are currently monitoring at Ashkhabad draws down."

"That could explain the trucks. But where did the two hundred new T-72 tanks and three squadrons of MiG-23s come from? Those are reinforced squadrons, Freddy. That is one big air regiment, over a hundred aircraft. Just what the *hell* is going on?"

The room was silent. The Director tried to form an answer. It was increasingly obvious the President had been briefed by another source. Only the Air Force could provide that depth of analysis. He made a mental promise to even the score. "Sir, it's necessary to keep this minor buildup in perspective. True, it is noteworthy but not critical—"

"Freddy, how many times have I told you I do not like surprises? I also do not like repeating myself. I want to know why those tanks and MiGs are there. Tell me, what would the Russians do in a situation like this?"

The question surprised the Director. "Ah, I suppose they would direct their Humint resources at the problem."

"Humint . . . human intelligence," the President said. "A fancy word for old-fashioned spies. Well, what does *our* Humint tell you?"

"We don't have agents in that area. It's incredibly difficult to sustain—"

"Freddy, the taxpayers of this country think the Company costs them approximately a billion dollars a year. That's the published figure. Everyone in this room knows the real number is closer to three billion. That's a lot of black money we hide for you. The taxpayers, and the President, are not getting their money's worth. Get me some answers."

After the Director left the room, the President drew on his cigar. "I want his resignation on my desk by tomorrow."

"Sir," Cagliari said, "that will really upset the Agency. Do we need that kind of turmoil now?"

"Why not? Maybe better now than later. The Company is just too politicized with Freddy running it. There's too much front and too little substance. We need some answers, and fast . . ."

2 February: 1000 hours, Greenwich Mean Time
1000 hours, Stonewood, England

Bill Carroll stood in front of the situation map of the Persian Gulf that he had tacked up on the wall of the biggest room in Intel. The two lieutenants and six sergeants manning intelligence had been delighted when Carroll asked them to dig out the current intelligence summaries on the situation in the Gulf for an update briefing to the wing. For the first time in months they were acting like an Intelligence section, passing information down to the crews.

Morgan and Gomez came into the room now, followed by the three squadron commanders, and sat down in the seats arranged in front of the briefing map. Carroll called the room to attention when Waters entered. "Please be seated," Waters said. "What have you got for us, Bill?"

"Sir, the 45th is earmarked for combat operations in the Gulf under Operations Plan ELK GROVE. Right now the Pentagon is looking for a deployment base for us to use. They're going to have to find one pretty quick if we're to be used there because the situation in the Gulf is getting worse every day. The Navy is predicting that attacks on oil tankers will heat up in the next few weeks, the head ayatollah's health is failing and Israeli intelligence has reported huge Soviet arms shipments out of Ashkhabad into Iran. They say it's all being shipped into southern Iran, but we don't know *where* the arms are going and *who* is getting them. We do know that large numbers of SAMs and Triple A for air defense have reached the Iranians. That's all I've got for now."

Waters turned to the men. "Get this out to the squadrons so they know what's coming at them." He turned to his weapons-and-tactics man. "Bull, I'm worried about the SAMs and Triple A. We're an air-to-mud attack wing, and air defenses like Bill just mentioned can chew us up good. What can we do about it?"

Bull Morgan's chin dropped onto his chest, as though illustrating what followed. "Low levels, Colonel. The crews are going to have to get down on the deck to get under the search-and-guidance radars and go at warp eight. Five hundred feet ain't low and four hundred knots ain't fast if you're trying to avoid SAMs and Triple A."

"Okay, Bull, get with Sir David and see if you can arrange for us to overfly the Stamford Military Training Area near here at low level. Let's see what our aerial assassins can do."

Waters, Morgan, and Pullman were in the control tower in the middle of Stamford MTA's target range. Morgan tuned the UHF radio to the common frequency the 45th would be using and cleared the first two Phantoms onto the range. "Let's see how close they can hit their scheduled time over target," he mumbled. They waited for what seemed an eternity. "Where the hell are they?"

"There, sir," a British Royal Army sergeant major said, pointing to the north, and looking, they could see the distinctive smoke trails the Phantoms left behind as two birds ran onto the range. Morgans' instructions to the crews had been simple: cross the target area at low level in pairs, keep your airspeed below six hundred knots and hit your TOT, time over target. "Seventy seconds late. I'd estimate their altitude at eight hundred feet, airspeed at four twenty, maybe four hundred thirty knots," the sergeant major said.

Morgan's ears started to turn red in embarrassment.

The phone rang, the sergeant major answered, hung up and turned to Waters, "Sorry, sir, the Rapier crew reports two simulated kills." Another pair of Phantoms overflew the range, almost two minutes late. Again the phone rang, reporting a simulated kill on the two birds. The next two F-4s never found the range, and Waters could see their smoke trails pass two miles to the west.

Waters walked out onto the catwalk surrounding the tower, motioning Morgan to follow him. His hands clenched the railing as two more of his Phantoms flew across the range, this time a minute early. "What in the hell is going on, Bull? They're all running in from the north and can't even come close to hitting their TOTs. The Rapiers are having a damned field day." Morgan could only shake his head.

For the next hour Waters watched and listened as his wing struggled across the range. Steve Farrell, the squadron commander from the 377th, hit his TOT to the second and crossed the range at three hundred feet close to 500 knots, and for the first time the Rapiers could only report a probable kill.

"At least one crew did it right," Waters snapped.

Now there was one scheduled TOT left. Everyone in the tower looked to the north, waiting to see the smoke trails. A Phantom flashed across in front of them, running in from the east, its sound wave shaking the tower's windows after it had disappeared over the tree tops.

"Bloody hell," the sergeant major yelled. "That bloke was below three hundred feet. Damn close to six hundred knots . . ."

Ten seconds later the second F4 slashed through from the south, kicking up a rooster tail of dust as spirals of wake turbulence fanned from its wing tips.

The sergeant major was in awe.

"Bloody fast, bloody low."

Morgan could smile for the first time. "Fairly and Locke. They split the TOT. Fairly was five seconds early, Locke five seconds late. I doubt if they saw each other." The telephone rang and the sergeant major relayed the Rapiers message: a probable hit and a definite miss.

Waters saw a glimmer of hope as he stared out the window. "Okay, Bull. We need to practice a mass raid stressing timing. I want to put a gaggle over a target so close together they'll wet their pants if they blow their TOTs."

Jack and Thunder were on one of their pub hunts, checking out the bars—the Brits called them public houses—trying to find one for a squadron party. Group Captain Childs had told them the Maypole was worth a try but they couldn't find it. Thunder's date, one Francine Thomas, finally asked two policemen who were parked beside the road. Francine was a buxom school teacher Thunder had met while giving one of his Friday tours to third graders from the base school.

Eventually they found the brightly lit building and a big parking lot no more than four hundred yards down the road. As they crowded up to the bar and Jack ordered drinks he also noted that there were some attractive women around, and this plus the obvious mutual attraction between Thunder and his Francine heightened his own need. It had been a dry spell for him. He'd had a notion about Sara, but Colonel Waters had taken care of that . . . He took a quick trip to the men's room, and when he came back to the bar saw that Thunder and Francine clearly didn't need him. Nobody else seemed to either, the place being full of couples . . . until he spotted someone he was sure he knew. It seemed almost too corny, like one of those old War War II movies with Robert Taylor, the Yank in England, or was it Oxford? and Eleanor Parker or somebody. But never mind, be grateful and accept that the lady he was looking at was, unless he was crazy, the haircutter. What was her name . . . ? An unusual one— Gillian, that was it. Quickly as he could he maneuvered through the crowd of tightly packed bodies toward her.

"Pardon me," he said, just as though he was Robert Taylor, "but haven't we . . . ?"

"You know perfectly well we have," she said, which was all the opening he needed. He reprised how she had saved him from an inglorious shearing at the hands of his squadron commander. They went back and forth like that for a while, the two girls with Gillian trying not to show their irritation at being left out, and then drifted through the crowd and out the door into the fresh air.

Watching them go, Thunder was a little surprised. Friend Jack hardly ever went for a girl that looked like this one. Mostly they were slim and young, very young, and obvious air-heads. This one, well-built and no child, hardly fitted that bill.

The sun was flooding his room, and Jack got out of bed to close the curtains. He stood in the middle of the room looking at Gillian, still asleep. Her long hair spilled over the pillow, framing her face and catching a ray of light. The soft morning light highlighted and accentuated her lovely, near-classic English features. No question, she was a new experience for him. She'd been straightforward in a way he wasn't used to, saying quite simply her need matched his. No cutsey-pie teasing. A woman. Her lovemaking had been at once gentle and fierce, not holding back, demanding and generous, too.

Rather than crawl back into the warm comfort of his bed Jack moved into the small kitchenette and started to make coffee, wondering how much longer before he'd have to send her home.

He had just begun to clean up the kitchen when he heard her start the bath water, waited until she was comfortably soaking and carried a cup of coffee in to her. He sat on the commode, talking about the Maypole and thinking how she was built for childbearing.

"I love all this hot water," she said, "it makes a bath so much more enjoyable when you don't feel guilty about using it all." They talked about the differences between Suffolk and Phoenix, Arizona, Jack's home.

Later, dressed and having a second cup of coffee, they kept the conversation light, but Jack knew he wanted to see her again. Or did he? . . . She was a woman, all right, and had normal womanly nesting instincts, he assumed. He was a flyboy, married to a warbird.

As though she were reading his thoughts, she put down her cup, found her bag, kissed him lightly on the lips and went out the door without a word.

No demands, no good-byes. A considerable woman, no question. He wondered if he was man enough for her.

The crews received their first surprise as they straggled into the base theater. Sharp-looking security police carefully checked the security clearance of each pilot and wizzo before they entered the auditorium. Most of them found seats in the rear with their squadron mates, but Mike Fairly dragged a reluctant Jack and Thunder to seats in the very front.

Bull Morgan stepped to his podium and shouted, "Room, ten-hut!"

The doors at the rear slammed shut and Colonel Waters quick-stepped down the aisle, stood to the side of the other podium.

"Seats, gentlemen. This is the mission briefing for your first large-scale raid," the wing commander announced as the lights dimmed and a map of the North Sea and southern Holland was projected onto the screen. Twenty-four Phantoms from each squadron would mount a two-pronged attack on the Dutch airfield of Woensdrecht. The crews gasped as the large-scale map of the base flashed onto the screen. Twelve aircraft from the first cell would run in from the north to attack the base, be off the target within two minutes and exit to the south. The second twelve aircraft would attack from the south thirty seconds later and exit to the north. "The first cell will attack the base from low-level simulating high-drag Mark-82s," Waters went on.

"The second cell will ingress at low level and pop onto their targets; you choose the simulated ordnance. Gentlemen, it's going to be hairy when you find yourself with twenty-three other birds in the same piece of sky and half of them going in the opposite direction."

The room was silent. The memory of how the wing had stumbled across the Stamford Military Training Area, barely able to find the target while Rapiers hosed them down, was still fresh. Finally a voice came from the rear: "Colonel, we can't do that—"

"You will," Waters cut him off, "but not right away. This is the graduation exercise of your first phase of training. Major Morgan will run through different tactics and techniques you can use. But each squadron will have to work up its own training program and fly this attack before it can move on to the next training phase. I expect the first squadron to be ready to fly it within two weeks."

Morgan called the room to attention and Waters walked out, leaving over two hundred very worried pilots and wizzos in his wake.

"I would suggest," Morgan boomed at the crews, "that you get your bodies down front, listen up and take notes. You are going to get your asses in the proverbial crack if you don't do this one right."

Jack twisted in his seat, all ears to hear what Morgan had to say and confident his squadron would be the first to attack the Dutch base.

Racer Two-One came off the range at Holbeach and headed home, looking for his wingman. He knew that Racer Two-Two should be coming up on his deep five o'clock for a rejoin but he couldn't see him. The lead uttered an obscenity. The mission had been perfect until he had lost his wingy after their last pass on the range.

"Racer Two-Two," he called over the radio, "lead is orbiting south of East Sturnham. Join up for recovery to home plate."

An affirmative answer told him that his wingman was headed for him. Finally his backseater confirmed that he had Two-Two in sight at their deep seven o'clock position. The lead started an easy right-hand turn to allow his wingman to close and join up on his left.

Who could have predicted what happened? It was, after all, an easy maneuver that the wingman had performed who knew how many times in the past. Nothing was mechanically wrong with the birds. But as the lead turned between the twin villages of East Sturnham and

Little Sturnham, Racer Two-Two smashed into the belly of his flight leader, instantly killing both crewmembers in Two-Two as the force of the impact crushed the canopies down onto them.

The engineers at McDonnell Douglas had designed the Phantom to withstand the ravages of combat, repeated hard landings on the decks of aircraft carriers and sustained high-G maneuvers. The Phantom was a hulking sixteen-ton monster that deserved its monicker Big Ugly. Big Ugly did not die easily. The engineers had done their work well. The pilot in Racer Two-One fought for control of his damaged bird as it sent him repeated signals that it could not stay in the air much longer.

He yelled at his backseater to eject alone, leaving him in the aircraft for a later ejection. His wizzo turned the valve selecting his seat for a single ejection and pulled the handle, separating cleanly from the aircraft at thirty-five hundred feet. The F-4 wanted to roll right and pitch down into the ground as the pilot turned it toward an open field, away from the village of Little Sturnham. With both hands on the stick the pilot managed to guide the Phantom away from the village before it pitched over into its final dive. The pilot reached for the ejection handle between his legs and pulled, ejecting from the bird as it flopped on its back, aiming him directly toward the ground.

A farmer watched the pilot hit the ground upside down, still strapped into his seat as the Phantom crashed only fifty yards behind the school. For a moment he could not move, horrified by the sight. Then he jumped off his tractor and ran toward the school, forgetting that he could drive there more quickly. He reached the yard along with the wizzo as the wreckage burst into fire. Both men ran into the school building, afraid of what they would find inside. To their relief no one was hurt and the three teachers were directing their small charges out the front door. The wizzo ran through the classroom's, checking for stragglers. Outside, he scanned the playyard, grateful to find it empty. The wail of sirens sounded in the distance.

RAF Stonewood learned of the crash through the civilian disaster net and immediately dispatched crash trucks and twelve security policemen to Little Sturnham. They drove through the village toward East Sturnham and to the site of the second crash, where they found the wreckage of the F-4 in a burning dairy barn full of bellowing cows. An eighteen-year-old security policeman ran into the barn in a futile attempt to rescue the animals. After bringing out four burning cows he watched a crash truck turn a fire hose on the animals. He drew his revolver and walked up to each cow and put a bullet in its head. The owner of the herd recognized the grief in the boy. "Thank you, lad. I couldn'a done it."

Sara watched her husband fight his inner demon, marking up a temporary win. Without words she had cleared the dinner table while Waters tried once again to write three terrible letters to next of kin. Sara waited, knowing at some point he would need to talk. Finally he did.

"My God, we've lost three aircraft under my command. For Cunningham that's three too many. For me too. I don't give a damn about the airframes; I just want the crews to get out . . . I don't know, maybe I'm pushing them too hard, demanding too much of them after Morris. But damn it, we're close to getting the wing on track. And with a little more time—but we're running out of time. Bill Carroll is keeping us up to date on the situation in the Gulf. He's translating Arabic and Iranian newspapers, listening to their news broadcasts on a shortwave radio and tying it together with the usual intelligence summaries we get from the Air Force. What he's telling us is scary. The place is unstable as hell, and there's a major buildup of supplies going on in southern Iran."

Time. How much? And how much could the men take?

Jack sat in the briefing room watching Fairly study the plan he had laid out for the squadron commander.

"It's ambitious, Jack, considering the way we performed at Stamford. How do you propose we train for it?" Fairly asked.

Jack was ready with his answer. He outlined a series of training missions in which flights of four Phantoms would practice low-level runs over the water onto targets in Scotland. The same flights would also practice lay-down and twenty-degree dive-bombing out of a pop maneuver on nearby gunnery ranges.

"How will you put it all together so we know they're ready and won't self-destruct?"

"We put a low-level mission together with a range mission," Jack said. "The first attack is hot and that's the only pass they get. They've got to be over the target plus or minus fifteen seconds."

Fairly stood and folded the maps. "Let's get over to wing and sell Bull. If we're going to run the first raid, we're going to have to beat the 377th." The two men hurried out of the building and nearly skidded to a halt in Bull Morgan's new office in wing headquarters. One of Muddy Waters' first changes had been to pull Morgan out of the 379th and make him the wing's weapons-and-tactics officer. Steve Farrell, the squadron commander of the 377th and three of his pilots and wizzos had beaten them to Morgan.

Morgan told them to come back in an hour. "You snooze, you lose," he said.

That afternoon they were back, Jack explaining the 379th's plan. When he was finished Morgan said, "Not bad for a virgin. Start taking notes."

For the next thirty seconds Morgan shot a series of questions at the pilot. After taking two pages of notes, Jack looked up, hoping the major was finished. "When you've got the answers to those questions, come back. If you want to be the first to attack Woensdrecht, get your tail in gear. The 377th has got its act together." Jack asked about the 377th's plan. Morgan said, "There's no freebies on this one, kiddo."

Activity on the flight line and in the squadrons kept building for the next two weeks as the two squadrons pushed their crews through a series of missions. Maintenance had to keep up with the 377th's and 379th's demand that all of their Phantoms be ready every day. The 378th, the tortoise of the piece, slowly built momentum.

The 379th came alive, and lights in the squadron came on early in the morning for the first Go's briefing. During the brief winter day the 379th tried to launch forty sorties. Maintenance protested, claiming they could not keep that many of each squadron's twenty-four Phantoms operational. At sundown the last go would recover and peace would again settle over the quiet countryside. But activity on the flight line was already revving up as Maintenance readied the birds for the next day's flying. The crews would return to the small briefing rooms in the squadron and rehash what had gone wrong on that day's missions and what to do to fix it. Wives had no trouble finding their husbands when they didn't come home. They just called the squadron.

Finally Jack and Fairly went back to Morgan's office to convince the big man their squadron was ready. But again the 377th had beaten them to Morgan and they had to come back later. When they did get to Morgan, Jack was determined to sell the 377th. "Major, this is really a simple attack. It looks bad because we have two gaggles of F-4s approaching from opposite directions. Looks like a setup for the Keystone Kops. We don't see it that way. It's a highly efficient way to quickly get in and off a target. It is a matter of timing, and time over target is the critical element. In real life the frag patterns from the bombs would be a big concern. Woensdrecht is a big base so we're using three thousand feet or twenty seconds for frag clearance between deliveries."

"Convince me your crews can do it," Morgan told him.

"We've run low levels to the ranges in the Wash. Every one of our crews hit their TOT within ten seconds."

Morgan drummed the table with his fingers. "Make me an offer I can't refuse."

"No offers, Major. This is our show all the way or someone else does it."

Morgan grinned, allowed a grin, nodded. "You've got the mission. But I've got to fly as tail-end Charlie to evaluate the mission." Morgan meant that as the last aircraft across the target he would be following the other aircraft and could tell if they had met their TOTs and not gotten lost on the low-level route. In combat it would be a very dangerous slot.

"You're gonna have one pissed crew," Jack said. "But you've got it."

On the morning of the raid all of the 379th's Phantoms stood ready on the ramp. Waters and Gomez had driven down the long line in the DO's pickup.

"Impressive," Gomez said. "Good for Maintenance. Fairly tells me this is all comm out. Let's see if they can do it without talking on the radios." Gomez turned the truck's two UHF radios on.

A pickup sped down the line waving a yellow flag that signaled the crews to start engines. In rapid-fire sequence the Phantoms cranked while the crew chiefs hurried to disconnect power, button up panels and pull wheel chocks. A crew chief ran to the front of his bird and gave a thumbs-up. When each flight of four aircraft was ready, four rear canopies came down in unison, followed by the four front canopies. Each flight of four taxied to the takeoff end of the runway where quick-check crews from Maintenance ran around each plane giving it a final inspection, checking it for hydraulic leaks, tire cuts and panels that might have jiggled loose.

Fairly had selected a young crew, Broz and Ambler, to lead the mission. Jack objected, but Fairly overruled him. "I know you can do it, Jack. But you can't lead every mission we fly. We've got to give some others a chance. And none of us is forever . . ."

The first four Phantoms now taxied onto the runway, a green light from the tower flashed and Broz led the first two birds in a formation takeoff. Ten seconds later the second two took off while the next four taxied into position, awaiting a green light. Twenty seconds later two more rolled down the runway, repeating the sequence. In less than three minutes twenty-four Phantoms had taken the active and launched in total radio silence.

The two colonels sat in the pickup. The launch was okay. Now they had to wait.

The first cell of twelve aircraft were broken up into three flights of four as Ambler guided them on a low-level route over the North Sea at a leisurely 420 knots using two stopwatches and his compass for dead reckoning to back up his inertial navigation set. The four aircraft flew in pairs, two thousand feet apart, while the second flight of four followed Broz two miles in trail.

Jack was in the third flight two miles behind the second. Like Bull, he was flying as tail end Charlie. It fell to Broz and Ambler to make each checkpoint on time or the entire cell would have to abort their part of the attack. At each checkpoint Jack would lift his plane to three hundred feet and make a comm out-turn with his wingman onto a new heading for the next leg, slam the bird back down on the deck. Sweat poured from both men as they labored toward their target.

"No way the Dutch are going to let us carry live ordnance over Woensdrecht," Thunder said. "Besides, it'd shoot our fuel-flow right through the roof."

"That's why they have tankers, me lad. And that's why we're going to hit one after we come off target. Like for real."

As they coasted in-between the Dutch islands of Voorne and Goeree south of Rotterdam Thunder switched on his radar, whose effective range for navigation was limited because of their low altitude. At forty miles the first traces of the Dutch coast started to paint on the scope.

"Damn," Thunder said, "Ambler's got us on course, on time." He switched the radar back to standby.

Jack lifted his aircraft to one thousand feet as they flew up the Haring Vleit, one of Holland's inland estuaries. "I wish the Dutch would let us get down in the weeds on this one. No real low-level into the IP, no ordnance, just overfly the target."

Thunder grunted and turned the radar back on. He broke their Initial Point, the Dutch village of Akker, out of the ground clutter on his scope.

"IP two minutes, on time," he said.

Jack concentrated on turning the IP exactly on time as he accelerated to 480 knots.

Each pair of Phantoms in the twelve aircraft cell overflew the IP at precise twenty-second intervals. Jack varied his heading slightly to separate from his wingman for a pop onto the target they had selected —the control tower—carrying his pop high to give Thunder a chance to check visually how the raid was developing. Thunder could see the smoke trails of the second cell splitting into two arms as it converged on the base from the south. "If they're early, we're dead." This was turning out to be no milk run.

On the ground a Dutch officer noted the exact time each bird overflew its target. The first cell took exactly one minute and forty seconds to attack the base. Jack rejoined his wingman on the southern edge of the base as the second wave started their attack. By splitting into a pincer movement the inbound F-4s left an escape route up the middle for Jack's cell.

Jack and Thunder twisted around, back and forth, as they tracked the inbound attackers flashing by them on both sides. "Hot damn," Jack shouted. "We did it. Right on time." Easing the throttles back, he decelerated to 420 knots and flew out the Wester Schelde, the waterway that led to Antwerp, then joined up with his flight and headed for a rendezvous with a tanker. He could hear Thunder humming. One hour twenty minutes after takeoff they recovered at Stonewood.

"What do you think?" Tom asked Waters as they watched the Phantoms taxi back in.

"Depends on what the crews think," Waters said.

The crews crowded into the squadron's main briefing room, exhilarated by how they had beat up the Dutch base. Then the phone call they were waiting for came—the Dutch officer reported that all twenty-four aircraft had made their times over target within five seconds. Jack was standing in the back of the briefing room, when Bull pounded him on the shoulder, congratulating him.

"Bull, as long as we made our TOTs it was pretty much a piece of cake. Why did the Old Man make such a big deal out of it?"

"Confidence builder, maybe. For you and Maintenance. Waters doesn't want to waste any of you budding aerial assassins." His shark grin was back in place, "But wait till the next one, buddy. You're in for a surprise."

The next day the 377th launched on their raid, determined to repeat the success of the 379th. After watching them launch, Waters and Gomez joined Bull by the 379th duty desk. The command post soon called with the news that six Phantoms were ten minutes out, and a voice from down the hall sang out, "They can't hack it." The building echoed with jeers and catcalls.

"That's probably C.J.," Bull grinned. The major picked up the mike to the squadron's PA system, "You mud movers, come on out of this den of iniquity and meet the latest addition to the wing." The two colonels, Morgan and a puzzled 379th wandered out onto the concrete apron to await the latest arrivals.

"Who the hell is C.J.?" Jack asked Morgan as they stood waiting.

"Charles Justin Conlan," Bull told him, "an absolute madman. And if you think he's crazy, wait until you meet his bear."

"This guy has a pet bear?"

"C.J. is bringing in six G-models for us from the States."

"Oh . . . great." Jack had forgotten for the moment that a wizzo in an F-4G was called a bear. "How did the old man get Wild Weasels? I thought they were all dedicated to NATO and that the big-boy F-16 wings wanted every one the Air Force owns to support them."

"You'll get your answers tomorrow," Morgan told him as he started to pace back and forth.

In the distance Jack could see the telltale black exhaust trails of five Phantoms approach the base at twelve hundred feet. "I thought the regs called for radar approaches after a ferry mission," he said. "That looks like an overhead recovery. What the hell sort of formation is that? There's only five birds, where's the sixth?"

Morgan shook his head, laughing at Jack's questions. Overhead recoveries are flown out of an echelon formation and these five new birds were coming down final in a perfect vee-formation.

As they crossed the approach end of the runway, the tail-end Phantom on the left arm of the vee peeled off first, bleeding off airspeed and circling to land. At precise five-second intervals the F-4s broke formation in order, working up and around the vee.

It was when the last plane was on downwind that the sixth bird shot down the runway at twelve hundred feet and 600 knots. At mid-field the new pilot reefed the fighter into a climb, heading for the cloud deck above them. As he disappeared into the clouds a few of the sharper-eyed observers could have sworn the pilot aileron rolled the F-4G.

"I don't believe *that,*" Jack muttered.

Morgan smiled. "C.J.'s calling the tower right now with the exact altitude of the cloud bases. Good information for them to know when the 377th recovers."

Now the five Wild Weasels taxied in and lined up in front of the crowd. They did not shut down engines but waited until the sixth bird had landed and taxied into the lineup. On an unspoken signal they cut engines in unison, the front six canopies opened together, followed by the six rear canopies. The solo pilot almost leaped out of his bird, scrambling down the recessed footholds on the left side of the fuselage. Once on the ground he twisted off his helmet, revealing a bald head with a brown fringe of hair above his ears. Jack thought immediately of a Trappist monk as he studied the skinny, freckle-faced major. "That's a fighter pilot?"

"C.J. is all of that," Morgan said. "If that bothers you check out his bear." Jack switched his attention to the man climbing out of the rear cockpit. "That's Stan-the-Man Benton." They watched as a young, pudgy version of Winston Churchill reached the ground and unzipped the breast pocket of his flight suit, actually pulling out a stogie to complete the image. "They say he's close to being an alcoholic," Morgan said. "Probably goes with the territory if you fly in C.J.'s pit."

Waters had stood on the ramp during the recovery of the G models. As C.J. walked up to him the wing commander wondered how much he could let Conlan get away with before he'd have to jerk him back into line. Conlan was, after all, infamous for his high-spirited approach to air-defense suppression with the Wild Weasels. If it wasn't for his airmanship and tactical abilities, he would have been court-martialed long ago.

C.J. saluted Waters, and with a fly-boy insouciance better suited to an old "Steve Cannon" comic strip, said, "I'm here, Colonel. You can start the war now."

An eerie quiet descended on the base as fog muffled noise and gave a ghostlike quality to images flitting through the mist. Maintenance needed the break in flying to finally bring the wing's fleet of F-4s into top-hole condition.

On the second morning after the arrival of the Wild Weasels, Major Yaru-Lau announced the wing's combat status had reached a one and Waters congratulated Leason on his accomplishment—the wing had made it past the first big hurdle.

After the morning briefing Waters called Fairly aside. "Mike, I'm putting the Weasels under Steve Farrell in the 377th. But it's Bull's job to teach people how to fly with them. He's going to need help. Pick a pilot to be your squadron weapons-and-tactics officer to work with him and the Weasels. Have your man at a meeting in Intelligence today at 1300. By the way, your troops did good at Woensdrecht."

Fairly picked up the hint. "Jack Locke will be there at 1300."

"Good choice," Waters said.

Jack was pleased at the news he'd be the squadron's new weapons-and-tactics officer but disappointed when Fairly told him he couldn't have Thunder to work with him.

"I've got other plans for the wizzo. You'll have to do this one on your own," Fairly told him and walked away. Time Jack got weaned from his wizzo.

In the back vault of Intel, Group Commander Childs had shown up with Waters, who proceeded to introduce the men to C.J. and his bear. "We're going to start training for an attack on Ahlhorn," he then said, pointing to a German air base on a wall map of northern Germany. "For us it will be the equivalent of an attack deep into enemy territory. Alongside of it, Woensdrecht was a piece of cake. Ahlhorn will be defended by the Tactical Leadership Program at Jever." He pointed to another German base near the North Sea. "They'll challenge us with an active air-defense, which is where the Weasels come in. We're going to have to fight our way in, suppress the base's air defenses and fight our way out." The colonel looked at Jack. "This one will not be a piece of cake."

"Colonel," Jack said, "the only rough thing about Woensdrecht was the low level and timing over the North Sea. Flying at a thousand feet and 420 knots to an IP like we did in Holland isn't flying low or fast. And that's our best tactic for penetration into any target. The Rapiers at Stamford proved that . . ."

Sara was right, Waters thought. There was a lot of Locke that reminded him of himself when he was a new young fighter pilot. There was a potential in Jack beyond anything in Morgan or Conlan when they were upcoming jocks at Red Flag. But he still had a long road to go and plenty to learn from C.J. and Bull.

"Good point, Locke. Group Captain Childs will explain the low-level flying structure in Germany. After he's finished, get into bed with C.J. and Stan and figure out how you're going to integrate the Weasels with your tactics. Okay, that's it," and he left.

Childs threw a blue three-ring notebook on the table in front of them. "That gives the story of flying low level in Germany. You can legally operate between four and seven hundred feet most everywhere until you're in a low-flying area; then you can descend to two hundred feet. Ahlhorn is in a low-fly area. However, the RAF likes to operate at two hundred feet wherever we please, but we do avoid most villages and built-up areas. Mustn't upset the natives too much—"

"Don't the Germans file violations like crazy?" Jack broke in.

Childs smiled. "Let us just say that the low-level structure in Germany is one way we remind the Germans that we were not invited there."

For the rest of the afternoon and the next morning, C.J. and Stan worked with the small group. Stan outlined the way a G-model worked and how they could detect and electronically counter radar-guided threats. C.J. took over and covered the three different missiles the Weasels carried that homed onto the radar-transmitting guidance signals to SAMs and Triple A. With a Weasel in the area, a radar operator led a short, exciting life. "There are several ways we can integrate our operations to get you onto and off a target, but in most cases what the old heads used to say is still right—'tell me what the threat is and I'll tell you what my tactics are.' Okay, time we chase our bodies over to the base theater to hear Bull shake up the troops with the Ahlhorn mission."

Jack met Morgan outside the theater as the crews crowded in for their next briefing. While they waited Jack said, "Tell me about C.J."

"Strange case," Morgan said. "Supposedly he's not even that good a pilot, but he's been asked to join the Thunderbirds *twice*. He's written articles on strategy for the Air University Review and been called simple minded. You figure it out. The guy's kicked out of a Pentagon assignment after an arrest for drunk driving. He also wrote a satire on official policies. It is not worth your career to be caught with one of the bootleg copies at the Puzzle Palace, but rumor has it that Sundown keeps a framed copy in his bathroom. Maybe that's C.J.'s secret weapon . . ."

Bull finished up his briefing with: "Some of you are wondering why an old bird like the F-4 should still be so alive and well when the F-15s and 16s are eating up the sky. It's because the Phantom can do *many* things well and has two engines and two crewmembers. It can take a lot of battle damage and still survive in a high-threat environment. It also offers a damn creditable air-to-air counter against the latest MiGs, especially since being retrofitted with the AIM-9L Sidewinder. Sure, the new birds can do any one of the things it does better, but none can do all of them as well. I've been talking about the Phantom's potential. It's your job to make it live up to that potential. The man in the cockpit *still* makes the difference."

* * *

Jack and Thunder had been visiting Eastern Radar. When they turned at the roundabout in front of Gillian's shop, Jack got Thunder to pull over, jogged around the corner to the shop and found her behind the desk scheduling appointments.

"How would you like to see the base this afternoon? The 378th is launching a mass gaggle on Woensdrecht. You might enjoy it. Pick you up at one?"

Before she could answer he had run back to the waiting car.

"He *does* seem sure of himself," one of the stylists who worked for Gillian observed.

Gillian said nothing but was thinking how glad she was he'd come back.

Jack was glad he had planned on finishing Gillian's tour of the squadron by watching the 378th crank engines and taxi out to the runway. The activity and the precision of the engine start and canopy drill fascinated her.

"Can we watch them take off?" she shouted over the noise.

Jack's answer was to commandeer a pickup truck and drive out to the takeoff end of the runway, beating the taxiing Phantoms, then hand Gillian a set of Mickey Mouse ear protectors as the Phantoms arrived and the first four lined up on the runway.

When the pilots lit the afterburners the shock wave rocked Gillian back as the Phantoms thundered down the runway. Ten seconds after the lead started his takeoff the second pair started to roll and the vibration of the noise pulsed through her body, seemingly reaching every nerve and bone. As the second flight of four taxied into position she took a hesitant step toward the runway, but Jack held her back. She shook off his hand and stood there, meeting the force of the noise alone until all twenty-four aircraft had launched.

The silence after the launch was as deafening as the noise had been. Gillian turned to Jack. "Oh, my God . . ." She reached out and put her hand on his cheek, surprising him by the warmth of her touch. They stood there for a moment, not saying a word.

"I don't know what happened to me," she said. "I think it must have been the incredible noise, the power of it . . . it excited me, I admit. That *is* the secret isn't it? I mean, the power in those beasts. Controlled and caged and *you* fly them—like riding a whirlwind." She seemed to blush. "Is that too silly, Jack? I don't care . . . No wonder it draws you in so . . ."

Jack drew Gillian into his arms. She had it right, no question. She knew . . . knew him, which excited and even scared him a little . . .

"What am I going to do with you?" he said, pulling her to him.

"Well, you can start by letting me show you London. You've given me part of your world; it's my turn to show you some of mine." For starters, she added to herself.

The London that Gillian first showed Jack included an aunt's elegant home in Mayfair, meeting her friends in a variety of pubs, and the theater. Over breakfast Sunday morning Jack told her that he now wanted to play tourist and see at least one of the standard sights.

Gillian checked the weather, found that it would be cold and *sunny* . . . a miracle in London. "That's it then," she told him. "Greenwich by river." They caught the tour boat for Greenwich at Tower Bridge, and Jack saw why the famous observatory should only be seen from the river. The rigging of the clipper ship *Cutty Sark* dominated his first impression until he saw the expanse of the buildings designed by Christopher Wren.

In bed early Monday morning, Jack reached out for Gillian—she wasn't there. A sudden hurt, an ache of loneliness hit him before he realized he was panicking, that she had gone no further than the bathroom. When she came back to bed he pretended to be asleep, not wanting to let her know how he felt . . . still confused—even afraid —about what was happening to him.

The next day when Thunder decided he'd had enough of waiting around for the Ahlhorn mission, delayed by the rotten weather, Jack grabbed at his suggestion that they get a pass and try some skiing in the Alps. Without saying as much, it was an escape from more than the tedium of waiting for the weather to clear . . .

19 March: 1930 hours, Greenwich Mean Time
2030 hours, Davos, Switzerland

The cold of the Alps and getting to the hotel in Davos that they'd been booked into made them almost nostalgic for the wet but tolerable English countryside. Never mind, they'd determined to have a time and proceeded to begin with a quick trip to the bar, which was crowded with some especially succulent women, including two who identified themselves only as Jane and Diana. The getting together didn't take long—everybody knew what everybody was there for, including but not restricted to the slopes.

And the next day, after a run from the top of the Weissfluhjoch down the Parsenns-Klosters trail, Jack and Thunder again got together at the bar with the ladies, who this time were conversing in French, with two men, a Frenchman named Paul and another, an Arab, named Reza.

Paul was especially interested to hear that Jack and Thunder flew F-4s, and soon let them know that he and Reza flew fighters, that he himself was actually a test pilot. They promised to talk more the next day.

Early in the morning, after a restless night, Jack decided to try the sauna, and found it was coeducational, with Jane already there, as though waiting for him . . .? A very nice coincidence. What the hell, he was supposed to be getting away from the pressures, personal included. She was sitting on a middle bench and patted the place beside her. She turned to him when he sat down, apparently taking his erection as a compliment. After that, there really wasn't much to say. What happened was sex, a purging. So why didn't he feel more satisfied?

Meanwhile, Jane's friend Diana was languishing and despite her advances, not having any luck with Jack's remarkably built buddy Thunder, who seemed to have found somebody else he preferred.

The Arab, Prince Reza Ibn Abdul Turika, of the Saudi royal family, was, on the other hand, pleased with his good fortune. He was impressed with the two American flyers and also listened carefully to the Frenchman Paul Rainey celebrate the technical merits of the French Mirage 2000 fighter as opposed to the much older U.S. F-4. He understood that the French government had given Paul the tough assignment of convincing him that his government should purchase new delta-wing Mirage 2000s.

Jack's arguments came down to the crucial difference being the relative skills of individual pilots. Paul then asked the two Americans to come with him to the airfield near Nancy, where they were conducting a combat evaluation of the Mirage. He'd arrange a demonstration ride for them, he said.

The next day at the airfield the weather was cold and cloudy. When they got to the hangar Jack stopped dead in his tracks. "For God's sake, where in hell did you get *that?*" He was referring to the lone occupant of the hangar—a pristine F-4E.

Paul then proceeded to tell how the F-4 was a gift from the Ayatollah in 1980, who was paying back the French for giving him asylum during the Shah's regime—and particularly enjoyed giving a plane that had been given to the Shah originally by the Americans. The French had shipped the plane in crates to Nancy, and their technicians had only recently reassembled it and trimmed the engines. They had only flown it twice, Paul said.

"What are you going to do with it?" Jack asked him.

"We want to fly it and use it as a standard for comparison. Maybe you would like to fly it for us?"

Reza watched the exchange closely, understanding that Paul obviously assumed his Mirages would perform well and impress Reza as compared to the older American Phantom. But then he added an unexpected zinger of his own.

"Jack, I would like to fly against you in the Mirage."

Paul protested, sure that Reza, a newly qualified pilot in the Mirage, would hardly be able to stack up against the two highly trained American pilots. But Reza insisted, and he was the potential customer. So Paul salvaged matters by urging that at least he should fly with Reza in another Mirage as his wingman. The fight would be documented, shot for shot, by video gun cameras.

Paul Rainey gave them a map and Thunder noted the location of the French GCI radar site in the center. He figured Paul would probably use it to find them and receive vectors into the engagement, which would put him and Jack at a real disadvantage. "Well, they've got to find us first," Jack said. "We get low and loiter in the weeds, hide from the radar and try to make them burn up fuel looking for us. Once they get low on fuel we'll engage them. We've got to make them depend on a visual contact to engage us—that's the only way I can see to offset their radar. So . . . we've got to keep below a hundred feet and you've got to track them without locking onto them with our radar . . . their warning gear will probably react even to the search mode of our radar, so keep your search time to a minimum and your radar in standby. Think you can handle all that till it's time to engage?"

Thunder said he could, thoroughly caught up in it now. Both of them were pushing to the back of their minds any second thoughts or possible consequences of what they were doing. They were fighter jocks. Consequences were for field grade officers and Pentagon paper pushers . . .

Jack taxied slowly, watching Reza and Paul takeoff, wanting the Mirages to consume as much fuel as possible while he stayed on the ground. He felt Thunder take control of the rudder pedals with his big feet and weave the bird back and forth down the taxiway. Thunder, Jack knew, was just prancing, enjoying himself, looking forward to the coming engagement.

In the control tower the controller remarked to an observer that the Americans were crazy, that they'd have no chance against the Mirages if they couldn't even taxi straight.

Actually Jack was being less crazy than he'd ever been on a flight, understanding the odds against him and Thunder. Paul, a top test pilot, was a better pilot in sheer technique than he was. But he was also betting that Paul wasn't so much of a technician, hadn't practiced or thought about air-combat tactics in a long time . . . not his bag. In fact, Paul had already made an error by taking off before the Phantom, and Jack stalled another ten minutes on the runway after he had received clearance to take off, claiming gyro-stabilization problems. When the controller saw Jack finally make his takeoff and come out of afterburner and level off at one thousand feet and 350 knots airspeed, he said, "*Merde,* he flies slow. The American is in no hurry to be eaten by Paul."

Once out of sight of the tower Jack dropped down to a hundred feet and skirted the area they'd picked for the engagement, entering it on the side opposite the base. He dropped lower and skimmed the tree tops, heading for the radar site. "Time for a bubble check," he said. Two miles out from the radar antenna he increased his speed to 420 knots, a better maneuvering speed, then pulled up in time to fly over the dome covering the antenna, clearing it by less than ten feet as he stroked the afterburners.

The operators in the radar site had been searching for the Phantom and weren't able to respond to Paul's request for information. The tower had broadcast Jack's takeoff time to them, and the delay in finding the Phantom was worrying the Mirage pilots. When Paul did realize Jack was using fuel conservation as a tactic he zoomed to a higher altitude to save his own fuel, penetrating the cloud deck at eight thousand feet, which forced him to rely on his radar and information from the radar site. He broke out of the clouds at twenty-four thousand feet, entering the envelope that, in fact, the Mirage had been designed for. Just then the radar site radioed that they had "found" the Phantom, that it had buzzed the radar head at a crazy low altitude.

Paul understood that the American would stay low, forcing him to come down to engage, and began to work his radar, using the pulse Doppler set to find the low-flying Phantom . . .

At Thunder's direction, Jack now fell in behind the two Mirages and trailed them around the area from twenty-five thousand feet below, hiding in their blind spot . . . the radar on a fighter is in the nose and so it is blind at its rear . . .

Reza was enjoying the Frenchman's predicament, remarking that it didn't look good if they couldn't find the target. Paul silently invited him to drop dead . . .

Finally Jack decided it was time to engage and let them know where he was. He told Thunder to get ready to lock onto one of the Mirages and stay locked on. He climbed to five hundred feet to let the GCI find him, then after pausing a few seconds went back to seventy-five feet, once again dropping off the GCI's scope. He counted to ten and told Thunder to lock on . . .

"The Phantom is at your six o'clock, five miles in trail, altitude five hundred feet," the radar site told Paul. As Paul received this unpleasant information, Reza broke in with, "I have a radar warning; they are locked on and tracking me at my six o'clock."

Paul checked his fuel gauge. "Follow me, I'll take the lead." He put the nose of the Mirage over and did a Split-S toward his six o'clock, immediately acquiring two targets on his scope as he plummeted through the cloud deck. He selected the one on the right, locked on to track it and told Reza to lock onto the left target. Paul's target turned out to be moving at only eighty miles per hour and he had to assume it was a fast-moving car. He broke lock and relocked on the other target. He came up empty. His and Reza's radars were interfering with each other, giving false readings. But Paul now called on his skills and led the Mirages in a steep dive through the cloud deck—not a simple dive but one that turned and reversed course as Paul maneuvered to bring the Phantom to his twelve o'clock position and keep it there. Reza's performance as a wingman wasn't too shabby either, remaining welded to Paul's wing throughout the tricky descent . . .

Thunder was twisted around his seat, straining for a visual on the Mirages. His radar-warning gear was screaming that the other birds were at his six, and he spotted them as they broke out of the clouds. "Tallyho," he called over the intercom. "Bandits, six o'clock, eight miles plus, high on us."

It was enough for Jack to engage. Thunder had just told him that the two Mirages were over eight miles behind him at a much higher altitude with their noses on the Phantom. He check-turned thirty degrees to his right, kicking them out of his six o'clock position and visually acquiring them. Then he accelerated to 420 knots and climbed to twenty-five hundred feet to gain the minimum room he needed to maneuver in. He watched with growing excitement as the two Mirages closed to his six. Then he waited . . .

Paul's acute senses told him they were going too fast and would overshoot the Phantom. Yet, the radar indicated a much slower overtake speed. Trusting his senses, he called for speed brakes and slowed the Mirages as they closed to within three miles of Jack's tail. Jack's speed control was faultless as he reversed course, pulling four Gs through a one hundred thirty-five degree bank, bringing his nose head-on to the Mirages. The American's timing was perfect as he simulated a snap gunshot at Paul's Mirage. He had cut his counterturn so close that the two Mirages had to take evasive action.

Paul zoomed out of the flight, expecting Reza to follow him, but Reza wanted to engage. He pulled his nose up, using the vertical to reverse course before Jack shot by. Now Reza was going back the way he had come and expected to see Jack in front and below him. But Jack, using his speed brakes, was still directly under Reza, turning to the left and diving for the ground. Reza, seeing how close they were, again pulled up his nose and turned to the right away from Jack. He wanted to maneuver away from the ground and get room to turn back on Jack . . .

Except Jack had only feinted in his hard turn to the left and rolled under and sliced back to the right, turning after Reza. He cleared the ground by two hundred feet and rolled out behind the Arab, right in the heart of the launch envelop for a Sidewinder missile. He then simulated AIM-9 missile launch two on the retreating Mirages . . .

Reza, trying to find Jack, heard Paul call out, "Bingo fuel." He glanced at his gauge and realized that they had to scramble for home. Nothing to do about it. No fuel left for maneuvering. Take the humiliation of defeat or flameout . . .

After calling the tower to enter the pattern, Jack came down final, but instead of landing he snapped up the gear and flaps and flew down the runway at one thousand feet, executing a roll as he passed the taxiing Mirages. "I wish you hadn't done that, old buddy," Thunder said as they circled to land. Our French-friend is going to be eating nails as it is."

He was, of course, right. Reza was fascinated and exhilarated by the experience but let them know that Paul was far from amused, that he had, in fact, asked that they be declared *non grata* by the French government. He quickly arranged private transportation for them at the international airport in Luxembourg, and they were soon back at Stonewood, without time to make any good-byes to any ladies. It seemed, for the moment, that they'd gotten away clean and free.

5 April: 0845 hours, Greenwich Mean Time
0945 hours, Stonewood, England

Waters had joined the three men around the map of the Persian Gulf that Bill Carroll had spread out on the work table in Intelligence.

Carroll plotted the coordinates he'd been given that morning. "That's it, Ras Assanya," the lieutenant told the group. "Never heard of it and there's nothing in my records about it."

Chief Pullman bent over the map. "Why is the air base located near a neutral zone?"

"That's an old map that needs updating," Carroll told him. "The neutral zone is now part of Kuwait. They stuck our deployment base in the middle of nowhere."

With a pair of dividers Waters measured off two hundred fifty nautical miles and swung an arc on the map using the base as the center point. "Someone had their act together when they picked Ras Assanya for our deployment base. Our effective area of operations is the head of the Persian Gulf. And that at least makes us a significant deterrent to any would-be Alexander the Greats."

"*And* a significant target," Carroll said. "Sir David, our information is that British contractors built the base. Can you get us any pictures, plans?"

The group commander nodded. "You have a problem," he began. "Base survival will be a major factor in the success of your operations out of Ras Assanya. You need to be prepared to deal with air attacks, commando raids and naval bombardment. Fighting for your base is something you Yanks haven't done since the early days of World War Two."

"How in the hell do we get our troops ready for that?" Chief Pullman grumbled. "Home is supposed to be safe."

"The first step is to get everyone's attention," Childs said, and outlined how they could do that by staging a training raid on Stonewood. He proposed using four F-15s from Soesterberg in the Netherlands launching out of Stonewood to defend against attacking aircraft from NATO's Tactical Leadership Program. "Once your people have seen what a well-planned attack can do, then we can teach them how to fight for their survival while they launch and recover fighters on combat sorties."

"Well," Waters said, "let's get cracking. Time's no longer on our side."

* * *

Jack stood on the ramp with Morgan and Conlan, watching four F-15 Eagles taxi into the hardened bunkers near the squadron and noting the big black letters painted on the tails of the taxiing aircraft. "I've never seen the CR tail markings before. Who are they?"

"That's the designator for the 32nd Tac Fighter Squadron out of Soesterberg in the Netherlands. Probably the best group of air defenders in the Air Force," C.J. said.

"If they're so hot, how come they're so unknown?"

C.J. shrugged. "They don't holler about it, they just do it. They've won the Hughes Trophy twice in a row. For an air-defense squadron that's the same as winning the Super Bowl. They only have eighteen birds and are tucked away on the corner of a Dutch air base. For them, small is better."

Ten RAF umpires now walked out onto the ramp and dispersed as the four F-15s cranked their engines for a launch. Six minutes later Stonewood was attacked as four thousand awe-struck Yanks straggled outside to watch the "show." The F-15s slashed down on eight German F-4s that led the attack and treated the spectators to a tight turning engagement over their heads. While the F-15s were occupied, the first two Tornados overflew the flight line at two hundred feet, then dropped down to one hundred to egress the target. In rapid-fire succession sixteen more Luftwaffe and RAF Tornados attacked Stonewood. While the Tornados cleared the base, a series of single U.S. and RAF F-111s attacked.

An evaluator came up to Jack, told him he was dead, then marked a big *X* on the squadron's door with chalk.

Suddenly the base was deathly quiet, and the four F-15s started to recover, low on fuel. An umpire surveyed the area. "Quick way to die. Yes?"

At the debrief of the attack in the main hangar a lone RAF officer took the makeshift stage in front of a screen and introduced himself. The first photo on the screen shocked the crowd into silence: it was a picture of a dozen charred bodies in a bombed-out hangar. "This is how this hangar will look in an attack. At 1406 this afternoon this was a functioning base. By 1417 twenty-four aircraft on a mass raid attacked and destroyed Stonewood.

Against a series of computer enhanced slides of destroyed buildings that bore an uncanny resemblance to their base and scores of dead bodies, the officer tallied their casualties. "We estimate that seventeen hundred of you are wounded, of which three hundred will later die. Eight hundred of you are unharmed, and approximately two thousand are a problem for Graves Registration. You ceased to exist as a base."

They believed it.

20 April: 1935 hours, Greenwich Mean Time
1435 hours, Washington, D.C.

General Cunningham's aide, Colonel Dick Stevens, reread the secret intelligence report from the CIA that detailed how the French had been given an F-4 by the Iranians and how two Americans had flown it against two of France's latest Mirages. He drafted a short one-paragraph memo summarizing the report, attached it to the cover and sent it into Sundown's office. Later that day Cunningham called his aide in. "All right, what happened?"

"Sir, it seems two of our people flew an F-4 against two Mirage 2000s flown by the French test pilot Paul Rainey and a Saudi Prince, one Reza Ibn Abdul Turika."

"Who were the Americans?"

"Lieutenant Jackson D. Locke, the pilot, and Captain James W. Bryant, the weapons systems officer, both assigned to the 45th Tactical Fighter Wing." Stevens did not have to tell Cunningham they were also the crew that had shot down the Libyan MiG.

"And the results?"

"Locke chased them out of the area, they never got a shot at the F-4. It ruined a Mirage sale to the Saudis, and the French government is furious. Not much they can do about it . . . The prince said that the American pilot turned out to be right, although he didn't elaborate."

Locke and Bryant . . . crazy bastards. Now they'd set themselves up for a court-martial . . . "You say they defeated the two Mirages?"

"Ate 'em alive, sir." The aide kept a straight face.

"I'll be damned."

Which ended the interview. As Stevens was closing the door he heard an unfamiliar noise in the general's office. It sounded like a series of sharp grunts and someone pounding on a table, followed by an ungeneral-like *"shit hot . . ."*

21 April: 0920 hours, Greenwich Mean Time
1020 hours, Mildenhall, England

A copy of the message ordering an investigation into the activities of Jack and Thunder while in France reached Blevins' desk the next day. He scrutinized the short text, ignoring the detailed intelligence references and which office was tasked with the investigation . . . Well, well, Muddy Waters' boys. Got you, you son of a bitch. He hit the intercom button to his aide. "Get me a car, I'm going to Stonewood."

Blevins ordered his driver to go directly to the 379th when they got to the main gate, then proceeded without advance warning into Fairly's office, slamming the door behind him.

Shortly. Lieutenant Locke and Captain Bryant were paged to report to the squadron commander's office. Thunder sensed trouble and wanted to warn Jack. He had been waiting for something like this to happen, not able to believe they were going to get away with their freelance adventure in France. He asked the Duty Officer to call wing headquarters and tell them a general was in the building before he followed Jack into Fairly's office.

Blevins started slowly, affecting a comradely attitude when he asked for an explanation of how they had come to fly an F-4 for the French. Jack caught Fairly's near-imperceptible headshake, warning him to remain silent. But the question was exactly the one that Thunder wanted to answer and he started to relate the entire incident in a low and unemotional voice.

"Captain Bryant . . ." Fairly tried to shut Thunder up, to let him know he shouldn't talk about an unauthorized flight involving a foreign government. Before he could warn Thunder, Blevins silenced him and told Thunder to continue. After Bryant had finished, Blevins turned to Jack and asked if what the wizzo had said was true. Jack, deciding to back up his backseater, confirmed everything the wizzo had said.

Afterward Blevins sat quietly for a few moments, then nodded, got up to leave and was on his way to the door when Waters came in without knocking. At the sight of his old nemesis, Blevins' cool began to evaporate. "Colonel, this is an investigation of serious misconduct on the part of your people. I am surprised that you seem to have lost control here," and then he proceeded, with some obvious relish, to fill in Waters on what he had just heard.

Waters was stunned, as well as furious at Bryant and Locke, two of his favorites. "I would appreciate disciplining my own people," he began. "And an investigation is always conducted through a wing commander . . ."

"Waters, I don't think you're capable of such an investigation or the necessary disciplining. I don't need to remind you that you are in my chain of command. Perhaps your problem, and theirs, is that you tend to become confused about that basic fact."

"Ah, yes. That is a truism," he smiled, infuriating the general. "But I do have one question, perhaps the most important question about the engagement with the Mirages." Blevins waited, breathing heavily, his face flushed. Turning to Jack and Thunder, Waters deliberately hardened his voice, "Who won?"

The men could feel Blevins rage vibrate through the room as he fought for control of his temper. The general stormed out of the room.

"Well, Jack, you've opened the proverbial can of worms this time," Waters said. "God, don't you ever stop to think about the consequences of what you do? Don't answer that; it's obvious. You're all stick and balls and no forehead. Okay, for now you two are going to have to sweat it out and let the system work you over. You're also restricted to base until it's finished. That's for your own good. Who knows, you might figure to do a little freelance stint over Moscow . . ."

Waters turned and left, worried about Jack's future in the Air Force. Damn it, I need you, he raged to himself. Morgan and C.J. are not enough. Blowing the Mirages away proved how good you are, no matter how dumb it was to fly that engagement. The colonel's natural optimism broke through his despair over the pilot. I hope what Thunder did will give you a second chance, he thought. By the time he left the squadron, his grin was back in place as he visualized Blevins' reaction to the news.

Jack and Thunder made a sort of unspoken pact not to hash over what they'd done and to try to make the best of their base confinement.

They called Gillian and Francine to meet them at the Officers' Club, and during dinner Thunder loosed some thunder by announcing that he and Francine were getting married. It wasn't exactly music to Jack's ears, inasmuch as he felt even more on the spot about Gillian. When he asked Francine if it wasn't sort of sudden, she smiled prettily, told him not really, but after their little vacation in France she thought maybe what Thunder needed was a little settling down. Jack immediately regretted the question, and even more the answer, and tried to change the subject. But no matter what they talked about for the rest of the evening the news hovered like a pall, at least as far as Jack was concerned.

The next evening, missing Gillian, Jack called her, asking her to dinner, and was told that she, all apologies, had another engagement. Another *engagement,* for Christ sake? What was going on? . . .

What was going on was that Gillian was being instructed by her friend Francine on how to force the *issue* . . .

"But it seems childish," she said to Francine. "I don't like playing games. Part of the best of what Jack and I have is the honesty between us—"

"Like what happened in Switzerland and France?" said Francine. "We don't discuss it . . ."

"Damn right, you don't. Because if you did that would probably be it . . . Look, honey, I agree, games can be foolish, but if they work? . . ."

Gillian sighed, and decided to go along, or rather hold out, at least for the rest of the week.

The Third Air Force's Judge Advocate had definite feelings about his coming meeting with General Blevins. Waiting, he again went over the way he was going to present the results of the pre-trial investigation. Impatiently he glanced at the clock, decided to walk over to the general's office fifteen minutes early.

He found Blevins in his chair, waiting eagerly for the report, but after he got it the color had risen in his face and the judge advocate was afraid the man was going to have a heart attack.

"Do you mean to tell me"—Blevins tried to take a deep breath— "that they are going to get off on account of some damn technicality about evidence?"

Trying to keep his voice under control, the JAG answered: "Yes, sir, it comes down to that, you might say. It would also now be all but impossible to sustain a case against Locke and Bryant with the evidence available to us. It appears that neither the Arab prince nor the French pilot, Paul Rainey, will volunteer to testify at a court-martial, and it would be impossible to compel them to. The bottom line, sir, is that no lawyer would touch this case—"

"Are you positive about the technicality?" Blevins' voice was subdued.

"Yes, sir, afraid so, sir. When you asked Bryant and Locke for their account of the incident without first reading them their rights against self-incrimination you ended for all practical purposes the chance of bringing them to a court-martial. The law is very clear, sir: because you are in the chain of command of the convening authority for the court-martial, evidence illegally obtained cannot be used . . ."

"What the hell do you mean illegally? Anyway, I thought that stuff only applied to civilians."

"Whatever made you think we lose our civil rights because we are in the Air Force? Let me explain further. Both Locke and Bryant acted as subordinate officers in answering your questions. As I understand it, Colonel Fairly tried to keep the men silent, thereby protecting you, but you overrode him. I'm sorry, sir," he said, suppressing his pleasure, saluted and walked out.

28 April: 1605 hours, Greenwich Mean Time
1105 hours, Washington, D.C.

When General Cunningham heard the news about Bryant and Locke getting off, he couldn't help but be partially pleased, but he was also concerned about their reaction and what the result might mean for the consequent attitude of the men toward military authority, in particular their misunderstanding of just what had and hadn't happened. He called in his aide Colonel Dick Stevens. Chewing furiously on an unlit cigar, Cunningham said, "Dick, I want you to get the word to Waters and those swingin' dicks in the 45th—I'm pissed."

Stevens raised an eyebrow.

"Locke and Bryant figure they've beaten the rap, right? That General Blevins is a pompous jerk and they could show him up. *Right?*"

Stevens said nothing. He knew better.

"Let me tell you something about Blevins. And get this to them. Blevins is a *career* officer. He's given his life to the Air Force, to something real corny, like the defense of his country. He isn't planning to get out next year and work for some damned defense contractor and make a bundle. He isn't looking for a rich wife or membership in some fancy club or a chance to hit the lecture circuit and clean up at ten thousand a crack. No, he's just a career officer, a guy who isn't very popular, who cares a lot and can turn off almost anybody. But you get out this message—I'd rather have one Blevins than a hundred hotshot flyboys who think service is an extended vacation. They may be smarter and prettier and younger, but right now they're nobody I want to depend on, the way they're behaving. In fact right now, if I saw one of them, I'd likely throw up. So get that message to them too. Who knows, maybe it might even penetrate-their thick heads after a few hundred hours. It better, is all I can say. It damn well better. That's all."

When Stevens had left, Cunningham slumped back into his chair and shook his head. He may have laid it on a bit thick, but Dick would get the word out. The more he thought about it, the more Cunningham decided he'd done pretty damned good. Especially since he personally couldn't stand that pompous son of a bitch Blevins.

2 May: 0800 hours, Greenwich Mean Time
0900 hours, Stonewood, England

The men gathered around the flight planning table in Intel's vault looked up when Jack entered the room. He looked all business as he pulled up a chair and sat at the far end of the table, listening to C. J. Conlon and Morgan and Carroll and Gomez argue about the plan for the wing's attack on the German base at Ahlhorn. C.J. and Morgan were hassling about whether the Wild Weasels should surge ahead of the main strike force or escort them in. Jack got up and peered over Carroll's shoulder at the large-scale, detailed map of northern Germany. "It looks like an updated raid on Woensdrecht," he said, his first words since entering the vault. Waters and the weapons-and-tactics officers from the 377th and 378th had just arrived. Jack picked up the planning map from the table, pinned it on the wall next to a larger map of eastern England, the North Sea, the Netherlands and northern Germany, then overlaid both maps with a large sheet of acetate and picked up a grease pencil.

"What if we run the Ahlhorn attack as an integrated exercise with Ahlhorn, TLP at Jever and the 32nd at Soesterberg . . . ? To hit Ahlhorn, we've got to fight our way in and out of Germany. Our opposition will be launching from Jever and Soesterberg. So . . . I'm proposing we attack all three bases at once in a three-pronged raid. We make them fight for their bases while we sneak our main attack force onto Ahlhorn. We don't tell them which is our primary target, they've got to figure that one out. We've got to concentrate our Wild Weasels on the air defenses at Ahlhorn. But I think we can con Jever and Soesterberg into thinking they're the main target if we send one Weasel on each of those raids to act like . . . like a red herring, I guess you'd call it.

"Hauling bombs in an attack would cause us fuel problems. We fly a split-mission profile: high altitude–low level–high altitude and hit a tanker on our way in and out. We fly the low level part over land, into and off the target. Regardless of the base we hit it's minimum time in bad guy land and over target. We've got to get them looking where we ain't."

He sat down, dropped the grease pencil on the table, and watched.

Waters was obviously pleased, not to mention surprised. He didn't know Jack had it in him. Or rather wondered if he'd ever get it together. He looked around the hushed room. "Tom, Bull, C.J., what do you think?"

"Should work," Tom said. "Wish I'd thought of it." C.J. only nodded and walked up to the wall map, planning his tactics.

Morgan was out of his chair, swinging at his imaginary sparing partner. "I want Soesterberg," he grunted.

"Good, then let's do it," Waters decided. As they walked out of Intel, Waters stopped Jack. "Where did you get the idea for this attack?"

Jack half-smiled. Actually seemed embarrassed. "Believe it or not, I read a book, by Liddell Hart, that Thunder gave me while we were sweating out the court-martial. He talked about the indirect approach to strategy. Seemed like a good idea. Still does."

The two colonels looked at each other and left.

"What a surprise," Gomez said as they walked down the hall.

"That Jack read a book?" Waters smiled.

"No. Well, he's changed. Or at least seems to have . . . I'm worried, though. That mission, too damn many things can go wrong. Think our crews can hack it? We'll be in deep *kimshi* with Sundown if we lose another bird."

Waters only nodded, and Gomez changed the subject. "Any more feedback from the Puzzle Palace or Third Air Force about the fizzle on Jack and Thunder's court-martial?"

"Only that they lucked out, and got a blivet from Sundown. My guess is that that's part of Jack's newfound religion . . ." And added to himself that Blevins, a canny in-fighter, wasn't likely to let it go at that . . .

Chief Pullman took a quick survey of wing headquarters that afternoon, sauntered into the command post and cornered the on-duty controller.

"What combat status we reporting today?"

"A one, Chief. No problems except for night sorties. Not enough of them. The Old Man's got a waiver and we're reporting that in the remarks section."

Satisfied at last that no surprises were waiting for his colonel, Pullman left the command post and headed for the NCO club, where he found the bar nearly deserted. The place didn't fill up at quitting time as it used to, the bartender told him. Still, fifteen minutes later Chief George Gonzaga, Maintenance's first shirt, sat down next to Pullman at the bar and ordered a beer. "Didn't know your stomach let you drink, Mort," he said.

"It seems to be cooperating these days. How's things down in the trenches, George?"

"Busy. We're launching more sorties than ever. Don't know how much longer the birds can take it."

"Getting behind on scheduled maintenance then, right?" Pullman asked.

"Nah, right on schedule."

"Then behind on meeting your scheduled flying time?"

"Nah, we're actually ahead of the time line and might have to request additional flying time."

"The birds are starting to break more?"

"Not a bit."

Another chief master sergeant entered the bar that was hard to ignore. Chief Curtis Hartley stood slightly over six and a half feet tall and was built like a weight lifter. Pullman motioned for him to join them. "How's the Security Police business?"

Hartley grunted. "Not good. The Old Man is using my sweet black ass for target practice these days."

"Gawd, it's big enough. Hard to miss," Gonzaga told him.

"Colonel Waters has got us training like mad; perimeter defense, intruder exercises. You name it."

"Your troops can't take the strain?" Pullman asked.

"Naw, they love it. Especially when they hear about Waters getting on my case." The three sergeants spent the next three hours complaining happily to each other about how rotten things were.

All activity in the command post stopped. The men sat behind their telephones and radios and waited. The board plotters had finished marking up the birds as they reported in on status. Seventy-one aircraft stood ready to launch on the Ahlhorn raid. Only one plane had not checked in on status: 512.

"I can't believe that," Leason snapped, picking up the phone and jabbing the button for Maintenance Control. "Get 512 on status or start building a scaffold." Ten minutes later Leason's phone rang. The DM listened and hung up, then leaned back in his chair and grinned at Waters. "The damn battery failed when they put power to the aircraft. No big deal replacing the battery but you have to pull the backseat to get at it. Normally about a two-hour job. The crew chief turned into a madman, dove into the pit head-first without removing the seat, got twisted around somehow and got the battery out and a new one in. Not by the book, but it's done. They had to pull the chief out by his feet."

Waters nodded. "Make sure your troops know they did a good job. I don't recall ever hearing of a wing getting all its birds up at once."

The digital master clock flashed 1305 and the first wail of cranking jet engines could be heard. Waters took a deep breath and tried to relax as his wing headed for the North Sea.

Bull Morgan checked over his eighteen-ship cell as they came off the tanker and headed into the letdown point seventy-five miles off the Dutch island of Vlieland. Six of his birds stayed at altitude to act as a combat air patrol while he led twelve down onto the deck, coasting in at two hundred feet over Vlieland. He turned south, running in over the Ijsselmeer, the old Zuider Zee the Dutch were slowly draining, stealing land from the sea. As long as his flight remained over water they could hug the deck. His flight took spacing as they separated into pairs for the attack on Soesterberg. Touching shore, he inwardly groaned as he lifted his flight to the mandatory one thousand feet the Dutch demanded when flying over land. The first whiplash of a search radar activated his radar warning gear, but he believed it was too late, that the defenders would not get the F-15 Eagles setting alert at Soesterberg airborne in time. He was three-and-a-half minutes out.

NATO had been watching Soesterberg's reaction to the impending attack and duly noted the late warning of the inborn fighters. The 32nd had four Eagles airborne but they were in a Combat Air Patrol (CAP) over Ahlhorn, the base they thought would be attacked.

Meanwhile, Bull's F-4s overflew the base and then headed back out the Ijsselmeer, switching to a CAP role. NATO recorded the time of the attack and calculated that the runway had been cratered and would not be operational for two hours. The American and Dutch base commander conferred on where to divert the airborne Eagles and how long they could engage the attackers . . . Clearly the first phase of Jack's plan had worked.

While the fight over Soesterberg was developing, Jack led a thirty-six ship cell down the Dollart, the estuary of the Ems river. The cell broke up over the large mud flat at the mouth of the Ems onto different low-level routes leading to the six IPs they had selected surrounding Ahlhorn. Six minutes later Ahlhorn came under attack as the 45th crisscrossed over the base for eight minutes.

Jack maintained four hundred feet until they entered the low-flying area, then descended to two hundred feet as he turned over the village of Papenberg and headed for their IP. Sooner, his wingman, moved five hundred feet off his left wing as he pushed the airspeed to 480 knots. They split a radio tower that loomed in front of them, exactly as planned. Thunder and Sooner's wizzo kept twisting in their seats, looking for any bandits that might be in the area. The only other aircraft they saw had an "SW" for Stonewood on their tails. Telltale activity started to light Thunder's RHAW gear.

"Come on C.J.," Jack said, "now's the time to do your thing. Open up the door for us."

Strobes of jamming activity streaked Thunder's radar. "Looks like some bear is at work," Thunder said from the rear.

"Right," Jack said, wrenching the fighter into a sudden climb, snatching four Gs on the aircraft. "A damn Army helicopter—didn't he read the NOTAMs?" The Notice to Airmen had warned pilots about the operation and the chopper was illegally transiting the area. Only Jack's quick reactions saved them from a midair collision.

"Nice dodge," Sooner radioed, and was interrupted as a lone Luft-waffe F-4 chased a 45th Phantom across their path while a third Phantom sliced down onto the German. They could see the "SW" on the last F-4's tail. "There goes one sour Kraut," Sooner intoned over the radio about the developing sandwich.

He got no laugh, especially from Jack, who warned, "IP now," and jerked his bird onto a new heading while Sooner moved twenty degrees off Jack's heading, the two aircraft separating for the run onto Ahlhorn.

Two miles out, Jack pulled his nose up, rolling, and pulling back to the ground as he came down the chute, flying the wire down to bomb release. Meanwhile Thunder used their altitude to sweep the area visually, and sucked in his breath when he saw what looked like twenty F-4s converging on them from different headings. Unless everyone's timing was right, there would be a midair collision over Ahlhorn . . .

Jack pulled off his bomb run and exited over two F-4s that were running in on the target. On the ground, Group Commander Childs stood with the German commandant from TLP watching the attack. "An impressive show," the German colonel said.

Jack's flight of four joined up as they fell into a loose box formation and climbed to five hundred feet, coasting out eight minutes after coming off the target. They climbed lazily to twenty-four thousand feet looking for F-15s or F-4s out of Jever. His flight rendezvoused with a tanker and entered a race-track pattern, waiting for other members of their cell to join up. When eighteen birds were accounted for, they fell into trail behind the KC-135 and headed across the North Sea to Stonewood. As they did, Thunder monitored the radios, listening as the last half of their cell joined up on the second tanker. "All accounted for," he told Jack when the last two Wild Weasels checked in on the tanker.

Waters found Jack hovering over Bill Carroll, who was peering into the screen on his computer, calculating the various probabilities that would determine the success of the mission. Carroll kept pounding numbers into the computer as he scanned the debriefs from the crews and the reports from the NATO ground observers.

Carroll shook his head. "I'll have to run it all again, but it looks like we would of lost three birds on this attack. That's a four point two percent attrition rate. Jever was too tough a target and they got too many birds launched."

Jack groaned. Such an attrition rate meant that after seventeen maximum-effort missions like the one they had just completed, the wing would have lost half its aircraft.

The Ahlhorn raid had been a bloodbath for the 45th.

Forewarned is forearmed, went the conventional wisdom. But this was the Air Force.

*   *   *

General Blevins' secretary did not like the position she was in—between the proverbial rock and a hard place. The general was going to reprimand her either for interrupting him after announcing he did not want to be disturbed, even though he was alone in his office, or for not immediately showing the man in. She made two decisions and picked up the phone. "Excuse me, General"—she deliberately clipped her words, using her British accent to full effect—"there is a gentleman here who wishes to see you." She smiled at the nondescript British civilian in front of her.

"*Damn* it, can't you people follow directions?"

"I take it then, General, that I'm to tell the gentleman from MI-5 to come back at your convenience. Good-bye, General." She picked up her handbag and left.

"What's got into that twit now?" Blevins mumbled as he hurried to catch the visitor from British counter-intelligence before his secretary sent him away. "Ah, please come in," he said, affecting what he hoped was his best Bostonian accent.

The man followed Blevins into his office, closing the door behind him. He handed Blevins his ID and scanned the office, deciding that it was probably bugged, the Americans were so careless . . .

Blevins settled into his chair and smiled. "Not to worry. My offices are swept weekly for bugs."

Sir Louis Nugent asked me to speak to you—"

"Ah, yes, the chief of your section."

"Right . . . well, to come to the point, we have penetrated something of a spy net, IRA-based mostly. However, there are some interesting connections with Libya, and through them, the Soviets. We are not going to roll them up until we are certain of the extent of their penetration."

"Ah, yes, I see," Blevins picked it up, "they have penetrated into my area. Well, I'm not surprised. I do have some, shall we say, interesting personal problems that have been forced upon me." The general knew how to play the old CYA, cover your ass, game.

"Not quite, sir. One of the ring's agents has recruited a sixteen-year-old Irish girl to establish a liaison with an American colonel stationed at Headquarters USAFE in Ramstein, Germany. Apparently his duties bring him here quite often." The man snapped open his briefcase and laid a stack of glossy black-and-white photos on Blevins' desk. "We did not take these; they did." The photos chronicled the development of a love affair, the last four prints leaving no doubt about the intimacy of the affair. "Very professional, wouldn't you say?"

"Yes . . . well, this colonel has been passing classified information to the girl?"

"No. Not yet. We want to leave the girl in place and watch her. However, we want the colonel out of the way. He is in charge of the Inspector General's Operational Readiness Inspection team, the ORI, I believe you call it, and is really quite small cheese." The agent did not tell Blevins that MI-5 wanted to feed misinformation through the girl to the Soviets, and for that they needed the girl's talents to be directed elsewhere. "Really," the agent concluded, "at this point the affair is quite harmless, other than the girl's young age, of course."

"Of course, we shall discipline the colonel and end the affair," Blevins said.

The agent gave an inward sigh. "Not discipline, that would be unwise. We simply want you to use your offices to tell the colonel to end the affair. If the colonel is, as you say, disciplined, then it will be obvious that we are onto the girl. This must be done discreetly, appear altogether natural."

"Certainly, of course. We will be glad to cooperate with Her Majesty's government."

The agent then handed the general a card with the colonel's name; then, without shaking hands or saluting, left the office.

The plan did not immediately jell for Blevins. But a chance remark the next day that the 45th was due for an Operational Readiness Inspection set his mental processes to grinding . . . He told his new secretary to book him a seat on the next plane to Ramstein, preferably that day. He was *finally* going to teach Waters that his way of running the Air Force was the only way. And, he calculated, do the Air Force a favor in the process. Which, of course, had always been his mission. It was just that some idiots and malcontents didn't understand . . .

* * *

Doc Landis' cadence was perfect as he called off the decreasing altitude coming down the chute. The sight picture was also perfect as Doc sang out "Pickle." Jack instantly flicked the pickle button, releasing a practice bomb onto the target, then honked back on the stick, loading the F-4 with four G's in two seconds for a smooth pullout. He was looking for the other Phantom when the first blink of the master caution light caught his attention. He promptly broke out of the pattern, checked his warning lights, keyed his radio and told the range controller and wingman about his problem: "Holbeach Range, Toddy Four-One. My Utility Hydraulic System has failed. RTB at this time. Toddy Four-Two, join up and let's go home." The range controller and wingman, Toddy Four-Two, acknowledged his call as Jack headed for Stonewood.

The wingy slid into position on Jack's left side as they passed by Blakeney Point, scanned his underside and told Jack that he could see hydraulic fluid streaming down the belly of the Phantom.

"Roger," Jack acknowledged, "we'll take the barrier." Doc Landis started to read the emergency checklist for hydraulic failure when the low oil pressure light came on for number two engine. Before Jack could shut the engine down the oil pressure had fallen to zero, indicating an internal failure in his right engine.

Landis continued to read the checklist as Jack reviewed each step. "Isn't this the emergency the flight manual says to consider ejection for?" Landis asked, trying to keep his voice calm; this was no damn appendectomy.

"It is," Jack answered. "We've lost most of our control surfaces. The right wing is dead. It's easy to run out of lateral control authority. If that happens the only choice we've got is to lower the nose and reduce power to recover. That can be hard cheese close to the ground. How do you feel about it? Want to try an approach?"

"One ejection per lifetime is more than enough," the doctor muttered. "Let's do it."

Jack radioed the tower and declared an emergency as he positioned the Phantom to the west of the base for a straight-in approach.

"Toddy Four-One, Tower," Stonewood tower radioed the wingman. "The DO says to consider ejection. He says he's got lots of Phantoms, only one you."

"Tell him thanks but I think that I'll give this bird back to him."

Waters had joined Tom Gomez in the DO's pickup truck and they now followed the crash trucks out to the approach end of the runway, listening to the radio calls on the truck's UHF radio. They watched in silence as the disabled Phantom intercepted the glide slope and started to descend. "I think I'd rather eject," Waters said. "But it's Jack's decision."

Gomez nodded, well aware that neither he nor Waters would stay in command if the 45th lost another bird.

As the Phantom passed through two hundred feet they saw it begin to yaw to the right, but Jack brought the nose down and gained enough control to continue the approach. "He won't have enough altitude to do that again," Waters said, trying to sound calmer than he felt.

Gradually Jack reduced power to 200 knots, then touched down four hundred feet short of the barrier. The Phantom's hook caught the cable and snatched the big bird to a halt in the middle of the runway.

Waters grinned. "He makes it look routine. Your boy did good, Tom."

"Good enough. He survived. Name of the game, I guess."

Doc Landis' wife pressed against his shoulder and glanced at the clock on the night stand. He started to caress her. His wife had never stopped being a sex object to him, thank God, and the feeling was mutual. "Doctor Landis," she murmured, "you better stop that or we won't get any sleep and you've had a rough day . . . you're a real goat, you know that? . . ."

He ignored her and kissed her neck, causing her breath to come faster.

"Jeff, stop it or I'll be as pregnant as Sara Waters. No wonder this place has such a booming birthrate, it overstimulates you men. No more flying for you on Mondays." And so saying, she returned his kisses, thankful to have her husband safely home, and more than willing to show it.

A team from the Inspector General's office at Ramstein, Germany, had managed to hit the 45th with a surprise Operational Readiness

Inspection, totally disrupting the base. Every one of Chief Pullman's contacts had fallen through and all the markers he had called in as due had misfired. The entire network of first shirts had let Pullman down. He would even some scores in the future. But in the meantime . . .

Five staff cars had driven on base and dispersed to pre-determined locations, one group to the command post as a simulated terrorist bomb exploded in a maintenance shop, creating a mass-casualty exercise. The inspectors at the hospital, in Maintenance and Security Police, all tight-faced, noted the reaction of the participants, taking endless notes and photographs. The order directing the wing to load its aircraft for wartime missions came at 1:00 p.m. and the wing had to load live ordnance on its F-4s. Munitions safety was of paramount concern for the inspectors as the wing entered into its next major event. The inspectors noted a munitions NCO had to borrow a checklist.

After listening to reports from his team that night, the IG's team chief, Colonel Peter Gertino, placed a call to Waters, telling the wing commander only that he would like to meet with him. He found Pullman in the office with Waters and Gomez and quickly proceeded to summarize the inspection. "Your Security Police were rated unsatisfactory. The command post was rated unsatisfactory. Your loadout would have been outstanding except for the improper use of checklists; consequently my inspectors rated that event as marginal. The mass-casualty exercise was satisfactory. In sum, not a good beginning, Colonel Waters. Your people can still salvage this inspection, but they are going to have to work for it." He picked up his notes and left the office.

"It's a setup," Pullman snapped. The chief was fully aware of how the IG system worked and the way personalities at the command level could predetermine the result of an ORI. "We've sure as hell pissed someone off at Ramstein," he declared as he headed out the door to find Chief Walt Chambers.

"Walt," Pullman said, catching up with the IG NCO, "why rate the command post's performance as unsatisfactory?"

Chambers stared at the ground, would not answer.

"A no-win game," Pullman snapped. "They were meant to bust no matter what they did. You call that integrity? What gives?"

"Look, Pullman, I play with the big boys and I do what I'm told—"

"Yeah, well, you produce evidence that the controller committed a security breach, or change the rating."

"And if I don't?"

"Then you can be sure of three things the next time you see me: in thirty seconds I'll rip your heart out, kill your dog and rape your wife. Bet on it, sweetheart."

The next day as the IG team initiated a second mass-casualty exercise, Waters sat in the Command Post monitoring the radios as the exercise went down. Barely controlling his temper, he walked out, asking Gomez and Pullman to join him. Outside, he made sure no inspectors were around, then: "Chief, you're right. This *is* a setup. Any ideas why?"

Pullman and Gomez shook their heads.

"Cover for me. I'm going to play their game," Waters said, and walked off to his staff car.

Colonel Gertino was puzzled by the message requesting he see the RAF post commander and decided to ignore it. An hour later he received a phone call asking when he would be in Sir David's office. Again, he chose to ignore it. Ten minutes later a British NCO approached him, quietly spoke a few words and escorted Gertino to RAF base commander Childs' office.

"What's this crap about *arresting* me?"

Childs tossed a thin document at the American colonel. "It is obvious that you have not read the Technical Agreement on RAF Stonewood. Please do so now."

"This doesn't apply to an IG team—"

"Wrong. Read page twelve." Gertino found the passage, which stated that all wartime and inspection exercises would be in accordance with British and NATO rules and coordinated through the RAF. "You will conduct the remainder of this exercise under the rules of a NATO Tactical Evaluation and not those of your ORI or I will have you and your entire team declared *persona non grata* in the United Kingdom."

"But you and NATO are only concerned with flying and base defense. We measure other items, like munitions safety and use of checklists—"

"I won't repeat myself. Of course, you may launch all the sorties you wish and you may measure the wing's reaction to an air attack or intruders as often as you wish."

"An air attack is planned for this afternoon," Gertino mumbled.

"And how many aircraft can I expect to overfly my base?"

"None," the colonel replied. "We simulate it."

"Interesting, Colonel . . . no aircraft, no air attack. Well, then, please finish your inspection by Wednesday." Gertino was dismissed and left. Childs dialed Waters' number. "Muddy, I think you can expect a rather more fair evaluation now."

He was wrong . . .

Actually, Gertino had been in a near panic when he first tried to figure out just what Blevins really wanted. The general had not openly tied the 45th's failing an ORI to his silence about his girlfriend, still . . . the colonel cursed himself for ever becoming involved with the girl in the first place. He shook his head, still not able to believe she was only sixteen—or a foreign agent. The girl looked at least twenty and didn't seem to have a brain. But Blevins had promised him the affair would be handled very discreetly if he "acted responsibly" when he conducted Stonewood's ORI. It wasn't hard to put two and two together, especially after Blevins went on openly to knock Waters. The problem, though, was the wing was in good shape. In fact, when the inspection was completed Wednesday, by every measure that NATO used to evaluate exercises, the wing had passed. Gertino solved his problem of needing to fail the wing by directing his team to write *two* reports, one using NATO's standards, one using the IG's.

That night the team put a message on the wires announcing the 45th had failed their ORI and that a full IG report with supporting details would be published in a week. The message did not mention that there was a NATO Tac Eval report with different results.

* * *

The "Flash" message reached Stonewood late Thursday night, six minutes after it was given to the Pentagon's communication center for transmission. The message consisted of one line: Colonel Anthony Waters was to report to Colonel Richard Stevens in the Pentagon no later than 0800 hours local time Saturday.

Sara had wanted to come with him, but Waters told her he had to do this one alone. Friday morning she helped him pack and rode with him in Tom Gomez's car to Mildenhall. Gomez could not hide his concern. "There's no way Cunningham is going to buy the IG's report," he predicted, "not after he sees the NATO report."

"He's got to reconcile two different sets of standards," Waters said gloomily. "The IG's and NATO's."

"Muddy, the IG was on a damn witch-hunt—"

"Sure, but Cunningham doesn't *know* that. And that's what I've got to convince him of . . ."

When it was time to board the waiting C-5B, Sara placed her husband's hand on her stomach and looked seriously at him. "Remember that old one about keeping your priorities straight. This here is *numero uno.*" She kissed him quickly and walked off, hoping he'd gotten the message.

After takeoff, Waters opened his briefcase and reread the two reports that Pullman had back-doored for him. He tried to look at them from Cunningham's perspective, gave up and tried to sleep.

Memories kept stirring through him . . . of his first wife and his daughter Jennifer . . . hurt and loneliness . . . More images . . . He tried to pinpoint when his desire to become a wing commander had crystallized but couldn't . . . Other images raced through his consciousness leading him to Sara, and then when he assumed command of the 45th. A new awareness enveloped—*this* was what he was supposed to be, to do. But he could not do it alone. Sara made it possible, with her love, and understanding. And his allies—Childs, Gomez, Bull, C.J., Pullman . . . He also had a legacy to leave—Bill Carroll and Jack Locke. Damn it, he would make Cunningham understand. Or literally go down trying.

24 June: 2340 hours, Greenwich Mean Time
25 June: 0310 hours, Qom, Iran

The old man shuffled slowly through the seminary's main gate. His two bodyguards followed him, sleepy from being roused before three o'clock in the morning. The streets of Qom, the religious center of the Islamic faith in Iran, were deserted and poorly lit, not like the bustling thoroughfares of Tehran seventy-five miles to the northeast. The two young bodyguards became alert as the old Ayatollah made his way to the central mosque less than a hundred yards from the gate.

"Have you heard anything?" the taller of the two asked.

"Nothing. But his Holiness"—he nodded toward the Ayatollah Araki in front of them—"is very worried. That is why he is going to the mosque for the first prayers of the morning. Perhaps his devotion will move Allah to be compassionate."

Normally Araki made the first two prayers of the day in the privacy of his room. But the two men did not complain and pulled their robes tightly around them to fend off the cold of the early morning. The mullah who would call the faithful to prayer that morning opened the huge door of the mosque for the Ayatollah and bowed his head as the old man entered. The two bodyguards stopped at the back of the deserted open area in the heart of the mosque and knelt.

Araki followed the mullah to the front and knelt on a worn prayer rug that had been laid out for him. Slowly and with a conviction that had not grown dull from years of repetition, he repeated the *Shahada.* "God is most great. God is most great. I testify here there is no other God than Allah, and Muhammad is his prophet." The words were to purify his soul and renew his hope that the most holy of men, the Ayatollah Khomeini, still lived.

In less than five minutes he was finished and slowly rose from the prayer rug. He could see his two guards on the floor but there was something wrong—they were not praying, but were sprawled out, dead still . . . Vague shadows moved around the walls of the mosque. He knew what was coming and stood as straight as his arthritis would allow. The years of teaching students *erfan* would serve him well. He watched one of the restless shadows detach itself from the wall and walk briskly toward him. *Erfan,* the trait of having character and courage in adversity, and knowing that emancipation came only from spiritual truth. He believed what he had taught his students.

The shadow materialized into the shape of a young man dressed in camouflage fatigues. He was not devout. That was apparent in his athletic gait as he crossed the tiled floor.

"The Ayatollah no longer lives?" But Araki knew the answer even as he asked.

The man said nothing as he strode up to the rigid Ayatollah Araki, raised a pistol in his right hand, pulled the trigger, blowing the old man's brains out.

25 June: 0045 hours, Greenwich Mean Time
0415 hours, Kerman, Iran

The room in the Citadel of Kerman was silent as the radio operator worked the deciphering mode of the Russian-made Urgo S-21 transmitter. The Russian adviser was proud of his student for mastering the complexities of the field radio. The young Iranian had no trouble programming the radio for optimum contact with six different locations throughout Iran. His fingers had moved swiftly over the control pad, punching in the right numbers when he needed to shift frequencies to establish contact with Ashkhabad. "The Urgo is a masterpiece," the adviser told the operator, "but it takes an artist to make it work."

An occasional gust of wind came roaring off the central plateau of Iran to batter at the windows of the room, sending swirls of dust across the floor. The adviser hoped the weather stripping on the Urgo's case had not cracked. Poor quality control was a problem with the radio.

"Araki is dead," the radio operator finally announced.

Every head in the room turned toward the man sitting in the corner, waiting for his next command. Apparently, he was asleep.

"The cell leader in Qom reports that Araki died quickly," the radio operator said, continuing to decode the latest transmission.

The sleeping man's eyes snapped open. "Then it was merciful." The commander's gaze took in the room. "Is the list complete?"

One of the standing men nodded in answer.

"Then the Guardianship Council exists no more. There is no one for the masses to follow. Iran is without leadership. We will fill that void." He motioned to the Russian adviser. "In a few hours we will control the roads, and the convoys you have promised can move without interference. Send the messages to start them south."

The Russian tapped the radio operator on the shoulder and moved into his chair. He typed a short message on the keyboard and pressed the encryption button. When a blue light came on he keyed up the Ashkhabad frequency and hit the transmit button. "Done," he told the commander.

The commander of the People's Soldiers of Islam (PSI), the name the Tudeh had given to their army, stood and walked out into the Citadel's quadrangle. He stared at the clouds scudding across the early morning sky and climbed the stone stairs of the wall. His aide hurried after him with a great coat and threw it over his shoulders as he continued up the steps. At the top, the commander surveyed the small city spread out before him. "We will use the Russians," he said. "And in the end, we will be the masters of our country. We will be the servant of no man. It is the time of our jihad."

25 June: 0440 hours, Greenwich Mean Time
0740 hours, Moscow, USSR

The black Mercedes sedan hurtled down the center of Granovsky Street less than four blocks away from the Kremlin. A policeman had not gotten the word over his radio that a VIP was inbound to Borovitsky Gate and frantically waved traffic and pedestrians to the curb when he caught sight of the speeding car. He breathed a sigh of relief when the car shot past him and he saw the license plate with its distinctive MOC number. Someone very big was in a hurry. The foreign chauffeured car and license plates were a warning that he would not have enjoyed another Moscow night if an accident had happened at his corner. Since the gray curtains of the limousine were drawn, he had no idea who was in the car.

The barrier at Borovitsky Gate was up and the guard waved the Mercedes into the Kremlin. Comrade Viktor Rokossovsky had made the four-hundred-mile flight from Leningrad and the long drive from

Vnukovo II airport in time for the unscheduled Politburo meeting called by the General Secretary.

The Tartar who served as the General Secretary's bodyguard told the General Secretary when the Mercedes arrived so that he could time the walk from his office and enter the conference room immediately after Rokossovsky, denying Ulyanoff the opportunity to speak to the late arrival. The General Secretary stood behind his chair at the head of the table. "Thank you, Comrade Rokossovsky, for making such a quick return. Your presence is always to our advantage."

You fox, Ulyanoff thought. Rokossovsky makes it back in time from visiting his blonde mistress and you try to turn it to your advantage with a compliment. It puzzled Ulyanoff how Rokossovsky had gotten the word about the meeting. The Politburo's staff had not been able to locate his errant supporter. Lately, wisps of doubt about Viktor had been bothering Ulyanoff. Still, it made no difference. With Rokossovsky present, he could force a showdown with the General Secretary over Iran. He calculated he would be sitting at the head of the table in less than three days.

The General Secretary sat down and looked directly at Kalin-Tegov. "Developments in Iran are swinging in our favor. The Ayatollah is dead and the Guardianship Council has been eliminated. Our brothers in the Tudeh Party have taken control of the governing structure in Tehran but their political position is far from secure. The Tudeh are also moving their forces into position to block any renewed military adventurism by Iraq across the Shatt-al-Arab. Needless to say, the situation is very fragile. The Tudeh has asked for our help."

"We don't need to get involved in another Afghanistan," Ulyanoff grumbled. "But that was before your time, you wouldn't know."

"But a different situation," Kalin-Tegov said. "Perhaps if we are not directly involved . . ." He deliberately let his words trail off.

Ulyanoff's heavy eyebrows knitted together as he tried to judge the direction Kalin-Tegov was taking. His support was critical if the General Secretary was to be removed.

"Exploit the situation now," Rokossovsky said.

Ulyanoff almost twisted out of his chair. All doubt about Rokossovsky evaporated—he had joined the General Secretary. Only Kalin-Tegov stood between him and defeat. "We must proceed on the course we have taken," Ulyanoff urged. "The revitalization of our economy is most urgent and our armed forces need to be restructed. The damages of Afghanistan must be corrected—"

"We are not talking about a major deviation from our policies, Comrade Ulyanoff," the General Secretary said, "only how to turn this situation to our advantage."

"Is it to our advantage to engage in a misguided venture that could ignite World War Three?" Ulyanoff said.

"As Comrade Kalin-Tegov says, if we are not directly involved," the General Secretary pressed.

"But you have involved us," Ulyanoff shouted. "The buildup of material at Ashkhabad, the shipment of supplies into Iran, and now you have ordered trucks to start moving out of Ashkhabad. That is direct involvement without the consent of the Politburo—"

"The trucks have not yet crossed the border," the General Secretary said, acknowledging the accuracy of Ulyanoff's intelligence. "They can be recalled . . . And they only carry what has been promised the Tudeh. The question before us is, should we honor the request of the Tudeh for more aid? I believe we should."

A murmur of assent went around the table. Kalin-Tegov nodded in agreement. The lack of further discussion was the Politburo's way of voting on the issue. The General Secretary's position had been approved.

"I believe my office should direct the aid into Iran," the General Secretary said.

Ulyanoff started to protest that as head of the Defense Council he had that responsibility, but another round of agreement swept the table.

"Comrade Rokossovsky," the General Secretary said, "as a member of the Defense Council, I want you to work on this problem."

The young man quickly nodded as the General Secretary stood, thanked the group and left the room.

Ulyanoff sat in his chair, sick at the rapid, unwelcome turn of events. He had suffered a major policy defeat. Too many members of the Politburo had deserted him. His maneuvering for ultimate power was stopped dead. He had been displaced by a younger generation. He glared at Rokossovsky. "Who told you about this meeting?"

"The Comrade General Secretary, of course."

He got to his feet and walked slowly to the door. Kalin-Tegov joined him in the corridor and gently placed his hand on Ulyanoff's shoulder. "Your dacha is a fine home for raising great-grandchildren," he said.

And the Tartar was standing in the hall, smiling at him.

25 June: 1155 hours, Greenwich Mean Time
0755 hours, Washington, D.C.

Stevens nodded at Waters and motioned him to a chair in Cunningham's outer office. Muddy fought to control his emotions, found some comfort by calculating how many colonels had sat in the same office cooling their heels, waiting for bad news. I'll probably be here most of the morning, he thought, while Sundown lets the tension build . . . Two minutes later Stevens escorted him to the general and remained standing near the door.

Cunningham looked up from his desk. *"Why?"*

"The IG team concentrated on procedures and not results, sir."

"And what were the results?"

"What we did is in the NATO Tactical Evaluation report the team wrote. My wing failed the ORI based on procedural criteria the IG has developed, and that's the basis of the message they sent out—"

" . . . I didn't know the team also conducted a Tac Eval . . ."

Waters felt a twinge of hope. Cunningham had lived with the two-tiered inspection system in NATO for years. But he had had serious misgivings about using NATO procedures to inspect his Air Force. He found the system acceptable only as long as ORIs were conducted separately because of the different rules and procedures.

"What were the results of the Tac Eval?"

"We did well, sir. The details speak for themselves—"

"Two things confuse me. Why did the IG conduct the two inspections together, and how do you know the results and details when I don't?"

Waters decided to be totally open with the man. "Sir, the inspection started as an ORI but the Technical Agreement with the RAF calls for a NATO Tac Eval. When it became obvious the investigation team was not aware of the agreement I requested that Group Commander Childs straighten out Colonel Gertino, the team chief. My first sergeant back-doored copies of the reports from the typists."

"Pullman at work, I gather."

Waters was astonished the general knew his first shirt.

"Okay, now I've got two sets of results. One based on my system, the other on NATO's. That sucks, Waters. The IG team is telling me that your wing is not ready, and I have to believe them."

The doubt that Waters had been hoping to build on was gone. "General, please read the two reports before you make up your mind. The examples the team uses are the only ones they could find. Six months ago you sent me to get the wing ready to deploy into the Gulf. We *are* ready. It's true, we've done things differently. But that's because we didn't have time to—" Waters stopped when he heard the excuses in his own voice.

Cunningham made a short, choppy motion toward the door with his left hand, signaling the interview was at an end, and that Muddy Waters had lost his wing.

Waters fought down the bile in his throat, saluted and left. Cunningham stared at the open door, then said to Stevens, "Get a list from Third Air Force of possibles for a new wing commander for the 45th . . . hurry up, but no rush."

As Stevens closed the door behind him he heard a crash from inside the office that sounded like something large being thrown across the room.

Cunningham's unhappiness about what had happened to Waters was put in a shadow by the ominous intelligence reports out of the Persian Gulf. Long experience had taught him not to ignore his forebodings, especially those based in experience and educated speculation. He left home early Sunday morning for work, telling Ruth he wouldn't be long. The halls of the Pentagon were their usual early Sunday morning quiet as he went directly to the Watch Center. Sergeant Nesbit saw him walk onto the main floor and warned the on-duty watch commander that he was about to have a guest.

Cunningham walked into the battle cab, disregarded the two men and sat down at the center console, staring at the big situation boards. He asked the colonel to call up the Persian Gulf display and sat puzzling out the likely intentions behind the newly emerging force dispositions. Taken individually, they did not appear so ominous, but together . . . "Get some analysts up here," he ordered.

Don Williamson was on duty, responded to the buzz from the cab and hurried up the stairs with his new assistant. The general motioned the two analysts to sit next to him and began to talk in a low voice. "What's the Tudeh doing around the southern edge of the Plateau of Iran?"

"Our latest reports," Williamson said, "indicate that they're organizing around Kerman and are holding the bridges as tax collection points."

"Which means they're controlling the bridges."

Williamson nodded.

"Okay, find out the latest status of the Ayatollah and update supply movements in both Iran and Russia. I want to see the latest Iranian order of battle. Include what the Russians have given the Tudeh with the Iranian armed forces."

After the analysts left, Cunningham directed, "Get my aide up here and recall the battle staff."

The two analysts returned to the cab forty-five minutes later. Stevens and the three generals who made up the Watch Center's battle staff were also on hand. Williamson keyed up the center board, displaying an entirely new disposition of forces inside Iran.

"The Ayatollah's current status?" the General demanded.

"Uncertain, sir. Either very ill, dead or his power base is slipping. The Iranian Communist Party, the Tudeh, are moving to gain control of the country and have requested help from volunteers who believe in their version of Marxist Islam. We're monitoring a massive movement of Farsi-speaking Shiite Muslims from Turkmen in the Soviet Union and Afghanistan into Iran. They're calling themselves the People's Soldiers of Islam, the PSI for short, sir. Radio broadcasts from Teheran indicate the Iranians see this as a chance to win out for good over Iraq."

"Goddamn, it's happening." Cunningham sighed. Bill Carroll's scenario was starting to unfold. "Shit's going to hit the fan in the Persian Gulf, no question. The Iranians have over a hundred fighters now, mostly MiG-23s, and are moving a quarter-million men into position to attack Basra." His electronic pointer flashed on the map around the head of the Persian Gulf, outlining the Iraqi city on the border between Iran and Iraq. His mind was racing now . . . "The Russians have given them enough supplies to crack Basra wide open. If that happens the Iranians will have a clear path into the oil fields of Iraq, Kuwait and the Arabian Peninsula. We damn well can't let Basra fall.

"Also, the Soviets are stockpiling supplies in Turkmen just north of the Iranian border. If those supplies reach the Iranians it'll double or triple their capability and give them the strength they need to exploit a breakthrough at Basra. *Gentlemen, we cannot let those supplies reach them.*"

The general's pointer moved down the map to the Strait of Hormuz at the southern end of the Persian Gulf. "At least there's no buildup at the Strait opposite Muscat and Oman. But we can't let the Iranians position troops and amphibious forces that can cross the Strait and attack Saudi Arabia through Muscat and Oman. We've *got* to keep the Strait of Hormuz open. Okay, here are our four major objectives if we're to win this thing. First, we provide the Arab military alliance, the—"

For a moment Cunningham drew a blank, could not remember the name of the United Arab Command; he closed his eyes, forced himself to relax, and the name flashed out of his memory banks . . . You're getting old, you old fart, forgetting stuff simple as that . . . "The UAC, the United Arab Command, we give them the supplies they need to hold the line at Basra. Second, we get the Rapid Deployment Force or the 45th into the Gulf to hit at the troop and supply buildup in front of Basra to take the pressure off the UAC, and they've got to keep at it until they get the job done. If any of those supplies in Turkmen move south into Iran, we hit them. Third, we strike at any military buildup at the Strait of Hormuz, prevent a flanking attack across the Strait into the Arabian Peninsula. Fourth, the Navy keeps the Strait of Hormuz open."

Cunningham was rolling now . . . "We haven't got a bunch of time.

Get all this into an intelligence summary, send it to Navy, Army, and the 45th. Activate the War Room, Nesbit. Joint Chiefs of Staff only. Order the 45th at Stonewood to go standby for deployment."

As Cunningham stomped down the stairs, the watch commander turned to Williamson. "How did he see all that before we did?"

The analyst shrugged. "I would say it's because he's a general and we're not. Truth to tell, the old son of a bitch has always acted sort of nuts to cover his smarts. I'm glad he's on our side."

26 June: 1408 hours, Greenwich Mean Time
1508 hours, Stonewood, England

The guards at Stonewood's gate were carefully checking each car onto the base. Jack noticed the gate guards were doubled and armed with revolvers and M-16s. When he saw them turn two dependents away he knew that the recall was not a practice. One guard stopped him and methodically checked his ID. "The base is sealed, Lieutenant. You won't be allowed off until everyone has reported for duty and the recall is terminated."

The squadron was in a turmoil of organized activity. The big portable mobility bins were being packed and Bull Morgan was strangely subdued. He pulled Jack aside. "This looks like for real. The boss has been at the command post for over an hour and the base is sealed up tighter than an old maid's snatch. Minimum communications went into effect an hour ago, no outside phone calls except through the command post. Be back here packed and ready to move at six tomorrow morning."

Chief Pullman did not have to raise his voice as he called the auditorium to attention when Waters walked in. "Seats, please," Waters said as he took the stage. He looked at the packed theater. "Ladies and gentlemen," he began, wondering if this was the last time he'd address the 45th Tactical Fighter Wing before Cunningham relieved him, "we're on hold, waiting for a launch order to deploy to the Middle East. We're not the only unit on alert, and the President hasn't yet decided who will be sent into the Persian Gulf . . . From here on, everything I say is classified secret. If we launch, our destination will be Ras Assanya, an air base located on the Gulf. The transports will launch two hours before the fighters and one-hop it to our destination. Their job is to get the ground crews in place to receive the fighters. We will launch the fighters in flights of twelve, twenty-minute intervals between flights. Each flight will rendezvous with two tankers and go chicks-in-trail. I will lead the first flight from the 377th.

"When we recover at Ras Assanya, expect confusion, because we're going in there fast. But I want the birds immediately turned for combat sorties. Load out the first four birds for air-to-air and place them on air-defense alert, even if that means the crews have to sit under the wings. Load the rest out for air-to-ground. Get your squadrons organized and be ready for whatever. I'm told there are quarters and messing facilities available but have no idea as to their quality or condition. Be flexible, stay loose."

RAF Stonewood was normally an immoderately noisy place, resounding with activity. Now an unusual calm and quiet descended on the base as the last of the transports were loaded and the last F-4 towed into the launch lineup on the ramp, a freshly painted star still moist from its latest coat of paint. Muddy Waters stood with Jack in front of the squadron after the pilot returned from pre-flighting his aircraft, tail number 512, and like the rest of the wing, he waited . . .

III

THE WAR

28 June: 1340 hours, Greenwich Mean Time
1640 hours, Ras Assanya, Saudi Arabia

The last of Waters' flight came off the tankers while they were still over the Gulf of Suez in route to their base at Ras Assanya. Tanker lead had wished them luck, checked out and turned his flight of two KC-135s toward their recovery base in Italy, leaving them on their own. After calling for a fuel check, Waters broke his flight of twelve Phantoms into three flights of four, ordering them to take four-minute spacing between each flight. "Make it an overhead recovery, circling to land," he radioed to his flight leads.

He anticipated a message to be waiting when he landed, relieving him of his command. I probably just made my last decision, he thought. The colonel turned his flight eastward, heading across the Arabian Peninsula. How easy it all seemed, he thought. So simple. Twelve months ago he had been the module commander of a reccy RC-135 orbiting over the Mediterranean and contemplating retirement. Now he was married, about to become a father and leading the last attack wing of F-4s into what looked like a real shooting match. Things happened fast, he thought. Well, at least he'd had the six months Cunningham had promised him to get his wing combat ready. And the wing *was* ready, damn it, regardless of what the general believed and what the ORI said . . .

Bill Carroll was waiting in a pickup truck when Waters shut down his engines. The wing commander had never seen the Intel officer so agitated in the two years he had known the young man. Bill's got the job of giving me the bad news or taking it to me, he told himself. He clambered down the side of the fuselage, determined at least to show his wing how to meet serious personal adversity, which, he calculated, would be his last lesson for them. Carroll held the door open for him and rushed around to the driver's side. Before starting the engine, he blurted his news.

"We've got our first frag order."

Waters stared at him in disbelief, feeling like a condemned man getting a stay of execution. A *frag* order—the operational message sending fighter aircraft into combat, detailing the missions the aircraft would fly, identifying specific targets, time over target, call signs and ordnance. Now here it was . . .

The Intel officer told him that the 45th was ordered to attack a supply dump at Bandar seventy-five miles east of Basra and a troop concentration at Ramshir twenty-five miles northeast of the supply dump. "Sir, we don't have reccy photos, no threat estimates, *nothing*. They want us to hit ASAP but no later than tomorrow morning."

"Bill, it fits with the Intelligence Summary we got from the Watch Center. Those troops are probably headed to the dump for resupply. From there they'll move up and attack Basra." He fought down a feeling of exultation and concentrated on how to use his one chance to lead his wing into combat . . .

The COIC, Combined Operations Intelligence Center, was in disarray when Waters and Carroll came in. Waters was ready with his first orders: "I need three runners." Carroll pointed out three sergeants. "Find Maintenance, the 377th and the 378th. Tell them to send a liaison officer or NCO here with a radio to relay orders. Go." The three sergeants ran out of the room. "Bill, have your troops find the charts, plotters, markers, whatever the crews are going to need to plan the attacks. Get a weatherman up here, show me the targets on a map—and the frag order."

Chief Master Sergeant George Gonzaga from Maintenance hurried into the room three steps ahead of C.J. and the two squadron commanders. "George," Waters said, "turn the first two squadrons for an air-to-ground mission. Load the 377th's birds with Mark-82s, the 378th's with CBUs, the Weasels with Shrikes."

While Maintenance downloaded the centerline fuel tanks, refueled the birds and uploaded the ordnance Waters had ordered, the men clustered around the map and studied their targets. Bull Morgan lumbered into the room with the weatherman in his wake. Rapidly Waters explained the situation: "I want to hit these two targets ASAP, but we are dealing with a lot of unknowns. Brief your crews to attack the targets like we did Woensdrecht. Here's where our practice runs can pay off. The 377th will go against the supply dump at Bandar with Mark-82s, the 378th will attack the troop concentration at Ramshir with CBUs."

Chief Gongzaga stuck his head in the door. "The first four birds are loaded out for air-to-air like you said at Stonewood, the crews are standing by. We can launch them using the radio in Maintenance Control's van or reload them with Mark-82s." Waters could have kissed the man for not forgetting and becoming confused. He needed the four jets for a Base CAP, a Combat Air Patrol flying a protective umbrella over the base.

"Good. Have Maintenance Control launch the first two into a Base CAP. Tell them to set up a radar search pattern. I don't want any uninvited guests to overfly the base right now." Gonzaga took off to relay the message on his brick. Within minutes they heard the two aircraft take off while two airmen from Communications hooked up three UHF radios in the COIC.

"There are two major differences on this attack," Waters said. "First, we don't need tanker support. The supply dump at Bandar is one hundred and thirty nautical miles away; the troop concentration at Ramshir is one hundred and fifty-five. Both are within low-level range. Brief to ingress at low level and to recover at high level after coasting out, threats permitting. Second, we don't know what the threats are around those targets. So expect a normal Soviet defense array of SAMs and Triple A."

Waters turned to the weatherman, a major. "What's the weather doing?" The major was ready. The weather was clear and would remain so, and the moon was almost full and would be up at 2010 that evening. "Okay, gentlemen," Waters said, looking at the group, "you know what your men can hack better than me and you know the three times we can attack—now, during the night or in the morning. Ideas?"

The group was unanimous they should try for a launch in one hour while surprise was still on their side, and hit the targets just before evening twilight obscured the ground. The men hurried out to make it happen.

Outside, Chief Gonzaga reported to Waters that eighteen birds were loaded, four more would be in five minutes. "Major Conlan has checked in on status, ready to launch," the Chief added. Waters was impressed by the fast response of his wing.

"Okay, Chief, level with me. How are you getting the birds turned so fast? You're taking a short cut. What is it?"

A smile split Gonzaga's brown face. "We're downloading the centerline tanks, then uploading the munitions while we refuel. About half the bunkers have refueling points in them so we don't need to use refueling trucks." Waters said something about uploading munitions and refueling at the same time being dangerous. "Colonel, we're using Israeli wartime procedures. We figured if they can make it work so can we. Of course, the Air Force wouldn't approve since it wasn't their idea."

Bill Carroll joined them as they listened to the first of the Phantoms crank their engines. "Colonel"—Carroll had to yell to be heard above the crescendoing noise—"we've got sixty-seven birds in from Stonewood. There are five stragglers that Lieutenant Locke will bring in tomorrow."

C.J. was the first to take off and never lifted above two hundred feet as he led his wingmen north over the Gulf toward their target, the troop concentration at Ramshir. The 378th was launching first since they had to penetrate the deepest to reach their target. C.J. kept scanning the sky, looking for hostile aircraft that might try to intercept them. Since they were flying without a CAP, they would have to jettison their loads and fight their way home. Stan's constant flow of "no activity, weak search radar, no sector searches, no activity, nothing" was nice to hear . . . Fifteen minutes after takeoff he coasted in over the point of land they had selected as the split-point for the two arms of their attack on to Ramshir. They were feet dry and in bad-guy land—Iran.

He lifted his bird to eight hundred feet to insure that the string of aircraft stretching behind him to Ras Assanya would hear his transmission. "It's a go on Hot Dog," he transmitted, committing the 45th to battle. Unless they were jumped by MiGs, the attack would continue. He dropped his bird back on the deck.

"They got us with a search-radar and tried to interrogate our IFF," Stan now reported. "Lost us now, but someone is very good on that end."

C.J. thought, We're seven minutes out. He pushed the throttles up, touching 540 knots and descended to one hundred feet. Sweat poured down his face. "Thirteen miles south of Ramshir," he told Stan as he lifted his bird to eight hundred feet and started to circle the target, challenging the SAMs and Triple A to come active, to turn their radars on. Nothing. He continued his arc, visually acquiring the target. "Goddamn, look at that!" He was circling a mass of people running for trucks and buildings. He did not see a single slit-trench or bunker.

Stan twisted his head away from the bank of scopes and radar warning gear in front of him, surveyed the target, grunted and went back to work. "Arm 'em up," he said, reminding C.J. to make sure the AGM-45 anti-radiation Shrike missiles were ready for employment. "I've got a load on an SA-6," he yelled, happy at last. One of the fifty-two antennas the Wild Weasel sported had detected an operator turning on the radar in the control van of a surface-to-air missile battery in preparation for a launch. "Follow the bug," he told C.J.

The pilot turned the nose of the Phantom toward the threat and centered the target symbol of his head-up display. When the plan position indicator showed he was in range, he mashed the trigger on his stick. The missile leaped off the missile rail on the left pylon and homed on the signal it was receiving from the SAM site. The radar van of the SAM disappeared in a puff of smoke and flame. "How do you say piss off in Farsi?" Stan muttered.

C.J. zoomed up to eight thousand feet, still looking for MiGs. Stan reassured him the RHAW gear was quiet. The pilot watched as the first cell of twelve aircraft approached the troop-staging area from the west on a laydown run with the CBUs. They came off the target as sporadic tracers in the fading light indicated someone was pulling in the welcome mat. The second wave of attacking Phantoms from the east started to pop onto the target, homing onto the tracers.

The attackers could not see the carnage the CBUs spread over the area. The canisters holding the CBUs would drop off the wing pylons when the pilots hit the pickle button. As they fell, the canisters would open up like a clam shell, spewing hundreds of baseball-sized bomblets over a wide area. Each bomblet would spin, arming as it fell. Some would explode immediately on impact; others would bounce high into the air before exploding and raining their lethal charge over a wide area. Others would bounce and then lie dormant, waiting for a time-delayed fuse to activate or someone to jiggle it, setting it off. In some three minutes the 378th had worked over the troop concentration area, effectively disabling its personnel. C.J. and his wingman took one last sweep of the area, still looking for MiGs and radar activity, and exited to the south, finally closing the door behind the retreating Phantoms.

The first Phantoms started to recover fifty-two minutes after C.J. had led the launch. The birds flew down final at twelve hundred feet in flights of two or four and circled to land. Waters stood beside a pickup with Tom Gomez and Mike Fairly at the roll-out end of the runway, counting the birds and checking them for battle damage. One after another, the planes rolled past, the pilot or wizzo giving them a thumbs-up. Gomez and Fairly had recovered too late in the stream of traffic from Stonewood to take part in the attack and could not believe they had missed the first mission. When the last of the F-4s had cleared the active, Waters turned to them. "In less than twelve hours we flew three thousand miles, turned, and launched fifty-four birds against two targets. And all recovered with little or no battle damage. Your men did good." To put it mildy, he silently added.

29 June: 0800 hours, Greenwich Mean Time
0900 hours, Stonewood, England

But unlike that from Ras Assanya, the launch out of Stonewood had not been perfect and five jets had aborted, not able to join the string of Phantoms headed for Ras Assanya. Locke was not surprised when his centerline fuel tank would not feed. He had taxied back in to face the worried crew chiefs. The two young sergeants vowed to get a new centerline tank that would feed if they had to cycle through every tank on base. Finally Colonel Bradley had driven up in his truck and told Jack that he was to lead four other Phantoms in a straggler flight and to go with only two tanks if they could not get a centerline to feed. After three fruitless hours of trying to get all the birds ready, Bradley had sent them all into crew rest, deciding they would launch the next morning. Jack had tried to contact Gillian, but the base was still sealed tight.

At 9:00 A.M. on Wednesday morning Jack taxied out with the last of the wing's fighters following him. "Hell of a way to go to war, one tank short and a day late," he said to Thunder.

"At least we're going," Thunder said. "I'd hate to be left here." Since he had a different load then than the other four fighters, Jack told the other four pilots that he would make a single ship takeoff; they would follow with formation takeoffs with twenty-second spacing between pairs. The five ships took the Active with Jack in the lead as the tower cleared them for takeoff.

Thunder had now broken Ras Assanya out on the radar scope. "It looks like a boot," he said, and indeed, the peninsula the base was located on did look like a boot that had the top of its leg stuck onto the mainland and the flat of the sole and heel pointing out to sea. They landed first and were not prepared for the intense heat when they popped their canopies.

"Son of a bitch," Thunder muttered, "just like Egypt." On the ramp that was a hubbub of activity, a Follow-Me truck appeared on their right and escorted them to a newly constructed concrete bunker where a ground crew was waiting to park them. They were still in the cockpit when Bull Morgan drove up in a jeep, tossed them two cold beers, bundled them into the jeep and headed for the new COIC. "What the hell's wrong with overhead recoveries these days?" he demanded.

"Regulations call for single-ship radar approaches after a ferry-leg," Jack said quickly, ready to defend himself.

"Start thinking like a fighter pilot. Visibility is no problem, you can see forever. Always get your flight on the ground ASAP. You're too vulnerable in the pattern in a combat zone. But glad you decided to make it. Too bad you missed the first go yesterday. We launched against two targets and plastered them. Come on in and look at the results," Bull said, leading them into the COIC.

Jack and Thunder joined a crowd of pilots and wizzos around a large collection of reccy photos pinned to a wall. The high-resolution photos vividly recorded the destruction the CBUs had spread, among the soldiers. Jack shook his head. "And they thought napalm was bad stuff." He was stunned by what his wing had done. The war was over, he figured, and he had missed it.

29 June: 1045 hours, Greenwich Mean Time
0645 hours, Washington, D.C.

The colonel briefing Cunningham on the results of the 45th attack concluded with the standard, "Any questions, sir?" His stomach was churning as he watched Sundown's fingers drum on the arm of his chair in the briefing room. After what seemed an eternity the general shook his head and the colonel beat a hasty exit. Cunningham did not mind keeping the large group waiting while he considered the situation at Ras Assanya. The 45th had been in place less than four hours and had inflicted serious damage on the forces operating in Iran. If he could believe the briefer, the attack had relieved pressure on UAC forces holding the line between Iraq and Iran at Basra.

Still, the lack of damage to the 45th had made it look too easy, too much like a milk run, and two colonels had deliberately commented within his hearing that they could have done better. Cunningham had raked the two men with a quick look, convinced they didn't have a clue about the developing situation in the Gulf. But Waters did, and he had a young Intel officer to stay on top of it . . .

Cunningham now probed the intentions of his adversaries, what they were likely to do with the forces they were committing into the

Gulf *and* how they would respond to this latest setback. The buildup and positioning of forces gave the Tudeh and their allies a distinct tactical advantage and, he was sure, they would not fold their tents and steal away because they had suffered one major loss. The PSI, the People's Soldiers of Islam, was still an Islamic Shiite organization with a strong penchant for martyrdom. Now they had another enemy to throw themselves against: the 45th.

Ras Assanya. The name kept pounding at him. Without a word to his staff he hustled out of the room, telling his aide to get Brigadier General John Shaw into his office immediately.

Cunningham told Shaw: "The President wants to convince the hotheads in the Gulf to cool their water." He didn't smile at the unintended pun. "Unfortunately his hands are being tied by critics in Congress and some of the media that's scared of another Vietnam. The President's advisers are telling him that he was lucky even to get the 45th in place, and he's under a great deal of pressure to get out of the Gulf. He has taken the Rapid Deployment Force off alert and is keeping most of the naval task force in the Gulf of Oman, just outside the Strait of Hormuz.

"Since we got the 45th into Ras Assanya, I want to make it a force strong enough to hurt the PSI and make them back off. We're going to reinforce the wing through Third Air Force and I'm making you Third Air Force's Director of Resources, Material and Personnel. Set up the logistic support necessary to ensure the effectiveness and survival of the 45th . . . Make it a base that can fight a war."

After Shaw had left, Cunningham buzzed for Stevens. The colonel entered the office and stood waiting, expecting what was to come. "Dick, how long have you been sitting on Third's list of possible replacement commanders for the 45th?"

"I had it Saturday night—"

"So why didn't you give it to me then?" The general was calm, no anger in his voice.

"Because, sir, I wanted to read both inspection reports first. That's why I ran out after you had finished with Waters. I figured he had them and wanted to catch him before he left. I hadn't read them when all this broke on Sunday so I waited to see what would happen. Besides, you didn't fire him on the spot; I figured there must have been some doubt in your own mind. I tell you, sir, I trust him. He said his wing was ready and I believed him. Events proved he was right—"

"What if you were wrong?"

"Well, sir"—the colonel risked a smile—"I was looking for a new job when I got this one."

"And you almost got one, in Leavenworth," the general said, dismissing his aide and keeping a straight face. After Stevens had left, Cunningham lit a cigar and paced his office. Dick Stevens just might be the first ground-pounder Chief of Staff. For sure he had saved one General Cunningham from a whopper of a mistake.

30 June: 0245 hours, Greenwich Mean Time
0545 hours, Ras Assanya, Saudi Arabia

The next frag order committing the wing against new targets had come in. The weapons-and-tactics officers from each squadron had gathered with Waters, Tom Gomez and the squadron commanders to allocate targets around the wing. The message from General Cunningham commending Waters and the wing on their deployment and first mission had sent the wing commander's spirits soaring but made Jack worry . . . The wing had set a standard of combat without him. He wondered if he could match it.

He found some relief by throwing himself into planning their mission against a line of heavy artillery that was pounding UAC positions near Basra. The 379th was tasked to attack with four Phantoms what looked like big howitzers on the reccy photos. Fairly had elected to lead a two-aircraft element against the northern battery while Jack would lead the second pair against the southern battery. His doubt started to build again as they went through the final briefing and stepped to their Phantom. Thunder pre-flighted the Mark-82 Snakeyes hung on the Triple Ejection Racks on the inboard pylons. He jerked a thumbs-up when he was ready to go.

Jack walked outside the bunker and urinated on the sand, noting that other pilots and wizzos were doing the same, then clambered up the ladder into his cockpit and strapped in.

A pickup truck drove by, streaming a yellow flag from a fender mount that signaled them to start engines. Maintaining radio silence, they launched over the quiet waters of the Gulf, and Thunder commented on seeing a lone ship that looked like a fishing trawler cruising nine miles offshore. Jack grunted, tried to stow his self-doubts and worries . . .

Fairly, leading his two-aircraft element, jinked his Phantom hard as he came off the target. He had flown a short curvilinear approach onto the gun emplacement, making it almost impossible to track his fast-moving fighter, and had acquired a late sight picture. His thumb flicked on the pickle button and the six Mark-82s slung under his wings rippled off, walking across the artillery tubes. The first bomb exploded short of the target, sending fragments and flying rock over a wide area. The second and third bombs bracketed the first 122-millimeter howitzer, shattering the gun, taking out its seven-man crew. The fourth bomb impacted on the ammunition dump between the gun pits, setting off a series of massive secondary explosions as the shells blew up. The fifth bomb landed directly in a gun pit, but it was a dud. The sixth scored a hit on the dugout that served as a command post, wiping out the eighteen men inside. Fragments from the five bombs and the secondary explosions in the ammo dump reached out over a thousand yards, adding to the destruction . . .

A seventeen-year-old Soldier of Islam had jumped for cover when he saw the Phantom start its run onto the gun emplacement. At first he thought the fighter was aiming for him, until he saw, with embarrassment, that he was well clear of the intended target. He jumped back onto his anti-aircraft gun, a Soviet-made ZSU-23-2, and raked the sky with a burst of twenty-three-millimeter high-explosive ammunition. The two barrels of the gun emptied eighty rounds into the sky in a rapid burst of fire. The teenager had been trained by his unit's Russian adviser, but he had not understood the man's explanations and, like the rest of the company, he detested the Russian for being a foreigner, even though he claimed to be Shiite and spoke fluent Farsi. Still, he was able to load and fire the gun, though he never saw the Phantom after it released its bombs.

One bullet hit the underside of Fairly's aircraft as he jinked to the right, but the bullet's fuse mechanism had jammed on impact and the shell did not explode. Fairly should have been able to recover the Phantom despite the battle damage it had taken. Unfortunately it was the "Golden BB," the lucky shot, the aircrews often joked about, and it struck the LOX bottle under Johnny Nelson's seat in the pit. The highly volatile liquid oxygen bottle exploded, shattering Nelson's seat and jamming the wizzo through the canopy. Fragments of the LOX bottle and seat ripped through the lower part of his body while the canopy crushed his skull. The stick went dead in Fairly's right hand as the Phantom rocked from its internal explosion. He automatically pulled the ejection handle between his legs, but nothing happened. He reached for the handles on the headrest of his seat and jerked them forward as the fighter spun out of control and into the ground, exploding on impact.

Waters and Gomez sat in the broiling pickup truck near the end of the runway listening to the radio traffic as the flights started to recover, each flight of four checking in with the tower as they called for landing clearance. Both men sucked in their breath when they saw a flight of three enter the pattern. Waters shot his DO a quick glance when they heard Jack's voice check the flight in with the tower. Jack was the *backup* lead . . . Mike Fairly was missing. Gomez gunned his truck toward the COIC to await the arrival of the crews for debrief.

Mike Fairly. Johnny Nelson. The names beat a constant punctuation into Waters as he listened to Jack's debrief. He wanted to ask questions, to interrupt the sergeant conducting the debrief, to get to the main point—the loss of Fairly. But he forced himself to let the young woman methodically plow through the series of detailed questions that reconstructed the mission.
"When did you last see Colonel Fairly?"
"When he rolled in on the target."
"Did everything appear normal at that time?"
"What's normal about taking on a battery of howitzers?"

"I'm sorry, Lieutenant Locke, I phrased that wrong. Did you see smoke coming from Colonel Fairly's aircraft or any unusual maneuvers on his part?"

"No."

"Did you see Colonel Fairly's aircraft impact the ground?"

"No."

"Did you see any parachutes in the area?"

"No."

"Did you see any wreckage?"

"Jesus H. Christ—! I was busy getting the flight together and getting the hell out of Dodge. Like Fairly taught me to do. Those people were hosing the goddamn sky down with missiles and Triple A . . ."

The sergeant, all cool and calm, finished the debrief. Waters put his hand on Jack's shoulder, hoping the pilot understood. Jack shook his head and left. The sergeant handed Waters the report, "I'll have to send it out immediately, sir. We'll have to list them MIA. Sorry . . ."

Waters only nodded, feeling he had failed Mike Fairly and Johnny Nelson.

That evening, the 379th gathered on the makeshift benches that doubled as an outdoor theater and chapel. They were joined by the other two squadrons and most of the wing. After the chaplain's opening prayer and a reading from scripture, Doc Landis got up from the front bench and stepped onto the stage. It was a dumpy man who stood before them, his hair in disarray and brown eyes moist.

"I knew Michael Fairly and John Nelson, Mike better than Johnny. At first I told the chaplain here that I didn't want to speak. But then I thought maybe I should. They certainly deserve a memorial like this service, but that's not why I'm here. I'm going to ask you to take a hard look at what Mike and Johnny were doing." The doctor paused, summoning the courage to go on. "They were killed because they were engaged in the business of destruction and killing people."

Jack started to get up and leave. Thunder's big hand grabbed his shoulder and pulled him back onto the bench. "Listen to what the man has to say. He was Fairly's best friend."

Doc Landis was looking directly at Jack. "The Mike I knew was a kind and considerate man and Johnny had a rare intelligence and believed in his God. Why should two such men choose to engage in the business of killing? The answer—they were trying to buy time. Time to make some kind of peace before this dirty little war we're in escalates to a bigger, uncontrollable one. They tell me that Mike and Johnny's epitaph is MIA. Missing In Action. In time that will be changed to KIA. Killed In Action. I hate those words. But if we here can't buy the world a little more time to stop this war, I wonder what our epitaphs will be. More to the point, will there be anybody left to write it . . . ?" He stepped down and headed directly for the exit.

"Thanks," Jack said to Thunder as they walked back to the COIC, where they would see if another frag order had come in for a new mission . . .

Waters found Jack staring at the mission-briefing boards in the COIC and sat down beside him. "Bull is going to be the new squadron commander, think you can handle that? I'll reassign you to another squadron if you want."

Jack shook his head and told him Bull Morgan was a good choice.

"Good. He'll need your help. See if you can find C.J. I want you and him to get together with Gomez and myself for some serious head-knocking tonight. I want to see if we can knock off a few more Gomers next time around without getting plastered ourselves."

30 June: 1910 hours, Greenwich Mean Time
2010 hours, Stonewood, England

A blue staff car left the wing headquarters at Stonewood. Brigadier General Shaw sat beside the chaplain as he drove slowly into the base housing area. The mothers that were watching their children play in the warm summer evening halted at the sight of the staff car and shepherded their wards home, relieved to see the staff car pass and not stop in front of their houses. Connie Fairly saw the car park directly in front of her house. She opened the front door, steeling herself.

1 July: 0930 hours, Greenwich Mean Time
0530 hours, Washington, D.C.

Cunningham scanned the message and threw it into his out folder. He chrewed his cigar to a ragged pulp and spat it into a waste basket. He called his aide. "The press will be looking for a statement about our first loss. Give 'em the standard answer and when they ask if we will stop flying missions or withdraw, tell them that is a decision above our level." He banged the phone down, shoved another cigar into his mouth.

The President dropped the PDB, the President's Daily Brief, onto his desk and spun his chair around to face the three windows behind him in the Oval Office. He focused on the pin oak planted in the President's Park by Dwight Eisenhower. To the left and further back he could see a white oak credited to Herbert Hoover. The office, the park, the trees . . . they would endure long after he left his place. It made one think about the so-called larger picture . . .

"It's developing as expected," he told Michael Cagliari, his National Security Adviser.

"The press is starting to talk about another Vietnam, sir. They're going to use us as shark bait."

The President almost grinned. "I think you mean you, not 'us.' Besides, you know the press, ready to go into an instant feeding frenzy at the first scent of a good story."

"Some senators and congressmen are beginning to circle as well. The conflict in the Gulf is turning into a classic set-piece limited war," Cagliari said. "It's got the potential to blow up in our faces."

"What doesn't, in this job? Mike, we can't lose sight of our objectives. I want to *stabilize* the region, keep the oil flowing our way and block the growth of Soviet influence. If by standing tough we can stop the fighting, which the Soviets exploit, we'll have made real progress on our long-range objectives."

"A lot of Congressmen are going to be reelected by beating you over the head on this. The press is going to help them."

"Screw the press. They want an issue that will dominate the headlines tonight. I got elected to worry about tomorrow. The government is supposed to make policy. The press is supposed to report it. Let's stop wringing our hands about the *reactions* to what we do . . ."

"Mr. President, you're confusing me. You started out sounding like Winston Churchill, now you've switched to Charles deGaulle."

The President leaned back in his chair and laughed. "Don't flatter me. They're in their own league."

The worry was back on Cagliari's face. "Mr. President, remember Nicaragua. There're some lessons there. The world's changed. Too many players can move independently of the major powers—"

"Mike, I understand you're worried we may not be able to control events in the Gulf. So am I. *If* that happens we'll just have to take our lumps and withdraw. History tells us democracies don't like to fight long wars. Right now, though, we have to gut it out. But I did not become President to be remembered for getting us into a major war. We are not in one. We've committed an Air Force wing to help the UAC stabilize the situation. That's all."

The President walked over to a carved chest, raised the lid and a small bar lifted up. "Let's have a drink. Your usual?" Without waiting for an answer he poured Mike Cagliari a straight sour mash whiskey over the rocks and scotch for himself. He handed Cagliari the drink and sat down beside him on the couch.

"There's still the problem of the press, Mr. President. They want a news conference—"

"Not yet, damn it. Let 'em stew a little."

"They're not going away and your press secretary is taking a helluva beating."

"Okay, okay . . . it's an Air Force wing doing the fighting—let Cunningham handle it. About time he earned his four stars."

Cagliari downed his drink, got ready to leave.

"Mike, what kind of tree should I plant in the park?"

"Ironwood, sir," Cagliari said, not missing a beat.

Cunningham submitted to the press conference at the direction of his Commander in Chief.

"General, can you tell us who decides what targets the 45th will strike?" a reporter asked.

"The President, through the Joint Chiefs of Staff," he said, starting to work a cigar.

"Does that mean the President selects or only approves the targets?"

"The President approves the overall operations."

"Who recommends the operations or targets to the President?"

"The JUSMAG, the Joint U.S. Military Advisory Group, to the United Arab Command in Dhahran. It coordinates the requests of the UAC and transmits them to the Joint Chiefs for presentation to the President." Cunningham braced himself for the next question.

"Do you mean the *Arabs* are picking our targets?"

"I wish that you would read the background papers we supply before you come to these conferences. I think that question has already been answered. Here goes again. We are providing the UAC, the United Arab Command, with military support in critical areas where they are weak. It's their job to pursue the war, ours to make sure that the gaps are plugged. For example, we mostly provide them with intelligence and logistical support. The Navy is ensuring, as it has for some time, that the Strait of Hormuz stays open. And the 45th flies interdiction and suppression missions against selected targets the UAC can't hit. Until the UAC can fly its own tactical air missions, we want to prevent their ground forces from being overrun. That's why the UAC coordinates its requests through JUSMAG. We want to keep the participation of the 45th to a minimum and only use them when and where they are needed . . ." Cunningham glanced at his watch, noted that he had gone three minutes past the scheduled end of the conference. "I'm sorry but we're out of time. You'll have to excuse me; thank you for your attention." He stomped off the stage. No wonder, he thought, Reagan played deaf with reporters, blaming helicopter noise.

3 July: 0200 hours, Greenwich Mean Time
0500 hours, Ras Assanya, Saudi Arabia

Jack found himself deep into it when he turned to the task of blending tactics and mission planning for the 379th. The situation on the ground was simple enough: the People's Soldiers of Islam were trying to push across the Shatt-al-Arab into the city of Basra, the Shatt being formed at the confluence of the Tigris and Euphrates rivers in Iraq, where they joined to empty into the Persian Gulf. Swamps on each side of the wide river formed a natural barrier between Iraq and Iran, and only at Basra, sixty miles upstream from the mouth of the Shatt-al-Arab, did a narrow isthmus of hard ground and sand provide a corridor through the swamps and into the Arabian Peninsula. The UAC had thrown up a strong defensive line centered on Basra, and as long as that line held, the People's Soldiers of Islam were stalemated on the eastern side of the river.

Bill Carroll pointed out how critical it was to interdict any buildup on the eastern side of the river and how the targets that had come down for their first missions had supported that goal. "Someone at JUSMAG has their act together," the Intelligence officer said. "They want us to cut into the muscle of the PSI deep enough to make sure the UAC can hold at Basra. But the PSI is regrouping and bringing in SAMs, most SA-6s, 8s and 9s. It's going to get hairier out there. The PSI hasn't committed MiGs against us yet, but they will. And we've established that the fishing trawler Thunder reported is a Soviet intelligence-gathering ship out there to monitor our radio transmissions. As long as it stays in international waters, our Rules of Engagement say we can't touch it."

So the pieces for a war were all in place as indicated on the board, Jack realized, envisioning an updated military chess board spread across the desert of Arabia. He and his buddies were among those pieces, and just as in any chess game, strategy could dictate that they be sacrificed for the sake of a checkmate.

3 July: 1000 hours, Greenwich Mean Time
1300 hours, The Saudi Arabian Desert

Mashur Ibn Aziz al-Darhali, a first cousin of Prince Reza Ibn Abdul Turika, was also thinking about sacrifice and survival as he drove his Mercedes 500 SEL along the lonely desert road running southwest from Dhahran. His contact had been most insistent that he make this rendezvous, and when he had refused, as befitted a prince of the royal family, the swarthy foreigner had asked him if his son was old enough to assume responsibility for his family. Mashur had ignored the remark but carefully noted the time and place of the meeting. As he approached the one hundred-seventy-kilometer marker he slowed to meet a rapidly approaching silver Mercedes. Both cars stopped at the kilometer marker on opposite sides of the road. The rear door of the silver Mercedes opened, and he was signaled to join the occupant in the rear seat.

The man was most polite and thanked Mashur for understanding his need to meet on such a lonely stretch of highway. The two men worked through the protective labyrinth of indirection and double meanings the Arabic language provided until Mashur divined the man's simple request: he wanted a list of the targets the 45th would be ordered to strike twenty-four hours in advance.

Mashur protested that he was only a minor functionary in the United Arab Command and did not have access to such information.

The man smiled and asked him if King Fahd would be interested in Mashur's backing of the fundamentalists who seized Mecca's Grand Mosque in November of 1979 and had seriously threatened the monarchy.

Thoughts of a beheading in a public square with a short sword on sand-covered ground churned Mashur's stomach. He had only been an immature youth at the time, rashly dabbling in politics. Nonetheless, he carefully noted the time and place to pass on the information to his contact. On the drive back to Dhahran, Mashur rationalized that he was not betraying his family or his king, only punishing the infidel Americans for their worship of false gods. Indeed, he would be serving his king, his country and above all his God . . .

5 July: 0200 hours, Greenwich Mean Time
0500 hours, Ras Assanya, Saudi Arabia

Some *frag* order, Jack thought, as he tried to decipher the long message detailing the targets for the wing's next missions. He had been through the message twice and still had not made sense out of many sections. Thunder had tried to help, only to find himself equally at a loss. Jack then had gathered up their notes with the message and searched through COIC until he found the sergeant he was looking for. "Hey, Casey, can you interpret this stuff for us?" The phlegmatic sergeant heaved his bulk into a chair and had the message sorted out in less than ten minutes.

Thunder marveled at the speed of the sergeant and how he added words and meaning to the seemingly garbled text. Jack was equally impressed. "Hey, Sarge, I thought a frag order was supposed to be short, a fragment."

"Yeah, it's supposed to only be a fragment of the day's total Operations Order. In Nam a wing would only get the part that applied to them. Over here we get the whole damn thing." He pointed out the part of the frag order that tasked the Saudis to fly a Combat Air Patrol to protect the 45th from any MiGs that might jump them.

Again the sergeant impressed the men as he plotted the six targets on the briefing boards, double-checked the accuracy of each plot and told them to check his work while he searched his files for reconnaissance photos and materials for each target. He then queried Intel's computer by entering the latitude and longitude of the center point of the target area, and a high-speed printer spat out information updating the defenses in the area. The sergeant whistled as he read the printout. "SAMs and Triple A are growing like weeds. Looks like the PSI is getting serious about the war."

Carroll's face was a mask as he bent over the reconnaissance photos and measured the distance from the FEBA, the Forward Edge of the Battle Area, in front of Basra, to the six targets. "These look like good targets." He let out his breath, satisfied the wing was getting worthwhile frag orders. "We're going after artillery batteries, a decent troop concentration and two supply dumps. All of this stuff has been recently moved up. I'm willing to bet the PSI is getting ready for a major push against Basra." The 45th was being used for tactical interdiction, precisely as Cunningham had explained to the reporters.

Jack planned to attack each target with six aircraft divided into flights of two. The men worked backward, first selecting three IPs around each target area. They wanted to find a feature on the ground a pilot and wizzo could easily find and recognize, one that would point them into the target and still help them avoid the growing number of SAMs. Once the points were identified, Jack assigned two crews to each IP and let them plan their own low-level route.

The number of red rings on the map that signified known SAM sites worried Jack. After mulling it over he decided to use a "get-the-hell-out-of-Dodge" option. "I want to saturate Gomer's command and control network and give 'em too many threats to sort out at one time," he told the men. "We get everyone in and out fast while the Wild Weasels open the front door by keeping the air defenders busy. We've got to keep our time in bad-guy land to a minimum." Together the men decided on the timing for each flight to ingress the target area and coordinated their TOTs.

They finished by selecting their escape routes and turning it over to C.J., who agonized his way through the plan, making sure his Weasels would be in position to suppress the enemy's ground defenses that would be brought to bear on the attacking Phantoms. "I can't knock them all out," he said to Jack. "But I can get their heads down while you're in the area, especially if I can get Colonel Gomez to buy your idea. Then I'll be able to cover you better."

"C.J., you've got a screw loose somewhere. You're going to have the Weasels all over them like stink on shit."

C.J. accepted the compliment.

When the planning was completed they briefed Waters and Gomez on the mission. Waters listened carefully, calculating the wing's chances of success. The timing of the raid made him think of the Ahlhorn training exercise that Jack had planned. Doubts started to nip at the edge of his mind, and the thought of losing more crews nipped even more. "Has Intel run this through their computer and come up with an expected attrition rate?" he finally asked.

"Yes, sir," Thunder told him. "Bill calculates about one percent. That's because we only have to take on ground defenses and not worry about being jumped by MiGs. According to the frag order the UAC is providing us with a CAP—Saudi F-15s."

The way Jack had assigned each flight a relatively simple and quick attack and then blended them all together with timing fascinated Waters. But his nagging doubts remained. "Okay," he told them, "give me a few minutes. You've impressed me." He got up, stretched and motioned Gomez to follow him outside.

"Tom, it looks fine on paper, like Ahlhorn did. But something says it's too aggressive. What's the weakness? What am I missing?"

"It looks great to me," Gomez said. "I wish we could fly our own CAP in case MiGs jump us. But the UAC is supposed to have their F-15s up and in the area. Exactly how far they'll come into bad-guy territory to cover us is anybody's guess. Besides, we haven't seen a single bandit yet.

"I'm more worried about the damn call signs the frag has assigned to us. It's hard enough remembering your own name when the heat is on, much less what Old Joe Blow is being called today. When I have to warn him about a missile coming his way or need to call him back onto a new target I've got to get his name right the first time. We need to use tactical call signs."

Gomez waited, then said, "C.J. needs more birds for air-defense suppression. He wants to try an idea Jack dreamed up and mate an F4-G Weasel with an F-4E as a wingman and use the Weasel to direct the E onto threats that come up. That will double his strength and allow two birds for suppression on each target . . . Muddy, I'm sure this attack'll work. Look, let me fly and I'll abort the mission if things start to hell in a hand-basket. Jack's planned a beauty. We really shouldn't waste it."

The DO's confidence was the deciding factor. "Okay, Tom. Ops is your show. Go with the mission as planned, use tac call signs, give C.J. his wingmen, and abort the mission if things get too hairy up there. I've got to get over to the Security Police and work on base defense with Chief Hartley, so get this thing on the road."

Bull Morgan led the first eight planes onto the active runway. Six of the Phantoms were pregnant with bomb loads destined for the first target. A Weasel and his wingman taxied with them. Forty more Phantoms stretched out behind them, broken into similar cells. Jack was sandwiched between the second and fourth cell; he had picked the third and most heavily defended target for himself. There had been no lack of volunteers to fly with him so it was easy to pick his five other crews at random. C.J. had also opted to fly with Jack's cell and followed them onto the Active, his F4-G Wild Weasel teamed with an E model from the 377th. C.J.'s bird bristled with anti-radiation

Shrike and Harm missiles while his wingman was loaded with CBUs and three AGM-65 Mavericks, electro-optically guided and not dependent on enemy radiations for homing.

Jack's flight took off on a southerly heading, turning back to the north as the formation fell into place. As soon as they were positioned he started to descend, hugging the water as the cell flew up the Gulf.

Twenty-five miles before they coasted in at the mouth of the Shatt-al-Arab, the first tell-tale flickers of radar activity started to light Thunder's Radar Homing and Warning receiver. "Can you sneak it down a little lower?" Thunder asked.

Without breaking radio silence Jack led his flight down to seventy-five feet above the calm and smooth surface of the Persian Gulf. They coasted in undetected and now were flying over the marsh land along the coast.

"Bandits two o'clock high, four miles, going away," Jack warned his flight, breaking radio silence as he sighted enemy fighters. "The Gomers are up today, where in the hell did they come from?"

Streaks of vertical contrails pillared the skies as the PSI's air-defense system started to react, indication that Morgan was already at work on his target. Jack concentrated on the orbiting enemy fighters he suspected were looking for his flight. But the Phantom's camouflaged paint blended with the land, and the Floggers could not pick them out. Jack pushed their speed up to 480 knots, seventy miles out from their targets, and climbed to two hundred feet. "Split now," he commanded, and the eight fighters broke, each pair going its own way, with C.J. taking the most direct route to the target in order to arrive seconds before the attack. "Glad we hadn't planned to come back this way," Jack said, trying to ease the building pressure. Sweat poured as he kept inching down to the deck.

Thunder directed them along a series of short navigation legs leading to their IP. "Arm 'em up," he told Jack, who toggled the last switch that activated his weapons-delivery system, glad for the reminder. He'd been concentrating on the MiGs and had forgotten to throw the Master Arm switch and so wouldn't have been able to pickle off his bomb load.

"IP one minute," Thunder announced.

"IP in sight," Jack replied over the radio. "Sooner, split *now.*" The two aircraft broke onto separate headings in order to strike the target from different directions. Sooner would hit the target exactly twenty seconds after him, gaining the separation in time he needed to miss the debris kicked up by Jack's bombs. Jack stroked the afterburners, pushing the Phantom as fast as it could go that low to the ground. Until they shed the drag created by their six Mark-82 Snakeyes, their maximum speed was 540 knots and their rate of fuel consumption was enormous.

"Tallyho," he shouted as the storage dump that was their target surged into his left forward quarter panel on the windscreen, just where it was supposed to be. He jerked the nose of the bird skyward into a pop maneuver, rolling and bringing the nose back onto the target before they climbed too high. His thumb hovered on the pickle button as the altimeter unwound and the pipper on his target ring walked to the target. As he flicked the button, a shadow flashed across the top of their canopies. "What the hell . . ." Jack yelled, pulling off the target and jinking to the left.

"A SAM," Thunder said, his voice remarkably calm. "Sooner in sight; come left and he'll cross in front of you." A hard wrench to the left brought them onto a southerly heading, and Sooner skidded his jet across and above them, falling into place two thousand feet abeam Jack for their egress. A series of secondary explosions from the storage dump marked the two fighters' exit, but they did not notice. Their CAP was nowhere in sight. What was going on? Something was wrong. Very wrong.

"Fish, *eject! eject!*" a voice crackled over Guard, the radio channel reserved for distress calls.

"Goddamn. C.J.'s wingman," Jack said.

"Bandits, eight o'clock, on us," Sooner shouted over the UHF radio. Before Jack could react a stick of smoke reached up and enveloped the leading enemy aircraft in a fireball. The second bandit broke off, presenting the plan-form of a MiG-23 as it turned away from them. The attacking MiG had been shot down by one of the PSI's SA-6 missiles . . . The problem of sorting out friendly and enemy aircraft for the ground air-defense systems had worked to Jack's advantage. This time . . .

As they coasted out, heading south for Ras Assanya, Thunder spotted two Phantoms from their cell. Jack joined them up and called for a fuel check. All four were low on fuel. He climbed the flight to eighteen thousand feet, conserving fuel as much as possible. Fifteen minutes later the flight touched down, forty-nine minutes after taking off . . .

When they arrived for their debriefing at the COIC, C.J. was waiting for them, already finished with his debrief. White streaks of dried sweat etched his flight suit. His face was haggard with fatigue. He walked with them to their debrief, asking if they knew about any losses. "I heard someone yell for Fish to eject, that's all," Jack told him.

C.J. nodded. "Yeah, I heard that call. I think someone behind us bought it too. They were waiting with everything, including the goddamn kitchen sink. We still managed to shut the SAMs down, but MiGs were all over the place. I didn't see any friendly CAP at all. I can't handle *both* SAMs and MiGs . . ."

"We ran into the same thing," Jack said. "We did see four bandits on ingress but they didn't see us. I mean, we were down in the weeds. A SAM almost speared us just as I pickled and we got jumped by two MiGs outbound. One of their own SAMS assholed the lead son of a bitch. The other MiG beat feet, lost interest I guess."

C.J. sat with them through their debrief before they went into Ops, where they found Waters, his face gaunt and lined. Motioning to them, he sat down, still staring straight ahead. "Tom Gomez is missing. What went wrong?"

"Oh God," from Jack.

"I'll tell you what happened," C.J. exploded, "there was no CAP!" He started walking away, then stopped abruptly. "Excuse me, sir. Give me a minute . . . I didn't want Colonel Gomez to fly with the tail-end flight. It's too dangerous back there and he knew it." The major's eyes were fixed on the floor.

"The UAC were fragged for a CAP," Waters seethed. "Where the hell were they? Why didn't Tom abort the mission?" A feeling of failure sickened him and he silently swore at the UAC pilots for not covering his wing.

"It was okay when we went in," C.J. said. "The shit hit the fan when we came out."

Waters could only shake his head, anger building in his chest, then walked out of the COIC, slamming the door behind him.

"Not my idea of a war," Thunder muttered, and headed for their trailer while Jack made his way to the mailroom. When he saw his empty box, he walked away, talking to himself. "What's wrong with her? Out of sight, out of mind, I guess." Back in the trailer Jack took a quick shower and flopped onto his bunk. Thunder had already sacked out. But sleep wouldn't come for Jack as thoughts of Gomez and Gillian intermingled. Gillian . . . he had written her the day he arrived at Ras Assanya, giving her his new address. He had struggled to find the words to tell her how much he felt about her without seeming sappy. He was feeling miserable, sorry for himself and guilty about that . . . after all, it was Gomez who had just been killed. But still . . . Gillian was the woman he had decided to settle on, or at least hoped he could. He remembered that local fair that he and the other officers were encouraged to go to for PR purposes, mingle with the civilians, put a good face on the Yank overseas, and how the two girls from the village had propositioned Thunder and himself, and how when he gave it a pass, Thunder told him that he figured maybe Makeout Jack was finally growing up. Now he wondered if he hadn't just been suckered . . . Of course, feeling as he did, it never occurred to him that his letter had been lost in the mail. During the confusion that marked the first few days at Ras Assanya his letter had been mistakenly sent to the APO in New York and not to Stonewood. There it ended up in the dead-letter file. If he had waited a few days before writing or sent a second letter, Gillian would have gotten the letter in one or two days. But he couldn't know any of that . . . God, he was tired, tired, and finally escaped into a fitful sleep . . .

After dinner, Thunder had roused him and insisted he eat . . . Jack wandered into Intelligence and sat studying the reccy photos that showed the Bomb Damage Assessment (BDA) from their mission. The six targets had been obliterated and the PSI's drive against Basra blunted. But looking at the targets, he felt hollow inside.

Waters walked in on him then. "It doesn't do any good to brood on it. We take our losses and go on from here . . ."

"Maybe there were other ways we could have done it—"

"Jack, it's self-indulgent to go blaming yourself for what happened. Your planning was right on. The results on the photos prove that. We plastered them." The wing commander studied the BDA photos. "And we paid a price . . ."

"Yes, sir. Two birds out of forty-eight. That's over four percent attrition—"

"It's worse than that," Waters said, not sparing him. "Six of the birds had battle damage and two won't fly again; we were lucky they even recovered. That puts our aircraft attrition rate at eight percent. I don't worry about losing birds when we recover the crews. There are lots of E models floating around the National Guard and Reserve units that can be ferried in." Waters stopped, not wanting the young lieutenant to assume all the burden for the wing's casualties—that fell to him. He searched for words . . . "Jack, you based your planning on not having to deal with a MiG threat. When the MiGs showed up, the mission should have been aborted. That was Tom's job, that's why he was there. Intel says a MiG got him when he coasted in, before he could abort the attack. I have to accept that. What I'm trying to say is that when the threat changes, we've got to change—and fast. Otherwise, we lose our friends and aircraft. Jack, you have a natural talent that helps put us right at the tip of effectiveness. You lay out attacks that bring what we've got, our capability, to bear on the enemy. You put six birds on each target and tied it together with nearly precise timing. And because of it, we clobber the bad guys. This mission today would have been textbook perfect except for one thing—MiGs— which we saw for the first time."

Jack could rationally accept everything the colonel was saying, but an inner fire drove him on, making him want to hurt the enemy, to keep hitting, not to back away. "Colonel Waters, I think I know how we can prowl around and prey on the bastards without getting hosed down."

"Prowl like a wolf, Jack?"

"Exactly, sir. Let me work on it."

8 July: 1400 hours, Greenwich Mean Time
1500 hours, Stonewood, England

Gillian's shop was unusually full now, many of the patrons being Americans; it kept her and her staff of stylists happily busy. Gillian was less happy about the level of gossip that swirled around the place, especially gossip about the way the Air Force notified next of kin when a man had been lost in combat. Talk about the number of trips that General Shaw had made in his staff car to base housing struck her at times as the lucky ones keeping score on the less fortunate. She thought a little more of the "there but for the grace of God go I" might be in order.

On the other hand, she had to admit some of her reaction was intensely personal, having more to do with Jack and her failure so far to hear from him. Not even a note about how he was doing, where he was . . . God, she missed him, no use denying it. She concocted stories for herself about why she hadn't heard from him, that he was too busy, that he was, after all, a combat pilot . . . At least there hadn't been any word that the worst had happened, and for that she had to be grateful.

Margaret, her oldest-in-service employee, asked her why she didn't talk to her American friend Francine; surely she'd heard from Thunder. But, of course, she would have done that if she could have . . . Francine had gone back to the States, not able to stand the waiting and anxiety. Gillian had no place to go, no place to hide her emotions. How much longer, she wondered, could she take it . . . ?

9 *July: 0925 hours, Greenwich Mean Time*
1225 hours, Dharan, Saudi Arabia

The sergeant laid the folder on General Mashur Darhali's ornate desk. The United Arab Command in Dhahran had assigned Darhali an office with furniture and staff that befitted a prince of the Saudi Arabian royal family. "The list you asked for, sir." The sergeant stood back from the desk at attention and waited for the general's next order.

"I need a map to understand this. Get one and an intelligence officer up here to explain this moving target." When the sergeant had bolted from his office, Mashur walked over to the copying machine in the far corner and ran a copy of the only target the 45th would be receiving in forty-eight hours. Prince Mashur Ibn Aziz al-Darhali calmly folded the copy and buttoned it into the breast pocket of his tailored uniform shirt, then sat and waited for the sergeant to return as he scanned the list. He wondered why his contact wanted the list so far in advance.

When the sergeant returned with the intelligence officer he directed the man to plot the target on the map, playing out his charade. He briefly scanned the map before turning both list and map over to the sergeant and dismissing the two men. He noted it was one P.M., the time he normally quit for the day.

That afternoon Mashur made his way through a fashionable jewelry store to a table displaying heavy gold chains and necklaces. The casual disarray on the table did not indicate the value of each chain, most of which cost more than a car. He fingered one after another until he was joined by his contact. They did not speak to each other but examined the chains. When Mashur left, a folded note was lying under a chain. The contact picked the note up with the chain and made his way to the counter, casually throwing sixty thousand *riyals* on the counter and not bothering to wait for his change. Neither Mashur nor his contact noticed the women who followed them out of the store.

10 July: 0600 hours, Greenwich Mean Time
0930 hours, Teheran, Iran

The men gathered around the table did not have the crisp look associated with high-ranking officers, and the chaos in the villa they were occupying bore little resemblance to a military headquarters. But their determination matched that of any professional soldier in the Middle East. "It's a good plan," the commander of the PSI said. "As Allah wills, tomorrow the Americans will attack the slow-moving convoy we have prepared as a lure. We must use this opportunity to destroy them. Prepare the Fedayeen for battle as the Americans will inflict casualties among our martyrs. But these foreigners will in turn be destroyed." Carefully the men selected locations for their SAMs and Triple A, creating a trap for any aircraft that might attack the convoy.

The air-group commander was the only pilot among them and approved of the overlapping rings of defensive fire surrounding the trap they were setting. "Your missileers and gunners must not fire after the Phantoms come off the convoy," the pilot repeated, worried that his pilots would fall victim to their own ground defenses. He had been insistent that the ground defenses work separately from his Floggers.

The men surveyed their handiwork. Every air-defense resource they possessed was marshaled in defense of the long convoy carrying men and supplies southward to the Strait of Hormuz. The commander of the PSI spoke in a low voice. "We will lose some of our soldiers and valuable trucks when the Americans attack. I know many will penetrate our rings of fire. But they will come and we will be waiting. We will receive messages when the Americans take off and our MiGs will be able to launch at the proper moment to meet and attack them." He did not tell the hushed men that one launch-warning would come from the Soviet trawler and another from a coastal watch-team that was moving into place disguised as fishermen. Some things were better kept secret even from the faithful.

11 July: 0400 hours, Greenwich Mean Time
0700 hours, Ras Assanya, Saudi Arabia

Because the 45th had three air crews for every two Phantoms, Waters had established a rotation order for assigning crews to fly combat sorties. Jack's and Thunder's name had not come up for the wing's fourth mission against the convoy and so they found themselves sitting on the sidelines. Jack had suggested they try using corridor tactics, his only input to the mission. He and Thunder occupied their time by working on Jack's latest idea for a small group of aircrews to roam at night and prey on selected targets. He was thinking of calling it "Wolf Flight."

When the crews had moved to the aircraft Jack walked into the makeshift command post at the rear of the COIC and found an empty seat next to the acting DO, Lieutenant Colonel Steve Farrell. His impatience grew as the crews checked in on status, ready to start engines and taxi. He admired Waters' cool and tried to imitate his relaxed attitude. He glanced at the big situation plot map, where two airmen were marking the location of friendly and hostile aircraft along with the day's targets. His worry even slackened a notch when one airman plotted an orbit over the Gulf and marked it "CAP-UAC."

"It's nice to know our Arab allies are flying a Combat Air Patrol today," Jack said.

"They're up," Waters said. "The UAC tells me we have a dedicated CAP for this mission. I'll believe it, though, when it happens. The crews have been briefed to jettison their loads and abort the mission if they see or hear MiGs in the area and no friendly CAP is around. It's one hell of a target, Jack. A major convoy strung out for over twenty miles along a narrow road and headed for the Strait of Hormuz." Jack nodded and wished he was going.

The Long Track radars that fed early-warning information to the SA-6's fire control first detected the inbound Phantoms. The missile operators slewed the target-tracking antennas of the Straight Flush fire-control radar toward the attackers and raised the triple-mounted missiles into a launch position. The first Wild Weasel detected the H-band frequency of the tracking radar and sent a Shrike down its beam, destroying the tracking radar and control van. Neighboring sites immediately placed their radars on standby and went to a visual launch mode. The string of Phantoms behind the lead Weasel dropped to two hundred feet above the ground, below the minimum altitude of an SA-6. The Weasel and his wingman were blasting open a corridor onto the convoy.

Two soldiers on the ground fired shoulder-held SA-7 Strelas at the F-4s as they flew past. But the fast-moving F-4s were doing jinks back and forth and hoped the 1.5-Mach missiles could not match their turns and catch them before running out of fuel.

Radio communications warned close-in defenders the attack was underway and three batteries of ZSU-23-2 Triple A came active. The gunners of the rapid firing, two-barrel twenty-three-millimeter guns spewed the sky the moment they saw the aircraft, not waiting to establish a tracking solution. Before a Weasel's wingman could pepper the area with CBU, driving the open-gun pit crews to cover, one ZSU laced a Phantom with a short burst. The big fighter cartwheeled into the ground and the next bird in the stream of attackers had to fly through its fireball. The wingman rolled in and pickled two canisters of CBU onto the ZSU-23-2, creating seventeen Shiite martyrs.

Twelve self-propelled ZSU-23-4s maneuvered into position with the convoy. The four-barreled guns, mounted on a tank chassis, had kept pace with the trucks, providing them with running protection. The tracking radar on the ZSU's fed tracking data to SA-9 SAMs, a small missile with an infrared seeker-head similar to the SA-7 Strelas. But the SA-9 was mounted on a scout vehicle, had a larger motor and warhead and was a far more lethal weapon . . .

The 45th started to work the convoy, hitting the lead truck first, bringing it to a grinding halt. The SA-6s behind them kept the Phantoms from popping too high for a bombing run, and the twenty-foot missiles streaked overhead whenever the operators thought they could launch. The second flight's lead Phantom started his pop and was raked by a ZSU-23-4. But only two bullets struck the left wing. The pilot jettisoned his load on the way up and ballooned as he checked for battle damage. His wizzo detected a new threat on his RHAW gear, an SA-8. He called for the pilot to turn twenty-degrees off the threat so as to visually acquire the missile. The pilot shouted "Tallyho" as he turned into the missile and pulled up, generating an overshoot when the ten-foot-long SA-8 could not turn with him—the missile's command guidance tried to make the turn, but the missile broached sideways and tumbled out of control.

The pilot searched for the second missile he knew was coming— SAMs were always launched in pairs or triplets—and found it. Again he turned into the missile, causing it to overshoot as he slammed the Phantom back down onto the deck. But he had bled off his airspeed to 300 knots in avoiding the two missiles. The wizzo jabbed at the chaff-and-flare button, shooting flares and small canisters of chaff from the dispensers on the wing pylons, leaving a trail behind the plane in an effort to deceive the missiles. But a ZSU-23-4 gunner now had the relatively slow-moving Phantom visually and mashed his fire-control trigger, sending over five hundred rounds at the F-4 just as an SA-6 exploded three feet under the fighter's belly. The one-hundred-seventy-five-pound warhead broke the Phantom in two and the warbird vanished in a burst of smoke and flames. The second SA-6 that had been launched at the Phantom could not find a target and went ballistic.

"Bandits two o'clock high on me!"

"Abort!"

"Jettison!"

These calls wracked the radio frequencies as the first MiGs were sighted rolling in onto the lead F-4 coming off the head of the convoy. A Phantom pilot turned hard into an oncoming Flogger and selected guns while his wingman tried to maneuver into a sixty-degree cone behind his lead to provide him protection. The wingman never saw the Flogger that popped up at his own six o'clock and launched an Aphid air-to-air missile at its minimum range of sixteen hundred feet. The missile leaped off its pylon under the glove of the variable swept-wing and was still accelerating when its infrared heat-seeking head found the Phantom's right tailpipe, exploding, destroying the aft section. A classic air-to-air kill: the victim never saw his killer.

Bull Morgan was leading the last flight of four and twisted in his seat, looking for the bandits and his CAP. When he couldn't find the promised friendly CAP, he ordered his flight to jettison their loads hot, hoping for luck to destroy a chance target. They cross-turned one hundred-eighty-degrees and headed for the Gulf. As they did, Bull ordered his flight into a "fluid four" . . . The second lead pilot moved into a line-abreast position roughly six thousand feet away from Bull; each wingman flew two thousand feet away from his lead on the extreme outside of the formation, slightly back, porpoising to a high-and-low position.

"Fox Three." Bull ordered his flight to select the only air-to-air weapon they were carrying. His flight was at least in a good defensive formation for maintaining a visual lookout for bandits as they ran for feet-wet. And Bull kept cursing the missing CAP under his breath as he searched the sky. He finally found the sons of bitches orbiting over the Gulf, well clear of any threat.

The first Mayday call reaching the Command Post jerked Waters, Farrell and Jack to their feet and out the door, piling into the wing commander's pickup. Jack rolled into the truck's bed as Waters gunned the engine and sped for the approach end of the runway. They skidded to a halt beside a crash truck, the UHF radios inside the trucks tuned to the control tower's frequency. An ambulance with Doc Landis soon joined the three waiting men, worry written on the doctor's face. Slowly, they counted the returning Phantoms.

Bull's flight came down final, the first to land. "We launched thirty-six," Waters said, and each man started an internal count. The colonel visibly flinched when the third recovering flight checked in with three. The stranglehold of tension eased some when the straggler appeared, declaring a Mayday. They scanned the sky as eight more birds entered the pattern. "That's twenty," Waters counted. The lone ship called the tower, declaring he was going to eject. "Nothing wrong with a nylon approach and landing," Waters said. They watched the aircraft turn inland before pointing out to sea, crossing the runway at four thousand feet.

Jack offered Waters binoculars he had found in the pickup, but the wing commander only shook his head. The lieutenant then focused them on the Phantom, examining it for battle damage. Half of the vertical stabilizer had been shot away and both tail pipes had major damage. Heavy smoke was streaming from the right engine. Immediately after crossing the runway both canopies flew off, and in quick succession the back and then the front seat rocketed above the dying F-4. The Phantom continued its glide out to sea, curling to the left while chutes streamed behind the men, snapping open as the seats fell away. The parachutes drifted back to the runway while crash crews ran toward them and the plane crashed into the Gulf. "The Martin-Baker wins again," Waters said, referring to the ejection seat and grateful for the results.

A flight of three checked in with the tower, but this time there was no straggler and any sense of relief Waters felt was quickly swept away. "Twelve more to go, twenty-three accounted for," Waters intoned. Two more flights of four called the tower as the men heard a calm voice on the UHF declare a Mayday—it was Sooner from the 379th. Jack held out the binoculars for Waters and this time he took them, scanning the sky. He found the Phantom's characteristic smoke trails, marking the path of two returning aircraft. Waters reached into the truck and grabbed the radio's mike. "Tower, this is Zero-One." The control tower acknowledged, recognizing the standard call sign of a wing commander. "Are those two the last inbounds?"

"Roger, Zero-One. No more inbounds at this time," the tower confirmed.

Waters threw the mike back into the pickup. "Three missing . . ."

Sooner's voice came over the radio. "Good afternoon, Rats Tower. Declaring an emergency at this time, I'll be taking the barrier."

Jack caught the cool detached tone. Sooner playing the macho fighter pilot in charge of the situation.

"State your emergency," the tower replied.

"Rog tower. Smoke and fumes in the cockpit, rear canopy jettisoned. Utility hydraulic pressure out, left-hand generator out, bus tie open, numerous holes in the aircraft, loud complaints from the wizzo."

Jack noted that Waters was not reassured by Sooner's black humor. He picked up his mike, mashed the transit button. "Sooner, this is Zero-One, recommend ejection."

"All the same to you, Boss, I'll give this one back to Maintenance." It was the reply Jack would have made. "Blowing gear down, now."

"Sooner, your right main gear did not come down," the wingman radioed.

"Rog, no big deal, I was taking the barrier away."

Waters ran his mental checklist of what systems Sooner had lost; no anti-skid, no nose-gear steering, no afterburner ignition. *It was too much.* "Sooner, this is Waters, deep six that puppy, we don't need it."

"No sweat, Boss," Sooner said, starting his approach.

They watched as the Phantom touched down, a perfect five hundred feet short of the arresting cable, holding the right wing up. Sooner lowered the nose gear onto the runway short of the cable, just as the emergency procedures for the F-4 called for. And they watched in horror as the nose gear collapsed, knowing what would happen next. The Phantom bounced onto its nose and ground-looped into the right wing, skidding over the cable toward the edge of the runway. The crash trucks were already moving with Doc Landis in the ambulance close behind. The aircraft's nose buried itself in the dirt and the fighter pitched onto its back, kicking up a shower of dirt as it skidded to a halt.

Waters swung his binoculars onto the cockpit of the upside-down plane. He saw no smoke or flames. A silver-suited crash-and-rescue fireman ran up to the rear cockpit, which was missing its canopy, and threw himself on the ground, reaching in, unstrapping the wizzo. Flames started to engulf the aircraft as he pulled the backseater out and dragged him to Doc Landis. Another fireman was trying to break through the front canopy.

The crash truck pushed against a wing tip in an attempt to raise the bird off its back so the fireman could pop the front canopy and release Sooner, directing its water cannon onto the fuselage, trying to extinguish the building flames. Another crash truck arrived and directed its water cannon onto the fireman but had to play back to the other truck to cool it. They could see Sooner trying to break through the canopy with a canopy knife as the flames mushroomed over the two trucks, and engulfed the fighter. Waters watched the trucks back away, cannons spraying, as the lone fireman ran out of the flames.

Waters smashed his fist into the pickup's door. "Overconfidence, damn overconfidence . . ."

And a sickening feeling of responsibility ate at Jack as Sooner burned . . . Was he the one who had taught Sooner overconfidence . . . ?

The C-141's engines were still spinning down when the forward hatch opened and Brigadier General John Shaw jumped down onto the ramp at Ras Assanya, somehow managing to shake Waters' hand, shove his flight cap on and return the salute. "Welcome to Rats Ass, John," Waters said, glad to see his old friend. "How's Beth?" The two spent a few moments trading more small talk, postponing the reason for the general's visit.

"Beth's fine, enjoying the auld sod. Got a letter for you from Sara. That what you're calling this place, Rats Ass?"

"One of our wizzos in his cups came up with it at the O' Club and it sort of stuck," Waters said, tucking the letter in a pocket for reading later when he could savor it in private.

"You've got an Officers' Club here with booze?" the general asked. "I thought the Saudis wouldn't permit any alcoholic beverages in the country."

"They ignore it. We're just across the border from Kuwait and pretty much isolated. The Kuwaitis and Saudis contracted with an English firm to build the base for the Rapid Deployment Force, but neither of them wanted it in their own country. The Kuwaitis didn't because they're worried about having more foreigners in Kuwait. They've been outnumbered by foreign workers for years and are sensitive about it. The Saudis wanted it in Kuwait to keep foreign influence and ideas out of their country. Of course, foreign arms are another thing. They compromised by ignoring the border. The Saudi border post is located on the coast road south of the base, and the Kuwaiti post ten miles north of us. We're sort of like a no man's land."

"Sounds like an Arab-type solution, all right," Shaw said, and turned to the reason for his visit. "This has to be fast. MAC's holding the C-141 for me and I've got to get to JUSMAG in Dhahran for a conference about the wing's stand-down from flying combat missions. But I wanted to talk to you first and see the place for myself."

Waters bundled the general into his pickup and gave him a quick tour of the base as they drove to the COIC. Shaw waited until they were inside the COIC before going into the stand-down. "Cunningham called yesterday about the President ordering a stand-down from combat. Congress is putting him under a lot of pressure to withdraw from the Gulf area and wants to implement the Emergency War Powers Act if we hang around. They also like to believe the Iran–Iraq war is really over. Sure, like Israel and the PLO are ready to kiss and make up. There has also been a strong reaction in the press because of your losses. Some are claiming we're getting our butts kicked . . ."

"We've taken some hard hits on these targets." Waters was leaning over a map, pointing out the targets they had hit. "But look at the results. Intel says the pressure is off the UAC and that the PSI is forced to regroup. And supposedly the Soviets aren't coming through with the resupply the PSI is crying for." Waters spread in front of the general the reccy photos that chronicled the destruction of the convoy. "We only got half our birds on target before we had to cut and run when MiGs jumped us. We still managed to pulverize the first half of the convoy and broke up any attempt to reinforce the Strait of Hormuz . . . And check this out." Waters handed him the photos confirming the BDA of the mission Jack had planned. "Those six targets were totally destroyed. That mission took the pressure off Basra. John, we're doing what we came to do."

"But the *cost*, Muddy. We can't sustain that. Ten aircraft in two weeks. That's an overall attrition rate of over five percent. And the rate is increasing. And you've lost thirteen men. That generates too much heat for the politicians to take—"

"Like the Marines in Beirut," Waters broke in, bitterness in his voice. "A suicide terrorist blows up their barracks and kills almost two hundred and fifty Marines and the U.S. bails out. Their sacrifice is for nothing." Waters was standing over the table, leaning on his arms, head bowed. "These casualties hurt." He looked up, masking his deeper feelings. "John, can you get a waiver on the restriction against wing commanders flying in combat? I can't keep asking my men to do something I'm not allowed to do."

Shaw nodded, understanding Water's dilemma.

"If we can get a dedicated CAP or even fly our own CAP," Waters added, "we can cut our loss rate and do what we were sent here for."

"Muddy, there's no way the UAC is going to let you fly your own CAP. You know that. They claim that's the purpose of *their* Air Force. There's a lot of Arab ego tied into that decision . . . What's wrong with the CAP they're flying?"

"They're airborne, but they won't go into SAM envelopes or escort us in. If we can get the Floggers off our back we can suppress the SAMs and Triple A. Jack Locke has worked out a way to hit the Gomers without a CAP and avoid getting plastered. We need to change the way we're fragged though. Interested?"

"Locke, huh? Okay, let's talk to your tiger and see what he has."

"What about the C-141? I thought it had to get going," Waters asked.

"One of the nice things about being a general, Muddy, is that the plane will wait."

Jack, Thunder and Carroll clustered around the flight-planning table briefing Shaw on Jack's idea for a Wolf Flight. "General, I'm proposing we launch sorties at night to hit targets not heavily defended. We run against them in flights of two at low level and beat feet if the threat gets too hot. That's it."

Shaw was surprised at the simplicity of Jack's plan. "How do you know which targets aren't defended?"

Carroll picked it up. "We get reconnaissance photos of the area every afternoon. We can pinpoint the latest location of the SAMs and Triple A. The PSI only has so many SAMs and can't cover every target. We pick a target they aren't defending and plan a low-level to it around the known defenses. The RHAW gear on the F-4s can warn our crews if unexpected defenses start to pop up and we abort the mission."

"I see you let their last defense posture determine which targets you pick—at the last minute." The general thought for a moment about Waters wanting to change the way they were ordered into combat. "You need a list of approved targets to pick from, not a detailed frag order."

"There's another reason," Carroll said. "They were waiting for us at the convoy. I don't know how they knew, maybe dumb luck. They might have psyched out our method of selecting targets—we've been going after big stuff. I don't know, maybe an intelligence leak. Also, no matter how we try to keep our communications down, that Soviet trawler offshore can monitor us as we load out and broadcast early warnings. We know it radios our launch times. As long as it's in International Waters, we can't do a damn thing."

"So you do surprise launches any time during the night." Shaw was almost sold. "What about the MiGs?"

Jack allowed a grin. "The PSI has piss-poor GCI coverage. They'll never find us rooting around in the mud at night. Besides, I don't think your average PSI Flogger driver has the *cajones* to come down into the weeds at night and mix it up with a Phantom. General, Thunder claims we can do the low levels. I think we deserve a chance to nail the bastards."

"So do I, Jack. You three get packed, you're coming with me to a conference at JUSMAG. We've got some convincing to do . . . Muddy, Chief Pullman is going crazy at Stonewood with nothing to do. Mind if I use him until you get back?"

Waters agreed, knowing well that inactivity was the one thing Pullman could not handle.

Shaw pulled a memo out of his briefcase while they waited for the men to return. "I've got a nitpicker from Third Air Force for you." The general, it seemed, had come to Ras Assanya for another reason. As director of personnel for Third Air Force he was carefully appraising Waters, looking for signs of physical exhaustion and, more importantly, emotional fatigue. "Plans and Intel claims your use of tactical call signs is giving away too much info. They've ordered you to stop them and use the variable call signs assigned in the frag order." He waited to see how Waters would react.

Annoyance and amusement flashed in Waters' brown eyes. "Tell Blevins we tried that and can't make it work. We'll do it if someone will come out here, fly a few combat missions and show us how it's done. Maybe Blevins would like to volunteer. What we're doing works well and I can't see fixing something that isn't broke. But like I say, I'm always amenable to someone leading a combat sortie and showing us a better way."

"I'll be pleased to relay that message, Muddy." Shaw smiled. Both loathed Blevins. "Who do you want to replace Tom?" he asked, easing into a more touchy subject, still evaluating Waters' reactions.

Waters kept his emotions under tight rein. "Steve Farrell, the 377th squadron commander. I want to give C. J. Conlan the 377th."

In spite of the man's fatigue, Shaw decided, Colonel Waters was firmly in control of himself and his wing. But Shaw also knew the intense pressure and burden of responsibility for leading a wing in combat would eventually take its toll, and his friend Muddy would inevitably start to make mistakes. Once a wing was committed to combat, it turned into a machine that consumed people for its fuel. Its commander became the driving force behind it, pumping his people into the maw of war, in large part determining who survived. It was a hellish burden that few sane men could carry for long.

17 July: 2245 hours, Greenwich Mean Time
2245 hours, Over the Atlantic Ocean

Most of the passengers of this flight back to Washington were asleep on the Boeing C-137B, the version of the 707 the Air Force used for hauling VIPs. Cunningham sat alone in the rear compartment, enjoying the solitude and the comfort of the big leather armchair. Smoke filled the air as he puffed on one of the fine cigars that Ruth had found for him in London. Probably a Havana with its label removed. Just like Ruth, she does spoil me. He checked the sleeping compartment to see if she was sleeping comfortably. His wife had never been able to rest on protocol trips like the one they were returning from and he worried about her health. He watched her sleep, curled up in the middle of the bed, quietly closed the door and returned to the armchair.

As he turned his attention to the rough draft of a proposal John Shaw had given him in London, he thought of an ambassador's daughter, Abigail, who had cornered him at an embassy reception in London and asked if he knew a Lieutenant Jack Locke, an F-4 pilot. The young lady, more out of her dress than in it, though within the limits set by the latest style, had more than a passing interest in the pilot. He told her he did know the lieutenant, who was currently with the 45th Tactical Fighter Wing at Ras Assanya on the Persian Gulf. She was impressed with *him* that he knew about a lieutenant and told him so, and a fleeting image of what the young lady might look like without clothes brushed his consciousness, a diversion he didn't much indulge in these days. Well, fighter pilots will be fighter pilots, he told himself, remembering his days in F-86s when the world . . . never mind the world . . . when he was young.

The reception in London for NATO commanders had not been a complete waste of time and the general had been able to spend a few minutes talking with John Shaw about keeping the 45th operational in the Persian Gulf. Shaw had hurriedly explained the plan Jack Locke had put together for cutting the wing's losses. The lieutenant had convinced the JUSMAG that it would work but they needed higher approval to implement it. The young pilot's idea had teased Cunningham with its possibilities, but the conference's full schedule had forced him to put it aside. He had told Shaw to give his aide Stevens the rough draft of the proposal that Shaw had banged out on a portable typewriter on the flight in from Dhahran.

Now Cunningham leaned back in his chair and turned his full attention to Locke's proposal. The 45th had been committed to combat for two weeks and had hurt the PSI, reinforcing the UAC as the President had planned. Cunningham speculated how it had turned into a trade-off: the situation was nearing stabilization but at a cost of downed aircrews. Now the cost was causing political problems. The general began to play a game of "what if," mulling over future possibilities, the probable reactions of the players and the counter-moves they would make. Carroll had accurately called the Soviet reaction. *Glasnost* was still the announced policy, the Soviets claiming what was going on in the Persian Gulf was a local matter and shouldn't confuse Soviet–American relations. That's what they said . . . Men and supplies were still reaching the PSI but not in significant amounts, not enough so far to cause the U.S. to increase its role in the Gulf. Fair enough, he decided, that's the game we played with you in Afghanistan—keep the conflict going on a low burner until the other side gets tired of playing and goes home.

We're close, he decided, close to stabilizing the situation on terms acceptable to the United States and its allies. But if we pull out now, the military situation will tilt in the PSI's favor. It was a limited-war situation that fascinated the general, calling for all his skill in resolving it without allowing it to escalate into a bigger conflict. And the 45th was the key—he had to keep them in place a while longer, flying missions, wounding the PSI. But the political game dictated that it had to be done with minimum losses. No more Nams. The general thought about the proposal in front of him . . . F-111s would be perfect for the type of mission Locke was proposing, but F-111s would be interpreted as a deliberate escalation.

He cursed his Arab allies who would not give the 45th a dedicated CAP and refused to let the 45th fly its own. Either solution would cut the 45th's losses. His advisers had convinced him that it was a question of Arab ego. The old macho perspective saw the ultimate use of a fighter aircraft in an air-to-air role, which was the arena the UAC had reserved for their own air force. They wanted to engage in so-called clean situations, where it was only fighter against fighter and not risk their expensive planes on escort missions into hostile territory. But if they let the 45th do it for themselves, it would make them look bad. He understood the irrationality of what was happening, and refused to accept it as a permanent condition for his Air Force.

So . . . he'd try to keep the 45th in the game by using Locke's Wolf Flight while he tried to find them a CAP. He tallied what he needed to make Wolf Flight work, focusing on the 45th, letting his thoughts spin down. Waters, you're on the cutting edge and you've got to keep your wing fighting until I can get you out of there some kind of a winner. Otherwise the sacrifices your people are making will be for nothing. And to think I almost canned you . . .

19 July: 1230 hours, Greenwich Mean Time
1530 hours, Ras Assanya, Saudi Arabia

The men crowded around the largest flight-planning table in the COIC studying the message and photos that made Wolf Flight a reality. The message was much simpler than a frag order: a long list of map coordinates identifying targets the 45th could attack at will. What interested Waters the most were four general-target descriptions at the end, allowing the 45th to strike any identified troop concentrations, command posts, fuel dumps or artillery batteries that were in Iran and within a hundred-mile arc of Basra. Carroll had two of his sergeants plotting the targets on a large wall map.

The men made room for the wing commander when Waters joined Thunder. "Piece of cake, sir," Thunder said. "I've never seen such clear photos and they're one to fifty thousand, the same scale as a topo chart. And no distortion." The crews used topographical charts for target planning. The wizzo held up the photo and chart of Ras Assanya for the colonel to compare. "I can use these to update our navigation charts and go any place we want."

Waters didn't much care for the note of overconfidence . . . it could be a killer. Studying the photo with a magnifying glass, he had to be impressed by the high resolution. "This one was taken around noon," he told them. "You can pick out my truck on the isthmus. That was the first time I had driven it out there." He had been inspecting Chief Hartley's perimeter defenses before noon.

Cunningham had ordered two reconnaissance versions of the Stealth fighter to deploy secretly into a remote base in the wasteland of Rub al Khali, the "Empty Quarter" of the Arabian Desert, to support the 45th. Cunningham had welcomed the chance to test the Stealth fighters in actual operations. These photos were the first products of a new camera that relied on computer-rectified, reticulated optics and high-resolution film that imaged far beyond the normal photographic spectrum. The spooks at the salt flat of Al-Ubaylah were delighted.

"When can you be ready to launch your first sorties?" Waters asked Jack.

"The wizzos are driving this one, sir. Whenever they're ready."

"Tonight," Thunder said quickly, throwing himself into selecting his route and updating his map using the photos they had just received. Waters motioned for Jack and Carroll to join him in the command post, leaving the men to work up the mission.

"Problems?" he asked the two young officers.

Jack replied: "Night deliveries will be a little tricky until we get the hang of it. The weatherman says it's going to be clear as a bell and the moon is in its first quarter, sets at three-thirty this morning. We should have good visibility. I checked with Bull. He prefers night operations because you can see tracers from Triple A or a SAM's plume in time to dodge them."

"That Soviet trawler is going to cause us problems," Carroll said. "But tonight we'll probably catch them asleep. Hell, they throw out the anchor and even turn off their radar. They'll hear our engines start and probably will figure it's late-night engine runs by Maintenance. But we won't surprise them twice, and they'll start sending launch warnings. We don't know how fast the PSI can react or if they'll throw MiGs against us. The whole idea of Wolf Flight is to avoid threats and recover every bird we launch. It's the same old problem—we can't handle both threats."

Waters leaned forward in his chair. "Now's the time we have to take a calculated risk. Even if the MiGs do launch I don't think they can find one or two birds at night down in the weeds. The Flogger Gs they're flying don't have a look down-shoot down capability. Tonight, let's bet on surprise being on our side. Like on our first mission. We'll reevaluate after every mission. Bill, keep watching for increased GCI coverage by the PSI and faster reaction on scrambles. That will be the first clue the MiG threat is heating up." They returned to the mission planning room, where C.J. and his bear were waiting for them.

"No way you can do this without help," C.J. said. "Stan-the-Man claims this stand-down is bad for his nerves and wants to get involved. It's a perfect mission for a Weasel and we aren't doing anything."

Jack turned to Waters: "Colonel, we are dealing with a lot of unknowns tonight. Wouldn't hurt to have a Weasel as a wingman."

Waters nodded, pleased that Jack was showing some caution.

It was agreed to launch eight birds in flights of two, pairing an E-model with a Weasel. Each flight would hit a primary target and if no threats were encountered, would go on to a secondary flight. They finished flight planning two hours later.

"Briefing at 2300 hours," Jack announced, sending them to get whatever rest they could find as the tension started to build.

The briefing that night started with a weather and intelligence update. Nothing had changed and Carroll had some reassuring news. "We launched a training sortie this afternoon and had it monitor the trawler for radar emissions. Nothing. The targets for tonight are in front of Basra and we're doing the usual: interdicting a buildup by the PSI."

Jack took over then and covered night-time delivery techniques. "Remember," he said, wrapping up, "from now on you're part of Wolf Flight, and if you can't hack night low levels going in and coming out fast, tell me now before you buy the farm."

Wrango, a pilot from the 378th, asked about their call signs. "You're a 'Wolf,' " Jack answered. "Learn to recognize each other's voice on the radio and keep the chatter to a minimum. Intel says the PSI monitors all our communications so we'll use that as a weapon. When the Gomers hear 'Wolf,' I want them diving for cover, convinced that the meanest fucker on the block is coming after them personally with a five-hundred pound bomb. Instead of a name we'll each have a number. I'll be Wolf Zero-Nine. You pick your own number and keep it."

At 1:08 A.M. the quiet of the early morning dark was shattered as eight Phantoms started their engines simultaneously. When their inertial nav systems were aligned they raced for the runway in pairs, maintaining radio silence. The tower saw the first two birds take the Active and blinked a green light, clearing them for takeoff. Each pair of birds made a formation takeoff to the north and never lifted above two hundred feet as they headed toward their target. Seven minutes after engine start, the base fell silent . . .

The PSI watch team that had been inserted to monitor takeoff activity at Ras Assanya heard the Phantoms start engines but had not reached their observation point in time to discover what had happened. The Soviet trawler offshore that served as a listening and radar watch post for the PSI never detected the activity . . .

C.J. moved his Phantom as close as possible to Jack's, determined to weld himself to Jack's wing. The sweat rolled off his face as he fought to maintain position, using the dim green luminescent formation lights on Jack's bird for a reference. Flying formation at night, that close to the ground and fully configured for combat was adding up to the most demanding mission he had ever flown. He was so close to Jack that they were even cycling together in response to the ground turbulence.

"Right turn to zero-six-four coming up in thirty seconds," Thunder warned his pilot.

Jack lifted the flight up to four hundred feet for the turn, spun them onto the new heading and immediately jammed them down to two hundred feet once they were wings-level on their new course.

"He's good, damn good," C.J. muttered under his breath.

Thunder's call of "ten minutes out" cued Jack to arm up his bird as they headed for the truck park that was their first target. Jack had decided that CBUs would be the best ordnance to use, giving him coverage over a wide area. C.J. had a mixed load for defense-suppression and would drop his CBUs on the secondary target they had selected on their escape route, a haphazard array of barrels and crates that looked like a supply dump. He would only use his anti-radiation missiles if a SAM site challenged them; otherwise he would return with the valuable missiles. They turned the IP and made their target run. Jack listened to Thunder count the seconds down to bomb release and at the count of five saw the truck park flash up in front of him. The laydown delivery was right on.

Thunder twisted in his seat and scanned the target. "I counted four secondary explosions," he said. "We got something that time."

The two Phantoms headed toward their next target.

C.J.'s backseater concentrated on his RHAW gear, waiting for signs of SAM activity. Thunder guided them to their secondary IP, and again they ran in on the target. Except this time C.J. dropped his CBUs while Jack moved out to the right and slightly above him, keeping him in sight, not wanting to become separated at night.

Again, Thunder scanned the target. "Maybe one secondary," he reported. "I saw a small flash that might have been something." The small flash that Thunder had seen was the fuel tank of an auxiliary generator exploding.

Coming off the target Jack made a gut decision. "Head straight for home plate, Thunder; let's get the hell out of Dodge." Thunder punched the base's coordinates into the nav computer. As Jack selected Nav Comp on the Navigation Function Selector Panel the bearing pointer on the Horizontal Situation Indicator slewed to the right, pointing to Ras Assanya. Jack wrenched the Phantom onto the new heading.

"Where the hell we going?" C.J. rasped over his intercom to his bear.

"Rats Ass," Stan told him. "No reason to get off our planned route."

"Not good." Thunder was studying his chart, working out where they were headed. The terrain was flat, and he and Jack had spent hours over charts, identifying landmarks and significant features. What worried Thunder now was that the reccy photos had proved the charts to be out of date. "There's a village on the nose—"

"Split," Jack yelled over the radio. Both pilots immediately separated, pulling five Gs as they split apart, flying around an unlit radio tower on the outskirts of the village. Jack's quick recognition of the shadowy line of the tower that had loomed up in front of him was the only thing that saved them. As it was, his left wing tip nicked one of the guy-wires that supported the tower, snapping it and ripping off the red position and join-up lights on the wing tip.

"Goddamn. Thunder, tell me when there's a tower in front of us, you mind? That's what you've got the chart for."

"Will do," Thunder answered. "Except there *was* no tower on the chart. I can't read what's not there . . ."

Less than an hour after engine start the eight Phantoms had all recovered safely at Ras Assanya, and the sixteen men walked quietly into the COIC for debriefing. Any sense of jubilation had been replaced by a crushing fatigue that replaced the slowly shredding tension from the mission.

Waters found Jack and Thunder looking at one of the reccy photos after their debrief with Intel. Thunder was using a magnifying glass to pinpoint the tower they had barely missed. "You can hardly see it," Thunder said. "Our charts need some serious updating."

"I'm sorry, I blew it and yelled at you." Jack looked at his friend, taking the blame. His backseater happened to be his closest friend.

"What the hell." The wizzo smiled. "Like they say in the movies, 'cheated death again.' "

"Maintenance tells me you had some battle damage," Waters said.

"Not battle damage," Jack told him. "I clipped a radio tower's guy-wire. After we came off C.J.'s target things were quiet. I decided to make a straight dash for feet wet. That's when I snagged the tower. There was no reason for deviating from our planned route. My fault."

"Okay, Jack, you learned something—like when *not* to improvise. Don't worry about it. We've got lots of wing tips. Wolf Flight worked as advertised. Let's keep it up."

The man's going to make it, Waters decided. He'd seen in Jack that rare combination of flying skill, intelligence and charisma that could lead. And now Jack was really growing up, recognizing and owning up to his mistakes.

21 July: 1130 hours, Greenwich Mean Time
0730 hours, Washington, D.C.

Cunningham was experiencing a rare feeling: contentment. It had started with a phone call from the National Security Adviser telling him the President was favorably considering his request for deploying a squadron of F-15s to Ras Assanya and wanted to discuss it with the general. The colonel conducting the early morning command briefing did not recognize the look on Sundown's face as the results of the first Wolf mission were flashed on the screen. The man thought he was in serious trouble and was dismayed when Cunningham only grunted a curt, "Thank you."

The next briefer was a colonel that Cunningham did not recognize. "Good morning, sir. I'm Colonel Charles Bradford, Office of International Affairs. The government of Iran has filed a complaint with the International Red Cross. They claim that we employed a secret terrorist weapon on civilians in violation of the Geneva Convention. At this point it appears that two of the Wolf Flight overflew an Iranian village at an extremely high rate of speed and very low. The location and time of the complaint match up with the egress of Wolf Zero-Nine and Wolf One-One. Reliable sources report the jet-wash damaged some structures, collapsed a radio tower and thoroughly roused the local population. There were also some minor injuries." The colonel seemed to be enjoying the briefing.

"What's so goddamn funny, Colonel?"

"This is the first known classification of jet fuel as a secret terrorist weapon, sir. We think it's in line with all Air Force policies on cost effectiveness," Bradford said with a straight face.

Cunningham, not especially amused, dismissed him and got to

business. "Okay. I want max publicity on Wolf Flight, get the press looking at them while I try to get the President to come on line with a squadron of F-15s to fly CAP for the 45th. Emphasize the losses we've taken and make the Wolves look like heroes. The valiant band of brothers and so forth. Tell the JUSMAG to concentrate on selecting targets for the Wolves and keep them flying every night. And get an F-15 squadron at Langley ready to deploy." The general left then, optimistic about his chances of getting F-15s into Ras Assanya within a few days. Of course he was also running the risk of escalating the war, but you always did that when you started shooting.

He motioned for his aide to join him. "Stevens, send a 'well done' to the 45th. Also check out a Colonel Charles Bradford of International Affairs. Tell him I want a briefing on the international reaction to our involvement in the Persian Gulf this afternoon." Another candidate for Cunningham's inner circle was about to be tested by the general.

28 July: 1800 hours, Greenwich Mean Time
2100 hours, Ras Assanya, Saudi Arabia

The "well done" letter reached Waters' desk one week later. The wing commander carried it into the Wolves nightly mission briefing and read it to the assembled crews. "Not bad. You're starting to get people's attention. But don't let down, don't get complacent. Tonight is your ninth mission and we're hurting them. Keep at it. Waters sat down to listen to the briefing. The familiar routine washed over him and he missed the details, thinking of how he was starting to sound like a football coach, pumping his men up at half time. He supposed it was necessary, but he'd damn sight rather be flying than sitting on the sidelines.

29 July: 0928 hours, Greenwich Mean Time
1228 hours, The Saudi Arabian Desert

Five more to go, Mashur thought as he passed the three-hundred-kilometer marker on the highway leading deep into the desert south of Dhahran. Even in the air-conditioned comfort of his BMW, sweat laced his back and the palms of his hands. The same silver Mercedes was waiting for him at the kilometer mark, and the rear door swung open as soon as he stopped. With a supreme effort he covered his fears with a characteristic put-on of bravado.

"We want the daily frag order for Wolf Flight," the man demanded, not hiding his meaning behind the intricate grammar of the Arabic language. "They have flown nine times against us and are like pinpricks that go deeper with every thrust." The man did not reveal the full impact of the 45th's Wolf operations. At first the PSI had discounted the attacks. But night after night they came back, never at the same time, always hitting a significant target. The total effect of the raids was cutting into the muscle of the PSI. "You will give us what we need to destroy them."

"There is no daily frag order for Wolf Flight, only a long list of targets. I have not seen the list; to ask for it would be dangerous," Mashur told him, hoping for a reprieve. "I am useful to you only as long as I am trusted—"

"*Get it.*" The man turned his head and looked straight ahead, his eyes invisible behind dark sunglasses. Mashur's panic swelled, almost choking him as he moved slowly back to his car, his strutting gone.

30 July: 1600 hours, Greenwich Mean Time
1900 hours, Ras Assanya, Saudi Arabia

The excitement Bill Carroll felt was contagious. "This is the best target the spooks have found. My God, it's a targets officer's dream come true." He kept pointing to a building on one of the reccy photos that had been delivered that afternoon. "It's a major headquarters near Basra. It's the best target we've run against. Everything correlates, communications, location, personnel, the works. Hitting a headquarters is like ripping their brain out."

Carroll would never learn the source of his intelligence or the complex Stealth reconnaissance program that had been ranging with growing confidence over the entire Middle East . . . A reccy flight would recover at al-Ubaylah in the early afternoon from a mission over Iran and taxi into an underground hangar. The entire camera package would be removed from an equipment bay and rushed to an underground Intelligence complex where its film would be removed and processed for evaluation by a team of photo interpreters. At Cunningham's direction the same RC-135 that Waters had commanded would land at al-Ubaylah for a crew change. The latest intelligence from the RC-135 would be rushed to the Intelligence complex and correlated with what the photo interpreters were discovering. Another team would sanitize the information and photos by removing any hint of sources and by deliberately degrading the quality of the photos. By late afternoon, an unmarked courier, a small business jet, would land at Ras Assanya delivering the latest information in time for Wolf Flight to select its targets . . .

Waters studied the target now, trying to solve his dilemma. A message had come in the day before giving him permission to fly on combat missions and he wanted to do it before some general changed his mind again. But he did not want to preempt one of the crews and possibly damage the skyrocketing morale of Wolf Flight. Wolf Flight was proving so successful that Weasels would only fly as a wingman when a target was heavily defended. The E-model's own RHAW gear was more than adequate to warn a Wolf to abort a mission, jettison his load and return to base. Of the thirty-six sorties launched over a period of nine nights only three had been aborted. The trawler was broadcasting attack warnings when the Wolves launched, and MiG-23 Floggers had been scrambled. But the PSI did not have the GCI coverage or a ground observer tracking net that could react in time to direct the Floggers onto the Wolves. Not too shabby, Waters thought.

"If any of you troops want a night off," Waters said, "I know of an old man that would like to go along as a wingy." Cheers greeted his announcement; they had all heard about the message.

"Whoever heard of a Wolf Zero-One being a wingman?" one irreverent voice asked.

"Some people will do *anything* to fly," another put in.

Waters bent his head in mock shame.

Thunder whispered to Jack. "He wants to go bad but he's leaving it up to you."

Jack gave him a puzzled look.

"Wolf Flight is your baby and he won't take it away from you," Thunder said.

Jack nodded . . . "I think Doc Landis wants to ground me for a while while he cures me of the clap." Jack said it with a straight face. Now everyone started to volunteer their slot for Waters, and one wizzo suggested they should make the wing commander a WSO so he could get a night off.

"Colonel, if you want to lead a flight, I'll be your wingy," Jack offered, and within a few minutes it was arranged with Stan-the-Man flying in Waters' pit.

The mission that Waters laid out for them was significantly different from the previous sorties. The wing commander pointed out that an identified headquarters merited much more attention and that both Phantoms would split at the IP and both would hit it. He would go first, using a new version of the Maverick they had received—the Maverick had been designed as an electro-guided anti-tank missile. The wizzo's radar scope became a TV screen that repeated what the seeker head was imaging. The wizzo drove the scope's target cursors over a high-contrast part of the target and locked on. The seeker head memorized the contrast, and when the pilot hit the pickle button the Maverick launched and homed in. The new Mavericks the 45th had received used a double-infrared seeker head that was very sensitive to heat signatures created by buildings, vehicles and people. Waters calculated that a headquarters would be very "hot" indeed at night.

At the prearranged time eight Phantoms of Wolf Flight hit their start buttons. But the number-two engine of Wolf One-Nine would not ignite when the RPM wound past fifteen percent. The wingman tried again, and still no ignition. It was an automatic abort for the pair of One-Nine and One-Eight. The remaining six birds fast-taxied for the runway. Waters and Jack were the last to take off since they had the closest target. Instead of hugging the water at two hundred feet, as Jack would have preferred, he lifted them up to four hundred feet, explaining that an old man's reflexes weren't that good. Waters reasoned that the trawler would send a launch warning no matter what altitude they ingressed at. But he was wrong; it was the PSI's coastal watch team that was sending the warnings. The trawler crew was apparently being lazy and not too concerned about detecting launches; it just monitored the watch team's frequency and repeated their warning over another frequency.

Waters used the higher altitude and pushed his throttles up, increasing his indicated airspeed to 480 knots over water. Stan kept grousing about the lousy RHAW gear in the pit of the F-4E but seemed satisfied that no search radars had found them. At the IP, Waters called, "Split," slight pause, "*now.*" He punched his clock, starting the second hand as the two fighters moved off on separate headings, losing contact with each other in the night. It was a new tactic for the Wolves and one that would make a rejoin very difficult.

Stan was concentrating on the image on his radar scope as Waters ran for his pop point. "A great picture, I think I've got the heat signature. It's glowing like a bonfire."

Waters grunted in acknowledgment, concentrating on wiring his speed at 520 knots and maintaining his compass heading as the clock ran down the seconds. He would pop at exactly one minute, eight-and-a-half miles in from the IP. He was using basic dead reckoning. As the second hand flicked onto sixty seconds Waters pulled the nose up, trusting Stan to get an early lock-on. Their RHAW gear came alive with chirps and barks of audio warning as air-defense radars found them.

"Locked on. Cleared to pickle," Stan said as he punched the chaff buttons on his left console. He did not, though, hit the flare button, knowing flares would draw attention to their part of the sky and might distract Jack, who should be rolling in right behind them. Stan would use flares and more chaff once he sighted a missile plume.

Waters rolled his Phantom one hundred thirty-five degrees and pulled its nose to the target, apexing at nineteen hundred feet, a tight pop. His finger flicked twice on the pickle button, sending two Mavericks on their way. Their sensitive seeker heads had pinpointed the target and homed in, allowing Waters to launch and leave. The explosions would serve as marker beacons for Jack to drop his load of Mark-82s on, which would do the real damage.

Waters keyed his radio, "Zero-One off hot." He had to tell Jack that he was clear of the target and the Mavericks were on the way. "SAM launch, eight o'clock," he warned Stan. The SAMs' rocket plumes were easily seen in the dark.

"Rog, Boss." Stan acknowledged. "Tallyho. No radar activity, probably an SA-9. Break—*now.*" Waters wrenched the Phantom's nose into the oncoming missiles, turning his tail away from their IR-guided seeker heads as Stan punched his flare button. Four flares shot out behind the F-4 and exploded, capturing the missiles' guidance head and sending them clear of the F-4. Six Mark-82s flashed in the night, and Jack was off the target. "Come right to one-three-five degrees," Stan directed. Waters envied his calm. "Thunder's found us with his radar. That interceptor symbol on the RHAW gear is from an F-4 radar."

Waters glanced at the small scope and saw an aircraft symbol at their four o'clock position, closing on them.

"Flash your anti-collision light," the bear directed. "Give Jack something to home on visually."

Waters bounced the flasher switch on, then off.

Stan had twisted in his seat to ensure they only flashed for a moment. When the anti-collision light did not come on, he said, "No light, boss. Make sure the fuselage switch is in the bright position and try it again."

Waters toggled the switch from DIM to BRT and hit the flasher switch again. This time the anti-collision light on the leading edge of the vertical stabilizer flashed twice and went out.

"Thanks, Stan," Waters said. Damn, I'm rusty, he thought. No wonder this is a young man's game . . .

"No problem, boss," Stan said, knowing how easy it was to lose your edge.

"Tallyho," Jack radioed. "Check right. Zero-One."

Waters did not acknowledge and "check" turned twenty degrees to the right as Jack had ordered.

A shadow slid over them and dropped into position on their left wing, materializing into the angular shape of an F-4. Jack was back in formation and they were on course.

"He's good," Waters said. "He made the rejoin look routine."

"They're *both* damn good," Stan added . . .

In the debrief the men found out how good Waters was. Without notes he ran through the entire mission, pulling from memory headings, speeds and altitudes. "We ingressed into the target at a different airspeed and altitude primarily to add more variables to our method of operating. I don't know if the Gomers monitored that phase of our flight or not. But if they did they now have plenty more factors to consider when they engage us. The idea is to make the situation more complicated for them, not us, and we're doing it." The colonel concentrated on the IP-through-escape phase of the mission, asking if Jack had any trouble acquiring the target.

"Not with the Mavericks acting as Willie Petes," Jack said, alluding to the white phosphorous marking rockets that slow-moving Forward Air Controllers used to mark targets.

"Yeah, but these Willie Petes hurt like hell and are accurate," Stan replied. "We need to use more of them. Beats the hell out of wide-area ordnance." The bear obviously preferred the rifle-bullet-through-the-heart method to the shotgun approach when dropping lethal ordnance. The bear was well named.

2 August: 1320 hours, Greenwich Mean Time
1650 hours, Tehran, Iran

The man removed his dark glasses when he entered the hospital room in Tehran. He studied the general lying in the bed . . . one leg was missing, the heavy bandage on his head confirmed he had lost an eye and the left side of his face was mangled. The man shuddered at the sight, thanking Allah it was not him; he preferred a quick and clean martyrdom. He suspected he had been summoned to the hospital for a very important reason when he made his normal courier run. The People's Soldiers of Islam commander's hawklike eye glared at the man from the silver Mercedes. "We monitored the radios of the devils who did this to me." The voice coming from the mass of bandages was not weak and had lost none of its command. "Find out *who* this is— this Wolf Zero-One—kill him. No—tell me and *I* will arrange his death."

Suddenly, without knowing it, Anthony Waters was in a personal war with a fanatic whose new mission was the death of an aging, well-married American colonel.

3 August: 0308 hours, Greenwich Mean Time
0508 hours, Athens, Greece

The phone call from the dispatcher woke Dave Belfort first. The C-130 navigator stared at his watch, noting that they had been in crew rest ten hours, the minimum the regulations allowed. He staggered to the window and twisted open the wooden shutters, marveling at the beauty of the first touches of sunrise across the Aegean. The busy street below them that led into the heart of Athens was quiet in the early morning dawn, a rare condition. "Come on, Sid." He shook his pilot, Sid Luna, awake. "A C-141 diverted into Athens for engine problems. We've got to pick up their passengers and get them down to Ras Assanya. I'll shake out Toni and the others."

An hour later the sleepy C-130 crew met the commander of the advanced party for the F-15 squadron going into Ras Assanya. "Where in the *hell* have you been?" the lieutenant colonel demanded. "We've got to get to Ras Assanya to receive and bed down twenty-four F-15s that are going to be landing there in eight hours."

The C-130 crew was started by the short man's barrage.

"Excuse me, Colonel," Belfort said, "it's a five-hour flight. We'll get you there with over two hours to spare."

"That's not enough. It's time you trash haulers earned your keep. Unplug your asses and get us in the air." The lieutenant colonel then stormed out to the waiting C-130.

"I'd say that Lieutenant Colonel Rupert Stansell has more than a touch of the Napoleon complex," Dave Belfort said, taking the man's name from the passenger list.

"More like an Adolf, if you ask me," Toni D'Angelo put in . . .

Five-and-one-half hours later the C-130 taxied off the runway at Ras Assanya. Much to the relief of the crew, the lieutenant colonel ignored them and stalked out of the Hercules toward the tall colonel wearing a flight suit waiting by a pickup truck.

Dave and Toni made the walk to Base Ops to file a new flight plan back to Athens while the C-130 offloaded. The dispatcher told them to expect at least an hour delay in getting the flight plan cleared. "The Arabs have been replacing foreign ATC controllers with Saudi nationals. The system is starting to bog down." Toni shrugged her shoulders. C-130 crews were used to delays for many reasons. They returned to the Hercules and were sitting on the ramp in the shade under the wing when the first F-15 touched down after making a radar-controlled approach. "I thought fighters did overhead recoveries," Toni said. An hour later the C-130 taxied out to take off as the last of the F-15s landed. They waited for a C-141 on final to land before they took the Active . . .

Captain Mary Hauser looked out of one of the small windows of the C-141 as the cargo plane taxied in, catching a glimpse of the C-130 taking off. The GCI controller from Outpost had been assigned to a new radar control post, Caravan, to furnish ground control to the F-15s. The Air Force also wanted her to determine if Caravan could be used as a cover for an intelligence-gathering operation. For Captain Mary Hauser—The times they were a-changin'.

4 August: 1000 hours, Greenwich Mean Time
1300 hours, Ras Assanya, Saudi Arabia

The order lifting the stand-down from daytime missions came in that morning. A frag order detailing three targets for the 45th arrived by courier two hours later. General Mashur al-Darhali had also seen and copied the frag order that directed the 45th to bomb the railroad-and-road complex leading to the Strait of Hormuz. Intelligence confirmed the People's Soldiers of Isam was shifting some men and supplies toward the south.

Carroll pointed out to Waters the PSI's growing number of amphibious and assault landing craft. "This could mean a military buildup that will allow the PSI to use those ships to strike across the Strait of Hormuz right into Oman. Not only will that give them control of *both* sides of the Strait and the ability to seal it off, but they'll have a beachhead on the Saudi Arabian peninsula."

The frag order made overwhelming sense.

Stansell had insisted that his pilots be thoroughly briefed on the entire operation before they flew CAP for the 45th and the main briefing room in the COIC was filled to overflowing as the F-15 pilots settled in for their orientation briefing, eager to start flying combat. Jack and Thunder stood in the back of the room, listening to a fresh echo of their own words when they had first arrived. Now the refrain

. . . "It's the only war we got" . . . didn't seem so funny to the two veterans.

The room was called to attention when Waters and Stansell entered and took their seats in the front row. But when Captain Mary Hauser stood to outline local Ground Control Intercept procedures and capabilities Stansell interrupted her. "Captain, are you to be in charge of controlling F-15s? We had expected someone more senior to be in charge—"

"I am a fully qualified master controller and have commanded units in the past, Colonel"—Mary wasn't too surprised by this boring outbreak of old-fashioned sexism. "If my rank is bothering you, captains normally run radar posts—"

"I was thinking of someone with more experience." Stansell's face was going to red. "We're the premier F-15 squadron in the Air Force. That's why we're here. Don't you forget it."

Jack couldn't take any more of it, and Waters was about to bust. "Colonel Stansell, excuse me." Jack spoke just loud enough to catch Stansell's attention. "I've worked with Captain Hauser before. She's the best GCI controller I've run across."

"And what in the hell would an F-4 driver know about what makes a good GCI controller?" Stansell shot back. Heads pivoted toward Jack. Stansell now smiled indulgently and decided to administer the coup de grace: "Fighter aircraft don't need a backseater."

Jack returned the smile and lowered his voice, making everyone strain to hear what he was saying. "We"—he nodded toward his wizzo —"were being controlled by Captain Hauser when we got a MiG. I believe that's one more than anyone else in this room can claim. I believe that's testimony to her ability as a controller."

A round of approval via applause and even whistles from the middle of Stansell's own F-15 pilots broke the heavy tension.

"Off-hand," Thunder said to Locke, "I'd say Colonel Stansell isn't the most popular fellow with his own troops."

The shrill siren-like sounds of cranking F-15 engines blended with the blunt roar of the F-4s. Crew chiefs hurried to button up the panels on the F-4s and marshal their birds into the taxi flow of the combined mission as the first eight F-15 Eagles taxied rapidly out of their bunkers, bringing their canopies down in a synchronized routine. Twelve of C.J.'s squadron followed, loaded out for SAMs and Triple A suppression. Another eight F-15s fell into place followed by thirty-six lumbering, bomb-laden attack F-4s. The last eight F-15s then taxied out, completing the strike force.

Waters twisted about in the cockpit of his F-4 to see if his entire package had taxied. A pickup truck pulled up alongside and the driver gave him a thumbs-up followed by a zero formed by his thumb and forefinger: there were no dropouts; the strike was formed. A green light flashed from the control tower and the Eagles roared down the runway in pairs, quickly lifting off and reaching for the sky, not needing to light their afterburners.

The fighters headed southeast. C.J. and his wingman split off from his flight and headed for the Russian trawler that was moving inshore trying to monitor the takeoff visually. The two Phantoms dropped down, skimming the smooth green cellophane of the Gulf. They could see figures running on deck as they bore down on the trawler. C.J. clicked his sight on and told his wizzo to lock on with his radar. "That should get their attention." The two Phantoms stroked their afterburners, pulling up and barely clearing the spy ship, which rocked under their jet-wash. The two birds rejoined as the trawler turned back out to sea. "If we can't touch the bastards, maybe we can scare them away," C.J. observed.

The PSI watch team on the coast had been warned about the launch and had no difficulty counting the birds as they took off. The radio operator was encoding the launch warning when a small British commando squad attacked. The twelve men from the SAS moved with precision and speed as they annihilated the team. Each man, but one, took out his assigned target within twenty seconds. The lone survivor had escaped to the latrine under the floorboards. The attackers methodically searched the area for the missing man until the leader motioned the unblooded member of his squad toward the latrine. The man scampered soundlessly across the open ground until he was within ten yards of it. In passable Arabic he called out a name: "Amini, come out. The fighting is done." When nothing happened he repeated it in Farsi. Slowly the man climbed out of the muck. And a single shot took off the top of his head.

The commando leader checked the stopwatch on his wrist. "Message?" he rapped. The shake of a head told him that the PSI watch-team had not gotten off a warning message. He wiped the sweat off his blackened face. "Bloody hell," he added in a crisp British accent, "even an unscheduled trip to the loo can't stop us."

Jack and Thunder sat on the beach and counted the jets as the strike force completed their launch. Since Wolf Flight was scheduled to fly that night, they were not part of the strike. They saw C.J. buzz the trawler in the distance but doubted it would do much good. "He'll radio the Gomers," Jack said. "At least he'll have the count wrong."

"He'll be back out there tonight when we launch," Thunder said. "I wish we could do something about him."

Jack tried to think of a way to discourage the trawler from monitoring their takeoffs. "We need a different type of intimidation . . ."

While the trawler did not get an accurate count of the launching aircraft, its crew was able to relay the exact time of launch to the PSI's waiting air-defense command net. The MiGs were standing by and scrambled to meet the Americans. Mary Hauser was at her radar console analyzing the multiple targets appearing on her scope. Her right hand flashed over the buttons on her IFF panel. Without looking, she selected the mode that interrogated the Floggers' IFF. "Let's see if any of you gentlemen have your IFF's on," she said under her breath, hitting the interrogate button. Every target responded. Mary nodded in satisfaction and quickly counted eighteen bandits. "So, you assume your IFF is secure. Never assume anything in this business . . ."

"Stormy." Mary keyed her transmit button, calling the lead F-15. "Bandits, ten o'clock at eighty-five, angels thirty." The short transmission by the GCI controller alerted every Eagle pilot to the inbound threat, telling them hostile aircraft were coming at them from sixty degrees to the left, eighty-five nautical miles away and were at thirty thousand feet. By only identifying the lead F-15, she hoped to confuse any enemy monitoring her radio frequency; they would have to sort out who "Stormy" was and the number of F-15s.

The F-15s turned to the left, into the Floggers. The radio crackled with commands as the F-15s used their radar sets to break out the MiGs and assign each Eagle a target. Then the PSI started communications jamming. Only the GCI site had the brute power to override the jamming, and Mary Hauser's cool voice could be heard as she paired up targets and F-15s, rapidly calling the Eagles to new, jam-free radio frequencies. The F-15s surged away from the F-4s and met the MiGs head-on while the attack birds dropped down to the deck, still over water.

Much to Mary's surprise the F-15s did not mix it up with the MiGs but launched their radar missiles from a front aspect and then blew on through the MiGs, zooming out of the flight. The symmetry of the engagement shattered as the MiGs dodged the missiles and scattered over the sky. The MiG pilots were startled to find no F-15s to contend with and switched their attention to the F-4s, which they had no trouble finding, their camouflage paint standing in stark contrast against the bright green of the gulf.

C.J. swore at the F-15s, angry at their poor tactics. He pushed forward the radio transmit button under his left thumb on the throttles to transmit an abort, and in his anger broke the switch off. Before he could tell Stan to transmit the message he heard Waters aborting the mission and ordering the Phantoms to jettison their loads. C.J.'s left hand moved over the weapons-selector panel, choosing what he would jettison. He punched off the F-15 type fuel tank on his centerline but kept the two valuable Standard Arm anti-radiation missiles carried on each inboard pylon, then toggled his pinky switch under his left little finger on the throttle to guns.

The voice of Stan-the-Man came over the intercom. "Bandit, left eight o'clock, coming to your nine, low. Hard left, engage." He could have been at the bar ordering a round of drinks, for all the excitement in his voice. The Flogger was not in a position behind C.J. to launch a missile and was closing in for a gun kill with its twenty-three-millimeter cannon.

Without first looking for the bandit, C.J. wrenched his bird to the left as Stan had directed. When the MiG pilot saw the F-4's nose turn and point directly at him, he chose to disengage, break off the attack,

turned slightly to the right and accelerated ahead. But the Flogger
pilot had given C.J. too much room to turn onto him. He should have
pointed his Flogger directly into the Phantom. As it was, the thirty
degrees he gave C.J. would cost him his life. With his Phantom still
in front, at the Flogger's eleven o'clock, C.J. now pulled his nose up,
not wanting to shoot past the MiG in the opposite direction, and used
the vertical to turn into the MiG. He was still on his back and pulling
the nose toward the ground when the Flogger slashed into his sight
ring. C.J. always flew with a "stiff sight," reducing the amount of lead
fed into the sight-picture, a mode especially suited for a close-in fight.
Now he mashed the trigger for a snap shot, sending a stream of
high-explosive bullets into the MiG. Over thirty rounds tore the plane
apart.

But there was no momentary exultation in the kill for C.J. He
immediately checked his fuel and rolled ninety degrees for a belly
check, looking for bandits beneath him. He was a professional going
about his business. He would celebrate later.

"Shit hot," his wingman yelled over the radio. "I'm at your six,
come off right." C.J. turned one hundred eighty degrees to the right
and rolled out, heading for Ras Assanya. His wingman fell into place
on his left and slightly above him in a tactical formation. Homeward
bound.

Jack and Thunder were still sitting on the beach when the first of
the Phantoms started to recover. Jack glanced at his watch. "They've
aborted the mission; something must have gone wrong." They stood
in the hot sun and counted the returning planes. The worry they both
felt lessened when a returning Phantom entered the pattern and did
a victory roll as it passed down the runway. "The Eagle drivers aren't
going to like that," he said. "Looks like one of C.J.'s Weasels got a
MiG."

"It was C.J.," Thunder said. "I caught the tail number."

"I only counted forty-seven F-4s," Jack said. One Phantom was
missing. "Let's get over to the COIC and find out what in the hell went
wrong." They pulled their flight suits over their trunks and ran across
the hot sand.

They found Waters in the crowded main briefing room of the COIC talking to Bull Morgan. The returning air crews were waiting for their turn to debrief and most were sitting dejectedly, not talking.

Stansell came into the room and marched up to Waters. "What went wrong?" the little colonel demanded.

Waters glared at him. He had seen bravado used as a smoke screen for a foul-up before. "I was going to ask *you* that question."

"We engaged like we briefed," Stansell shot back. The room went silent. "We plan and practice to shoot the bad guys in the face, blow on through and take on the next wave of targets. We maintain our flight integrity and use our head-on ability to the max extent possible—"

"That would be nice if you managed to shoot someone down," Waters said. "As it was, you didn't get a single kill and left the area. We were right under the MiGs, still over water; they had no trouble finding us. We were lucky, they only got one. That's my eleventh loss. At least the others got over Iran—for whatever that's worth. You didn't help, you just got in the way."

Waters cut it off, turned and walked out of the room. Each loss his wing suffered made it increasingly difficult for him to keep pushing his crews into combat. As the war ground on, his chief concern was slowly shifting away from the mission he had been assigned and onto the survival of his aircrews. The Pentagon might not understand that. Well, they dealt in paper, not people.

Bull Morgan was experiencing a different reaction. He had seen his wingman explode in a fireball when an Atoll missile, fired by a MiG that had maneuvered behind them, found its target. When Stansell started to leave the room after Waters he found his way blocked by Bull's bulk, which materialized in front of him. The corded strength of Bull's neck muscles caused arteries to visibly pulse. He stuck a finger in the middle of Stansell's forehead. "Stick around to fight next time or I'll squash your fucking head."

Stansell stood his ground. "Maybe a court-martial will remind you of the difference between a lieutenant colonel and a major. Don't threaten me—"

"Not a threat, Colonel"—Bull's finger punched a tattoo on his forehead—"a promise that you'll be giving your testimony with freshly rearranged brains."

Jack hurried up to put a hand on Bull's shoulder, feeling the man's knotted muscles ripple in anger. "Your turn to debrief," he said, leading his squadron commander away.

Ten minutes after Stansell's own debrief he walked across the freshly paved street to the small set of trailers that served as wing headquarters, where he found Waters' office door open. "Come in, Colonel Stansell. I had a feeling you'd be along."

"Okay, I'm a bastard. I know that . . ." Stansell's self-appraisal caught Waters' attention. It was probably the only thing the two men agreed on—Waters sure as hell didn't like the bull-headed way Stansell ran the F-15s. True, both men had combat experience in Vietnam, yet both had come away with totally different reactions. For Waters it had demonstrated that most men want a leader who trusts them, leaves them to do their job and is capable of gutting out the hard decisions and never losing sight of the mission of tactical fighter aircraft. Mostly, Stansell had found that war was a means of demonstrating his control over people, which flattered his ego.

". . . and our tactics went wrong," the F-15 pilot went on, fortunate he couldn't read Waters' thoughts. Waters motioned him to a seat, and rocked back in his chair, determined to give the man a chance. "I was told not to lose any birds. In fact, it's my number-one marching order. But our job is to protect you by shooting the Gomers down. So far, you've managed to do that better than we have. That bunch of prima donnas that I sit on will start doing their own thing unless I find a way to use them. My own wingman wouldn't talk during our own debrief. He told me that that it was my show so I could debrief it any way I wanted. Do you know what else he said?" The hurt in Stansell's voice was apparent, a condition Waters hadn't thought the man capable of. "He told me to win engagements in the air, not in the debrief."

"And?" Waters said, still waiting.

"We need to work out new CAP tactics with your people. What we did today obviously didn't work."

Waters continued to stare at the man.

"Okay, what *I* did today didn't work. *I* screwed up big time."

"Join the club," Waters said, standing up. The man was human, after all. Besides, he needed his F-15s. "I've canceled tonight's Wolf strike. Get your most creative tactics man with Lieutenant Locke and put them to work. Once they've worked something out we'll hear their plan. We only make necessary changes. Got it?"

Stansell nodded quickly, then said: "Would you object if *I* worked with Lieutenant Locke?"

"Okay, but don't pull rank. You're equals on this project and I'll tell him so." Again Stansell gave a sharp nod. "By the way, Locke pins on his captain's bars next Wednesday. It is about time he made it. Listen to him, he's good."

Stansell stood up, ready to leave. "Colonel Waters, please tell Major Morgan that we will stick around next time." It was as close to an apology as he could come. "And relay my congratulations to Major Conlan for getting a MiG." Stansell then left wing headquarters, looking for Jack Locke. His ego had taken a beating and his stomach was tying knots around his backbone. He felt a sense of shame, near-humiliation, that he not experienced since he was a fourth classman at the Academy in 1966. Only one way to shed that awful feeling: do better, and fast.

The stranglehold of tension that bound Waters' existence did not fade as he paced his office, not sure if the feisty Stansell really meant what he said. No question, he had to cut his losses, and for the first time he seriously doubted that he could make it happen. He tried to push his thinking into more productive channels, putting his thoughts of Mike Fairly, Tom Gomez and the others into a hidden niche, walling them behind the detailed bricks of running his wing. But the number eleven would not be contained, and it kept flashing its defiance, challenging him: fifteen crewmen either dead or MIA, eleven aircraft lost, all because of orders he had given, decisions he had made.

A vivid mental image of a brick wall materialized in front of him and collapsed, revealing Sara, her arms outstretched, offering him refuge. With an inner discipline he didn't know he possessed, he forced away the image. God, now I'm hallucinating. I can't run this wing or anything else if I'm coming apart at the seams. He picked up his phone, dialed, listening to each ring. Relief came over him when he heard the mild greeting. "Doc," he said, "I need to talk . . ."

The patient in Doc Landis' office was handed on to another flight surgeon and the doctor hurried over to wing headquarters, concerned about his most important charge. The heat slowed him to a more sedate walk, giving him time to think about the burden Waters must be carrying, and how eventually it would wear him down.

Somehow, Landis realized, he had to find the words to make Waters shed any *exaggerated* sense of moral responsibility for the men. There were certain words Landis could not use, words that would only reinforce the basic problem. The same strength that Waters gave to his command could not be used to help him. In spite of their losses the wing's morale was high and seemed capable of absorbing the shock of seeing their comrades shot down. Yet everything the doctor had seen and sensed as he talked to the men and women of the wing confirmed his original impression: the mortar holding the 45th together was a deep-seated trust in one Anthony J. Waters. But telling him that would only fuel the fire that was already consuming him.

The doctor found Waters sitting behind his desk, wading through a stack of paperwork. "Come on in, Doc, and shut the door." Fatigue lines etched furrows around his eyes and mouth. A tautness had driven out the vestiges of his once relaxed nature. Every physical sign pointed to a man being driven by his own inner demands.

"Don't tell me you've got the clap too," Landis said straight-faced.

The wing commander tried to force a grin that would not form. But it was the doctor's first chip in the wall of stress.

"Is that getting to be a problem?" Waters asked.

"No, not really. It's just about the only thing I seem to be treating these days, that and The Rats Ass Crude, our local variety of dysentery."

"Where's the clap coming from?" A sparkle of amusement was trying to creep into the wing commander's eyes.

"Not sure yet. Maybe from our imported ladies. There are certainly enough of them, and a few of our more resourceful airmen have found a way to break through the language barrier and expand their services." Indeed, over one hundred-fifty girls, mostly from Sri Lanka, had been contracted for to provide janitorial and maid services to the Americans. Waters nodded at the thought of the girls and how their small lithe bodies, large brown eyes, masses of dark hair and graceful movements as they went about their work cast an aura of grace and charm. He could understand why his men found them attractive and looked for a way around the chaperons that the contractors had provided to run the compound where the girls and other civilians lived.

"Colonel, all things considered," Landis went on, "I'm not surprised that they've managed to get their things together. At least money hasn't exchanged hands—yet." The grin that was more characteristic of Waters finally broke through. "East meets West, so to speak, with a bang. At least I haven't had any requests to marry. These girls strike me as being so giving and gentle that some of our troops are bound to fall sooner or later. It's the good old American way of war —marry the locals. But, that's not what I wanted to talk about, Doc. I had an hallucination or something like one a few minutes ago." And Waters proceeded to recount his images of walls and bricks as Jeff Landis sat in front of him, hunched over, elbows on his knees, clasping his hands as he listened, not wanting to say a word until the colonel was finished. As Waters talked the doctor's worry began to recede and Waters was finding the sounding board he needed to break his tensions against. The old Waters, he felt, was pretty much in place by the time he stopped talking. "I'm keeping too much bottled up inside me, aren't I, Doc?"

"Probably. Human beings need to share each other's burdens. That's what those girls are doing, sharing their loneliness and sense of dislocation with someone else. And I don't think you were hallucinating; your sense of reality is intact and you knew it wasn't real. Your subconscious was simply sending you a strong visual image. It's the price a sane man pays when he fights a war."

The doctor believed he had said enough and guided the conversation away from Waters and onto their current operations. When he left Waters' office he was reasonably sure that Waters was in control of himself and the wing. Not every commander was a Colonel Morris. Waters was made of sterner stuff.

Stansell finally located Jack on the beach hidden between two low dunes, sitting under a canvas canopy he had rigged, pulling on a beer and staring out to sea.

"You spend a lot of time here?" Stansell asked.

Jack handed him a cold beer from the cooler and motioned him into the shade of the canvas canopy. Stansell accepted it as a peace offering and sat down. "It's a good place to think. Not too many people swim out here even though the water is crystal clear. Doc Landis says there's some pollution and I guess the shark net is out there for a reason, but I haven't seen one yet." Jack continued to look out to sea, not wanting to tell the man that he felt better when he could concentrate without distractions on the men who had killed his friends.

"Colonel Waters asked me to get with you and work out some tactics," Stansell said, waiting for the reaction. He was uncomfortable in the heat and crawled out of his Nomex flight suit, sitting in his shorts.

"I've been thinking on it, Colonel. The main problem is that damn trawler. It's giving the Gomers our launch times and their reaction time keeps getting shorter and shorter. Hell, they were scrambled and jumped you before you coasted in. That's why Colonel Waters canceled tonight's missions. He figures we'd be jumped too."

Jack was somewhat mistaken about the significance of the trawler; actually it only provided confirmation to the PSI that the frag order they had received from Mashur was being implemented. Without knowing the time and targets that were going to be attacked in advance, the PSI could not react in time to intercept them.

"It's no big deal on changing tactics," Jack went on. "I think your idea of blowing through the Gomers is a good one, but I also think you got it back-asswards."

Stansell wanted to point out that an F-4 mud-mover couldn't have a clue about how to employ an F-15, then remembered Waters' words about listening to the pilot and strangled his reply.

"The MiGs come at us in waves," Jack said, "and I want to use that against them. Break your Eagles into three flights, about like you did last time. When your first flight of Eagles encounters MiGs, shoot them in the face with missiles just like last time. *But* instead of blowing on through and leaving the fight, stick around and fight. The F-15 can out-turn any Flogger built, it should be a turkey-shoot for you. Then the second flight of Eagles should blow on through, stuffing any bandit they can in the face. It's the second flight's contract to meet the second wave, the third flight's to meet the third wave."

"What if there's a fourth wave?"

"We should be off-target by then and headed home. There'll be enough F-15s in the area to confuse them and we can defend ourselves at that point."

Stansell thought it over. His inclination was to change things, make it more complicated, vary the way they would engage the MiGs. It upset him that he couldn't think of anything better under the circumstances. Like most officers, especially action-oriented ones, he wasn't an introspective person, rarely bothered to look at himself. Now for the first time in his career he realized someone else's way of thinking was very probably better than his own . . . and it had taken a lieutenant to make him face up to it. Well, a lieutenant going on captain, he reminded himself, trying to find some consolation.

No denying it, this Jack Locke had the potential to be a first-rate leader, maybe even a combat commander. "Jack, I'd be glad to be your sponsor if you want to transition to F-15s."

"Thanks, I appreciate your offer, but I'll stick with Big Ugly for a while longer. At least until this is over." And added quickly, "Besides, I've got to get Thunder home and married. It's something Colonel Fairly trusted me to do." Jack's voice quieted. "He was my squadron commander and flight lead when Thunder and I got a Libyan MiG. He bought it on our second mission here."

Stansell heard him loud and clear—and the underlying need for revenge.

Waters sat and listened to Jack's proposed change in tactics for the Eagles and agreed with him about the early warning the trawler was giving the PSI. "We've got to slow down the reaction time of the Floggers or we're dead in the water, pun intended."

"Let's get the Navy to come in and blow it away," Stansell suggested.

Bill Carroll shook his head. "Maintaining the alleged neutrality of the Gulf is one of our major political objectives. The U.S. isn't about to provoke a neutral, including the Soviet Union—at least they're officially neutral so far. We need to jam the hell out of that trawler."

Jack was on his feet. "Okay . . . what if a big, unidentified neutral ship with one hell of a jammer happened to show up when we launch and parked next to it?"

"Could work, but where are we going to find one of those puppies?" Waters asked.

"I know where, but I'll need to go to Riyadh and talk to an old . . . acquaintance."

Waters rocked back on the hindlegs of his chair, quickly running through what Jack had said, not wanting to delay his answer too long before the rivulets of doubt would form. "Why do I get the feeling that I don't want to know any more?" he said, and smiled. "Take three days and see if you can get what you want. After that, get back here and lay it all out. You'll probably scare the hell out of me but that's what I get paid for."

Jack thought for a moment, then: "Can I take Carroll here with me? Might get some use out of his subtle tongue."

"Might as well. Bill needs a break. Now get going."

Waters waited until Jack and Carroll had left the room. "Well?" he said to Stansell.

"You're right. He is good. But aren't you worried about what he's trying to arrange in Riyadh?"

"A lot," Waters told him. "But . . ." He wanted to demonstrate to Stansell how he worked, believing the man could add more to the wing's operation if he accepted his way of ordering and leading. "But I've got to take the calculated risk and trust him or word will get out that I've got the 'disease of the colonels.' "

"The disease of what?"

"The main symptom of it is when you tell your troops to do something and then reject it after they've done it because it's not what you wanted. Great for buying shoes but a lousy way to inspire trust and confidence."

Stansell was beginning to understand why the morale of the 45th, in spite of its losses, was so high, and why young and promising pilots like Locke were more than willing to stay with the wing . . . Waters was one hell of an officer.

6 August: 1415 hours, Greenwich Mean Time
1715 hours, Riyadh, Saudi Arabia

Jack and Carroll were shocked at the prices of the modest hotel they had found in Riyadh. After a hurried consultation they decided they could afford the cheapest double room for one night; then they'd have to find another, much less expensive hotel if they had to stay a second. Once in the room, Bill flopped onto one of the narrow, hard beds and dialed the number Jack had given him. His fluent Arabic proved to be the key, and Jack soon found himself listening to the cultured Oxford accent of Prince Reza Ibn Abdul Turika. Within an hour they had checked out of the hotel, been driven to the prince's residence and ushered into separate, wondrously plush bedrooms.

A discreet knock on the door announced the prince. "Jack, my friend, I am pleased to see you." Reza extended his hand. His soft leather loafers, slacks, and open-necked silk shirt were Côte d'Azure and not Arabian. "Please introduce me to your friend. My servants are impressed by his Arabic. It is rare for an American to have such mastery of our language as your Captain Carroll." He led the two men into a large well-appointed lounge and indicated seats for them on divans around an ornate coffee table.

A servant wheeled out a covered trolley that proved to be a portable bar and proceeded to mix a dry martini for Reza. "You Americans have developed a most civilized drink with good English gin. It may be one of your more important contributions to the world's culture."

Carroll understood what the prince's martini implied—he was Arab. Outside his residency Reza would act like a Saudi; only in the privacy of his home or abroad would he be the modern man. A slim, remarkably beautiful woman in tight jeans and a tailored shirt joined them and was introduced by Reza as his wife. Carroll wondered how in hell Jack had met this Saudi prince.

"You no longer, how do you say, have your hair on fire?" Reza said, smiling at Jack. His wife had asked to be excused, aware that her husband was turning to the purpose of the men's visit.

"I guess the war can make even a flyboy grow up fast," Jack said.

"And how is your black friend . . . Thunder?"

"Well, matter of fact, he's busy planning our next mission. Otherwise he would have come along with us."

"Ah, yes, your Wolf Flight is famous. Your American newspapers seem to believe you to be a new Lawrence of Arabia while they condemn our small war of survival. I suspected Thunder was a force behind your successful night missions. It's too bad that all the resources of the 45th can't be used against the People's Soldiers."

"Well, we figure we could do more if a Soviet trawler monitoring our launches was somehow stopped from warning the PSI that we're coming. The trawler gives them time to scramble against us before we hit our targets."

Okay, there it was . . . out on the table.

"Yes, Jack, I understand your problem. But as long as the trawler stays in international waters there is little that can be done about it. You understand we cannot compromise the status of the Gulf . . . it must not become a battleground. It has been an old problem with the Iranians and Iraqis, we dare not enlarge it . . ."

"Maybe if we could borrow an oil tanker to act like an iron curtain around the trawler, something might be done about it," Jack said, and then, speaking quietly, he laid out what he had in mind.

When he had finished, Reza nodded. "I believe I can arrange that. Jack, our way is different than yours and what you are asking for involves political exchanges. It is Byzantine politics. Think of it as a labyrinth with many passages we must go down at the same time."

Reza could not, of course, tell them about his cousin who was passing on the frag order to the People's Soldiers of Islam. The Americans could not be expected to comprehend the power struggles that went on in the Saudi royal family, requiring that Mashur be protected. At least, he thought, Mashur will be in England attending the Farnborough air show for the next few days. The Americans would also find it confusing that religious leaders in his country were crying for the Americans to be expelled . . . and under other circumstances he would also like to seem them go . . . but he and those of more practical bent appreciated how much his country needed the 45th . . .

8 August: 1200 hours, Greenwich Mean Time
1500 hours, Ras Assanya, Saudi Arabia

Two days later Reza's small Gates Learjet deposited Jack and Carroll at Ras Assanya. Thunder was waiting with a pickup and drove them to the COIC, where Waters was anxious to hear about their trip.

"Reza has some Japanese friends who will be happy to even a few old scores. An oil tanker will be available when we get our next frag order," Jack told Waters.

"Can we trust him?" Waters asked.

"Can we afford not to, sir? . . . There's something else, Colonel. Something there's no question about. We need to change the way we get out of bad-guy land and work on bagging a few MiGs. We figure it's time to even the score."

The first shrill whines of the starting engines jarred Jack out of his sleep. It would be the first strike since they had aborted with the F-15s. At first he had felt relief when the frag order came in two days after he and Carroll had returned from Riyadh. The targets indicated the PSI was again pushing at Basra, trying to break it open. But the United Arab Command was tenaciously holding, taking heavy casualties. This time the 45th was fragged against the transportation net in an attempt to freeze movement of men and supplies away from the FEBA, The Forward Edge of Battle Area—the front. But doubts were starting to build—was his plan too ambitious, was he relying too much on Reza? And if it was, and if he was . . . well, the thought of dying in a grubby little war helping the Arabs—as a group, people he didn't particularly like—wasn't one he relished. Still, he did like Reza, the only Arab he knew personally. Whatever, it bothered him sometimes that he was fighting for political goals old men in comfortable rooms had chosen for him. But then he remembered Doc Landis' words at Mike Fairly's memorial service: ending a small war before it became a larger, uncontainable war was what it was all about. And there was another thing, something very simple and deep: he wanted to hurt the enemy that had killed his friends. He wanted his revenge. But were the sacrifices worth the results? Only when he snapped the gear and flaps up on takeoff could he stop brooding and find his answer dropping bombs on a hostile target. It was simple then: them or us, kill or be killed.

The trawler's radar operator studied his scope, watching the big blip move toward them. He had noticed it thirty minutes earlier but had decided it was one of the rare ships that still chanced the run into Kuwait. He carefully plotted the new position of the ship, confirming its course. "Konstantine," he called out the open door of the stifling hot cabin that served as the radar shack on the trawler, "there is a large ship bearing down on us. Have the lookouts check on it and tell the captain. It is not in the shipping channels."

"Impossible," the mate said. "It would have to be out of ballast to be in these shallow waters. They don't do that." One of the lookouts solved the argument by calling in and reporting that an oil tanker riding high in the water was bearing down on them but should pass to their left, between them and Ras Assanya. Konstantine ran out to the bridge's wing and focused his binoculars on the ship. "Get the captain," he snapped. Every eye on the trawler studied the tanker.

The captain came onto the bridge, still half-asleep and rubbing his chin. "Identify him," he said, focusing his binoculars on the ship. "We will report him to the International Maritime Commission. At least his insurance rates will rocket for being out of the shipping channels—" He froze as he saw the bow of the tanker start a swing toward his trawler, putting them on a collision course. "Hard to starboard," he ordered the helmsman, turning his much smaller craft away from the looming mass of the tanker brushing past them. Well, at least the idiot must realize where he is and return to the proper channel—

"Fighters!" the aft lookout reported in. "I count over thirty headed north, are launching . . ."

"Why didn't you report them sooner?" the captain barked into his headset.

"The tanker was in the way. I cannot see through steel, Captain. Ask the radar operators why they have not reported it."

The captain knew the 45th maintained strict radio silence and his operators had to rely on radar to pick up launching aircraft out of Ras Assanya. But why hadn't they reported anything? "Captain, we're being jammed," the chief radar operator told him, answering his unspoken question.

All doubts he had about the tanker vanished. It was a trick of the Americans. But whose tanker was it? They had not been able to identify it. "Radio a warning," the captain told his operators, hoping the air-defense net would receive the message in time to react.

"Captain," the mate told him, "all our radio frequencies are being jammed. The jamming is very close to us. It must be from the tanker." The two men ran back out onto the open wing of the bridge. The tanker was slowly turning, staying close to the trawler. Until they could stand well clear of the tanker, they could not overcome its jamming.

"We've got to outrun the tanker. Turn to the north; find another frequency. They can't jam everything we have . . ." The mate could hear the building panic in the captain's orders. Soon he would be in command of the trawler and not the old fool who swilled cheap vodka and slept past six in the morning. The radio operators rapidly cycled to new frequences as they searched for an open channel to transmit a warning message. But as soon as they found one the automatic frequency sweep on the tanker's jammer would lock on them and override their signal. As the trawler tried to draw abeam of the tanker the huge ship again turned into the trawler, forcing it to turn eastward and continuing to cast its shadow over the trawler's radio frequencies.

After seventeen minutes, the jamming ceased and the tanker stood clear of the trawler, signaling, "Can we be of any assistance?"

The captain swore and beat on the railing, fully aware the Phantoms were reaching into Iran.

The captain of the oil tanker *Tokara Maru* stood on the starboard wing of the bridge, concentrating on the Russian trawler as his ship turned south, his weather-beaten face impassive while the trawler disappeared behind him. The captain stood almost five feet ten inches, tall for a Japanese of his generation, and at sixty-three years of age, his rigid discipline and self-control masked the satisfaction he felt. He turned now and walked into the spotless, air-conditioned bridge.

The officer of the watch saw him turn and warned the helmsman that the captain was coming. The old man was a perfectionist.

The navigation officer was still awed by the captain's piloting of the 150,000-ton ship—small by supertanker standards—around the trawler. Only the officer of the watch acknowledged the captain's entrance with a crisp bow. The captain glanced at the radar, fixing the location of the trawler and his ship, and walked out onto the port wing.

"He hates the Russians," the helmsman said *sotto voce.*

"Most Kuril islanders do," the navigation officer put in. "He was forced to leave with his family in 1945 when the Russians took over their island, Kunashir.''

The bridge became silent when the captain reentered and stood beside his chair—he seldom sat down. ''How long to the rendezvous with our escort?''

''Forty-six minutes,'' the navigation officer told him. ''We are in radio contact with the British frigate and Dutch minesweeper the United Arab Command has arranged to escort us through the Strait of Hormuz. The frigate sends a 'well done.' ''

The old man focused on the horizon. ''Please relay the message to the crew and tell them I am most satisfied with their performance. Now we must return the *Tokara Maru* safely to the open sea. She is my last command.'' He silently reprimanded himself for saying so much, but he was pleased with his crew. He had not been allowed to tell them about the coded radio message from the company's headquarters in Yokohama that asked him to take his ship into the Persian Gulf as a jamming platform for the Americans. He had only told them that the next voyage would be dangerous. They had volunteered to the man. The captain's face relaxed. The men on the bridge exchanged furtive glances. Their captain was very pleased.

This time, without warnings from either Mashur or the trawler, the strike force was able to reach its targets unopposed, hugging the deck and trying to avoid early-warning air-defense radar. Without MiGs to contend with they were able to fly around the last known positions of SAM and Triple A sites. And their intelligence was current, courtesy of the Stealths.

It was, of course, impossible to avoid all the defense sites, and they deliberately challenged a few emplacements, relying on surprise and hoping to catch the PSI at their early-morning prayers. Waters was leading the first attack flight and was nearing his IP. Sweat poured off his face as he concentrated on picking up the small cluster of buildings located at the junction of two dirt roads that his wizzo had selected as their Initial Point. It flashed into his front left-quarter panel, exactly where it was supposed to be. As his flight flew over the buildings he could see six figures still kneeling on the ground next to their trucks, looking at the fighters turning above them. They would soon be on their radios, warning the railroad marshaling junction an attack was imminent and fighters were inbound. Well, they would have to be damn quick; he was less than a minute out.

So far the PSI had not reacted. Waters doubted it would be as smooth getting out. It depended on the last half of Jack's plan. Two miles out from the junction he pulled in a pop maneuver, seeing the railroad junction with eight boxcars on sidings for the first time. He rolled in and pickled his bombs off. Before the bombs exploded he could see figures running for cover. He jinked the Phantom hard as he escaped, not taking chances, expecting to receive ground fire. His wizzo told him the other three planes in his flight were safely off target; their six o'clock was clear and no bandits were in sight. Waters was too old a hand to relax and concentrated on getting himself and his wingman out of the target area. They headed southwest, toward the city of Basra, an escape route they had never used before.

Jack's plan had been simple: egress over Basra, the pivot point of the whole conflict. He had maintained that the UAC would never be able to coordinate its own air-defense network sufficiently to allow the fighters through. But if the UAC ordered its own Triple A and SAMs to remain at weapons-tight, only shooting at aircraft positively identified as hostile between 8:00 at night and 7:00 each morning, the 45th could hit its targets early in the morning and sneak through before the gunners started shooting at everything in sight. The UAC had agreed and sent out the order the day before. Mashur was still in England, taking a prolonged vacation . . .

The last of the Phantoms exited over Basra at 6:44 A.M. with MiGs in hot pursuit. The escorting F-15s had turned around and were sorting the MiGs out, each Eagle driver picking his target. For the next six minutes the embattled inhabitants and defenders of Basra watched as the F-15s met the MiGs over their city, engaging in classic aerial combat. Instead of zooming through the oncoming Floggers, the first flight of Eagles stayed and mixed it up, with most of the agile fighters using the vertical to turn with the slightly smaller MiG-23 Floggers. From the ground it looked as if the Eagles had hinges on their tails as they flopped over, always keeping their nose on a MiG. For the MiG pilots it was a terrifying experience, seeing the F-15s turn so quickly and not being able to disengage, to escape. The sky filled with the smoke trails of Sidewinder missiles and the falling wreckage of six MiG Floggers.

The second flight of Eagles ripped through the fight, heading for a second wave of oncoming MiGs, and the deadly ballet repeated itself as three more Floggers fell out of the sky. The third wave of MiGs opted not to engage and ran for home.

Stansell had forbidden his pilots to pursue the MiGs back into hostile territory, and so once the sky had been swept clean he ordered his birds home. His words crackled over the radio, "Recover as briefed," which also meant no showboat victory rolls.

At the debrief in the COIC Waters saw how closely success and morale were linked. One of the F-15 pilots had produced a case of champagne and toasts were being intermingled with an occasional dousing. Stansell walked in then, looked around and made his way through the crowd to wing commander Waters. "We did good," he said.

"*You* did good. I saw you didn't let them do victory rolls on recovery. You've got a bunch of disciplined pros flying for you. Maybe next, though, you ought to let 'em. They've earned it. But of course it's your decision—"

Their exchange was interrupted by an announcement over the loud-speaker, "Your attention in the COIC. All, repeat all, aircraft have safely recovered."

Cups were refilled and the crews turned and looked to Waters. But before he could find the right words, Bull Morgan took over. "Gentlemen, to our commander, Colonel Waters."

The reccy photos being projected on the screen of the main briefing room told a tale of destruction and success—the wing had stopped the latest flow of men and supplies before they could move into position to attack Basra. Every pilot and wizzo was there, listening to Carroll as he recounted the BDA from that morning's mission and confirmed seven of the nine MiG kills. Two of the Flogger pilots had been captured, more or less intact, and were undergoing "interrogation" by the UAC.

After the briefing Waters told Jack and C.J. in Carroll's small office that JUSMAG wanted them to launch Wolf Flight that same night for a cleanup on specific targets. Reports had it that the PSI was moving at night and forming convoys at transloading points. Those points were the new designated targets.

"They'll be waiting, Colonel." Carroll, from previous flights, was almost certain there was an intelligence leak in the UAC.

"I know, but we've hurt them. Now's the time to keep punching," Waters said.

"I think we need to go back to pairing a Weasel with an E model for this one." Jack was already committed.

C.J., the bald-headed major, agreed. "They'll be expecting us when the moon is up. We ought to hit them right at the end of evening twilight, just after it gets dark and before the moon rises. We need to do something different on this one."

"Mostly, we need to get them looking where we ain't," Jack said. Jack didn't like having his targets picked for him. It felt too much like a setup.

As for Waters, his training and experience told him to press the attack, hit the enemy when he was hurting. Sure . . . except some gut instinct told him to scrub the mission, quit while they were ahead. But the USAF didn't pay him to go by his gut instincts . . .

Jack let Thunder do most of the planning, pulled up a chair in front of the big area map on the wall and stared at it. "Hey, come here a minute," he said. "That damn trawler is back on station and Reza doesn't have another oil tanker to run interference for us again. It'll warn the PSI when we take off, like before. Besides, they're expecting us now, which makes hitting the targets pretty damn risky . . . But how about if we *let* the trawler know when we've launched? The first flight will get high enough so the trawler can paint them on its radar. Instead of flying welded wing, the two birds will move, say, two thousand feet apart. We make it look like two strike elements on their radar, hope they'll think we're flying our normal close formation and assume they're seeing four aircraft. Keep low so they'll have a rough time tracking but high enough to divert their attention away from the six birds we'll launch right after the first two. Those six will be going after the real targets, and they'll have to get down in the weeds to avoid radar detection. They'll fly together and go right over Basra again, only this time they will be on an easterly heading, inbound to the target. Since it's at night the friendlies'll be at weapons-tight over Basra. Besides, they should be looking to the east and we'll surprise them as much as the Gomers. Once clear of Basra they head directly for their targets, but instead of turning south to escape, they head north before turning westbound and getting out of enemy territory. It'll be a long low-level and that means we've got to have a KC-135 waiting for inflight refueling once we're in friendly airspace over Iraq. At the same time the first flight draws all the attention to itself, hits the closest target we can pick and beats feet home, providing the diversion we need to get the other six in."

Carroll said, "It could work for the six, but questionable for the two who serve as a diversion."

A quick look at Thunder told Jack that his pitter was willing. "C.J., you game to be a volunteer?" Jack asked.

"Why not?" It's the kind of ride Stan-the-man likes. We'll join you. Now we need to sell it to the Old Man."

Waters listened to Jack's latest plan for launching Wolf Flight and had to admit the pilot was creative in devising new ways to deceive and attack the enemy. But he was the one who had to decide whether to launch or cancel. He wanted time to think, not be forced into committing the lives of his men so fast. Except time was what he didn't have.

He made his decision. "If we can get an airborne tanker it's a go," he said, and quickly left the room. All the elation he felt from the morning's successful raid was overwhelmed by the possible consequences of his "go" decision.

The telltale flickers of the trawler's search radar lighted Thunder's warning gear immediately after takeoff. Jack dropped low to the water while C.J. moved up, letting the radar positively identify him. They used the warning gear as cues, porpoising up and down, making sure the trawler could periodically paint them on radar as they flew downtrack. Jack could barely see the soft green formation lights on C.J.'s bird in the growing haze and darkness when he violently rocked his wings, signaling C.J. to collapse into a tight formation. The major slid his fighter onto Jack's wing and they dropped down to the surface of the water, changing course trying to elude search radars.

Unexpectedly C.J. slowed down to below 300 knots, too slow for the area they were in, then broke silence with a short transmission. "Aborting, engine failure, frozen." The major's number two engine had lost its oil pressure and frozen, the compressor blades not turning and consequently creating a ferocious drag for the remaining engine to overcome.

Jack started to turn with him and return to base before realizing that he *had* to continue the mission. He jerked the Phantom back onto course and headed into the night alone. "No choice," he said to Thunder. "We've got to hit the target to keep the MiGs looking for us."

"New heading three-two-nine degrees in thirty seconds," Thunder replied, navigating to the target. Then: "Contact, IP," Thunder told him. Jack saw the crosshairs on his scope move out and freeze on an indecipherable glob while the bearing pointer on the Horizontal Situation Indicator (HSI) swung and pointed to the IP. Jack cut the corner and headed straight for the Initial Point, wanting to drop his bombs and run for home. But without the protection that C.J. offered him from SAMs, he felt naked. "Contact, target," Thunder said, and again the radar crosshairs moved over a bright return on the scope.

This time, Jack did not cut the corner and flew over the IP, giving Thunder time to refine the placement of his bombing cursor. The visibility improved as they started their bomb run. Jack selected visual mode for the delivery when he saw the outline of trucks and buildings on the near horizon in front of them. His thumb depressed the pickle button when the target-pipper on his sight was centered on the buildings, and six bombs rippled off, walking across the farm buildings the PSI had recently turned into a fuel dump. The impact on the ground was instantaneous as the fuel exploded, lighting the sky and silhouetting the lone Phantom against the night. Jack jinked hard, going as fast as he could without lighting his afterburners and giving the enemy a beacon to find him. He was just turning south when an explosion rocked the Phantom, almost twisting the stick from his grasp.

Neither he nor Thunder saw the SA-9 that was homing on the heat-signature of their tail pipes. The turn south had rotated their hot exhaust away from the missile's infrared guidance head. The guidance program then tried to follow the Phantom through the turn by feeding cutoff into the missile's trajectory. The guidance-head lost the heat signature halfway through the turn but went into a memory mode and speared Jack's bird on the lower left side, below the cockpits. Most, not all, of the small warhead's charge was absorbed by the variable ramp that led into the air duct of number one engine and the bulkheads surrounding the cockpit. The J-79 engine, damaged when it sucked in debris from the explosion, did continue to operate, sending out signals that it was hurt.

The pain was a lion to be tamed, but Jack had never dealt with a lion before. The lion walked through him, clawing and ripping. "Thunder, talk to me, babe . . ." Silence. He wanted to twist in his seat to check on his friend, except the lion wouldn't let him as it came on him, bringing a fog that threatened his consciousness. Jack fought it, fought the lion trying to drag him into the encroaching fog . . . "Okay, check. Fly the goddamn airplane," he ordered himself, going through the routines he had practiced so often to analyze and handle such an emergency. "Thunder, *talk to me.*" He wasn't sure if he had said it aloud so he repeated it, and again still no answer. He could feel the fog now, numbing, confusing him—the lion snarled and the searing pain brought him awake as two thoughts battered at him: fly the bird; help Thunder . . .

He labored to quiet the lion. What's the matter with me? Fly the jet. He checked his instruments, started to navigate home. The engine instruments were normal; no, the oil pressure on his number one was a little low, but still within limits. Concentrate on basics: breathing, bleeding, bones—the three *B*s of first aid. Where had he learned that? Fly the airplane. His internal monologue continued as his hands went through their assigned tasks. Forcing his eyes down, he checked his feet, directing his flashlight at the floor. Nausea came over him when he saw his feet soaked with blood.

Where's that damn lion when I need him? Shock is there, has to be. Stop the bleeding, be quick about it. With his left hand he ripped the first-aid kit out of its pouch on his survival vest, shook it apart into his lap, unwrapped the large compress bandage. He patted his right side with his left hand. Nothing. Switching hands on the stick, he patted his left side. Just below his hip he felt the warm, sticky wet.

He was near the leak. *"Fix the leak."* A simple problem of maintenance . . .

The lion came again from nowhere, challenging him with pain. He
had reduced the problem to basics. He looked at his left hip. A flow
of blood was coming out of his upper left thigh, not pulsing or heavy,
which would have meant an artery had been severed. Why couldn't
he feel it? Shock? He grabbed the bandage and stuffed it into the flow
of blood. The lion snarled as he tightened the bandage around his
wound, stopping the flow of blood.

Again he scanned the instruments, checked his fuel, calculated the
course home. Looking outside, he searched for a recognizable land-
mark, anything to point the way back to Rats Ass. Automatically he
scanned the instrument panel yet again, an ingrained part of his flying
routine. He noticed the bearing pointer on the HSI was pointing at his
one o'clock position. How had he missed that? He recycled the select
switch on his HSI to the navigation computer mode and watched the
bearing pointer slew back to the same position and the mileage indicator roll to 128 nautical miles. "Thunder, baby, I love you," he said.
In his last few seconds of consciousness Thunder had punched the
coordinates for Ras Assanya into the navigation computer, showing
his pilot the way home.

"All right now, Thunder, baby, what's the matter with you?" He
reached up to his right and twisted the far right rearview mirror on
his canopy bow, adjusting it to see into the backseat. He could only
make out the top of Thunder's helmet in the dim glow of the light
given off by the instruments. Gently he rolled the F-4 onto its back
and started a climb. The maneuver straightened Thunder out and
forced his inert body into a sitting position. While still climbing he
rolled the Phantom upright and leveled off. He directed the beam of
his flashlight into the rear cockpit and could now see Thunder clearly
in his rearview mirror. Thunder's helmet visor was busted and splat-
tered on the inside with blood, and his shoulders were bloody. Please,
God, not a head wound . . . but he knew one was likely. A cold
determination came over Jack to recover the big fighter. With Thunder unconscious and with a head wound, an ejection would be fatal.

The only defense Jack had against the fighters no doubt searching
for him was the ground, and so he dropped the Phantom down to the
deck, skimming the flat marshlands that bordered the coast. The

mileage indicator clicked to 112 miles as he saw the faint outline of a bay in the dark. He knew where he was and changed heading slightly to the east, heading in a direction away from the base. He could only hope the MiGs were being deployed as a blocking force directly between the target they had struck and Ras Assanya.

The glowing Master Caution Light caught his attention. How long had that been on? He punched it off and checked the warning panel on his right. "The "Check Utility" pressure light was illuminated and the Utility Hydraulic Pressure gauge read zero; he had lost his primary hydraulic system. He ran over the systems he had lost and what he would have to do; no brakes, no gear lowering, no flaps. He went over the emergency procedures that he had spent hours drilling into his memory: blow the gear down, blow the flaps down, lower the hook, take the arresting cable stretched across the approach end of the runway. Hell of a time to have to act like a Navy carrier pilot . . .

Eighty-five miles out from Ras Assanya the oil pressure on his number one engine fell to zero and he had to shut it down before it froze up and created the same intolerable drag C.J. had encountered. Without a choice, he started to climb, gaining the altitude he needed to fly the disabled aircraft—the telltale buzz of a strong search radar came through his earphones, the enemy had found him.

"Well, I've done this one before," he said to his unconscious wizzo. Of course, if Thunder were okay, he'd jettison the bird, but he wasn't, so get on with it. He remembered the emergency landing that he and Landis had made at Stonewood when they had lost an engine and their Emergency Hydraulic pressure. The conditions had been perfect for an emergency landing that time and Tom Gomez had still told them to eject. Now the option wasn't available when he wanted it the most. He keyed his radio, calling the tower at Ras Assanya. "Rats Tower, Wolf Zero-Nine, Mayday, Mayday." For the first time, he was aware of the loud wind noise in the cockpit.

"Roger, Wolf Zero-Nine," the tower responded. "You are weak and barely readable. Say position and emergency," the tower controller answered, and at the same time hit the alarm button to the crash trucks and hospital clinic . . .

Lieutenant Colonel Steve Farrell, waiting out the recovery of Wolf Flight in the tower, did not hesitate when Jack told him about their battle damage and the condition of the Phantom. "Wolf Zero-Nine," he radioed, "recommend controlled ejection. Overfly the base and point that pig out to sea. Eject when you are over the runway, we'll catch you and the bird will glide for two miles before it crashes, well clear of us."

"Negative," Jack replied. "Thunder can't take an ejection. I'm taking the approach end barrier."

Farrell acknowledged Jack's decision and keyed the crash radio, telling the crash truck, clinic and Waters about the emergency.

"Boss," Farrell said to Waters, "if he prangs on the runway he'll close us down. The rest of Wolf Flight is still airborne and we have to recover them—"

"They've got a tanker and can go someplace else. If they have to land here for an emergency or for fuel we'll bulldoze Jack's bird off the runway."

"What if the crew is still in the plane?"

The knot of decision grew tighter for Waters. "They go with the jet if they're still in it." Waters ran for his truck, wanting to be on hand to do what he could . . .

The tall crew chief stood beside the crash truck, watching his Phantom, 512, come down final. His hand was on the collar of the crash team's leader. "I'm going with you," he told the man. "I'll pop the canopies open for you—"

"Get your hands off me, and you ain't coming with us; you'll get in the way . . ."

"You hurt my bird and I'll squash your head, shithead. Personally, you hear?" The crew chief threw the man back into the truck . . .

Doc Landis sat in the ambulance, waiting. If anybody could pull this off, Locke could . . .

Unconsciousness was starting to swirl around Jack again as he fought for control of the wounded F-4. The airspeed needle hovered around 280 knots, over fifty knots above the recommended airspeed for final approach. But whenever he inched off the power he could feel a loss of control and had to inch the power back in. It was going to be high-speed approach and touchdown. As he brought the Phantom over the approach lights he carefully bled the power off, inching down to 240 knots, on the very edge of controlled flight. He ripped the throttle of his good engine aft as the gear slammed onto the runway. The F-4 bounced back into the air, its hook missing the arresting cable, but the big rudder exerted enough authority to steer as Jack fought to stay on the runway, and the hook snagged the second cable two thousand feet further down the runway, jerking the Phantom to an abrupt halt.

The ambulance reached the Phantom seconds after the crash truck, and Doc Landis held his breath as he received the unconscious pilot and wizzo that the rescue crew handed down to him.

12 August: 1300 hours, Greenwich Mean Time
1400 hours, Stonewood, England

The shop buzzed with its normal Friday afternoon gossip as the wives from Stonewood streamed in, getting their hair coiffed for the weekend. The wives had an excursion on for Stratford-on-Avon Saturday and Sunday, so Gillian and her people were busier than usual. From the comments, some less subtle than others, it seemed a number of the ladies were using the trip as cover for a weekend with someone other than the husband. Gillian was glad when Beth Shaw arrived. She liked the older woman, a straight-on set who disdained gossip and obviously cared about her husband and his cadre.

"Is something wrong, Gillian. You seem upset . . ."

"No . . . I guess it's because we're so busy." And changing the subject, "What's a stand-down, Mrs. Shaw? Everyone keeps talking about it."

"Well, it seems the wing has stopped flying combat missions, at least for the time being," Beth told her. "Everyone is hoping that it will become permanent and the men will be coming home. Haven't you heard about it?"

"The shop keeps me so busy I don't have much spare time," she said, deciding not to tell Beth Shaw she deliberately ignored the newspapers, TV and any talk of the war, afraid they would remind her too much of Jack.

"Yes, well, the wing has been so successful in its last few missions. Thankfully, no one was lost. One crew was wounded but they landed safely. There are rumors that feelers have been extended on both sides to stop the fighting. It's in the morning papers." Beth knew a good deal more, thanks to her husband's recital of the 45th's proud record, but she also knew that a general's wife had to button up, as he put it. Still, no harm in talking some about what was in the papers. "The two wounded men were a Captain Locke and a Captain Bryant, I believe. Did you know them? I understand Captain Jack Locke is considered quite a catch . . ."

Gillian stood back, the comb trembling in her hand. Jack and Thunder? She didn't even know. What a damn fool she was. She wanted to ask Beth Shaw to tell her *everything* she knew . . . and yet . . . did she really want to know? Wounded, she'd said. Thank God, Jack was still alive. And Thunder. Damn it, why did she care so much? It was one sided; he didn't even care enough to write. *Stop it,* she ordered herself. Stop pretending. You damn well do care . . .

Beth Shaw didn't miss the expression on Gillian's face, or the moisture in her eyes. "Oh, I'm sorry, you did know them . . ."

"Yes," Gillian said, fighting for composure. "And now, Mrs. Shaw, I think we're just about done."

15 August: 2215 hours, Greenwich Mean Time
1815 hours, Washington, D.C.

The National Security Adviser preferred meeting in the Oval Office, the nation's pinnacle of power and authority. He also hoped the President was not recording their conversation. Ever since Nixon . . .

The agenda was the status of the Gulf war, and what both he and the chief executive tended to consider a fortunate turn of events. The last two raids by the 45th had been successful, more so than they had any right to expect, and the supply buildup by the PSI had been set back by at least two months. The main strike had caused most of the damage but the follow-up night missions by Wolf Flight had made a significant contribution. Neither of the men knew why the one target had been selected for the lone attack by an F-4 at night, but they were quite willing to accept the results since the 45th had managed to locate and destroy a huge petroleum dump. After all, fuel-storage areas were on the approved targets list, so the wing did not need specific permission to attack it. And since no aircraft had been lost, the war had suddenly taken on a much more positive coloration.

"We're getting positive noises the PSI wants to stop fighting and talk," the adviser said. "Our intermediary is, of all people, North Korea. Makes sense in a way, though. They're all more or less in the Soviet orbit."

"And what are the Soviets doing?"

"So far, little. Reports indicate that they are disenchanted with their allies. No wonder . . . the leadership of the People's Soldiers of Islam is prickly as hell, tough to influence, not to mention control, politically. We figure part of this is because the PSI is searching for a face-saving device to stop the fighting. Maybe, sir, we should give it to them. Saudi Arabia is interested in negotiations. The royal family is coming under a lot of pressure by various religious factions to throw *all* foreigners out of the country. A sort of Middle East Boxer's Rebellion may be brewing."

"So what do you suggest?"

"Perhaps if we withdraw the F-15s and most or all of the fleet out of the Gulf of Oman, they might interpret that as a de-escalation."

"Look, I need action on the diplomatic front," the President said. "My people are taking major hits from the press and in Congress on this. They won't take such attacks forever and stick by me. They may not be Sunshine Patriots but they sure as hell aren't about to play Valley Forge."

"I understand . . . but they should at least give us some time to maneuver. We can send confirming signals back to the PSI. I suggest through Algeria as well as North Korea. Withdraw the fleet now and pull the F-15s later, when we need to sweeten the pot."

The President nodded. "It's all in the timing; it's got to be right. Send the signals and watch for a reaction. Like you say, we'll withdraw the F-15s later . . . You know, I hate all this pussyfooting. We're involved in a war . . . short and long term. My damn blood pressure is off the charts."

As for the future of the 45th Tactical Fighter Wing, it was never mentioned.

The photos of the petroleum dump burning in the night were the capstone of the morning's situation briefing. General Cunningham joined in the general enthusiasm. The results of the two raids by the

45th had exceeded his planners' expectations. The recovery of all his aircrews made him think momentarily about firing a couple of the planners for being too damn cautious. The two wounded men were safe in the hospital at Wiesbaden, where their condition was reported as stable and improving.

Cunningham was pleased when Locke was identified as the pilot who had volunteered to create a diversion for the rest of his flight and in so doing hit a secondary target that turned out to be a major petroleum-storage area. And this was the man some people wanted to court-martial. Fortunes of war? Good planning? Dumb luck? Whatever, there was no denying Locke's and his wizzo's tenacity in attacking the target after their wingman had aborted. And they had paid the price, taking a hit by a SA-9 SAM, being wounded, and still landing. Locke, it turned out, had been more severely wounded than Bryant, but hadn't lost consciousness until he managed a remarkable landing with one engine out and no utility hydraulic pressure. The general decided he would sign an order awarding both Locke and Bryant the Air Force Cross, the decoration second only to the Congressional Medal of Honor. It was up to Waters and Third Air Force to recommend them, but that should be no problem . . .

Cunningham had a tougher decision to make about the KC-135 tanker pilot. Or rather about the tanker pilot's wing commander, one Colonel Simmons. The idiot had recommended a court-martial for the pilot after he had flown his tanker into Iran to rendezvous with a Wolf that had been hit by Triple A and was leaking fuel like a sieve. The KC-135 pilot had taken a chance but knew in advance there was not likely to be much Iranian air defense in the area. He'd maneuvered his tanker into position and made a hookup after the Phantom flamed out—a terrific performance. The tanker had dragged the F-4 home, pouring more fuel into the sky than into its engines. It was the sort of action Cunningham applauded and wanted his pilots to be capable of when necessary. What the hell was the matter with his commander's . . . did they have something against smarts and guts?

The general stomped out of the room. "Ask that genius Simmons what medal he's recommending for the tanker driver," he said to his aide, well within the hearing of everyone in the room. Even the commander of the KC-135 unit would get the implied message about the court-martial. In his office now, Cunningham told his aide Stevens,

"Hold all calls for about twenty minutes. Dick, am I getting soft? Not so long ago I would have sacked Simmons."

"Probably," Stevens replied, keeping a straight face as he quickly departed.

Sinking into his soft leather chair, Cunningham folded his hands across his stomach, closed his eyes and attacked the problem that had kept him awake most of the night. What were those sons of Allah, the PSI, going to do next? The President's National Security Adviser seemed to have all sorts of faith in the negotiations that were starting, but to Cunningham's mind it looked very much like the beginning of a song-and-dance routine . . . or as his mother used to say, all butter and no potato. Every intelligence estimate he'd seen indicated the PSI were still a force to consider in spite of the recent beatings they'd taken. And he didn't like the U.S. fleet being withdrawn to Diego Garcia in the Indian Ocean to encourage negotiations.

Never mind . . . his instincts, educated instincts, told him the 45th was not done fighting. He called his aide. "Dick, arrange a commander's conference for me at Third Air Force early next week. I want to take a hard look at what's going on in the Gulf. Have the commander of JUSMAG and Waters there."

He relit his cigar. He'd decided on some action. He was feeling better.

17 August: 0630 hours, Greenwich Mean Time
1000 hours, Teheran, Iran

The commander of the PSI had ordered his aides to lift him from his hospital bed in Teheran and helicopter him to his headquarters when he received the news of the latest attacks by the 45th. The military situation his generals were now laying out on the big chart table enraged him. He motioned an aide to wheel him away, his good eye blazing with hatred. He was not going to accept the stalemate his enemies had created.

Two doctors proceeded to lift the frail little man into a hospital bed that had been rushed to the headquarters and tried to monitor his vital signs, but he waved them away and motioned to an aide, speaking in a barely audible voice. Within minutes a group of men were gathered around the bed in a council of war. "The Americans have blocked our *jihad,*" he told them. "But our holy war must go on. For now we must try to negotiate an end to the fighting—but only until we can resume the *jihad.* Our Soviet allies"—he spoke the word like a curse—"ask too much for the supplies we need to continue. We will not be their lackeys. We will not allow them to build bases in our country. But we must negotiate from strength. Remember, we still have the means to punish our enemies. We will not be treated as powerless children at the negotiating table but as equals. And we *will* have our revenge."

He lay back in his bed, trying to gather his strength. Finally, he motioned to his valued agent and courier, the man from the silver Mercedes. "Why weren't we warned of these latest attacks?"

"Our spy Mashur al-Darhali was ordered to England to attend the Farnborough Air Show. We did not know of the attack," the man answered, handing the commander a thin folder. "Darhali will live only as long as he is useful. I do not trust Saudi princes who claim to support us." The bedridden man studied the photo in the folder. "Is this the one that leads the 45th?"

"Yes. His name is Anthony Waters. He is only a colonel."

The commander's eyes squinted as he brought the photo into focus. Every feature of Waters' face stood in sharp relief as hate flowed through the old man. His voice took on strength. "Begin the game of negotiations, but delay. Gather our forces at Bushehr and wait for the weather conditions to favor us. We will demonstrate our strength by destroying Ras Assanya. And with it the presumptuous colonel . . ."

23 August: 1135 hours, Greenwich Mean Time
1235 hours, Mildenhall, England

Sara was waiting with John and Beth Shaw when the C-141 bringing Waters to the commanders' conference taxied up to the terminal at Mildenhall. Beth marveled at the grace of the young woman in her eighth month of pregnancy, remembering wryly how her own pregnancies had blown her up. As she watched Sara rush into Muddy Waters' arms, she also noted the lines around the colonel's eyes that hardened into deep furrows. Muddy had changed, been changed by command . . . Similar things were going through her husband's mind as he observed his old friend, understanding now what he had only seen on his visit to Ras Assanya. Anthony Waters had found himself in the lives of the men and women who served under him.

The conference Cunningham had called opened with Colonel Charles Bradford, Cunningham's latest protégé, giving a quick update on the situation in the Gulf. He pointed out a military buildup around Bushehr, the Iranian air base located on a bay one hundred forty-five miles due east of Ras Assanya across the Persian Gulf. "Fighting has stopped. But negotiations with the PSI are stalled as the buildup at Bushehr gains momentum. I believe the PSI will strike out of Bushehr at the UAC, perhaps at Ras Assanya, in order to strengthen their position at the negotiating table."

Cunningham leaned over the table, coming to the reason for the conference. "The President is personally calling the shots on this one. It's his call if the 45th will be used again in combat, if it will be reinforced or withdrawn. Our job here is to figure out what the Air Force can do to protect Ras Assanya while the President negotiates us out of the Gulf."

For the next two hours the men assembled faced up to how they were to accomplish that job. Not with mirrors or rah-rah but with tactics that would put the 45th on the line as never before. As Captain Bryant would say, "So what else is new . . .?"

That night Sara cradled into her husband's arms, making sure he could feel their child growing inside her. The deep pleasure she felt was conditioned by the knowledge that she would only have him for this night, after which he would return to his wing. It was only a fantasy, and so impossible, but she wanted to run away with him, escape to a place they could never be found. And then reality crowded in, and she returned to the reality of this man who had changed her life, fulfilled it. Be grateful for the moment, Sara, and show it. And she forced her fears into the shadows and gently caressed her husband.

The next morning Sara rode with her husband to Mildenhall, determined to stay in control of herself. She had a bad moment when Waters' flight was announced over the PA system and felt the too familiar panic that she was losing her husband. Together they walked to the waiting C-141, and after he kissed her good-bye she stood for a moment, waved as he entered the open hatch, then turned quickly. At least he deserved not to see her tears.

31 August: 0725 hours, Greenwich Mean Time
0925 hours, Wiesbaden, West Germany

The physical therapist ran her fingers lightly over the freshly healed wound and down the pilot's leg. "Roll over," she commanded. Her fingers moved gently down his back, tracing an old scar on his right side. She slipped her fingers under the elastic of his shorts and pulled them down, inspecting his buttocks.

"Didn't know I was wounded there," Jack said, not exactly suffering from the inspection that was interrupted as Thunder walked into the room and, overhearing the remark, told him, "She's checking out your brains, hero."

The girl recovered by bustling around, full of professional advice. "You're not ready to start exercising yet, maybe in another two days; we mustn't open the wound . . ." She handed him his robe and crutches, wishing his buddy would drop dead. This one was a live one, but like most of them, he got away . . .

In the solarium Jack said, "As soon as they let us out on convalescent leave I'm going to Stonewood and try to find out why Gillian never wrote. I might not like the answer but at least I'll know."

"Like I told you, maybe she never got your letters." Thunder didn't know that Jack had only written once. "Why don't you phone her while you're here?"

"I can't chance that. Something went wrong. I've got to try to straighten it out face to face. If I'm lucky . . ."

"What?"

"I want to marry her. Can you believe it?"

Thunder shook his head. "I'll try, old buddy. But what about the therapist with wandering hands?"

Before Jack could try an answer an orderly ran up and handed him a shred of yellow paper, saying, "I've never seen a flash message before."

Jack scanned the short message and handed it to Thunder. "Well, at least it's nice to know we're needed at Rats Ass," he said, at the same time irritated that once again his so-called personal life was on hold.

"They're holding a C-5 at Rhein-Main for you," the orderly said.

"It's got to be important if the Boss wants us back this fast," Thunder said. "Waters doesn't usually hit the panic button."

Jack limped down the hall after Thunder, forcing thoughts of Gillian to the back of his mind, wondering about the summons from Waters.

The big transport plane's lower deck was loaded with cargo and two batteries of SAMs that Jack had never seen before. Each battery consisted of three small trailers: one had a turret that held four short missiles; the second, an optical tracker; the third, a compact radar that resembled a cone-shaped hat sitting on top of a square box.

Jack found an empty seat on the upper passenger deck next to the Army lieutenant in charge of the new SAMs, and during the flight into Ras Assanya the lieutenant told how he had been selected to field-test the latest version of the British-made Firefly Rapier. He seemed to delight in describing how the system's radar could simultaneously scan for aircraft and track a target. The high probability of a kill that the lieutenant claimed for his SAMs made Jack hope the PSI never got hold of any of them.

31 August: 1555 hours, Greenwich Mean Time
1855 hours, Ras Assanya, Saudi Arabia

The ramp was full of equipment and people waiting to onload when the C-5B taxied to a halt at Ras Assanya. By the time they deplaned most of the cargo was out of the back and two loadmasters were motioning equipment into line and up the forward ramp. Jack scanned the bunkers in the rapidly fading light. "The F-15s are gone . . . ?"

Their confusion increased when Stanstell stopped his pickup truck and motioned for them to hop in. "Appreciate the lift, Colonel," Jack said, "but what in the hell is going on?"

"We're digging in. That group on the ramp is the last of my squadron and equipment. The President ordered us to withdraw two days ago. You'll hear all about it, but first you've got to see Doc Landis for a clearance to go back to work."

Doc Landis was the only person in the clinic and was sorting out equipment and packing it into small boxes designed for use in the field. "We're dispersing the clinic into four bunkers around the base," he said. "That's where everyone is." He led them to a wall map of the base and pointed out where they could find the temporary aid stations. "If you haven't got the picture yet, we're preparing for an attack." He lifted Thunder's flight cap and examined the WSO's head, checking his eye movement and reflexes. "You'll be ready to fly in a few more days." He motioned for Jack to drop his flight suit and sit on the examination table, gently probed the new flesh on Jack's thigh, concerned over the depth of the scar. "The quack who patched you up knew what he was doing. You're only a few weeks away from flying. Start some leg-lifts tomorrow. About five, twice a day to start with."

They found their wing commander in the command post section of the COIC talking to a sergeant they did not recognize. Waters introduced Master Sergeant John Nesbit, telling them that the sergeant was detached from the Pentagon to set up and run a direct communications link with the Watch Center. "He worked for Tom Gomez," he added, giving Nesbit instant acceptance. "Rup, if you're going to catch that C-5 you'd better shake it."

"Sorry, boss, I'm not going. My wing wants me to write up an after-action report, have it ready when and if Cunningham asks for it."

"Your wing needs—"

"Shee it," he drew the obscenity out into two words. "My wing's got more colonels than it knows what to do with. The way I see it, we'll be back when the fighting starts back up, and I'll need to be here to get the F-15s in action. In the meantime I can help you out."

Waters nodded. "I need all the help I can get. Our Rapiers came in on the C-5. Get them sited and camouflaged before morning. I want them to be a big surprise for the Floggers. Then chase over to the Security Police and find out how Chief Hartley is doing training his latest batch of volunteers and reinforcing the perimeter."

Stansell found that Hartley had done everything but dig a moat and said so.

"Right, sir. We dig a ditch and turn this place into an island."

"Chief, do you have any idea what you're saying? The narrowest part of the isthmus is almost two thousand feet wide. And what happens if it floods before we finish? What about the road to the mainland? We can't cut that."

"Colonel, we've got three bulldozers on this base. Let's use them." Stansell keyed his brick and relayed the chief's request to the command post. An hour later, a NCO arrived with the first bulldozer and listened in shock to the chief's directions.

"We start bulldozing from both sides of the road toward the water. We turn the road into a causeway and bury demolitions under it. Make the cut at least thirty feet wide with steep sides. Push the dirt into an embankment on the base side. That will give us ridge to fight from. I want ten feet of water in it." The sergeant tried to argue with the chief, telling him it would take days to move that much earth. "Sarge," the chief said wearily, "am I speaking in a language you don't understand? Don't tell me why you can't do it; I only want to hear how you're going to do it."

The sergeant shut up and went to put his bulldozers to work.

When Stansell asked the chief what else he wanted he was not surprised by his request: "Mines," and he gestured toward the water surrounding the base, "plus some boats to lay them with." Stansell headed back to the command post to see what he could find.

Waters put Jack to work helping move the command post into a new concrete bunker, and Carroll kept trying to explain why the wing was not being withdrawn while negotiations were underway and that Waters was driving the wing into a deep defensive crouch, as Cunningham had ordered at the conference at Third Air Force. "We're getting reports of increased terrorist activity between us and Kuwait," Carroll told him. "Only armed convoys are moving down the coast road and they're coming under heavy attack. The last two have been turned back."

"That's our only land link," Jack said. "Sounds like we're being cut off."

"Looks that way. Waters figures we'll be getting some attention pretty soon. He's using everyone and everything to hunker down and prepare for attack. What a pisser to be the last man killed in this shitty little war," Carroll said. And Jack thought, Who could argue with that?

The third day after returning from the hospital, Jack was asked by Waters to take care of a Saudi F-15 that had just declared an emergency for fuel and was in the landing pattern. Jack borrowed one of the few pickups on base and was waiting on the ramp when the F-15 taxied in. The canopy raised while the engines spun down. The pilot took his helmet off—it was Reza. He climbed down the boarding ladder a crew chief had hooked over the canopy rails, looking very much the fighter pilot, and shook Jack's hand. "I can only stay long enough to refuel, but I must speak to your Colonel Waters."

"Byzantine politics again?" Jack ventured.

"I'm afraid so. And this is quite serious."

At headquarters Reza came directly to the purpose of his visit. "We have information that you will be attacked the day after tomorrow. It will come from Bushehr, before early morning prayers . . ."

As he said it Reza hoped the Americans would accept his warning and not press him for more information. He could not reveal that he had learned of the attack from the PSI agent who had been running his cousin Mashur, or how the agent had decided to switch sides. For a substantial price, of course. It had been decided by the UAC not to warn JUSMAG or the 45th. The UAC in their peculiar wisdom believed the PSI would only negotiate when it appeared they were winning and an attack on Ras Assanya would presumably create that illusion. The Arabs calculated that the attack would further weaken the PSI and make them less of a threat. So it had been decided to let the Americans serve as a pawn to be traded off for negotiations with the PSI. The prince did not agree. Sacrificing good allies did not match his own well-bred sense of honor, Byzantine or otherwise.

Waters thanked Reza for his warning, and Reza said he had to leave, since he had used the fuel emergency as a cover for his visit and his F-15 would by now be refueled and ready to go.

Reza had proved he could be trusted, but how big an attack was coming? In any case, Waters could see the political jigsaw puzzle was finally fitting together. And seeing it, bitterness took over. The 45th, it seemed, was nothing but a political pawn, at the expense of his

people. Well, this pawn had teeth and could . . . *would* . . . sure as
hell defend itself.

Carroll poured over the latest Stealth reccy photos, which supported the warning Reza had passed to the wing: the PSI was muster-
ing a waterborne invasion force one hundred forty-five miles to the
east in the bay of Bushehr. The large number of operational hovercraft
surprised Carroll. He calculated that the PSI could land a sizable force
on the western edge of the Gulf two hours and fifty minutes after
departing their launch ramps. "Not good," he told Waters when the
colonel walked into Intel. "Look at the MiG-23s they've deployed to
give them air cover." He flipped a series of photos of the air base at
Bushehr less than six hours old. "They have the capability of launching an attack anytime they want. If Turika's intelligence is good, that's
their intention. And look at the ships they've got around Khark Island
to protect the oil terminal. They can easily move them along with the
invasion fleet, more than doubling the number of surface combatants
they can throw at us."

Twenty minutes later, sixty-four officers and NCOs who commanded the units and sections that made up Water's wing crowded
into Intel.

"We're getting intelligence warnings of an attack in the next day,
two max. Pass it on to your people. I've requested airlift to evacuate
all non-essential personnel. Let's get as many of our troops out of here
as we can. Get back here with names and numbers ASAP."

Waters motioned for Carroll to join him. "Bill, somehow we've got
to bypass the UAC. They're playing fiddlefuck with us. Get an update
message to the Watch Center." He paused for a moment. "And transmit a copy to Shaw at Third Air Force.

"Jack, care to take a walk?" Waters unlimbered from his chair and
headed for the door. The colonel walked slowly. "We've got to defend
this base until they tell us otherwise. Give me a plan for a spoiling raid
against Bushehr. I want to discourage them, but we'll need the President's okay to launch this one. I got the message loud and clear from
Reza; our so-called ally, the UAC, wants to use us as a sacrificial goat.
No goddamn way."

"And I get your message, sir," Jack said, and took off.

4 September: 1220 hours, Greenwich Mean Time
0820 hours, Washington, D.C.

The main floor of the Watch Center was crowded with observers as the proposed spoiling raid against Bushehr unfolded on the center board. It was the first time that the analysts and technicians had seen the detailed exposition of the planning that went into an attack, and the numbers, timing, tactics and weaponeering held their attention as they saw the end result of much of their work.

Captain Don Williamson sat on a table, knuckles white as he clasped the edge and watched the computer analysis of the attack flash on the boards: probability of arrival over target, probability of damage to target, probability of recovery, expected losses–aircraft, expected losses–aircrews, expected battle damage, expected time to reconstitute, expected dollar cost. Williamson was a staff officer and would never experience the reality of combat, but unlike so many of his fellow ground pounders the numbers had a personal meaning for him ever since they had lost Tom Gomez.

The generals on the battle staff of the Watch Center saw a new dimension to their commander. Cunningham's carefully cultivated coarse image was gone and his keen intellect was in charge as he directed the watch commander to feed different commands into the computer. "Whoever planned this is no idiot. Name?"

The duto NCO activated his communications link with Ras Assanya and queried Sergeant Nesbit about the identity of the tactician who formulated the plan. "Sergeant Nesbit is manning the console at Ras Assanya, sir. He's asking Colonel Waters now." After a brief pause the sergeant gave him the name of Captain Jackson D. Locke.

Cunningham looked at the generals. "Consider what Locke has done . . . minimum time over target, minimum time in hostile territory, smart use of deception, and all worked into a tight package that only tasks the aircrews to do what they've been trained to do." For the first time in days Cunningham felt a sense of relief. Waters had trained his people well. Given a chance they should be able to fight and survive. He rolled an unlit cigar in his mouth as the old veneer fell into place along with his determination to execute the attack. "Dick, get me an appointment with the President."

                              *   *   *

The President's National Security Adviser gave a slight shake of his
head to the notion of launching a preemptive attack on the buildup
at Bushehr.

"I'm sorry, Lawrence," the President said, "but I can't let you
attack with the 45th, not now. We're at a very sensitive point in
negotiations; the 45th is good—too good for the moment."

Cunningham didn't take it as a compliment. "Mr. President, the
PSI has the capability to wipe Ras Assanya off the map. We've received a warning signal from a reliable source that that is also their
intention."

"*We* haven't received anything from other sources to confirm that,"
the Security Adviser said. "Maybe a minor attack to harrass the base,
nothing more—"

"A face-saving device by the PSI for negotiations, sir?" Cunningham shot back. "Don't bet on it—"

"Lawrence," the President intervened. "Those people at Ras Assanya are as important to me as they are to you. I am not going to
sacrifice them in the name of political expediency."

Bullshit, was Cunningham's unspoken thought. The President was
avoiding the issue, talking in generalities. "Mr. President, I ask you
—please return the fleet to the Gulf. At least that will discourage an
attack on the base."

The President shook his head.

"Then give me permission to let them defend against any attacking
force heading their way—"

"What did you have in mind," the Security Adviser challenged.

"I have in *mind* to launch a counter-attack against any hostile force
that enters a hundred-mile defensive perimeter around the base."

"*Out of the question.* That's almost in their own territorial
waters . . ."

The President took over. "Lawrence, my policies in the Persian
Gulf are coming under *severe* scrutiny and even attack in the press and
in Congress, as you well know. Too many people are willing to see the
area go under out of fear of being caught in another Vietnam. Congress, as you also know, is demanding the War Powers Act be imple-

mented. They *love* that act. That's the first step, as I see it, in a unilateral *complete* withdrawal from the Gulf. How would our allies in the Middle East react to *that?* Especially with negotiations underway?"

"We still need to defend Ras Assanya," Cunningham said, refusing to let the issue go down.

"A defensive perimeter of, say, fifty miles is justifiable," the President said, offering the general a compromise.

"That's less than six minutes flying time from the base. We need a hundred." Actually the general was willing to settle for fifty under certain conditions, and wanted to shift the discussion away from the details of any rules of engagement. As long as the 45th could meet attacking aircraft as soon as they broke the fifty-mile perimeter, the wing still had a chance. If the 45th had to wait until enemy aircraft penetrated to within fifty miles to *launch,* then the advantage shifted to the attackers. It was a case of not addressing the question and diverting their attention to another subject.

"It's fifty," the adviser told him.

"Will the fleet return if we come under heavy attack?"

"The fleet will support you but must remain outside the theater for now. It's one of our bargaining chips," the President said.

"Allow me to position MAC for a quick evacuation—"

"Can't do that, Lawrence. The PSI would interpret it as a signal of our intentions to withdraw unilaterally in the near future. As I've tried to make clear, negotiations are too delicate to send a signal like that at this time. I assure you I'll withdraw the 45th at the proper time but I will make the decision when to do that. Lawrence, don't overreact to this situation."

"I may have to consider other options," was Cunningham's reply, placing the possibility of his resignation in front of them.

The President had an answer to that ploy. "I'll only accept your resignation after this is successfully concluded. You will remain subject to my command until then."

Without another word Cunningham left the Oval Office reasonably satisfied that he had enough leverage to protect the wing. Did the President realize he'd given him that much? He suspected the smart bastard damn well did.

4 September: 1625 hours, Greenwich Mean Time
1925 hours, Ras Assanya, Saudi Arabia

Sergeant Nesbit's hands trembled slightly as he handed Waters the message off the high-speed printer. "Sundown is talking directly to the operator at the Watch Center," he told the colonel. "It's almost like being in the same room."

"Why doesn't he use the voice feature of the net?" Waters asked.

"Mostly because encryption and decryption is much faster and more accurate. We spend a lot of time synchronizing the voice scramblers when you transmit over long distances and some of it still comes through garbled," the sergeant told him.

"Okay, acknowledge that I'm here." Nesbit's fingers flew over the keyboard, then punched the transmit key. Moments later the printer spit out the message it had been holding for his eyes only. "Get Stansell and Locke in here," he ordered.

Jack couldn't believe the message. They were denied permission to strike at Bushehr? And had to establish a defensive ring around the base at only fifty miles? "Don't they know the basic correlation between time and distance? We've got to press this fight on *our* terms—"

"Calm down," Waters told him. "The President has made his decision and we've got to live with it. No one ever said you had to like it. Now get back to the drawing board. See what you can come up with to defend this base."

Waters proceeded to bring the base up to a pre-attack status. No sirens went off, no one ran to shelters. Instead, a last-minute positioning of equipment and personnel took place. Under the cover of darkness a convoy of trucks moved onto the narrow isthmus road that connected the base to the mainland and erected a series of radar reflectors intended to create a confusing pattern of returns on the radar scope of an attacking aircraft. A team planted anti-personnel mines and strung barbed wire on the beaches while two boats dropped mines into the shallow waters, forming a series of expanding rings seaward that any landing force would have to penetrate.

Meanwhile Jack and his people had come up with enough of a plan to present it to Waters, who nodded in agreement and told his Maintenance chief to download all bombs from the Phantoms and upload with air-to-air missiles.

Farrell could scarcely contain his elation as he brought his aircrews in for a new briefing.

Waters had sent most of the pilots and wizzos back to their quarters, telling them that they would have plenty of warning when the attackers sortied from across the Gulf.

Jack dragged a lounge outside and stretched out the Intelligence chief, Carroll. Neither man said a word as they stared across the taxiway that ran past the COIC, sharing the tension of waiting. Carroll, assuming the pilot had fallen asleep in the long silence, was surprised to hear: "Intelligence is really the key, right?"

"Yeah," Carroll replied. "It's an enemy and a friend. An enemy when it takes the form of that trawler out there that haunts every move we make, a friend when it tells us when the Gomers are going to attack."

Carroll started to doze off . . . only to see a big warbird that moved silently down the taxiway, towed by a small tug. The soft red glow of the cockpit's lights lit the crew chief's face as he hunched forward in the front seat, arms dangling over the sides of the canopy rails. Only the subdued hum of the tug's engine broke the silence as the F-4 filled Carroll's vision, its angular lines giving meaning to the name "Big Ugly." Then another image came to Carroll: the Phantom was totally functional, an instrument of caged power, lethal. But it was also a symbol of the system that made it work, a complicated organization that ranged from mechanics to the pilots that flew it. And like the system, it was incredibly complex, a machine designed to carry destructive power into a wide variety of hostile environments, from the air-to-air arena to attacking ground targets.

Its stark functional grace made it a beautiful machine, but only because of the way it fulfilled its purpose. A shudder ran through him as he realized that here, in the still of a desert night, he was mulling over such heady stuff as function, utility, purpose—and death. And coming to a conclusion about *beauty?* Maybe he'd been in the desert, and at war, too long, he decided . . .

"Okay, warbird," Jack said, shaking him. "You're in it now, just like the rest of us suckers." But, Carroll noted, he was smiling when he said it.

Waters and Farrell sat at the back of the room while board plotters behind Plexiglas sheets posted incoming information in grease pencil. C.J.'s squadron checked in first as each flight of four ships came on status. Waters cracked a smile when the commander of the 378th checked in. "Rup wanted to lead them," Waters said. "He claimed that they would shape up if someone kicked their butts out of the starting blocks. I reminded him that he wasn't current in Big Ugly but he could fly in the pit of the squadron commander's bird. You should have seen his face."

"He's Jenkins' *wizzo,*" Jack said, surprised that the egotistical little lieutenant colonel would submit to being number two in a fighter.

"Right, and he ran out of words when Jenkins told him that he would rather have Doc in his pit."

"Some people will do anything to fly," Jack said, wishing he could find a fast way for himself.

An announcement drew their attention to the situation board as the first plot of the incoming wave of ships was marked up. Their speed identified them as hovercraft and fast patrol-boat escorts, and the doubts that had been building in Jack's mind quieted some when the lack of enemy aircraft was confirmed. He had assumed the enemy CAP would hold their launch until the 45th launched its Phantoms. He nodded to Waters, his heart beating fast. "Now."

"Scramble twelve aircraft from the 377th," Waters ordered the controller.

C.J.'s twelve Phantoms were airborne six minutes after they were scrambled, each bird loaded with two external fuel tanks and eight air-to-air missiles.

"Do your thing," Jack said quietly, counting on the traweler to warn the PSI of the launch. The Floggers had to be coaxed into scrambling early if they were to separate the attacking boats from their air cover when they were inside the fifty-mile perimeter.

C.J. was the bait.

Waters selected the GCI frequency on the radio and turned up the volume. Jack studied the older man with envy. He had so much self-control. Seven minutes later they heard Mary's voice as she called out ten approaching bandits, sounding just as she had when she directed Jack and Fairly against the Libyan MiGs.

The even tone in C.J.'s voice shifted to rapid staccato as he ordered his flight to jettison their external tanks.

"They're still going to be heavy with internal fuel if the Floggers come straight at them," Jack said, unable to hide his worry.

Almost on cue C.J. ordered his flight to jettison a thousand pounds of fuel, configuring his birds to a better weight for the coming engagement.

Jack's visible relief brought a smile to Waters' face. "You've got to trust them to think," he told Jack. "Plus, have a little faith."

Mary's calm voice jolted them when she announced a second wave of Floggers approaching, bringing the total to twenty MiGs against C.J.'s twelve Phantoms.

"Scramble the 377th's last eight birds," Waters ordered, his body tense, "and order the first eight birds of the 378th to start engines." Again they waited while the inertial navigation systems in the Phantoms aligned. "C.J.'s going to be out there a long time by himself before I can get help to him."

The concern Waters felt for the skinny, bald-headed, freckle-faced major who had served him so well was now shared by Jack as he worked out the numbers. The roar of the launching F-4s penetrated the thick walls of the Command Post as the remaining eight 377th birds took off in pairs ten seconds apart. Jack glanced at his watch and ran through the numbers again. "C.J.'s got to hold 'em for three, maybe five minutes." A gnawing feeling of too damn much personal responsibility ate at him. C.J.'s flight had a good chance of surviving a *short* aerial engagement against superior numbers, but anything longer than a minute drove their odds into the ground. This was what ate away at Jack. C.J.'s life and the lives of the other men were dependent on how good his plan was.

The reverberation of the launching planes had not died away when Waters ordered the first of the 378th to taxi into position on the runway and hold.

Mary then announced a third wave of ten more bandits.

"Scramble those eight birds on the runway," Waters told the Command Post controller, "and order the next eight aircraft of the 378th to start engines and hold in their bunkers." With thirty bandits coming in their direction he did not want a stray MiG to sneak through and catch one of his aircraft sitting in the open. One by one, the eight Phantoms starting up checked in and Waters scrambled them in pairs. The launch continued until thirty-six aircraft, over half his wing, were committed.

The broken cloud deck at five thousand feet bothered C.J.: it provided a perspective he did not want, with the clearly etched horizon and soft bed of clouds forming sky boundaries. A pilot would not have to rely on his altimeter to warn him if he was too low. The single-seat MiG Flogger profited from it more than the two-place Phantom because the backseater in the F-4 could act as a verbal altimeter calling out low altitudes. C.J. relayed the cloud conditions to the GCI site and split his flight up, sending four Phantoms below the cloud deck while he climbed with seven and maneuvered to the south, not wanting to look into the sun, which favored the MiGs.

Mary's voice was crisp as she now directed the Phantom F-4s into the merge, engaging them in the largest single aerial battle the U.S. Air Force had fought since Korea.

C.J.'s wingman maneuvered into a following position before they slashed down onto the MiGs. The flight caught the Floggers in a pincers as the Phantoms converged on them from above and below, both sides wanting to reduce the number of opponents before the second waves arrived. The Phantoms then launched six radar missiles from head-on, downing one MiG, and destroyed flight integrity for the MiGs as they broke apart to avoid the missiles. The F-4s were still operating in pairs as they turned onto the Floggers. C.J. launched one of the radar missiles before he buried the nose of his bird and rolled to counterturn on the Floggers. From a distance it looked like he was tracing a downward *S* with the maneuver. Stan calmly told him where his wingman was and that his six o'clock was clear. After that the fight was one on one. Every man for himself. Radio commands blended into a babble of confusion as different pilots shouted warnings or asked for help.

A Phantom fell apart as gunfire from a Flogger raked its fuselage, and C.J. had to watch as the two crewmen ejected, the wizzo colliding with the MiG that had shot him down. Another MiG from the second oncoming wave rolled in on the pilot as he hung from his chute and squeezed off a short burst of twenty-three-millimeter cannon fire. The MiG pilot, concentrating on the kill, did not see C.J. fall in behind him and launch a Sidewinder. The MiG exploded before the pilot's parachute was hit. The man waved that he was okay.

A low growl-like sound came from the pit. "Got to fight fair, select guns and come hard left, bury your nose and you'll have another bandit." The captain could have been on a picnic for all the concern in his voice.

C.J. wrenched the big fighter around and saw another Flogger below him in a turning engagement with a Phantom. He flashed past, squeezing off a long burst, destroying the MiG.

"That's three," Stan announced. The growl turned into elation, and C.J. thought he had a madman in his pit. "Burners now, go for the moon. Let's come back in from the top." A Flogger shot by under them as they reached toward the sky . . .

For the next two minutes they twisted and turned, unable to take the offensive or shake off MiGs and head home. They heard three bingo calls announcing low fuel levels as Phantoms started to disengage and head home. The third wave of Floggers entered the fight as the eight fresh birds from the 377th cut through, closely followed by the eight planes from the 378th. C.J. rolled in behind a Flogger that started to jink and dive for the cloud deck, trying to shake off C.J.

"I've got a Master Caution Light, probably for fuel-low level," Stan said, apparently not bothered that they didn't have enough fuel to recover.

"Goddamn . . ." C.J. was angry at himself for not monitoring his bingo fuel more closely.

"Press it," Stan yelled at him. "We can get one more before we flame out and eject." C.J. stroked his afterburners, chasing the Flogger in a seventy-degree dive through the cloud deck . . .

Jack was pacing the Command Post as the first fighters recovered. Most of the Floggers had also broken out of the battle, forced to return home by low fuel. But six birds from the 378th were still engaged, making the MiG pilots continue the fight. The young woman posting the board checked off the recovering birds as they called in and circled the gap beside C.J.'s name when his wingman landed. Waters stood by silently, his attention drawn to the board as his right eyelid lightly twitched. "Colonel," Jack said, "we've got to launch against the hovercraft now if we're going to catch them when they hit the fifty-mile perimeter."

Waters shook his head, tried to force himself to concentrate. How many more open squares would appear on the board . . .? He played out the options he had to defend his wing. "Scramble the 379th onto the boats. Hold the last five of the 378th in reserve in case more MiGs are launched. Turn the recovering birds around quick as possible and put them on cockpit alert." He turned to Jack. "Go to the COIC and find out what happened to C.J."

Jack sat beside Carroll in the COIC and listened as the Intel debriefers talked to the recovered aircrews over the telephone hot lines to each bunker. The contractors had created a spiderweb of hardened underground telephone lines around the bunkers that could be repeatedly cut and still function. The aircrews would not leave the bunkers as the crew chiefs worked with the munitions loaders and fuel specialists to turn the birds for their next sortie. Slowly, the debriefers were able to patch together what had happened. It seemed the defense of the base had been successful, and twelve Floggers had been shot down. No one reported seeing C.J. go down, so Carroll reluctantly listed him as MIA for the initial Situation Report. "Only two against their twelve. That's a pretty good exchange rate," Carroll said to Jack. "Do you want me to tell the boss about C.J.?"

"I'll do it. You get in touch with the GCI site and find out what they know."

It was a triumphant Bull Morgan, with Thunder in his pit, that led the 379th down the final thirty minutes after scrambling on the attacking boats. After coming off target he had formed his twenty planes into flights of four and brought them home together, treating the base to an impromptu air show. After landing he headed for the COIC, bursting through the door of the COIC looking for Jack. He picked the captain up in a bear hug and threw him around in a circle. "Hey, you were right-on about using air-to-air missiles against them.

Worked like a charm on the hovercraft. They couldn't beat feet back home quick enough after we hosed down the leaders. Hell, we must've sunk half a dozen, set four on fire and scared them shitless . . ."

"Where's Thunder?" Jack finally managed to ask after getting his breath back.

"Still out at the bird trying to appease the crew chief. We picked up a few holes and the chief is pissed. You can't have him back, he's the best damn wizzo in the Air Force."

When he returned to the command post Jack found Waters and Bill Carroll in intense conversation. "Jack," Waters said, "according to Bill we've got ourselves a problem. He thinks the attack wasn't big enough or pressed the way it should have been. He figures there'll be a second attack . . ."

5 September: 0630 hours, Greenwich Mean Time
0230 hours, Washington, D.C.

The new display on the center board in the Watch Center told its own story and dominated Cunningham's attention as he sat in his chair, chomped on his cigar and listened to Don Williamson outline the developing situation. Every word the captain uttered was an unwelcome testimonial to the perseverance of the enemy. A searing pain in Cunningham's chest momentarily made him think he might be having a heart attack. But the pain was beyond physical . . . it came from the general's realizing he had underestimated the will of the PSI. "How long before the next attack?" he asked.

"The communications traffic the RC-135 is monitoring indicates they'll sortie from behind Khark Island within a few hours, around noon their time," Williamson said, trying to keep his voice even.

"When and where you figure they'll come ashore?"

"Well, the crossing will take about twelve hours. And I expect them to come ashore . . . here," the captain said, and pointed to a spot on the coast eleven miles north of Ras Assanya. "That's the only place where the channel is deep enough for their ships. They'll have to move down the coast and attack the base from the land side, forcing their way across the isthmus to capture the main runway."

Cunningham punched the transmit button, relaying the intelligence to the War Room. He calculated how long it would take the President and his advisers to react to this latest information. He wanted to start an immediate evacuation, but that decision belonged to the President and without his permission Cunningham couldn't even position a goddamned MAC aircraft for an emergency airlift. He drummed his fingers on the arm of his chair, hunched forward, scribbled out a message for John Shaw, who was responsible for managing Third Air Force's people and supplies, and gave it to the watch commander for transmission as he left for the War Room.

5 September: 0715 hours, Greenwich Mean Time
0815 hours, Mildenhall, England

Mort Pullman's stomach knotted as he read the message Brigadier General Shaw had handed him. Outwardly the message from Cunningham seemed almost routine: a cautionary statement from a commander to a subordinate about the protection of supplies and resources. "So Sundown thinks Rats Ass is going to get plastered by a bunch of ragheads . . . So what does himself want us to *do* about it?"

"I don't know, Mort," Shaw said. "I hope to God he's trying to tell us something we've missed."

Pullman reread the message and handed it back to the general. "This is no way to do business, General. If he wants us to do something, then tell us. We don't need to be playing guessing games—"

"Except Cunningham has to play politics with the big shots. The President's probably calling the moves and the general's hands are tied . . ." Shaw read the message again. "He says we can 'increase logistical support with the resources at our disposal to protect critical resources.' " Then it hit him . . . "Mort, what's our most important resource?"

"Man, I'm slow," Pullman said. "People."

"Right. We've got over twenty-three hundred of our people there. I don't know what it'll take or whose ass I'm going to have to kick, but I am going to get them out. I'm going to go down there. You in, Mort?"

"Count on it, sir. Half the goddamn Air Force owes me favors and I'll call in every one of them."

"Mort, your markers can't go that high. Who owes you?"

"The worker bees, General, the people that make things happen."

The general liked Pullman's style but wondered if he was mostly bragging. "To get down there it's a ten-hour flight in a C-130. We've got one Hercules at Dhahran now for logistical support into Ras Assanya. We'll use it. Send a message to the 45th and get it started on a shuttle into Dhahran. I'll see if General Percival can get us airlift from MAC."

Chief Pullman started calling in his markers the minute he sent the message to the 45th. The NCO in charge of Communications told him all circuits to the Persian Gulf were logjammed with heavy traffic and that even flash priority messages were running six hours late. "Sarge," Pullman replied politely, "how would you like your wife to learn about your girlfriend who told the Air Force you were *not* providing child support for your kid—the illegitimate one, that is."

"Chief, hey, give me a break . . ." Pause. "Well, I'd have to call a buddy at Chicksands and have him dump the circuits and restart the system with your message plugged into the flow—"

"Just make sure it's plugged in at the top. Sam, those are our people we need to get out—"

"And I'll probably get me a court-martial—"

"That's nothing compared to what your wife will get you. I'd appreciate that message going through in thirty minutes."

And the sergeant did it. Pullman next headed for MAC's Airlift Command Post to collar the NCO in charge of scheduling the movement of MAC's aircraft.

Shaw's problem was proving more difficult to resolve. General Percival wanted to support the 45th but Third Air Force did not have or schedule cargo aircraft. "John, you know how slow MAC works," Percival told him. "Unless airlift is specifically requested through channels they won't turn their aircraft loose—"

"True, very true," Shaw said. "But you can redirect airlift once it is on the schedule, just like I did with the C-130 at Dhahran."

"But only in my theater of operations, which happens to be northern Europe," Percival said quickly. At which point the phone rang. Percival answered, listened intently and gave his best imitation of

Cunningham's "yes" grunt before hanging up. "Well, well, a lot of Third Air Force's scheduled airlift missions have been suddenly canceled and MAC's got a free C-130 ready to go and sitting on the ramp. It seems Third Air has had a long-standing request for a haul to Ras Assanya that's now magically at the top of the heap. The request was lacking my signature . . . merely an oversight." The general paused. "Good luck, John."

Shaw thanked Percival and was out of his office. Pullman met him with a staff car at the front door. "Got to hurry, General. The Herky bird is waiting for us, engines running."

"We make a country-fair team, Mort."

"I'd say, General."

5 September: 0900 hours, Greenwich Mean Time
0500 hours, Washington, D.C.

The men huddled behind the President were reluctant to admit to themselves or to him the significance of the information displayed in front of them. At any other time Cunningham would have been amused by the sight of the President's advisers literally hiding behind the man they were supposed to counsel and support. At least there was no doubt in Cunningham's mind now that he had the undivided attention of his commander-in-chief. He waited impatiently, concentrating on the growing activity in the War Room.

The President, more hardheaded than his advisers, wasn't afraid to hear bad news. Not that he easily accepted it. "I expected nothing on this scale; I underestimated their intentions . . . What's their primary objective?"

"The capture of Ras Assanya," Cunningham told him.

"What would that do for them?" The President did have a flaw: he believed the men that moved the world's events were at least rational actors, and so if he knew what their goals were he could anticipate their actions.

"Get us out of the Persian Gulf, and for a long time," Cunningham said. The silence around the table presumably confirmed his statement.

"Why are you so sure they will attack within twelve hours?"

"Because, sir, there is no naval force in place that's strong enough to block them. By the time we can get our fleet back into the Gulf they'll be ashore. That's why they have to go in now, when they feel there's little resistance . . ."

One of the President's advisers handed him a note that he scanned and held up a hand, interrupting Cunningham. "General, I have just been informed that the PSI has made a new offer for a permanent cease-fire. The United Arab Command believes it's valid and urges us not to overreact."

"Mr. President . . . I believe that's a ploy to keep our fleet out of the Gulf. Sure, the PSI will be glad to negotiate *after* they've overrun the 45th." The general had no illusions about his enemy; he would not underestimate their ability or resolve again . . . "Please don't sacrifice the 45th." Cunningham could hear the pleading in his voice and didn't give a damn.

The President looked at him intently, then picked up an electronic pointer and flashed it on the screen, circling the cluster of ships poised to sortie across the Gulf. "I can't allow the 45th to be sacrificed as a quid pro quo for a truce. As long as the PSI keeps its ships in international waters we shouldn't attack them. But after their first attack, the intentions are obvious and nothing takes away our right to self-defense. If those ships move toward the west"—he directed the pointer on the screen towards Ras Assanya—"I will consider them a threat to the 45th. Tell the 45th to hit the S.O.B.'s the moment they head across the Gulf."

He was warming to it now. "And order the fleet back into the Gulf and have the carrier air group ready to launch in support of the 45th when they're in range. If that force attacks Ras Assanya, it will not return. Also, I want an orderly draw-down of Ras Assanya so it can be rapidly evacuated, but keep them fighting."

Cunningham was forced to reevaluate this President, realizing, if belatedly, that the man was one helluva geopolitician, willing to trade measured blows with an antagonist to advance the interests of the U.S. But playing the game only so far before reacting with the forces at his disposal . . .

Two hours later a Navy admiral announced to the President that the force behind Khark Island had sortied and was turning to the west. He pointed to the map of the Indian Ocean. "Sir, there is one hell of a storm building down there, an early-season typhoon. Our ships will have to reduce speed and the carrier will not be able to launch aircraft until they clear the area. It makes you wonder whose side God is on."

"Admiral, God is the all-time neutral in war, even though we'll claim he's in our camp. The Greeks called it *hubris,* pride, and you know what pride goeth before: the fall."

5 September: 1048 hours, Greenwich Mean Time
1348 hours, Ras Assanya, Saudi Arabia

Sergeant Nesbit ripped the latest transmission off the high-speed printer and handed it to Waters. The colonel scanned and added it to a growing pile of messages, then huddled with Stansell and Farrell trying to make sense out of the flood of information. "Everything," Waters began, "points to an attack in the next few hours. We can defend ourselves and are cleared in hot against anything that moves toward us. At the same time, we start to move our people out while maintaining the wing's combat readiness." Waters glanced at the board on the wall that tracked arrival and departure times of transient aircraft. There was only the C-130 that had been given to them for a shuttle. Without more airlift in the next ten to twelve hours he was not optimistic about moving many of his people before the base was attacked. "Rup, get as many people onto that C-130 as you can every time it lands. I'll holler for more aircraft . . ." He did not know about Shaw's C-130 that was seven hours away from landing.

Waters' mouth drew into a tight, narrow line as he scanned the board that listed only fifty-one mission-capable F-4s, a reminder of the losses his wing had suffered in less than ten weeks. The wing had eight other Phantoms with severe enough combat damage to make them of doubtful use. "Steve, use the four Weasels we've got left for air defense against the ships; load out twenty-two planes for air-to-air. Hang AGM-65s on the other twenty-five." He would use Mavericks against the ships.

Jack felt like a damn spectator as he watched the men go to work carrying out Waters' orders. Waters kept staring at the big situation map board, which for now was blank. Finally the colonel pushed his chair back and headed for the coffee pot. Jack joined him. "Sir . . . I want to get back to the squadron—"

Waters shook his head, then added, "Jack, I've been so busy the last few hours trying to bring things together I've forgotten about the basics. I want you—"

"Throwing me a bone, sir?"

"No. And stop feeling sorry for yourself. We've got to keep control of the air over the base. Start working on it and get back to me and Farrell."

In the COIC Jack realized the bone Waters had thrown him was keeping air superiority, controlling their airspace. The Air Force hadn't done that since the early days of World War II. Some assignment . . .

Sergeant Nesbit ripped another message off the printer and handed it to Waters. Immediately he summoned Carroll to the Command Post and handed him the message. Carroll sat down, feeling sick. "Much worse than I thought," he said. "They've got four assault landing ships and three small coastal freighters escorted by two frigates and three large Sherson-class torpedo boats coming our way. There must be another dozen or so small, fast boats they've mounted a machinegun or grenade-launcher on, running along with them. Colonel, that's a good-sized *fleet* for this part of the world."

"And we've got to stop them from coming ashore . . ."

The battle for Ras Assanya had begun.

5 September: 1205 hours, Greenwich Mean Time
1505 hours, Bushehr, Iran

The squadron commander selected to lead the first attack on Ras Assanya walked around his MiG-23, preflighting the four eleven-hundred-pound bombs hanging on the pylons under the fixed inboard wings. He patted one fondly, pleased that its target was the Americans. His plan was simple: twenty-four bomb-laden MiG-23s would take off in radio silence, fly at low level across the Gulf, avoid early detection and drop their bombs on the base. At the same time sixteen MiG-23s would launch as a CAP and escort them at high level, engaging any Phantoms that came to challenge them. The pilot commander thought it especially appropriate that they were using the Americans' own method of attack.

5 September: 1220 hours, Greenwich Mean Time
1520 hours, Ras Assanya, Saudi Arabia

The CAP launched first, as planned.

Mary Hauser's GCI radar detected them when they climbed above fifteen hundred feet. She warned the 45th of the inbound bandits and lowered the elevation angle of her search antenna, hunting for bandits on the deck. Her low-altitude coverage was very poor at that long range but improved closer to the radar head. A momentary flicker at one hundred ten miles caught her eye. She hit the sequence of switches that allowed her IFF to query Soviet transponders, and the screen lit up with five responses. "I can't believe it," she said aloud. "They won't turn off their IFF. Just like last time." Again she sent a warning to the 45th.

Jack sat next to Steve Farrell watching the board plotters post the MiG warnings. "I'm betting there's more than five on the deck," Jack said. "GCI's radar will get skin paints when they're inside eighty miles. Don't be suckered into going after the CAP."

Waters nodded and scrambled sixteen of his air-defense craft onto the runway, holding six in their bunkers. The first eight taxied onto the Active and held, waiting for a release from the Command Post, while the second group of eight held on the taxiway.

Mary's radar started picking up skin paints at ninety-two miles on the MiGs ingressing at low level. They're not that low, she told herself, and again warned the 45th.

The command post's frequency came alive, launching the waiting Phantoms, committing them against the bandits that were on the deck. Jack sat in the command post listening to the radio traffic and wondering if he could follow the directions he had given the crews: make them jettison their bombs and run like hell, don't hang around trying for a kill.

It was against everything they'd been trained for. The only thing he was grateful for was that he couldn't hear what they were calling him . . .

*   *   *

The MiG pilot leading the attackers on the deck saw his radar-warning receiver come to life and scanned the sky at twelve o'clock high, expecting to see the distinctive smoke trails of Phantoms high above them. The warning tone in his headset became louder, indicating the threat was closing in. He momentarily froze when he saw two Phantoms swinging in on him from his left eight-o'clock position and another two doing the same at his right two o'clock position. And they were all *below* him . . . it was a classic low-altitude intercept that had been turned into a pincers maneuver . . .

The lead Phantom pilot keyed his radio, "Tallyho, the fox," he called out, telling his flight the MiGs were carrying bombs, the ones they were after. The Flogger pilots, not expecting American low-level engagement, weren't able to counterturn or evade a fighter below two thousand feet. So they did the only thing they knew: jettison their bombs and make level turns back to base as the Phantoms shot through.

Five of the Phantoms managed to launch Sidewinders as they made one turn onto the MiGs, and three of the missiles traced their characteristic sideways guidance pattern, like a Sidewinder rattlesnake, through the sky to a target. One F-4 squeezed off a snap gunshot when he turned onto a Flogger, raking the fuselage and sending the MiG tumbling into the sea. For most of the Phantoms it was a one-hundred-eighty-degree turn through the Floggers' formation before they disengaged and ran for home. And because the Floggers had jettisoned their loads, it was all "one pass, haul ass" for the F-4s.

The Phantoms reformed into elements of two as they disengaged, the backseaters twisting in their seats, looking for the Floggers they knew were still out there. Mary monitored them as they ran from the bandits and assigned hard recovery altitudes: once inside a five-nautical-mile ring around the base the Phantoms would not leave their assigned altitude until cleared to land by the tower. The Rapier crews also copied the hard altitudes Mary was assigning to the Phantoms and dialed their IFF interrogators to the codes the F-4s would be squawking on recovery.

They were turning the base into the "flak trap" Jack had planned . . .

The MiGs flying CAP were not aware of the Phantoms until their comrades started yelling over the radio. Then they pushed over and headed for the engagement that was eight miles away and thirty thousand feet below them, not happy about engaging in a dogfight on the deck. When the MiG pilots saw the Americans "running away," four of them, sensing an easy kill, chased after the Phantoms. With the F-4s at known altitudes and their IFF transponders squawking the right codes, it was easy for the Rapier crews to break out the Floggers as they were lured into range. The Firefly radar operator of the Rapier battery at the north end of the runway used the track-while-scan mode to lock onto the leading MiG while placing his secondary-target symbol on the following Flogger. The operator hit the fire-control button and sent two missiles off the round turret toward the MiG, then immediately transitioned to the second target and rapid-fired two more missiles.

Both MiGs died within eight seconds of each other.

The other two Floggers lost their enthusiasm, lit their afterburners, dropped down onto the deck and ran for home. The tail-end MiG hugged the water at fifty feet and accelerated to 550 knots, the lowest and fastest the pilot had ever flown, but the Rapier battery at the south end of the runway tracked him down onto the deck and fired. The missiles found their target.

Nineteen minutes after launching, the first Phantom touched down and taxied rapidly back into its bunker to be refueled and rearmed for its next mission.

The squares on the board that tracked aircraft launch and recovery rapidly filled up, and there were no open spaces to indicate a plane missing. Waters sank back into his chair, closed his eyes and breathed deeply. He turned to Farrell and Jack. "Judging by the radio chatter, it was a turkey shoot." There was no elation or pride in his voice, it was a simple statement of fact. The PSI's best pilots had led the first attack and attrition had reduced their ranks.

Nesbit caught Waters' attention and pointed to the transient aircraft board. He had just grease-penciled in the ETA for another C-130 that was five hours out. "We might get out of this one yet," Waters said as he scanned the situation plot board, noting the position of the ships that were heading directly at the base, trying to estimate when they would be offshore. Such stuff wasn't his game.

"I'd like to know what happened to C.J.," he now said, more to himself than to the waiting Sergeant Nesbit. "There's a chance the PSI might have picked him up . . ."

The sergeant deftly typed a series of code words into the classified command communications set in his charge, waited a few moments, then typed in a series of instructions. A voice came over the transmitter, raspy and broken but understandable. "Hey, Reno, this is Nes, how do you copy?" The answering voice from the Watch Center came through much better. "Do me a favor, check with the analysts on the floor and see if they've got anything on a Major Charles Justin Conlan. We lost him today and think he might have been picked up by the PSI." The sergeant broke the transmission and turned in his seat, "Colonel, what you saw was a test of the voice circuits of the command net, only this one didn't get monitored or recorded."

Nesbit had to wait thirty minutes before the printer came to life and spit out that a message from the trawler off Ras Assanya had been intercepted. When Nesbit read it he wished he'd never asked. He ripped off the sheet of paper and handed it to Waters.

The anger Waters felt did not match the calm in his voice. "Jack, I've got a job for you. How's Thunder with the Pave Spike?"

Jack was puzzled by Waters' reference to the laser illuminator. The accuracy of the system was phenomenal but the aircraft carrying the laser pod had to orbit while the wizzo kept the laser's beam centered on the target until another aircraft could toss a "smart bomb" that would home on the reflected energy. The target had to be relatively undefended for them to hang around that long. "Good, but I imagine he's rusty. Anyway, I think those ships are too heavily defended—"

Waters shook his head. "I want you to illuminate that trawler while Bull tosses a bomb into the basket. We're going to sink that son of a bitch. Without an air cover you shouldn't have trouble."

"But why, Colonel? That trawler isn't going to help them now and it's a noncombatant."

"It *became* a combatant when it pulled C.J. and Stan out of the water and turned them over to a PSI patrol boat. The PSI executed them on the spot. I'm going to return the favor."

* * *

Jack set up a standard pylon turn around the slow-moving trawler, feeling naked, while Thunder illuminated the target. His back seater's crisp voice came over the radio signaling that he had a lock on and clearing Bull to toss his bomb. Bull Morgan's precision was legendary, but without some type of smart bomb, hitting the trawler would have been more luck than skill. Jack watched, fascinated, as the two thousand-pound bomb separated from under Morgan's F-4 and arced downward toward the trawler, and then as it picked up the reflected laser energy and refined its trajectory it showed a series of little jerks and wobbles as it fell toward the trawler. It impacted three feet from the point that Thunder had laid the crosshairs on and penetrated to the keel before its delayed-time fuse activated, and it exploded. The ship buckled upward, splitting in two and sinking a half-minute later. Jack broke out of orbit and headed for base.

It was twilight when Jack taxied in and swung the Phantom around on the concrete apron in front of the bunker, pointing its tail into the waiting cavern. As soon as he dropped F-4's arresting hook, one of the waiting crew chiefs connected a tow cable to pull it inside while the other attached a steering bar to the nose gear and signaled for power to the winch, which guided the Phantom into its nest. Since 512's bunker did not have in-bunker refueling, a fuel truck was waiting for them, hose outstretched and ready. Before Jack or Thunder could climb down, refueling was underway and a dolly had been wheeled under the Pave Spiker laser pod for downloading. A maintenance stand had been pushed up against the tail and a fresh drag-chute was being jammed into its compartment in the empennage. The gun-plumbers pushed a munitions dolly with three Mavericks already hung on a LAU-88 launcher under each wing for upload . . . The phone in the bunker rang. Jack and Thunder were wanted in the command post.

"The C-130 will be taking off on its fifth shuttle in a few minutes and will be back in two hours from Dhahran," Waters told the assembled men in the command post. "I want a hundred bodies on board every time it takes off. Have your people ready to go. We should have a second C-130 shuttling in around 2100. We'll pick the pace up then and should be able to move two hundred people out every two hours. Okay, that's it. Get back to your troops, tell them what's going down and make it happen."

"Jack, Thunder," Waters called, motioning them to follow him, and the three walked over to the COIC, where they found thirty-six aircrews waiting and eager for their chance to be assigned to a mission. Having an extra crew for every two aircraft should now pay off, Waters figured . . . the fifty-one mission-capable aircraft the 45th possessed were standing loaded and ready to go, but many of the crews had already flown two combat missions and all were dog tired. A fresh and welcome team was about to be rotated into the fight.

Waters got right to the point: "The ships coming toward us are about halfway here. We're going after them with twenty birds as soon as it's dark. You'll be using Mavericks so you can stand off, launch and leave. The four Weasels we've got left will go in with you and try to suppress their air defenses. Intel says they've got shipboard SAMs and Triple A. Your job isn't to sink them but to get them turned away. As long as they keep coming, we keep hitting them. The other twelve crews are CAP, but they'll sit alert in the bunkers. Any MiGs supporting those ships will have to come to us now. Our GCI will give us warning to scramble on them. Captain Locke will help you plan and coordinate the attack. That's it. Any questions?"

There was none, except from Jack: "Sir, can I fly *this* one?"

"No, you've flown once. You'll get another chance. For now I want you to hang around while these crews brief; you should be able to help. Then get some rest, it's going to be a long night."

Evening twilight had ended and the quarter-moon would not rise until two in the morning, creating the conditions Waters wanted: use darkness as a cover and at the same time catch the ships away from any coverage the MiGs might give them. Experience told him that Weasel operations forced the PSI missileers to shut their radars off and rely on visual sightings to track and fire, a bad nighttime tactic. Now, at 8:30 A.M., the big blast doors on thirty-six bunkers swung open and twenty-four Phantoms cranked engines. The other twelve crews sat in their cockpits, waiting for a scramble order on any MiGs that might challenge them.

The Weasels taxied out, the first pair turning onto the active runway, setting their brakes, the caged power of the J-79 engines driving the nose of each bird down, and rolling at the first green wink from the tower. In less than two minutes twenty-two aircraft followed them into the night sky.

Jack returned to the Command Post, joining Waters in what seemed an interminable waiting game. Both knew the risks without talking about them . . . The enemy ships mounted SA-N-5, a naval version of the Strela, nasty little missiles, and Intel had established that there were SA-8s and 9s on the decks. But who knew how many Triple A or Strelas they had to throw at the 45th? It was going to be tough, no question . . .

The Phantoms' pilots didn't have time for such thoughts as they skimmed the surface, eating up the sixty-five miles to the oncoming fleet. None had any illusions about getting onto the ships undetected and all hoped the eight minutes flying time would be too short a reaction time for the ships to bring up their defenses. Three minutes out, the bear in the lead Weasel reported he was picking up a signal. "Probably an SA-8," he told his pilot. He studied his radar for a moment. "I'm painting a lot of small craft in front of the big stuff." The pilot started doing easy jinks back and forth, which at their speed should, he figured, defeat Strelas, the small shoulder-held SAM that might be fired at them from a small boat.

The Ukrainian on the Shershen-class torpedo boat leading the fleet pressed his headset to his ears, listening to the constant flow of information being radioed by the *Sirri,* the Alligator-class landing ship that served as the fleet's flagship. The Soviets had given the PSI the *Alexandr Tortsev,* a four-thousand-ton amphibious assault vessel, and the PSI had renamed it the *Sirri,* following the Iranian practice of naming assault vessels after islands in the Gulf. Its main cargo deck was loaded with eighteen T-62 tanks and ten BTR-40P scout cars, all capable of wading ashore.

The radar on the *Sirri* had picked up the fast-moving attackers and was sending out warnings. When he was sure of the incoming track of the Phantoms, the Ukrainian picked up the small heat-seeking missile and waited. He caught a glimpse of the bird moving toward him at over 500 miles per hour. The man barely had time to swing the shoulder-held missile into the path of the F-4 and pull the trigger. He had time, however, to watch with satisfaction as the U.S.-made Stinger homed on the Phantom's tailpipe, scoring a direct hit. A small explosion then engulfed the rear-half of the Phantom as it tumbled into the water. The Ukranian silently thanked his Iranian allies and was pleased to know they had more Stingers.

The Phantoms had spread into a wide pattern, converging on the fleet from all points of the compass. They planned to attack simultaneously and for a few seconds saturate the defenders. The crews remembered Jack's description of the most likely survival tactic: "one pass, haul ass," or as Thunder put it, "shoot and scoot." A crew from the 378th zigzagged through the defenders, heading for the *Sirri*. Its Wizzo pinpointed its bright return on his radar and the Maverick's infrared seeker-head was sensing the unbelievably bright target at six miles. He drove the crosshairs onto the heat-signature and locked on. The pilot grunted when his wizzo told him he was cleared to pickle, then headed into a gap between two small patrol boats escorting the *Sirri*. He popped to twelve hundred feet to fire the Maverick and hit the pickle button, sending two missiles with their one-hundred-twenty-five-pound warheads toward the ship. But before he could jam his plane back onto the deck to escape, a crossfire of Triple A from the patrol boats ripped into the fuselage, building a huge fireball in the night.

The late pilot's wingman marked the crossfire, teeth grinding, and headed for the two escort boats. He was able to avoid the trap his lead had fallen into and rippled off two Mavericks at the boat on the right, then jinked hard, pulling to the deck and leveling off fifty feet above the water as a stream of tracers etched the sky above him. His wizzo noted that the two Mavericks had blown the patrol boat apart and that the *Sirri* was burning as they ran for home. At least some payback . . .

A crew from the 377th now arced across the water toward a heavily camouflaged Polnocny-class landing ship in the van of the fleet. The wizzo's RHAW gear was screaming its loud warbling cry at them, telling them they were in the beam of a guidance radar. He checked the RHAW scope and didn't see any flashing symbols that indicated a missile was tracking them, so he punched off the system's audio. Probably a malfunction, he told himself, willing to rely on visual warnings on the scope.

The crew never saw the two missiles that blew them out of the sky . . .

Wrango, a Wolf from the 378th, was tail-end Charlie. He circled the fleet three hundred feet off the deck, selecting a target, counted twelve fires and decided to hit a ship that was coming to the aid of a burning freighter. When his wizzo couldn't make the system lock on as he ran in, Wrango had to break off the attack run. "We'll have to come back another day," he told his Wizzo. But neither saw the stream of thirty-millimeter tracers reaching for them from the burning ship as they turned away, presenting their exposed belly to the ship. Two explosions promptly rocked the Phantom. Wrango's telelight panel flashed warnings at him as the stick shuddered in his hand and he had to fight to control the violently shaking plane as he yelled at his wizzo to retard the throttles while he ballooned to a higher altitude. For three minutes he kept up the fight for control as smoke and fumes filled the cockpit. Finally, unable to take his hands from the stick, he yelled for his backseater to eject them.

It was a clean ejection, the Martin-Baker performing as advertised, and they landed unhurt in the water less than a thousand feet apart. The wizzo had released his parachute risers when his feet touched the water and was pulling himself into his one-man dingy when he felt a sharp tug at his foot. Before he could check it . . . he figured his boot was caught in a parachute shroud . . . two more sharks hit him, one ripping off his leg, the other gouging him in the side. The man's scream carried a quarter-mile over the calm water. Wrango never heard it. Two sharks had hit him before he could release his parachute risers, and now his inflated parachute dragged him, lifeless, through the water.

Sergeant Nesbit handed Waters a note telling him the C-130 from Mildenhall had called in and would be landing in ten minutes with a VIP code-six on board. "What the hell's a general coming in here for?" Waters said, collecting Jack and heading for the bunker the wing was using to muster the next group to be evacuated. They found Stansell in front of the bunker when they drove up. "Rup, get all the women out quick as you can." Waters paused and looked at the clipboard Stansell was holding. "Get most of Intel out too." If the base was overrun, he sure as hell did not want Intel captured.

"Colonel," Stansell said, "the women aren't asking for any special favors, let's go with the priority we've established. Intel, okay, we don't need them now—"

Their exchange was cut off by the howl of the C-130 as it taxied to a halt in front of the bunker, the crew-entrance door opened and Shaw stepped onto the ramp as the engines spun down. Stansell was rushing the next group aboard the ramp at the rear of the Hercules.

"Well, Colonel Waters, you've got yourself into one hell of a mess," Shaw said, shaking Waters' hand. "What's going on here?"

Waters quickly filled him in, including how he was trying to shuttle his people out before the base was attacked by the oncoming fleet.

Shaw motioned at the C-130's flight deck, signaling Pullman to join them. "I need a command communications net. Is there one at Dhahran?"

Waters shook his head. "Dhahran only has a small message center. But Nesbit's got the 45th's command net up and working."

"So I'll stay here and scream for help. Maybe the Air Force will listen to a general that's on the spot. Chief, you go with the C-130 at Dhahran and keep the shuttle going from that end—"

"General," Waters interrupted, "wouldn't it be better if you ran the show from Dhahran? Things are going to heat up around here . . ."

Shaw gave him a drop-dead look, then pointed to the C-130. "Get going, Mort," and the sergeant ran back aboard as the number three prop started to wind up.

"It'll be a few minutes before the Hercules can take off," Waters told the general. "We've got birds recovering."

Jack drove the pickup as the three then returned to the command post, where the launch-and-recovery board was mute testimony to the high cost of attacking the ships. Four recovery squares were open and two planes that had made it suffered battle damage that made it doubtful if they would fly again. Shaw stood at the back of the room while Waters ordered Maintenance to turn the birds ASAP, Farrell to switch the crews on air-defense alert with the recovering crews, and Nesbit to check with the GCI site for movement of the fleet. "Jack, get with the crews and find out what happened. Work up some new way to go against those ships."

Jack looked away, not wanting to tell that he was fresh out of ideas.

Before Jack could take off, Nesbit relayed a report from the GCI site's radar: the invasion force and the ships were heading directly for Ras Assanya.

"We'll hit them again," Waters said.

A lousy situation, but Shaw had at least seen enough to convince him that Waters was in control of it. He watched Waters in admiration. The colonel's strength was the galvanizing factor that kept the men going. Muddy, he realized, was a for-real leader. It was something he'd never really accepted about his old friend until now. Shaw turned, commandeered Nesbit and his communications net and set to work spurring the shuttle on.

The situation-map board was a magnet that drew everyone's attention. A board poster had only to move toward it and the room went silent in anticipation. The latest plot showed the ships moving inside forty miles . . .

Jack leaned close to Waters. "We're going to try corridor tactics, Colonel, go at them with a series of punches at the same spot and try to blast into their center—go after the landing ships. But we're running out of Mavericks. And it seems they've armed their patrol boats with some new type of Strela"—Jack, who got his information from the crews, shared their mistaken impression that the Stingers the PSI were using against them were a much improved Strela. "We're going to try using AIM-4 Sparrows on them. I don't see a lot of difference between a fast-moving patrol boat and a slow-moving plane. Maybe a radar missile can keep their heads down."

The board posters started to mark up launch times as eighteen Phantoms headed toward the ships. Shaw pulled a chair next to Waters and watched the board rapidly fill with takeoff times. "MAC has been ordered to start a full-blown airlift to get you out of here," Shaw said. "There'll be a steady stream of C-141s and C-5s into Dhahran starting in about seven hours, and six more C-130s should be here in about ten hours. MAC has gone to a full wartime footing and lifted all peacetime restrictions but one: they won't risk C-141s or C-5s coming in here if the base is under attack."

"I see. Well, we need to talk to Rup," Waters said, picking up a phone that patched into the bunker. The colonel would have preferred to talk face-to-face with Stansell but didn't want to leave the Command Post or pull Stansell away from the bunker. "How many can you have out of here by morning?" Waters asked him.

Stansell ran the numbers for him. "I've sent seven loads out with seven hundred and thirty people. A shuttle takes about two hours, and with sunrise at 5:30 we'll get four more shuttles out of the two C-130s. That's about eight hundred more. Should have about sixteen hundred out by morning. We could sure use another Hercules or a C-141, Colonel."

"Sorry, Rup, this is all we're getting for a while." He hung up and turned to Shaw, who had been listening on an extension. He pointed to the situation board and the constantly advancing ships. "If we don't get those mothers turned around, they'll be on us in a few hours . . ."

Time dragged as the birds checked in and landed. The landing squares on the launch-and-recovery board filled, until three remained open. Waters looked across the board, checking the names of the missing crews, each name a hot iron in his gut. "Battle damage?" he asked, keeping his voice a monotone.

Three birds had taken hits and looked bad. Two others had minor damage and would be turned in a few hours. Two pilots and one wizzo had been wounded and were on the way to the hospital. "John," he said to Shaw, "I came in here with one hundred and eight crews and seventy-two F-4s. I've got seventy-six crews left and thirty-seven effective aircraft, maybe thirty-nine. I'm going to draw down to forty crews and get the rest of them out of here."

Shaw couldn't argue with it. The returning crews from the attack reported encountering two more frigate-type ships that put up a wall of fire and had to be avoided. Word went out for volunteers for a third attack that Waters wanted to throw against the ships, and sixty-eight crews packed into the COIC asking for the assignment. The room quieted when Waters walked in. He looked around, taking in each face. "You know what our situation is," he said. "We're fighting a rear-guard action until we can get the wing out. We've got to keep those ships away from the shore . . ."

Before he could go on they heard a distant whistle followed by an explosion. *"Artillery,"* Waters called out, and sent the crews running for bunkers. He went for the Command Post as they heard another loud explosion out to sea, followed by a brief flash that settled into a glow.

The frigate *Sabalan* had made a run at flank-speed past Ras Assanya, throwing a 4.5-inch high-explosive shell at the base. But shallow water had forced the ship to keep well out to sea, and so the shell had been for ranging. Before the frigate's fire-control system could adjust and lay the next round, the ship struck one of the mines that Chief Hartley had seeded around the approaches to the base. The following explosion ripped a forty-foot gash in the frigate's skin, and the ship now lay dead in the water as fire spread through its midsection.

A reprieve.

Shortly after two A.M. four Phantoms taxied onto the runway. The control tower had been abandoned and the controllers moved to a small bunker at the southern edge of the runway. One of them held up an Aldis Lamp, flashed the Phantoms a green light. The F-4s took off to the south, arcing out to sea as they sucked up their gear and flaps and armed their weapons. When they turned north they were less than two minutes flying time from the ships. After talking to the crews, Jack suggested they start a series of sorties directed at the edge of the fleet, throwing a stream of attacks against them, though not trying to penetrate, just whittling away at them with constant pressure. The four planes split and started to range around the ships. Within minutes the ships had started to move together, reducing their perimeter, a wagon train circled by Indians.

In the light of a rising quarter-moon one of the circling Phantom pilots caught an unusual movement at the nose of one of the ships and maneuvered until he could better make out what was happening, disregarding the streams of tracers that engulfed him. He dropped his bird onto the deck and retreated when he felt two thumps. Once he was clear of the ships he slowed down and climbed to six hundred feet, calling the command post. "Rats Ass Control, this is Wolf One-Four. Be advised the landing ships have their ramps down and landing craft are in the water. Also, Mayday, I've got two fire lights." He then pointed the Phantom toward the shore and within a minute was flying parallel to the beach on the east side of the runway. His wizzo pulled the ejection handle between his legs and they ejected, landing in the water two hundred feet off-shore inside the shark net, and waded ashore.

Broz watched Wolf One-Four's Phantom start to burn when he made the call to the command post. "Hey, Ambler," he said to his wizzo, "see those puppies heading for shore?"

"Roger on the puppies, Broz," the wizzo replied, "let's nail 'em."

"We're in." The pilot selected guns and dialed thirty-nine into the mil depression on his gun-sight for a ten-degree strafing run. "You don't happen to remember the max speed for using the gun, do you?"

"No, but make this one quick," Ambler told him.

Broz rolled in, jinking back and forth as his wizzo jabbed at the chaff-and-flare button while they bore down on the landing-craft heading ashore. A curtain of bullets and missiles rose in front of them as the pilot walked his pipper across three low silhouettes in the water. And then they were off, twisting and turning as they ran for safety. "By damn," Ambler shouted, "I do believe we're still alive."

"You're right, but we have got one sick bird." Broz keyed the radio, sending out a Mayday. Four minutes later the Phantom's hook snagged the cable stretched across the approach end of the runway, dragging the bird to a halt.

Blind luck, Broz sighed. Next time . . .?

The SAS team leader watched the F-4 strafe the boats before he motioned his twenty-eight blackened-faced men toward the beach. Silently, with an ease gained from repeated training sessions, they took out the advance party as it came ashore, making sure no warning messages were transmitted. The rising moon helped to light the approaching landing craft. While twenty-four of his men rushed to seed the beach with land mines, he called his four squad leaders together. "Look," he told them in a clipped British accent, "no heroics. Do it as planned and withdraw immediately. The clock starts running when the first boat runs aground. Do it bloody right."

The leading six scout cars grounded within seconds of each other and ran into a storm of machinegun and mortar fire. The few survivors stumbled ashore and started across the short strip of land, only to set off the freshly planted land mines. The brief opposition to the landing was not meant to be a resistance in the force, and the momentum behind the landing forced the second echelon ashore as the defending fire stopped.

The puzzled attackers worked their way across the deserted beach, setting off an occasional mine but not encountering any more ground resistance. Two phantoms roared overhead, strafing the beach and dropping CBUs. One of the Phantoms exploded as a SAM from a landing ship found its mark.

Four fast patrol boats started a run toward Ras Assanya eleven miles to the south, trying to bring their small-caliber guns and rockets into range. The boats were two miles offshore when the lead struck a mine. The remaining boats withdrew, not stopping to rescue the survivors.

A reprieve.

Stansell checked his watch: 3:15. He figured he could get in two more shuttles before sunrise. He watched the shadowy image of the C-130 as it took the Active. At first the lieutenant colonel thought a lightning flash had illuminated the base, but the loud concussion that followed warned that the base was coming under an artillery barrage. He dove into a slit trench, raised his head to check on the C-130. As the cargo plane began to move down the runway a flash followed by an explosion swallowed it in smoke. And like a dragon poking its ugly snout out of a misty cave, the Hercules emerged, accelerating out of the smoke, rolling down the runway and lifting into the air.

Stansell waited for the barrage to end, counting forty explosions. "So they've got a BM-21 ashore," he muttered to himself. And that worried him. If the PSI had managed to get the truck rocket-launcher within its nine-mile range, they could also hit the base with heavy artillery. He dusted himself off and keyed his brick, calling for the next round of men and women to report to the evacuation bunker. He ignored the fires burning at the far end of the runway and the wailing sound of the crash trucks that had rushed to the north end of the runway as soon as the barrage had ended. Now they found the burning hulks of four Phantoms on the taxiway, where they had been caught in the open during the rocket attack. As best they could tell, a rocket had scored a direct hit on the second bird in line and its exploding ordnance had destroyed the other three. An NCO ripped off his silver helmet, throwing up as the smell of burning flesh washed over him. Another fireman keyed his radio and called for a bulldozer to clear the taxiway as the trucks started to put out the fires.

The board posters in the command post erased the four tail numbers from the shrinking list of mission-capable aircraft. Waters counted the thirty effective aircraft now available to him. The board posters had started another list, marking up the total people evacuated. As one list grew shorter, the other increased. He turned to Farrell. "Steve, match one aircrew to each of those thirty birds. Round up the extra crews and take them out on the next shuttle."

"Colonel, I'm not going—"

"Steve, don't argue. Just *do* it. Artillery and rockets will eat us up. You know that." Waters walked through the command post ordering people out on the next shuttle. When he got to Nesbit, the sergeant told him that since he had just arrived at Ras Assanya he should be among the last to go. He also pointed out he was the only one who knew how to activate the self-destruct on the command-communications console. Waters accepted that, not knowing there was *no* self-destruct installed on the equipment . . .

Shaw handed Waters the latest message he had received. "I've been ordered out by Cunningham." He felt he needed to justify his leaving. "The President has ordered a full-scale evacuation since the UAC is hardly opposing the landing. They've only thrown one regiment against the beachhead. Maybe two thousand men. I wonder how long they can hold? Probably don't want to upset negotiations. Great allies, the pricks. All they have to do is hold on long enough for the Navy to get back in the Gulf. A day or two. Maybe. Anyway, it doesn't matter to them what happens to us." He shook Waters' hand, gathered seven men together and headed for the evacuation bunker.

Waters picked up the phone to the Security Police bunker. "Have the GCI controllers made it in yet? I ordered them in an hour ago."

Chief Hartley answered: "Sixteen of them have made it across the causeway. They say Captain Hauser is right behind them with seven more. Colonel, they reported seeing troops and scout cars. I think we may be cut off. Everything is awful quiet here."

*6 September: 0110 hours, Greenwich Mean Time
0410 hours, Dhahran, Saudi Arabia*

Sid Luna told his crew to wait outside the Airlift Command Element while he went inside. He was amazed at the number of people wandering around the ramp in the early morning, most of them wearing flak jackets and helmets like a badge of honor. The C-141 they had come in on was already taxiing out with a full load of people and he could see one C-130 on the ramp. The place—known as ALCE—was deserted except for one angry-looking chief master sergeant behind the high-topped desk counter.

"Say, Chief, if you've got a Herky bird, I've got a crew." Luna handed the chief a copy of the flight orders that identified his crew as available for staging out of Dhahran.

"Where were you when I needed you?" Pullman snapped, then angrily explained what was happening at Ras Assanya, how he could have used Luna to replace a crew that had been flying for over twenty-four hours, how they had received two messages, the first from the Pentagon declaring Ras Assanya to be evacuated, the second from headquarters MAC forbidding all flights into Ras Assanya since the base might be attacked.

"Chief, you've been on duty too long," Luna said. "My old man was a chief and he would have handled this one . . . like this. Get communications to request a retransmission of the message you don't like, claim it was garbled. Then get on the phone to the com center where the message came from and make sure they *really* garble it on the second transmission. Any chief worth his salt can do that."

Pullman nodded his thanks, surprised that he could learn from a trash-hauling captain.

"Relax. Chief, you're doing them a favor," Luna said. "MAC will get it all straightened out in about twenty-four hours. That's their normal run-around-with-their-heads-up-their-ass time. Now, you got a bird for us? We want to go aflying."

Twenty minutes later Toni D'Angelo was reading the start-engines checklist while Dave Belfort plotted a course into Ras Assanya.

6 September: 0345 hours, Greenwich Mean Time
0645 hours, Ras Assanya, Saudi Arabia

Jack stood defiantly in front of Waters. "Don't evacuate me out, Colonel. I'm the freshest pilot you've got. I've flown once; you know I'm ready. I can pound the bastards into the ground . . ." For Fairly and the rest, he silently added.

"Jack," Waters said, "you're still recovering; you're bound to be weak. In a jet that could jeopardize—"

Jack shook his head. "This is what I'm all about, what I've trained for. Colonel, you know I'm the best pilot you've got, and I'm not bragging. I'm ready for this . . ." He searched for more words to convince Waters. Finally: "Colonel, I'm at least good enough to get through this. Isn't that all that counts here?"

The words struck home. Besides, maybe he'd been overprotective of Jack. And if not the best, Jack was close to it, certainly the best technician in the wing. And with Bull Morgan, it was a helluva team . . . "Okay, okay, you're with Bull. Good luck—"

Jack was already half-sprinting, game leg and all, toward the aircraft bunker, where Bull was with his wingmen, Thunder and Craig, the latter a pilot from the 378th. He slowed, though, when he saw two medics rushing a wounded airman on a stretcher toward an aid station. The man was covered with blood-soaked bandages and leaving a trail of blood. Jack glanced inside a destroyed bunker and saw two body bags lying side by side. He hurried on.

The sun was well clear of the horizon, promising another hot, sweltering day, making Jack glad he had brought two canteens of water. Finding the blast doors of the bunker closed, Jack darted inside the small access door as another artillery barrage ranged over the base. The four men were sitting in a back corner of the bunker with the two crew chiefs, trying to ignore the pounding. Jack sat down and waited. After about fifteen rounds, the shelling stopped. "Just enough to crater the runway and keep us from taking off," Bull said disgustedly.

"Craig," Jack said to the big man he was replacing, "Farrell wants you on the next shuttle with him." The pilot's eyes went from man to man. When he saw no hint of condemnation he stood up, body aching with fatigue, reached out and touched Thunder's shoulder, his way of saying thanks for flying with him, pulled himself around, and left.

The phone on the wall rang and Bull picked it up, acknowledged the message and returned to the group. "The Gomers blew that barrage. Range is still too great and lousy spotters. Civil Engineers claim they'll have five thousand feet of runway open in around fifteen minutes. We're first up, people. Going after the artillery batteries. Take off to the south, clean the bird up, arm 'em up and swing back around to the north. Go straight for them, ripple off your Snakeyes and escape over land. Keep punching chaff and flares behind you all the way around. Get on the ground quick as you can; get turned and ready to go again." He stopped and looked at the men. "We've only got eighteen operational birds and maybe seven hundred people left to get out. From now on we're going to keep pounding at them, making them keep their heads down. Okay, let's do it."

For the next three hours Jack found himself on the treadmill Bull had briefed. On each launch he would hear Mary Hauser's cool voice telling them the sky was clear of bandits and then she would fall silent. When he taxied back in, the crew chiefs, refueling tanker and gunplumbers were ready to turn 512. Thunder would call their mission results in to the command post while Jack post-flighted the aircraft, looking for battle damage. The sorties were averaging less than twelve minutes from the time they taxied out until they were back in the shelter . . .

After their sixth sortie Bull and Jack had to hold south of the base as the Civil Engineers worked furiously patching holes in the runway with quick-setting cement and aluminum planking. To conserve fuel Bull climbed to eighteen thousand, where they found a C-130 also cutting lazy circles. When Bull called the cargo plane on Guard, asking about their status, a female voice answered, saying that like them the C-130 was holding and waiting for an opportunity to get in.

"I know that voice," Jack told Thunder.

"Right. Sounds like Toni D'Angelo." Both men were recalling the scramble a year in the past. Amazing . . . Jack, Thunder and the Grain King co-pilot together in the same piece of sky again, still involved in the same dirty little war for "allies" you could learn to hate.

Toni's voice came over the UHF radio now. "Got to go, can't get in this time. They're recalling us to try again later, won't let us hang around long if the runway isn't open."

They watched the C-130 head south, and after several minutes the tower told them to think about diverting to Dhahran, that the runway had just taken another barrage and was severely cratered, especially around the arresting cables, which eliminated any chance to take the barriers for a short-field arrestment.

"How much taxiway you got open?" Bull asked, thinking about landing on the wide strip that paralleled the runway. When the tower reported that only the taxiway between the aircraft bunkers was serviceable, Bull told them to clear any vehicles off. Minutes later Bull started his approach onto the narrow lane of concrete that connected the bunkers to the main taxiway, most of which was curved and twisted as it wound between the bunkers, and only on the southern edge did it straighten out for some three thousand feet—barely enough room for a landing rollout. Bull said he would taxi into the first open bunker to give Jack the wing-tip clearance needed on each side of the narrow path. "It will be tight; we can do it." Bull came down a short final and planted his aircraft hard onto the concrete. The drag-chute was streaming before he slammed his nose gear down and managed to drag his bird to a halt just short of a large crater, then headed into a bunker, nose first, not waiting to be winched in backward.

Sweat rolled off Jack as he made his approach, glad that Bull had cleared out of the way; it was going to be a tight squeeze. He drove his Phantom hard onto the concrete, repeating Bull's performance. The crew chiefs were winching 512 back into its bunker when Jack saw ten or twelve men pushing Bull's F-4 out of his bunker so it could be turned around and stuffed in properly. Bull's mask was pulled away, and he gave them a raised clenched fist.

"Beats diverting to Dhahran," Jack said, "but I don't want to do it again."

In the bunker Jack called Carroll and was told they were down to ten aircraft and still had five hundred people left to get out. He relayed that to Thunder, adding, "the C-130s have only gotten in twice since sunup. Runway should be open in about forty minutes, Bill says, and we're picking up Broz and Ambler for a threesome. Bill says it's getting grim in the first-aid bunkers." The image of the wounded airman on the stretcher forced its way into his mind, and he now understood why the infantry hated artillery . . . Thirty minutes later the phone rang and the three of them, Jack, Bull and Broz, were scrambled . . .

Bull's voice crackled over the UHF as he arced onto the beachhead for their seventh run at it. "Rats Ass Control, two tanks have broken out and are moving south along the coast. Coming your way." Before Nesbit could acknowledge the warning Bull radioed, "I'm in." He rolled in ahead of Jack, jinking furiously until his wizzo could lock on the lead tank. Jack saw Bull's first Maverick streak toward the tank, then after a slight hesitation the second Maverick shot out from under the wing, its smoke trail pointing to the second tank. Bull's right wing flared . . . and his F-4 disintegrated before the Mavericks destroyed the tanks. Jack broke off his attack and retreated to safety over the water, looking for Broz. "*What got him?* I didn't see a thing, no SAM, no puffs of smoke from the ground, *nothing.*" Thunder couldn't help.

What it was, what they missed, was a single round from an obsolete thirty-seven-millimeter Triple A cannon that hit Bull's right wing. The fuse in the small bullet had detonated its small high-explosive charge inside the right-wing tank. It was enough.

When Thunder pointed out the other F-4 orbiting low over the water Jack keyed his UHF, assuming flight lead, and told Broz to join on him. The young lieutenant whipped his plane around and rolled up on a wing, showing them he was still carrying two Mavericks. "Thunder," Jack said, "check out that ship at three o'clock."

Thunder identified it as an Alligator-class landing ship. They circled the *Sirri* at a respectful distance as it moved in an eastward direction, away from the beachhead.

"That's the baby that probably delivered those tanks," Jack said, thinking about Bull. He studied the vessel, sensing that something was unusual . . . "Count the antennas. I'll bet your sweet ass that's a command ship."

He keyed the radio. "Broz, I'm going to check this one out." His fingers ran across the armament switches, selecting the Mavericks. "Thunder, lock on that S.O.B. soon as you can." Adrenaline flowed; he needed to even the score for Bull. Abruptly he broke out of his attack run and headed for the base. Again he keyed his UHF, calling Broz to join up and switch over to the frequency for the command post.

"Rats Ass Control, Wolf Zero-Nine, flight of two." Nesbit acknowledged his call, Jack continued: "Lead bought it over beachhead, two tanks destroyed. Have observed an Alligator-class landing ship heading eastbound, away from beachhead. Ship has numerous antennas and signs of damage to superstructure. Standing by for words."

"Roger, Zero-Nine," Nesbit answered. "State ordnance remaining."

"Lead and wingman have two Mavericks each."

"Roger, Zero-Nine. Wolf Zero-One says your choice of targets, the ship or targets of opportunity on shore. RTB ASAP."

"Jack," Broz radioed, "it's a command ship, worth hitting even if it's leaving." Jack could hear in the lieutenant's voice the same anger he had felt moments earlier.

"Negative, Broz. That baby is loaded with SAMs and Triple A and it's out of the action. We'll split the beachhead for one pass. You take the north half."

Broz followed Jack down to the surface as they looped south of the base before turning inland to circle and attack the beachhead from the west . . .

Waters had been monitoring the exchange between Jack and Broz over the radio, and though he would never know if Jack had made the right decision about which target to attack, he knew Jack was going after targets on the coast exactly as he would have done . . .

The two Phantoms split apart as they turned to the east, skimming across the gravelly dunes, kicking up dusty rooster tails as they ran onto the beachhead. They were crossing the thin line of UAC defenders when a string of tracers came at them. Jack jinked around the tracers and then jerked his Phantom into a sharp break to the left as a SAM flashed by and exploded. He felt a thump but continued the run, hoping Thunder could find a target on his monitor screen that the Mavericks could home on. He waited to hear Thunder's pickle call. His telelight panel started to blink warnings at him, but without a fire warning light he was determined to press the attack.

"Cleared to pickle," Thunder shouted. Jack raised the Phantom just high enough off the deck to get a decent launch angle and depressed the pickle button twice, sending both his Mavericks toward the tanks his backseater had found.

Thunder had his head out of the scope and was checking their six o'clock position, stabbing at the flare-and-chaff buttons. Suddenly he called out, "Broz is hit!"

Jack had descended to fifty feet and was still jinking hard as he ran for safety. Another two missiles reached over them, not able to guide on the Phantom below a hundred feet.

Thunder saw Broz's Phantom buck from an unseen hit and then balloon up. Even in the bright afternoon sun the wizzo could see tracers reaching into the F-4, could see the rear half of the plane flare into flames as Broz climbed.

"Head south," Jack shouted over the radio, but Broz's F-4 bucked again, taking another hit as it turned toward the base. Jack crossed behind the lieutenant while Thunder laid a barrage of chaff and flares behind them, trying to create a diversion for the SAMs and Triple A to guide on.

Now Jack's bird trembled from another hit and then they were clear. "Hold on, Broz," Jack whispered to himself, "almost home." On cue the canopies of the flaming F-4 flew off and the two men ejected as the aircraft twisted into the sea. Jack watched them slip their parachutes onto the northern end of the base, not too far from his old beach camp. Both waved furiously, signaling they were okay. "There go two lucky S.O.B.'s," Jack said. But how much longer, he silently added.

The crew chief walked around 512, surveying the damage his Phantom had taken. Unable to contain himself he turned on Jack. "There are four, count 'em four, birds left that can fly, and she ain't one of 'em. Look what you done." He was shouting now, blaming Jack for the damage. "Engine change, new speed brake and flap for the right wing, gotta seal the wing tank, and more goddamn little holes than Carter's got liver pills. The hydraulic leaks don't even count."

Thunder hung up the phone after reporting their message and joined the two men. When the crew chief slowed his verbal barrage, the wizzo said, "Let's just fix it." The crew chief grunted in surprise and darted out of the bunker, leaving Thunder and Jack behind.

Within a few minutes he was back and opening the blast doors. Waiting outside were a dozen men and an engine on its dolly, still encased in a bright aluminum protective wrap.

"You fine officers believe in getting your hands dirty?"

Stansell ran into the command post just ahead of an artillery barrage, flopped down in a chair next to Waters, exhausted by the long ordeal of evacuating the wing. "They're persistent mothers," he said, listening to the regularly spaced whomps as artillery barraged the base.

"How's the evacuation going?" Waters asked.

Stansell shook his head. "Five hundred and eighteen left. I don't think we'll get another C-130 in until after dark. Any chance of evacuating over land?"

"We only have enough vehicles to move sixty, maybe seventy people. The coast road's been cut for four days and in this heat no one is going to walk very far. It was never an option." Waters tried to force his mind to work but fatigue was driving him down. He reached into his pocket and pulled out the bottle of pills Doc Landis had given him, wondering if he should take one. He needed something. Not yet, he thought, I've never used them and don't know what they'll do to me. And then he did something he never believed he could do. Sack out. To him it was like a cop out. "Rup, you've got the stick for about an hour. I'm going to sack out in the corner. Wake me if there's something you can't handle." He walked over to the corner, stretched out on the floor and fell into an instant deep sleep.

"Colonel, wake up." Stansell's voice cut through the deep fog of his sleep.

Waters sat up, feeling slightly dizzy, glanced at his watch. He had been asleep over three hours and it was almost sunset. He felt alert and rested. Sergeant Nesbit handed him a cup of hot coffee.

"What's our status?"

"Chief Hartley wants to blow the causeway," Stansell told him. "He's starting to take small-arms fire out there. We've lost contact with the GCI site and Captain Hauser never made it in . . . The engineers never got the runway open and are trying to patch together two thousand feet on the taxiway, enough for a C-130 to get in and out. Single-ship Floggers have tried to overfly us six times. Reccy birds, I figure. The Rapiers got 'em every time. So far. If we can hold on another six or seven hours, the Navy should be able to give us air cover. We're taking on artillery barrage every fifteen or twenty minutes. Over two hundred casualties now, sir."

The phone lines had been cut to the Security Police bunker and Waters had to use a radio to establish contact. "Chief, this is Zero-One. I agree. Blow the causeway."

"Roger, Zero-One," Hartley answered, "it's time. We're taking an occasional mortar round and can see movement at the head of the mine field."

"How long can you hold?"

"Maybe three or four hours, Colonel. But that's only a guess."

The chief signed off then, telling them he would report back when the causeway was down. He listened for a moment, looking at his watch. "These muthas are something regular." He calculated he had twelve to fifteen minutes to blow the charge under the causeway before the next artillery barrage would start. "Hey, with a little luck they might do the job for us with a lucky shot." The chief was talking to himself as he strapped on his helmet and closed the front of his flak jacket, then jogged the two hundred yards from his command bunker to the embankment the bulldozers had pushed up on the base side of his big ditch. He kept down until he reached the break in the wall that they had left for the road leading across the causeway. He moved quickly and lightly, darting into the observation bunker set into the embankment next to the road.

Macon Jefferson, holding the bunker with another man, felt a little better when he saw Hartley. "Time to blow this mutha," the chief told them. He quickly connected two wires to the actuator, a small box with two guarded switches and a timing dial. He set the dial to zero, lifted both guards and threw the switches. Nothing happened. "Don't look out," Macon said quietly. "There's a sniper out there." The chief looked anyway, counting seven craters on the causeway. A single shot hit the sandbagged opening inches from his face.

"Mortars must have cut the wires," the chief growled. "Why haven't you guys taken the sniper out? He can shoot. Maybe the next bastard won't be as good." He scowled at the fresh scar the bullet had left. He picked up an M-16, checked it. "Stick your helmet into the opening in three minutes, he ordered, jogging out of the bunker. He moved fifty yards down the wall and scrambled up the loose dirt of the steep bank, stopping just below the ridge. Carefully he scooped out a shallow depression that pointed toward the spot he judged the sniper fired from. "I got the angle on you . . ." The chief took off his helmet, laid his cheek against the stock, looked over the sight, and waited. He saw the flash before he heard the report when the sniper fired at the helmet flashing in the port of the observation bunker. Hartley swung the barrel ten degrees to the left and squeezed off a single shot. He could see the sniper's jaw and rifle stock come apart in the rapidly fading light. He checked his watch, calculating he still had seven minutes before the next barrage.

He jogged back to the bunker and picked up a fresh reel of wire, telling the men to cover him, then moved along the edge of the causeway to a spot near the middle. He knelt and attached the new wires to the leads coming from the charge planted eight feet in the earth, threw the old wires aside, reeled the wire out as he trotted back. Twenty feet from the observation post a series of shots erupted. Hartley surprised the watching men with a sudden burst of speed as he piled into the bunker. One shot had cut a bloody furrow across the back of his left thigh. "I told you he wouldn't be as good," he grunted, handing the new wire to Macon. "So I was wrong. Blow him while I stuff this leak." He shoved a wadded-up dressing into his wound and bound it tightly with a compress bandage from the first-aid kit on his belt.

The causeway erupted in a shower of noise, dust and dirt. Macon asked him why he didn't crouch when he ran. "Don't do any good when you're my size. Now get some shovels and fill this gap in," he replied, waving at the road cut through the embankment. He checked his watch and walked back to his command bunker to call Waters.

"Rup," Waters was saying to Stansell, "see if the Engineers can get three thousand feet of taxiway open. Enough for an F-4 to take off." Waters hadn't shaved in two days and his face and flight suit were streaked with sweat. Energy, though, still radiated from him. "After that, get over to the bunkers you're using for evac and make sure someone is in charge; then get back here."

6 September: 1710 hours, Greenwich Mean Time
2010 hours, Dhahran, Saudi Arabia

The crew of the C-130 was sprawled out on the cargo deck waiting for the order to launch another shuttle mission out of Dhahran. They were weary from repeated attempts to get into Ras Assanya and discouraged because they had only been able to land once. The overweight major who had taken over running the operation drove up in his air-conditioned truck and walked toward the C-130 with clipboard in hand. "I'm putting you into crew rest," he said. "Ras Assanya is reporting they have only two thousand feet of runway open. I'm not about to send you into that."

Toni D'Angelo turned and walked toward the flight deck, the men trailing her, and the major realized they were going to Ras Assanya no matter what he said. "Captain Luna," he yelled at their backs, "stop using Grain King Zero-Three for your call sign."

"Screw you," from Toni, climbing up the ladder.

Captain Luna dropped the Hercules down onto the deck when they were forty miles out of Ras Assanya, hugging the coast line. The moonlit night gave him plenty of visibility, and Dave's radar navigation kept him on the course he had to fly in order to be recognized as a friendly aircraft by the Rapiers.

Two miles out, Luna popped the bird to twelve hundred feet and dropped his gear and flaps, configuring for an assault landing. When he saw a flashing light at the southern end of the taxiway he queried the tower's frequency. No answer. He did not see the large crater that had been the tower's bunker.

He brought the Hercules down final with its nose high in the air, carrying as much power as he could. The moment his main gear touched down on the taxiway, he shoved the yoke full forward, slamming the nose gear down, raking the throttles full aft and lifting them over the detent into reverse. He stomped on the brakes, dragging the cargo plane to a halt.

A pickup dashed onto the taxiway in front of them and a figure jumped out with two hand-held wands and motioned them to back up. Luna threw the props into reverse and backed down the main taxiway until he reached another taxiway leading into the bunkers. The lone figure ran down the taxiway motioning him to follow, waved the Hercules to a stop in front of a bunker with open blast doors.

"My God, look at the litters lined up," Toni said, pointing to the casualties waiting evacuation. "How are we going to get that many on board?"

"We shut down and reconfigure for litters, that's how," Luna said.

"Captain, that takes thirty, maybe forty minutes," the loadmaster complained.

"We'll do it in fifteen. Get busy."

Chief Hartley was already in the back of the Hercules directing the offloading of mortar shells and anti-tank weapons they had been waiting for. He told them the base was expecting an attack across the isthmus connecting the base to the mainland at any time. "They been pounding the crap out of us for two hours. We got some gettin' even to do." The battle-weary and wounded chief bundled into his truck and went off with the load into the night.

The men tending the wounded swarmed onto the Hercules and helped the crew rig the stanchions that allowed litters to be stacked five-high. The wounded were then carried on board as soon as a set of stanchions were in place, leaving trails of blood across the cargo deck. Bill Carroll helped carry on board one of his sergeants badly wounded in a rocket attack. He strapped the litter into place and checked with Toni D'Angelo, who was standing at the rear of the cargo bay supervising the loading. "These are the ones our doc says can be saved if we get them to a hospital . . . The aid stations look like slaughterhouses."

Toni looked at his name tag and checked the passenger list that had been handed her. She found the captain's name at the top, indicating he had top priority to be evacuated. "We'll do what we can, Captain. Why don't you ride up front with us?"

It was an offer hard to turn down. God knew, Carroll wanted to get out of there, find his sanity again. He even started to pull himself up the steps leading to the flight deck, then abruptly stopped and hurried out through the crew-entrance hatch. "What the hell am I thinking of," he mumbled to himself.

"Okay, let's get the hell out of here," Luna yelled at his co-pilot as Carroll jumped off the C-130 and headed for the Command Post.

Toni snapped the gear handle up as soon as the C-130 lifted off while Luna held the big bird on the deck and pushed the throttles full forward, coaxing as much airspeed as he could out of the tired engines. "Ten minutes, babies, just ten minutes," he pleaded . . .

The enemy Flogger was also on the deck, trying to avoid radar-detection and engagement by the Rapiers. The pilot was trying to figure out a cover story to prove he had overflown the base on a visual reconnaissance as the air-group commander had ordered. Those fools, he thought, nothing is impossible for them when they don't have to do it! Well, let them try once and not take a hit from an American missile. He also couldn't understand why his superiors were so anxious to learn if the American base was burning. A huge silhouette flashed in front of him, heading south. He pulled up and rolled in behind the escaping airplane, recognizing the outline of a U.S. C-130 and seeing a solution to his problem. A confirmed kill would give any story he concocted the ring of truth.

The pilot carefully positioned his Flogger and closed to within three hundred meters, moving the pipper on his gunsight over the cockpit area. He squeezed the trigger and held it, emptying his twin-barreled twenty-three-millimeter gun into the Hercules . . .

The first five shells ripped into the left side of the cockpit, killing Captain Luna and Riley Henderson. A shell smashed into Riley's chest, tearing apart the upper half of his body. Blood and pieces of the flight engineer splashed over Dave Belfort as pieces of shrapnel cut into his face. Toni wrenched the yoke back, fighting for altitude, managing to control the Hercules and keep it airborne. Belfort un-strapped from his seat and moved across the flight deck, scooping Luna's remains out of his seat. "I still got it," Toni called out, and Dave grabbed the wheel and helped her fly the plane while she checked the overhead panel and radioed a distress call.

Meanwhile the Flogger repositioned for another attack and rolled in. The pilot selected an Aphid dogfight missile and placed his target-pipper on the left outboard engine before he squeezed the trigger. The missile streaked toward the Hercules and impacted outboard of the engine, tearing off the left wing. The C-130 spun to the left, out of control. Toni pushed the left throttles full-forward and pulled the right throttles aft, trying to use differential power to control the plane's flat spin. Just before they hit the water Belfort thought he heard her say, "I'm sorry, Dave."

6 September: 1955 hours, Greenwich Mean Time
2255 hours, Ras Assanya, Saudi Arabia

The lights in the command post flickered, then went out. Waters heard the backup generator kick into life, cough twice, and the lights came back on. Stansell had never stopped talking on the phone. Now he hung up and walked over to the launch-and-recovery board and marked tail-number 512 as mission capable. "Whoever laid in the hardened com lines knew what they were doing," was his only comment. He changed to 2049 the number of people evacuated out. "The second C-130 is taxiing out now. Three hundred eighteen to go." Waters listened for the sounds of a C-130 but couldn't hear the turbo-props through the thick walls. He was thankful that two shuttles had made it in since dark and most of the wounded had made it out.

He studied the boards for a moment, knowing what he had to do. Bitterness and frustration washed over him when he thought of the sacrifices his wing had made in trying to end this "little war." He almost lost control when Bill Carroll walked into the room. "Bill, you were ordered *out.*"

"Yes, sir, but I think I might still be of some use . . . I speak Arabic and Farsi—"

"Yes, you do. Get over to Doc Landis and stay with him. He'll need a translator." The Intelligence officer stared at him, catching the terrible implication.

The crew chief threw open the right blast door to the aircraft bunker and motioned the refueling truck to back in. He wanted to see if he could get the truck inside and close the blast door, but there wasn't enough room. He yelled at the pumper to get the hose out and connected. The pumper refused to be hurried and went about his duties with a studied nonchalance, an unlit cigar stump clamped in his mouth. "No way this here white man's piece of shit is going to get into the air," the pumper said, knowing how to rile the crew chief.

"Shut your mouth unless'en you want that cigar lit and shoved up sideways." He went through the servicing routine that had not been completed, even though he had already called his aircraft in as mission ready. "Well," he grumbled, "what do they expect? Bust my ass doing an engine change 'cause some pilot can't see shit comin' at him and now can't find anyone so I got to do the whole thing . . ." He was still muttering to himself when the pumper disconnected the hose and started to move his refueler away from the bunker. "Hey, if you see my partner tell him to get his ass back here," he yelled after the departing truck. "And I could use a ammo cart and a gun-plumber . . ."

The truck had moved about thirty yards down the ramp when another artillery barrage started to pound the base. That pumper's a dead man, the crew chief thought, returning to his work in the relative safety of the bunker, not feeling guilty. No time for that now. He slipped into the front cockpit, checked the switches and carefully adjusted the lap belt and leg harnesses, making the cockpit ready for the next launch. He crawled into the backseat and did the same thing. Finally he found some rags and started to wipe the bird down, removing any signs of dirt, oil or hydraulic fluid.

He cracked open the small access-hatch in the blast doors, peering into the night, and worried about his partner. He thought he saw some movement on the taxiway but it was hard to tell in the darkness. The intensity of the incoming rounds had slackened and given way to a steady deadly rhythm. "Whump-one-two-Whump," he counted, picking up the beat. He could see definite movement coming his way: the figure of the pumper materialized, pushing an ammunition cart, cigar still clamped in his mouth. The crew chief pushed the blast door open and helped the exhausted sergeant jockey the cart up to the right side of the Phantom's nose, swung a panel down and connected the feed head into the internal gatling gun. Then he grabbed a speed wrench and started to crank the gun over, feeding fresh ammunition into the drum.

"Okay, I need help turning this fucker—"

"What's wrong with them," the pumper shouted back, pointing at two motionless figures on the floor in a corner.

"Ah, them's the pilot and wizzo. They been bustin' their asses helping change the engine. They ain't used to workin'. Let 'em sleep." The two then helped each other, laboriously turning the wrench and reloading the gun. They had finished when the chief's partner staggered in with another man, carrying the last Sidewinder on base. They almost dropped the one hundred-eighty-pound missile before they could hand it over to the crew chief and the pumper. "Not bad, asshole." The chief allowed a grin as they slipped the missile onto the left-inboard rail.

A minute later the Phantom was ready and the shelling died away. An unusual quiet descended over the bunker.

"What the hell," the chief muttered as he settled down to wait.

The sergeant from Civil Engineers who reported into the command post was covered with dried sweat and caked dirt. His hair was plastered to his head with rivulets of fresh blood. "You've got three thousand feet," he told them, and sat down, shaking with fatigue.

Waters erased Jack's call sign on the board and wrote in "Wolf Zero-One." He motioned to Stansell, stepped into the passageway leading outside and put on his flak jacket and helmet. "Rup, I've got to . . . surrender the base before the shelling starts again." Stansell said nothing. "These lulls last about fifteen minutes; use it to get our planes out of here. Get the word to the crews and call Doc Landis and the evacuation bunker and tell them what's happening. I'm going to the Security Police bunker and tell them. They're the closest to the Gomers."

Stansell still said nothing. What was there to say? They shook hands, and Stansell went back to the command post as the Security Police's radio net began to broadcast a new warning.

The bunker's blast doors were partially open so Jack and Thunder could receive messages over the command post's radio frequency. Now they heard Stansell relay the latest warning he had just received from the Security Police. The repeated artillery shellings had finally cut the landlines to the bunker, so the Phantom's UHF radio was their only means of communication. "Close the doors," Jack told the crew chief. "There's a tank on the taxiway, coming for us."

"What you want me to do about that?" the crew chief said, pulling the doors shut with his partner's help.

"Control says we're scrambling as soon as they can knock it out with a TOW missile. Stand by."

"That's all they ever say—stand by." The crew chief could hear the clank of tank tracks and sporadic cannon fire moving toward his bunker. "They're going to standfuckingby too long," the crew chief said, disappearing into the back of the bunker. He rummaged around, finding two glass jars that he used for collecting fuel samples out of his Phantom. Hurrying up to the power cart, he twisted a valve and filled both jars with gasoline from the cart's fuel tank. He tore strips from the rag he had been using, soaked them with gas and stuffed one into the neck of each jar. He held up his handiwork for Jack to see. "Got a match?" Jack reached into the leg-pocket of his G-suit and tossed him a container of survival matches.

The crew chief dropped his webb belt with its heavy canteen and ammo pouch and shoved three matches between his teeth. Bending low, he peered out the access door, then ran toward the oncoming tank, making for the cover of the next bunker. He ran inside and set his jars down, unbuttoned his pants and urinated against the wall. Explosions and shell fire were coming from the tank's direction. He crept around the wall of the bunker on all fours, looking at the tank. It was firing pointblank into a bunker about seventy-five yards away. "Not my bird, you don't."

The tank pivoted on its left track and moved toward the next bunker on the other side of the taxiway not fifty yards away. "Oh, momma," he whispered, "the angles are right." He struck a match and lit the rags of both bottles, picked them up and ran toward the tank. The flames burned his hands, nearly making him drop the jars.

The gunner in the tank saw the light from the burning Molotov cocktails and swung the turret toward the running figure of the chief as he hurled them against the tank. The bottles shattered, the rags ignited the gasoline, the tank was enveloped in flames. Now an internal explosion sent a tongue of fire out of a hatch that had popped open.

The crew chief picked himself up, surprised he was still alive, and ran back to his Phantom, partially opening the big blast doors to the bunker.

Jack keyed his radio. "Control, Wolf Zero-Nine. 512's crew chief knocked the tank out. The taxiway is clear."

The guards at the Security Police bunker recognized Waters immediately and waved him inside. Chief Hartley was lying on his stomach on a table while a corpsman put a fresh bandage on his thigh. The crew chief sat up, pointed at the chair next to hm. "You shouldn't be here," he rasped at the colonel, "but the gesture is appreciated."

Waters searched for a way to tell the chief how he felt about what they had accomplished. He could only think of tired phrases, all of them wrong. "No gesture, Chief. How much longer can you hold your ditch?"

"Not long. They're using tanks like a bulldozer to build a causeway. That's one reason the shelling has stopped. They don't want to nail their own troops."

Waters stared at the wall in front of him. "Chief, I can't ask your men to do any more . . . I've got to . . . I'm going to surrender before the shelling starts again. Maybe we can scramble our last birds out of here before that—"

"Sir"—there was hurt in the crew chief's voice—"a tank waded ashore about five minutes ago and is on the taxiway. You must not have heard." He paused, startled by the look on Waters' face. "Don't worry, my men will knock it out."

He hoped it wasn't an empty boast.

"Roger, Wolf Zero-Nine." Stansell's voice was firm. "*Scramble.* Repeat. *Scramble.* Wolf Zero-Nine, you are now Wolf Zero-One. Recover at Dhahran. Repeat, recover at Dhahran. Good luck."

The crew chief and his partner pushed the blast doors open and fed power into the Phantom when Jack signaled them for engine start. They worked furiously buttoning up panels as the bird came to life. Finishing the last panel, the two men jerked the chocks from the wheels and gave Jack thumbsup. The chief ran to the front of the bunker and motioned them forward. Gunning the engines, Jack taxied out. As they rolled past, the crew chief came to attention and threw them a salute, the only way he knew to say good-bye to his warbirds.

Jack returned the salute, hoping he saw it.

"Hey, pard," the crew chief said. "The ragheads are coming from the north. I'm going south. Coming?" And the two men ran from the empty bunker.

Doc Landis looked at the beams over his head, visualizing the five Phantoms he heard taking off. He bent back over the wounded Security Policeman, trying to stop the flow of blood from a gaping wound in his back. "Bill, it won't be nice when they find out you are an intelligence officer," the doctor said. "I don't need you here. Doctor's orders . . ."

"Thanks," Carroll said, "but I'm not going anywhere. Waters' orders . . ." He had disobeyed his colonel once and wasn't about to do it again.

The Security Police radio net came alive with warnings of landing craft and tanks in the water moving toward the beach at the north end of the runway. Chief Hartley shook his head. "I guess this is it. Well, we've come a long way together, Colonel."

"Chief, we sure have . . ." He began looking for something to make a white flag out of.

Hartley wouldn't let it go. "You're the best damn boss I've ever had." And he started to weave, dizzy from the effort. Waters reached out and steadied him. "You made me want to do things I never thought I could. I appreciate that . . ."

The men still in the bunker looked up as they heard the sound of jets taking off. Waters counted them. In his mind's eye he could see his five warbirds lifting off, reaching into the clear desert night, their afterburners leaving pulsating beacons of blue light behind them. And Waters knew with a certainty now that Jack Locke was, no question, Wolf Zero-One.

The men reflexively ducked when they heard the shrill incoming whistle of artillery. Most of them heard the chief say, "Sweet Jesus," before the rounds walked through the bunker, tearing them apart, and killing the commander of the 45th Tactical Fighter Wing.

> *7 September: 0230 hours, Greenwich Mean Time*
> *6 September: 2230 hours, Washington, D.C.*

The President was standing in the War Room deep in the Pentagon, leaning over the table in front of his chair, propped on his arms. His jaw moved slowly, the only sign of his distress as he listened to the colonel standing in front of the situation map at the front of the room. The colonel's gray hair belied his youthful good looks, and his slow southern accent masked a quick, intense intelligence.

"The base at Ras Assanya has been overrun," the colonel said, using an electronic pointer.

A pain cut through the President's gut.

"A Navy reconnaissance plane is stationed over the area and reports that all fighting has stopped . . ."

"How old is that information?" National Secretary Adviser Cagliari said.

"Less than twenty minutes, sir. The United Arab Command is reinforcing a line between the Getty oil refinery at Mina Azure"—the colonel traced a line six miles south of the oil refinery located on the Persian Gulf—"and the beachhead the People's Soldiers of Islam have carved out." He circled the spot where the PSI had come ashore.

The pain in the President's stomach got worse. "Has the PSI attacked the oil refinery?"

"No, sir, their objective was the base."

"Oil . . . it always rears its ugly head."

The room was silent. Then the colonel picked it up: "Our fleet is moving into position, the vanguard, two destroyers and a frigate, passed through the Strait of Hormuz an hour ago. They're moving at flank speed toward Ras Assanya. The rest of the fleet is on-station in the Gulf of Oman." He pointed to an area southeast of the strait. "The Carrier Air Group is on standby waiting for the Go to launch a strike at the PSI."

The President wanted to be alone, have a little time to think before he acted. But time was what he did not have. The pain was turning

376

to anger. He had, after all, the means to destroy the PSI. Give the order and send more people into harm's way. He turned to Cagliari, who was now sitting next to him. "If I brought us up to DEFCON Two, would they get the signal how serious we are?"

"Wrong signal, sir. That would be announcing we're on the verge of a major war. The Russians couldn't ignore it; they'd increase their state of alert. They might even opt for preemptive moves . . ."

"Mr. President"—Cyrus Piccard, Secretary of State, broke into the conversation—"I've some room to negotiate here and try to stabilize the situation, the region . . . But I need a *restrained* military response." He waited, anxious to see if the President would consider other options.

"What do you need, Cy?" the President asked. The Secretary of State was a master at hiding his sharklike nature behind a facade of courtly manners and polite words.

"If you use the Navy and the United Arab Command, you can trap the PSI *at* Ras Assanya. Which makes them a bargaining chip."

"But they're holding over three hundred of our people prisoners," Cagliari said.

"True, which makes the situation more delicate," Piccard told him. "My people are in contact with the International Red Cross. We're asking for them to monitor the status of the prisoners. If you bring the Rapid Deployment Force to full alert and start moving advance elements toward the Gulf, that will send the signal we're considering military intervention. But we can send other messages. The Soviet ambassador is waiting for me in my office. The channels are open. Mr. President, if we do this right, we can hope to achieve our immediate objective: an end to the fighting."

"And that's a victory?"

"It's the best we can get without a war."

"But the cost . . ." The President's pain would not go away. Or his anger. It seemed so much for so little . . .

7 September: 1400 hours, Greenwich Mean Time
1700 hours, Moscow, USSR

The men waiting in the ornate room the Kremlin reserved for Politburo meetings could hear the new General Secretary's footsteps echo down the hall, and they all stood and applauded when he entered the room.

Viktor Rokossovksy, formerly the youngest and now the first among them, nodded, acknowledging the applause, and walked to the chair at the head of the table. He nodded again and sat down while the men continued to clap. He swept the table with an appreciative eye, stopping when he saw his old seat, now empty. Soon, he thought, one of my people will be sitting there. He could see the hard, satisfied look on Rafik Ulyanoff's face. Even Kalin-Tegov, the party's theoretician, looked pleased.

"Thank you, comrades," Rokossovsky said; his first official words as General Secretary. "Please be seated. We must not waste valuable time." The applause slowly died as the men sat down. "I'm concerned about the American reaction to their defeat in the Persian Gulf."

Ulyanoff leaped forward. "We're getting mixed signals. They've placed their Rapid Deployment Force on full alert but are not moving in mass. Our ambassador in Washington reports that the President seems to be looking for a negotiated settlement. There is a growing concern in the American press over the prisoners taken by the People's Soldiers of Islam. The situation is fluid."

"And the KGB?" Rokossovsky asked.

The pleasant-looking man who headed the KGB smiled. "Our agents report that the Iranians must negotiate. They no longer have the means to continue fighting."

"I'm considering that it would be in our interests to stabilize the Persian Gulf for now," Rokossovsky told them. "Especially if we can participate in the negotiations for a peace treaty. Your thoughts, please."

"That would be consistent with our philosophy," Kalin-Tegov said, "but we must reinforce any expansion of our influence in the diplomatic area with concrete developments inside Iran. Perhaps more non-military support to the Tudeh Party."

He did not add, nor did he need to, "For the time being."

Rokossovsky listened carefully to what Kalin-Tegov said. As the party's theoretician, he had made it possible for Rokossovsky to depose the former General Secretary. "Then this is an opportunity to show the world that we can be peacemakers."

"When it suits our needs," the party theoretician said.

EPILOGUE

9 September: 0905 hours, Greenwich Mean Time
1005 hours, Stonewood, England

Cunningham had to walk. The protocol officer at Stonewood had set up a welcoming brief, a tour and a luncheon to keep the general occupied until the F-4s arrived, and out of politeness he had sat through the welcome by Brigadier General Shaw. But during a coffee break he sought out Mort Pullman. "Chief, let's walk over to base Ops."

The general walked in silence, reflecting on the irony of the situation. The fighting had ended and the antagonists were scrambling to find a new way to live with each other while the press looked for scapegoats to blame for the "defeat." Yes, the PSI had overrun Ras Assanya and taken over three hundred prisoners, but now with the fleet standing offshore they couldn't give them back quick enough. The Saudis wanted the remnants of the 45th out of Dhahran, but were demanding the U.S. fleet remain in the Gulf. Most of the press in Europe was claiming that the U.S. had started World War III, but the NATO governments were mightily pleased that oil was still flowing.

And then a newly promoted Vice Air Marshall, Sir David Childs, had appeared in his office, telling him that the Prime Minister was under attack in Parliament because of British involvement in the Persian Gulf. But Her Majesty's government would not object if five F-4s happened to recover at Stonewood under routine training operations in the next few days. The general had thanked Childs and scheduled a C-137B to take him to Stonewood.

As they made the short walk to the flight line, a staff sergeant saluted them, saying, "Forty-fifth, sir." It was not the loud shout of the Army's "Airborne, sir," but a quiet statement of pride. More men and women passed them, each demanding a salute.

"Your people look sharp, Pullman. How do you do it?"

"I don't. They do it, general. They're proud of what they did."

The general shook his head. "I almost destroyed them and they're proud of it . . ."

"They don't see it that way, sir. You gave them a job to do without starting World War III, and they *did* it. The fighting has stopped. They're ready for next time."

Shaw met them as they entered base Ops saying the fighters were ten minutes out. The three men went out onto the flight line.

"General," Shaw said, "can we do something more for them?"

"You have something in mind?"

"I was thinking of a memorial . . ."

"You mean like the *Arizona* in Pearl Harbor? Something to remember a defeat? Lest we forget?" Even his own generals did not understand that for the last forty years his Air Force had not won a war. "*No.* A memorial marks the end to something. This is not over. Death and waste and stupidity don't need memorials, only memory so we won't underestimate an enemy again. I don't know about you, but there's nothing wrong with my memory. I won't make that mistake again."

"Will we have a second chance?" Shaw asked.

Cunningham was silent. He was fifty-eight years old, beyond normal retirement age, serving only at the pleasure of the President, who did not seem overly pleased with him. He studied Shaw, trying to fathom what was behind his troubled eyes.

"I was thinking of Waters, the others. Their chances are gone."

"Yes, and we don't have many like them left. Waters was a real combat commander. He could lead and people would follow. Do you know how rare that is? I had to tell his wife about his death. It was something I couldn't let anyone else do. You know, she was more understanding and stronger about it than I was. She said, 'Anthony understood the risks. He wouldn't have it any other way.' "

An honor roll of names scrolled through Cunningham's mind: Fairly, Nelson, Gomez, Conlan, Benton, Luna, D'Angelo, Belfort, Henderson, McCray, Morgan . . . He felt a deep *personal* accountability that he couldn't shove into a bureaucratic niche. Human beings had been killed because of the decisions he had made . . .

"No, I was wrong," he said. "They do need a memorial. Maybe not now, but in a few years when time has put this mess in perspective. When we can remember them for who they were and what they did."

The three men stood there together, silently committed to making it happen.

Jack sharply rocked the wings of his Phantom, signaling his flight to rejoin into close formation. The four jets started to collapse together into finger-tip formation when Jack's words broke the radio silence. "Echelon right." Smoothly and with precision the two wingmen on the left joined up and slid under the other three. The four wingmen then stretched out to Jack's right, each slightly behind the Phantom on his left, their wing tips almost touching.

Without scanning his flight, Jack checked in with Eastern Control. "Eastern, Poppa Kilo with four . . ." He stopped. He wasn't a Poppa Kilo on a routine training mission. Who was he kidding? And why? To appease the politicians? He was a Wolf, leading the 45th.

"Go ahead, Poppa Kilo, you are coming through broken," Eastern replied, a voice Jack recognized from a long time ago. Now he remembered the face that went with the voice, a warm, humorous man with the deep-seated professionalism characteristic of a British controller.

"Correction, Eastern. *This is Wolf Zero-One with four.* Request clearance direct to Stonewood for an overhead recovery."

Inside the control center every controller looked at the man directing the five fighters. They had, of course, heard what had happened to the 45th. They understood the political implications of acknowledging that now famous call sign. It would be one thing for Her Majesty's government to explain the transit of five fighters under normal operations; it was an entirely different matter giving aid to five of the combatants in a war that was being widely condemned by the opposition party in Parliament. The thought of what the press would do to the RAF was sobering.

The Englishman stood up, nearly at attention. "Roger, *Wolf Flight.* Cleared direct Stonewood. Descend to sixteen hundred feet at your discretion. I will clear all traffic."

"Roger, Eastern." Jack acknowledged the clearance.

"Welcome home, Wolf Flight," the controller added, looking around the room at the approving faces, and said quietly, "Bloody hell, it might be interesting here tonight."

The sound of the fighters turning onto final echoed through Gillian's salon, drowning out conversation. Margaret stopped her work and looked at her employer. "That's the wing. They're home. Jack's with them." She made it an announcement.

Gillian looked at the older woman, not quite believing her. "How can you be so sure?"

"I just am; he's a survivor." Margaret was carefully combing the woman's hair in front of her, her voice matter-of-fact.

"I don't know . . . he's probably dead like the rest of them. Look at those wives at Stonewood. Hoping and waiting . . ."

"Gillian, for God's sake, *go.* If he's there, he's going to need you."

Gillian stared at her, tears beginning to form in her eyes. What if Margaret was right? That Jack was back? "Oh, bloody hell," she said, running out of the salon to find him . . .

General Cunningham watched the Phantoms' final turn. He had been briefed that it would be a radar recovery with one aircraft landing at a time and about five minutes apart. But like every flyer on the ramp he knew that Jack was bringing the flight down final for an overhead pattern. Cunningham looked at Brigadier General Shaw, not concerned about the unauthorized change in landing. "You trained most of the crews at Alexandria South."

"Yes, sir. But Egypt was some time ago."

"What were they like then?" Cunningham asked.

"Typical fighter jocks, General. Hair on fire, young hell-raisers. That Captain Locke, especially. Got tangled up with the ambassador's daughter." Shaw paused, remembering not only Locke but Mike Fairly too . . .

"A regular skirt-chaser?"

"No, sir. A regular fighter pilot. One of the best."

Cunningham nodded and watched Jack execute a sharp break to the left as he crossed thirteen hundred feet above the approach end of the runway. Every five seconds a Phantom would peel off to the left, circling onto a short downwind leg, bleeding off airspeed and lowering flaps and gear before circling to land at intervals of two thousand feet. The symmetry and grace of the recovery pattern was testimony to the skill of the pilots. Cunningham knew how battle weary the birds were, and knowing, especially appreciated the precison of the maneuver. He also knew the scars the pilots and WSOs would carry for the rest of their lives.

On downwind Thunder called the landing checks, then added: "Looks like they've got a reception committee for us."

Jack extended his downwind leg, retracted the gear and flaps and held his airspeed. He rolled out on final and stroked the afterburners, accelerating straight ahead.

"Do it," Thunder said.

"Tower, Wolf Zero-One on the go," Jack radioed.

"Roger, Wolf Zero-One, report Initial."

Jack leveled 512 off at a thousand feet and shoved the throttles into full afterburner, touching 450 knots as he passed the tower. He snapped the stick to the right, executing a neat aileron roll. Neither he nor Thunder said a word—the roll itself announced the 45th had returned home. Winners. One after another the warbirds went around, each doing a victory roll as they passed down the runway. The noise was overpowering and constant.

"They did good, Shaw," Cunningham said.

"Good enough, General."